THE
Virtuoso

GRACE BURROWES

sourcebooks
casablanca

Published by Sourcebooks Casablanca, an imprint of Sourcebooks
P.O. Box 4410, Naperville, Illinois 60567-4410
(630) 961-3900
sourcebooks.com

Originally published as *The Virtuoso* in 2011 in the United
States of America by Sourcebooks Casablanca, an imprint of
Sourcebooks.

Printed and bound in the United States of America.
OPM 10 9 8 7 6 5 4 3 2 1

Praise for *The Virtuoso*

"Perfection...enchanting and stunningly sensual."

—*The Romance Reviews*

"Burrowes's exceptional writing and originality catch the reader and keep the story moving."

—*Publishers Weekly*

"Reminiscent of the heroines in Amanda Quick's romances... Another outstanding entry in a strong series."

—*Booklist*

"A charming tale."

—*Fresh Fiction*

"Filled with wonderfully touching relationships, interesting and intriguing characters, witty and delightful humor, and steamy and romantic seduction... Outstanding."

—*Night Owl Reviews*, 5 Stars, TOP PICK

"A splendid, sparkling, sensual love story—a keeper."

—*The Long and Short of It*

"Beautifully written, with a thrilling story, dialogue to love, and characters to care about, *The Virtuoso* is a wonderful book."

—*Dark Divas Reviews*

Also by Grace Burrowes

The Duke's Disaster

The Windhams
The Heir
The Soldier
The Virtuoso
Lady Sophie's Christmas
Wish
Lady Maggie's Secret Scandal
Lady Louisa's Christmas Knight
Lady Eve's Indiscretion
Lady Jenny's Christmas Portrait
The Courtship (novella)
The Duke and His Duchess (novella)
Morgan and Archer (novella)
Jonathan and Amy (novella)

The MacGregors
The Bridegroom Wore Plaid
Once Upon a Tartan
The MacGregor's Lady
What a Lady Needs for Christmas
Mary Fran and Matthew (novella)

The Lonely Lords
Darius
Nicholas
Ethan
Beckman
Gabriel
Gareth
Andrew
Douglas
David

Captive Hearts
The Captive
The Traitor
The Laird

Sweetest Kisses
A Kiss for Luck (novella)
A Single Kiss
The First Kiss
Kiss Me Hello

True Gentlemen
Tremaine's True Love
Daniel's True Desire
Will's True Wish

This book is dedicated to younger brothers, and specifically to my brother Joe, who has the ability to make hard things look easy and even fun—things like raising kids, Montana winters, and being a younger brother to six obstreperous siblings.

Joer, we are in awe of you.

One

"MY BEST ADVICE IS TO GIVE UP PLAYING THE PIANO."

Lord Valentine Windham neither moved nor changed his expression when he heard his friend—a skilled and experienced physician—pronounce sentence. Being the youngest of five boys and named Valentine—for God's sake—had given him fast reflexes, abundant muscle, and an enviable poker face. Being called the baby boy any time he'd shown the least tender sentiment had fired his will to the strength of iron and given him the ability to withstand almost any blow without flinching.

But this… This was diabolical, this demand David made of him. To give up the one mistress Val loved, the one place he was happy and competent. To give up the home he'd forged for his soul despite his ducal father's ridicule, his mother's anxiety, and his siblings' inability to understand what music had become to him.

He closed his eyes and drew breath into his lungs by act of will. "For how long am I to give up my music?"

Silence, until Val opened his eyes and glanced

down at where his left hand, aching and swollen, lay uselessly on his thigh.

David sat beside him, making a polite pretense of surveying the surrounding paddocks and fields. "You are possibly done with music for the rest of your life, my friend. The hand might heal, but only if you rest it until you're ready to scream with frustration. Not just days, not just weeks, and by then you will have lost some of the dexterity you hone so keenly now. If you try too hard or too soon to regain it, you'll make the hand worse than ever."

"Months?" One month was forever when a man wanted only to do the single thing denied him.

"At least. And as long as I'm cheering you up, you need to watch for the condition to arise in the other hand. If you catch it early, it might need less extensive treatment."

"Both hands?" Val closed his eyes again and hunched in on himself, though the urge to kick the stone wall where they sat—hard, repeatedly, like a man beset with murderous frustration—was nigh overwhelming.

"It's possible both hands will be affected," David went on. "Your left hand is more likely in worse condition because of the untreated fracture you suffered as a small boy. You're right-handed, so it's also possible the right hand is stronger out of habit."

Val roused himself to gather as many facts from David as he could. "Is the left weak, then?"

"Not weak, so much." David, Viscount Fairly, pursed his lips. "It seems to me you have something like gout or rheumatism in your hand. It's inflamed, swollen, and painful without apparent cause. The test will be if you rest it and see improvement. That is not the signal to resume spending all hours on the piano bench, Valentine."

"It's the signal to what? All I do is spend hours on the piano bench and occasionally escort my sisters about Town."

"It's the signal you're dealing with a simple inflammation from overuse, old son." David slid a hand to Val's nape and shook him gently. "Many people lead happy, productive lives without gluing their arses to the piano bench for twenty hours a day. Kiss some pretty girls; sniff a few roses; go see the Lakes."

Val shoved off the wall, using only his right hand for balance. "I know you mean well, but I don't *want* to do anything but play the piano."

"And I know what you want." David hopped down to fall in step beside Val. "What you want has gotten you a hand that can't hold a teacup, and while that's not fair and it's not right, it's also not yet permanent."

"I'm whining." Val stopped and gazed toward the manor house where David's viscountess was no doubt tucking in their infant daughter for the evening. "I should be thanking you for bothering with me."

"I am flattered to be of service. And you are not to let some idiot surgeon talk you into bleeding it."

"You're sure?"

"I am absolutely sure of that. No bleeding, no blisters, no surgery, and no peculiar nostrums. You tend it as you would any other inflammation."

"Which would mean?" Val forced himself to ask. But what would it matter, really? He might get the use of his hand back in a year, but how much conditioning and skill would he have lost by then? He loved his mistress—his muse—but she was jealous and unforgiving as hell.

"Rest," David said sternly as they approached the house. "Cold soaks, willow bark tea by the bucket, and at all costs, avoid the laudanum. If you can find a position where the hand is comfortable, you might consider sleeping with it splinted like that. Massage, if you can stand it."

"As if I had some tired old man's ailment. You're sure about the laudanum? It's the only thing that lets me keep playing."

"Laudanum lets you continue to aggravate it," David shot back. "It masks the pain, it cures nothing, and it can become addictive."

A beat of silence went by. Val nodded once, as much of an admission as he would make.

"Christ." David stopped in his tracks. "How long have you been using it?"

"Off and on for months. Not regularly. What it gives in ability to keep playing, it takes away in ability to focus on what I'm creating. The pain goes away, but so does both manual and mental dexterity. And I can still see my hand is swollen and the wrong color."

"Get rid of the poppy. It has a place, but I don't recommend it for you."

"I comprehend."

"You think your heart's breaking," David said, "but you still have that hand, Valentine, and you can do many, many things with it. If you treat it right now, someday you might be able to make music with it again."

"Is there anything you're not telling me?" Val asked, his tone flat.

"Well, yes," David replied as they gained the back terraces of the manor house. "There's another possibility regarding the onset of the symptoms."

"More good news?"

"Perhaps." David met his gaze steadily, which was slightly disconcerting. In addition to height and blond good looks, David Worthington, Viscount Fairly, had one blue eye and one green eye. "With a situation like this, where there is no immediate trauma, no exposure to disease, no clear cause for the symptoms, it can be beneficial to look at other aspects of well-being."

"In the King's English, David, please." Much more of David's learned medical prosing on, and Val was going to break a laudanum bottle over his friend's head.

"Sickness can originate in the emotions," David said quietly. "The term 'broken heart' can be literal, and you did say the sensations began just after you buried your brother Victor."

"As we were burying Victor," Val corrected him, not wanting to think of the pain he'd felt as he scooped up a symbolic fistful of cold earth to toss on Victor's coffin. "What in the hell does that have to do with whether I can ever again thunder away at Herr Beethoven's latest sonata?"

"That is for you to puzzle out, as you'll have ample time to ponder on it, won't you?"

"Suppose I will at that."

Val felt David's arm land across his shoulders and made no move to shrug it off, though the last thing he wanted was pity. The numbness in his hand was apparently spreading to the rest of him—just not quickly enough.

❦

"You seem to be thriving here, Cousin."

"I am quite comfortable." Ellen FitzEngle smiled at Frederick Markham, Baron Roxbury, with determined pleasantness. The last thing she needed was to admit vulnerability to him or to let him see he had any impact on her existence at all. She smoothed her hair back with a steady hand and leveled a guileless gaze at her guest, enemy, and de facto landlord.

"Hmm." Frederick glanced around the tidy little cottage, a condescending smile implying enormous satisfaction at Ellen's comedown in the world. "Not quite like Roxbury House, is it? Nor in a league with Roxbury Hall."

"But manageable for a widow of limited means. Would you like more tea?"

"'Fraid I can't stay." Frederick rose, his body at twenty-two still giving the impression of not having grown into his arms and legs, despite expensive clothing and fashionable dark curls. She knew he fancied himself something of a Corinthian, paid punctilious attention to his attire, boxed at Gentleman Jackson's, fenced at Alberto's, and accepted any bet involving his racing curricle.

And still, to Ellen, he would always be the gangly, awkward adolescent whose malice she had sorely underestimated. Only five years difference separated their ages, but she felt decades his senior in sorrow and regret.

"I did want to let you know, though"—Frederick paused with his hand on the door latch—"I'll likely be selling the place. A fellow has expenses, and the solicitors are deuced tightfisted with the Roxbury funds."

"My thanks for the warning." Ellen nodded, refusing to show any other reaction. Selling meant she could be homeless, of course, for she occupied a tenant cottage on the Markham estate. The new owner might allow her to stay on. Her property was profitable, but she didn't have a signed lease—she'd not put it past Freddy to tamper with the deed—and so the new owner might also toss her out on her backside.

"Thought it only sporting to let you know." Frederick opened the door and swung his gaze out to his waiting vehicle. A tiger held the reins of the restive bays, and Ellen had to wonder how such spirited horses navigated the little track leading to her door. "Oh, and I almost forgot." Freddy's smile turned positively gleeful. "I brought you a little something from the Hall."

Dread seeped up from Ellen's stomach, filling her throat with bile and foreboding. Any present from Frederick was bound to bring ill will, if not worse.

Frederick bent into his curricle and withdrew a small potted plant. "You being the gardener in the family, I thought you might like a little cutting from Roxbury. You needn't thank me."

"Most gracious of you, nonetheless." Ellen offered him a cool smile as he put the clay pot into her hands and then climbed aboard. "Safe journey to Town, Frederick."

He waited, clearly wishing she'd look at the little plant, but then gave up and yelled at his tiger to let the horses go. The child's grasp hadn't left the reins before Frederick was cracking the whip, the horses lunging forward and the curricle slewing around in Ellen's front yard as the boy scrambled up onto his post behind the seat.

And ye gods, ye gods, was Ellen ever glad to see the last of the man. She glanced at the plant in her hand, rolled her eyes, and walked around to the back of her property to toss it, pot and all, on her compost heap.

How like Frederick to give her an herb often used to settle the stomach, while he intimated he'd be tearing the roof from over her head. He'd been threatening for several years now, as winters in Portugal, autumn at Melton, a lengthy stint in London each spring, and expensive friends all around did not permit a man to hold on to decrepit, unentailed estates for long.

She should be grateful she'd had five years to settle in, to grieve, and to heal. She had a few friends in nearby Little Weldon, some nice memories, and some satisfaction with what she'd been able to accomplish on this lovely little property.

And now all that accomplishment was to be taken from her.

She poured herself a cup of tea and took it to her back porch, where the vista was one of endless, riotous flowerbeds. They were her livelihood and her solace, her greatest joy and her most treasured necessity. Sachets and soaps, herbs for cooking, and bouquets for market, they all brought a fair penny, and the pennies added up. Fruits and vegetables created still more income, as did the preserves and pies made from them.

"And if we have to move"—Ellen addressed the fat-headed orange tomcat who strolled up the porch steps—"we have a bit put by now, don't we, Marmalade?"

Himself squeezed up his eyes in feline inscrutability, which Ellen took for supportive agreement. The cat had been abandoned at the manor house through the wood and had gladly given up a diet of mice for the occasional dish of cream on Ellen's porch.

His company, though, combined with Frederick's visit and the threat to her livelihood, put Ellen in a wistful, even lonely mood. She sipped her tea in the waning afternoon light and brought forth the memories that pleased her most. She didn't visit them often but saved them for low moments when she'd hug them around her like a favorite shawl, the one that always made a girl feel pretty and special.

She thought about her first pony, about the day she'd found Marmalade sitting king-of-all-he-surveyed in a tree near the cottage, like a welcoming committee from the fairy folk. She thought about the flowers she'd put together for all the village weddings, and the flowers on her own wedding day. And she thought about a chance visit from that handsome Mr. Windham, though it had been just a few moments stolen in the evening sunshine, and more than a year had passed since those moments.

Ellen set her chair to rocking, hugged the memory

closer still, and banished all thoughts of Frederick, homelessness, and poverty from her mind.

❧

A life devoted to any creative art did not develop in the artist an ability to appreciate idleness, much less vice. Val had run his errands, visited his friend Nicholas Haddonfield, paid his duty calls to family—and that had been particularly difficult, as family was spread all over the Home Counties—and tended to every detail of his business he could think to tend to. He'd taken several sessions guest-conducting the Philharmonic Society Orchestra, because he'd promised his friend Edward Kirkland he would, but they were painful afternoons.

And amid all this peripatetic activity, his head was full of music. Mozart's *Requiem* figured prominently, but it was all he could do not to let his hands wander over any available keyboard, tapping out a little rendition of the simplest nursery rhyme.

He owned two manufactories that built, of course, pianos. One for grands, one for cottage pianos. They did a surprisingly brisk trade, and because the Americans in particular had decided snobbery required well-made English goods, many of the grands were shipped overseas at very significant cost to the buyers.

Val had been in the habit of personally playing each instrument before releasing it for sale. The temptation to sit down and dabble just a little…

Dabbling, for Val, could go on literally for days. Oh, he'd heed the calls of nature—to eat, sleep, and tend to bodily functions—but when a particular theme got into his brain, earthly concerns were so many intermissions in the ongoing concert that was his life.

Had been his life.

For the first time, Val was forced to consider what younger sons of the nobility actually *did* with themselves. They could apparently drink, whore, duel, and *what*? The Corsican had met his match at Waterloo, which left gambling.

It boggled the mind but certainly did not entertain for long.

Glancing at his cards, Val felt a wave of despair. Here he was, seated amid the power and plenty of the realm's aristocracy, and he was about to burst out cursing for lack of ability to play "Hot Cross Buns."

A fucking, bedamned nursery rhyme was denied him.

"Your turn, Windham," Darius Lindsey drawled. By some unspoken accord, Lindsey had become Val's latest carousing companion, though Val had his suspicions as to how this had come about. "Or not, if you'd rather cash in."

Val glanced again at his cards and felt the heavy irony of divine humor at work. In the two weeks since he had stopped making music, his luck had become uncannily good at all games of chance. The pile of chips before him was obscenely ample, but he was comforted to note Lindsey was managing fairly well, too.

Not so young Baron Roxbury, seated across from Val. The man was playing too deep, visibly sweating in the candlelight.

"You can't back out now," Roxbury said,

desperation in his voice. "Wouldn't be sporting in the least. A fellow needs a chance to win back his own, don'tcha know?"

"Believe you're about out of chips, Roxbury," Lindsey said. "Why don't we all call it a night, and things will look less daunting in the morning?"

"Not a bad idea," Val chimed in on cue, for he had no intention of spending the entire night watching Roxbury dig himself even deeper in debt. "My eyes grow tired. The smoke is rather thick."

"One more round." Roxbury's hand shot out and gripped Val's right wrist when Val would have swept his chips to the edge of the table. "All I need is one more."

"My dear," Lindsey's voice cut in softly, "I don't think you can make the ante."

"I can." Roxbury's chin went up. "With this." He fumbled in his breast pocket and tossed a document on the table that bore the ribbons and seals of legality.

"I'm out." Darius stood. "Roxbury, if you need a small loan to cover your losses, I'm sure it can be arranged until next quarter. Lord Val, you coming?"

"He can't," Roxbury answered for Val as the other two players murmured their excuses and left the table. "He owes me *one more hand*."

"He owes you nothing," Lindsey said. "You're half seas over and the cards aren't favoring you. Do yourself a favor and call it a night, Roxbury."

"One more hand." Roxbury held Val's gaze, and it was difficult for a decent man to decide what would be kinder: To allow Roxbury what he thought would save him or to minimize the man's losses.

One more hand, Val thought, the irony quirking his lips.

"One more." Val nodded, meeting Lindsey's exasperated glance. "But call for our hats and gloves, would you, Dare?"

Lindsey took the proffered excuse to leave but said something to the two men loitering by the door as they finished their drinks. With his peripheral vision, Val noted both sidled over to the corner and topped off those drinks. Witnesses, Val thought, realizing Lindsey brought a certain sophistication Val lacked to the suddenly dangerous business of gentlemanly idleness.

"Shall we cut for the deal?" Val asked. "Perhaps you can tell me exactly what you've tossed into the pot."

"An estate." Roxbury turned the top half of the deck over, smiling hugely when he revealed the knave of diamonds. "A tidy little property a short day's ride from Town, out in Oxfordshire. Been in the family but doesn't merit much attention."

"Doesn't merit much attention?" Val quirked an eyebrow and cut the queen of hearts—of course. He sighed inwardly as the little mi-re-do tune to "Hot Cross Buns" ran through his head. "My deal."

Roxbury shrugged in what Val supposed was an attempt at casual disregard. "It's not the family seat. Haven't spent a night there myself, so there's little point to keeping the place staffed, but it's worth a pretty penny."

"How many acres?" Val asked, dealing—with his right hand.

"Few thousand." Another shrug as the final cards

were dealt. "Home farm, home wood, dairy, pastures, a few tenants, that sort of thing." Roxbury picked up his cards, and from the man's expression, Val knew with sinking certainty this unstaffed, neglected, miserable little ruin of a country estate was all but his.

He could throw the game, of course.

Hot cross buns, hot cross buns.

One ha' penny, two ha' penny,

Hot cross buns.

He wasn't going to throw the game. The place might be useful as a dower property for a relative, or a retreat for Val that wasn't surrounded by friends and family. If it required attention, so much the better, because nobody sane spent the entire summer sweltering in Town.

Surrounded by pianos at every turn.

Val looked at his cards and almost smiled. Of course, a full house, queens over knaves. How fitting.

⁂

"This brings back memories," Darius said from his perch on a solid piebald gelding.

"The trips to university and back," Val replied from aboard his chestnut. They'd had good weather for their trip out from London, thank God, though this particular stretch of road was looking oddly familiar. "Jesus pissing in the bloody blazing desert."

"Original," Darius conceded. "But apropos of what?"

Val retrieved the deed from the breast pocket of his riding jacket and scowled at the document. "I am very much afraid I know this place."

"You know the estate or the town nearby?"

"Both." Val felt a reluctant smile tugging at his lips. "And if this is the place I think it is, it's in godforsaken shape. The roof was on its last prayers a year ago and the grounds are an eyesore."

"Famous. So why are you smiling?"

"It needs rescuing. It has good bones and a lovely setting, and it's just far enough from London I won't be plagued with relatives and friends. There's a decent tavern in Little Weldon, and a market, and the folk are pleasant, as long as you've no pretensions to privacy." Val tucked the deed back in his pocket and urged his horse forward.

Darius brushed his horse's mane so it rested neatly down the right side of the animal's muscular neck and put his gelding to the walk beside Val's mount. "You are telling me we are to bivouac in Oxfordshire among a bunch of toothless old men and church biddies?"

"Nonsense," Val said, his smile broadening. "Both Rafe and Tilden have a few teeth, and we'll be camping only until I can put a few rooms to rights."

"I see."

"Lindsey." Val peered over at him. "Didn't you and your brother ever camp in the home wood at Wilton? Play Indians, roast a few hapless bunnies over a fire, and swim naked in the moonlight?"

"I am in the company of a pagan." Darius smoothed his hand over the horse's already tidy mane. "If you must know, Trent and I were not permitted such savage pastimes, and I'd not have indulged in them if we were."

"You've never sat in a tree reading *Robinson Crusoe*?"

"Not once."

"Never snitched a picnic from Cook?" Val was frowning now. "Never pinched your papa's second copy of the *Kama Sutra* to puzzle over the pictures in the privacy of the hay mow?"

"He had no such thing in his library."

"Never crept down to the study in the dead of night and gotten sick on his brandy?"

Darius's brows rose. "God in heaven, Windham. Did Her Grace have no influence on her menfolk whatsoever?"

"Of course she did. I am a very good dancer. I have some conversation. I know how to dress and how to flirt with the wallflowers."

"But one expects a certain dignity from the ducal household. Did your papa have no influence on you?"

"A telling influence. Thanks to him, my brothers and I learned to indulge in the foregoing mischief and a great deal more without getting caught."

Darius eyed his companion skeptically. "And here I thought you must have been spouting King James in utero, reciting the royal succession by the time you were out of nappies, and strutting about with a quizzing glass by the age of seven."

"That would be more my brother Gayle, though Anna has gotten him over the worst of it. The man is too serious by half."

"And you're not?" Darius was carefully surveying the surrounds as he posed this question.

"I am the soul of levity," Val rejoined, straight-faced. "Particularly compared to my surviving brothers. But this does raise something that needs discussion.

The folk in these environs know me only as Mr. Windham, or young sir, or that fellow out from Sodom-on-Thames, and so forth."

"Sodom-on-Thames." Darius's brows drew down. "This isn't going to be like summering at the family seat, is it?"

"One hopes not." Val shuddered to think of it. "No womenfolk to drag one about on calls just to observe how decrepit various neighbors have gotten, no amorous looks from the well-fed heifers of the local gentry, no enduring the vicar's annual sermons aimed at curbing the excesses of Moreland's miscellany."

"So it wasn't all Indians, pilfered brandy, and erotica?"

"Not lately. The point I wanted to make, however, is I do not want to be—I most assuredly do not want to be—Moreland's youngest pup while I am among my neighbors here."

"You're a mighty strapping pup, but you are his son."

"I could be the size of your dear brother-in-law, Nick Haddonfield," Val retorted, a note of exasperation in his voice, "and I would still be Moreland's youngest pup, and not just to the doddering old titles His Grace battles with in the Lords. You try being the youngest of five boys and blessed with a name like Valentine. It wears on one."

Darius did not argue, which meant when they approached the Markham estate in the waning light, they did so in silence. Valentine was certain the silence on Darius's part could not be described as awed.

❧

In her five years in Little Weldon, Ellen had found evening was at once the sweetest and the most difficult time of day. Memories crowded closer at night, and even a good memory had an element of loss about it, for it was only a memory.

And she was acquainted with loss. If she'd known how brief her marriage was going to be, she'd have been a better wife. The sentiment was foolish, for she hadn't been a bad wife, not until the end, but she would have spent less time wishing she were in love with her spouse and more time loving the man.

As shadows lengthened over her yard, she spied Marmalade stalking his great, fluffy-footed way across the back gardens. He was a big cat, made all the more impressive for the fact that his fur was long, luxurious, and scrupulously groomed. The idea that such an animal—and bright orange to boot—could sneak anywhere was vaguely comical. As Ellen watched, he pounced among the daisies and pounced again but then sat back, exhibiting a sudden need to bathe, as cats will when their dignity is imperiled.

I'm like that cat. I don't fit in as an exponent of my species, and yet my dignity still matters to me.

Thoughts of that ilk required a fortifying cup of tea, lest the thinker become morose, or worse, lachrymose. As she filled her teakettle, tossed kindling on the hearth, and swung the pot over the flames, Ellen reminded herself she'd started her menses that morning, and every month—every useless, benighted month—that occasion filled her with sadness. When she had been married, the sadness made more sense, as it signaled yet another failure to provide Francis his heir.

She poured the boiling water into her porcelain pot, added the tea strainer, assembled a tea tray that included strawberries, bread, and butter, and took her repast to the back porch. Marmalade had arranged himself on the bottom step, taking advantage of the heat retained in the wood both behind and beneath him. As she sipped her tea, Ellen set her chair to rocking and tried not to set her thoughts to remembering, but the evening was peaceful, beautiful, sweet—and lonely.

Tonight, Ellen decided, she would wander in the wood, searching for herbs, or perhaps, just searching for a little peace.

❧

"A bit of work needed," Darius remarked, glancing around at the overgrown track. The front gate to the Markham estate, with stone griffons rampant on the gate posts and the wrought iron sagging, lent an ominous touch to the entryway.

"A bit," Val conceded. "But then, if the drive is not navigable, I will have to concern myself less with uninvited company."

"Are you planning on becoming eccentric?" Darius inquired as he steered his gelding past a pothole. "Or will it just overcome you gradually, like the vines obscuring Sleeping Beauty's castle?"

"We'll have to wait and see. For the present, I rather like all the rhododendrons."

Darius peered at the foliage. "They have misplaced their self-restraint."

The drive was lined with towering oaks that created

a dense canopy of greenery overhead. The understory had been taken over by the rhododendrons, and it being the proper season, they were awash in blooms. In the lengthening shadows, the pink, purple, and white flowers stood out luminously against the dark foliage and shifting dapples of sun.

Val rode on in silence until the manor house itself stood before him.

"Oh dear," Darius said softly, "and that is an understatement."

The house lay north-south in orientation, so the full impact of the westering sun hit the entire façade. The southern wing and the center section were unkempt and dilapidated. Shutters hung crookedly, windows were missing panes, porch bricks had come off and tumbled to the grass.

The northern wing, however, was a complete shambles. The slate roof was visibly sagging near the soffit in the front corner, three of the chimneys were on their way to becoming piles of mortar, the north-facing porch was listing hard to port, and as Val watched, bats flew out of the missing attic windows.

"Well, come on." Val swung off his chestnut. "The light won't last forever, and I've a mind to look around."

For Val, there was an incongruous sense of pleasure just looking at the place. Last year when he'd been ostensibly looking for property to purchase, he'd needed a key to gain access. This year, any number of broken ground-floor windows afforded the same privilege. Many a boy had obviously tested his aim against mullioned panes without thought to the cost of replacing them. Still, as Val gazed upon the wreck fate had dumped in his lap, he had the thought: *She's waited for me.*

In the mellow evening sunbeams, the house held on to a kind of dignity, despite disrepair, neglect, and abandonment. The native stone blended beautifully with the surrounding wood, while patches of wild-flowers splashed color in unlikely spots around the yard. Opportunistic saplings were encroaching, but a liberal use of imagination put the former serenity and appeal of the place within sight.

"The stables aren't bad at all," Darius said as he caught up with Val at the back of the house.

"A silver lining for which the horses will no doubt be grateful." Val's gaze traveled toward the largest outbuilding. "And the springhouse looks large and sound, and the carriage house nearly so."

"Where is your home farm?"

"That direction, being worked by a tenant most likely."

"You're fortunate to have stone walls." Darius frowned as he turned slowly where he stood. "They'll take some effort to repair, but the materials are at hand, and most of your tenants should have the skill."

"It so happens, while in Yorkshire enjoying my brother's hospitality, I acquired the skill. It's more a matter of wearing gloves, cursing fluently, and not being able to walk or rise from one's seat the next day."

"And who wouldn't enjoy such an undertaking as that?" Darius smiled as he spoke. "Are we going inside?"

"Not tonight." Bright morning light would serve

better for an inspection, and Val had seen enough for now. The place still stood, and that was what mattered.

Though why it mattered escaped him for the present.

"Let's peek inside the carriage house, though, shall we?" Val suggested. "There might be usable quarters above, and the first thing we're going to need is a stout wagon to haul supplies and debris."

"You're staying?"

"Think of the privacy." Val's smile widened at the incredulity on Darius's face. "The insipid teas and dances we'll miss, the scheming young ladies we won't have to dodge under the arbors, and the unbearable stink of London in summer we won't have to endure."

The pianos he wouldn't have to abstain from playing. Hot cross buns… Hot cross buns…

"Think of your back hurting so badly you can hardly walk," Darius rejoined as he crossed the yard beside Val. "The endless small talk at the local watering hole, the pleasures of the village churchyard on a Sunday morning, where no man escapes interrogation."

"You're not"—Val paused in mock drama—"*afraid*, are you, Lindsey?"

While giving Darius a moment to form the appropriate witty rejoinder, Val pushed open the door to the carriage house. No doubt because vehicles were expensive and the good repair of harness a matter of safety, the place had been built snugly and positioned on a little rise at the back of the house. The interior was dusty but dry and surprisingly tidy.

"This is encouraging."

Darius followed him in. "Why do I have the compulsion to caution you strenuously against going up those stairs, Windham? Perhaps you'll be swarmed by bats or set upon by little ghoulies with crossbows."

"Oh, for God's sake, what could be hiding in an empty old carriage house?"

❦

Ellen had meant to take herself off for a little stroll in the dense woods separating her cottage from the crumbling manor, but the chamomile tea she'd drunk must have lulled her to sleep. When she awoke, Marmalade was curled in her lap, the kneading of his claws in her thigh rousing her even through her skirts and petticoats.

"Down with you, sir." She gently put the cat on the porch planks and saw from the angle of the sun she'd dozed off only for a few minutes. Something caught her ear as she rose from her rocker, a trick of the time of evening when dew fell and sounds carried.

"Damn them," Ellen muttered, leaving the porch with a swish of skirts. Bad enough the village boys liked to spy on her and whisper that she was a witch. Worse was when they ran tame over the old Markham manor house, using it as a place to smoke illicit pipes, tipple their mama's brandied pears, and practice their rock throwing.

"Little heathen." Ellen went to her tool shed and drew a hand scythe down from the wall pegs. She'd never had serious trouble with the boys before, but one in particular—Mary Bragdoll's youngest—was growing into the height and muscle for which his brothers and father were well known. By reputation, he could be a sneering, disrespectful lout, and Ellen was more afraid of him than she'd like to admit.

She tromped through the woods, hopping over logs to take the shortest path, until she came out of the trees at the back of the old house. That view was easier to look on than the front—the roof wasn't quite so obviously ruined.

When Francis had been alive, this property had still been tidy, graceful, elegant, and serene, if growing worn. The years were taking a brutal toll, leaving Ellen with the feeling the house's exterior represented her own interior.

Time was slowly wearing away at her determination, until her reasons for going through each day without screaming and tearing her hair were increasingly obscured.

"You have started your menses," she reminded herself, "and this is no time for silly dramatics."

The voices came again from the carriage house, and Ellen's eyes narrowed. Heretofore, the encroaching vandals had left the carriage house in peace, and their violation of it made her temper seethe. She marched up to the door, banged it open with a satisfying crash, brandished her scythe, and announced herself to any and all therein.

"Get your heathen, trespassing backsides out of this carriage house immediately, lest I inform your papas of your criminal conduct—*and your mamas*."

"Good lord," a cultured and ominously *adult* male voice said softly from Ellen's right, "we're about to be taken prisoner. Prepare to defend your borders, my friend. Sleeping Beauty has awakened in a state."

Ellen's gaze flew to the shadows, where a tall,

dark-haired man was regarding her with patient humor. The calm amusement in his eyes suggested he posed no threat to her, while his dress confirmed he was a person of some means. Ellen had no time to further inventory that stranger, because the sound of a pair of boots slowly descending the steps drew her gaze across the room.

Whoever was coming down those stairs was in no hurry and was certainly no boy. Long, long legs became visible, then muscles that looked as if they'd been made lean and elegant from hours in the saddle showed off custom riding boots and excellent tailoring. A trim, flat torso came next, then a wide muscular chest and impressive shoulders.

Good Lord, he was taller than the fellow in the corner, and that one was a good half a foot taller than she. Ellen swallowed nervously and tightened her grip on the scythe.

"Careful," the man in the shadows said softly, "she's armed and ready to engage the enemy."

Those dusty boots descended the last two steps, and Ellen forced herself to meet the second man's face. She'd been prepared for the kind of teasing censorship coming from the one in the corner, a polite hauteur, or outright anger, but not a slow, gentle smile that melted her from the inside out.

"Mrs. FitzEngle." Valentine Windham bowed very correctly from the waist. "It has been too long, and you must forgive us for startling you. Lindsey, I've had the pleasure, so dredge up your manners."

"Mr. Windham?" Ellen lowered her scythe, feeling foolish and ambushed, and worst of all—happy.

So inappropriately happy.

Two

VALENTINE WINDHAM CONTINUED TO SMILE AT HER, an expression of concentrated regard that formed a substantial part of Ellen's pleasurable memories of him.

"Mrs. Ellen FitzEngle." Mr. Windham's gaze—and his smile—remained directed at her. "May I make known to you the Honorable Mr. Darius Lindsey, late of Kent, come to assist me in the assessment of damages on my newly acquired property."

Lindsey fell in with the introductions with the smooth manners sported by any well-bred fellow.

"You've bought this place?" Ellen kept both the hope and the dread from her voice, but just barely.

"I have acquired it, and apparently just in the nick of time. Do you often have to shoo away thieves and vandals?"

Ellen glanced at the scythe in her hand. "It's worse in the summer. Boys wander around in packs and have not enough to keep them busy. There's a very pleasant pond in the first meadow beyond the wood, and it draws them on hot days."

"No doubt they are responsible for my broken

windows. Perhaps they'll be willing to help with the repairs."

"You're going to restore the house?" Ellen asked, though it was none of her business.

"Very likely. It will take a good deal of time."

"Where are my manners? May I offer you a pot of tea, gentlemen, or a mug of cider, perhaps?"

"Cider." His just-for-you smile broadened. "An ambrosial thought."

"I take it you live near here, Mrs. FitzEngle?" Mr. Lindsey interjected as they left the carriage house.

Ellen gestured vaguely. "Through the wood."

"Well, darkness approaches," Mr. Windham said. "Darius, if you'll bring the horses along down the track, I'll escort Mrs. FitzEngle through the wood."

"That won't be necessary," Ellen replied. "I know the woods blindfolded."

"You wound me." His smile—and worse, his green eyes—put a hint of sincerity in the words, leaving Ellen to feel a little flip of excitement in her vitals. Oh, God help her, her tame, tired memories of his single previous visit did not do him justice. Either that, or Mr. Windham had become even more intensely attractive in the year of his absence. Dark hair slightly longer than was fashionable went with those green eyes, and if anything, in the year since she'd seen him, he'd grown leaner, taller, and better-looking than was decent.

"Despite the fact that periodic wounding keeps him humble," Mr. Lindsey spoke up, "I must ask you to humor my friend's suggestion, Mrs. FitzEngle. He will only want to inspect his wood come morning, in any case, so you are the ideal guide." He spun on his heel and strode off toward the front of the house.

"You are looking well," Ellen said, dusting off her long unused skills with small talk.

"I'm tired. Road weary, dusty, and probably scented accordingly. You, however, look to be blooming."

"You mustn't flatter me, Mr. Windham," Ellen replied, not meeting his gaze. He offered his arm, as he had once long ago, and she took it gingerly. "I did steal a nap after my supper."

"Did a handsome prince come kiss you awake?" he asked, matching his steps to hers. "Darius is convinced we've fallen into the land of the fairy, what with the rhododendrons, the bats in the attic, and the air of neglect."

"You're less than three miles from that thriving enclave of modern civilization, Little Weldon. I will disabuse your friend of his wayward notions."

"Oh, please don't. He's having great fun at my expense, and the summer is likely to try his patience if he bides with me for any length of time."

"You can't think to live at the manor." Ellen frowned as she spoke. She didn't want him so nearby, or rather, she did, and it was a stupid, foolish idea.

"We'll put up in the carriage house. It's clean and serviceable. There's a small stove upstairs for tea and warmth, and the quarters are well ventilated."

"And the roof is still functioning," Ellen added. They were passing through the woods on one of the more worn bridle paths. Nobody maintained the paths, but game used them, and Ellen did.

And nasty little boys did, as well.

She walked more quickly, all too aware that in these woods the man beside her had kissed her, only once, but endlessly, until she was a standing puddle of desire and anticipation. With nothing more than his mouth on hers, he'd stripped her of dignity, self-restraint, and common sense, probably without a backward thought when he'd gone on his way.

"Are we in a hurry?" her escort inquired.

"I would not want to leave Mr...." Ellen searched frantically for his name. Good lord, she'd just been introduced to the man.

"The Honorable Darius Lindsey," Mr. Windham supplied as they walked along. "His papa is the Earl of Wilton, with the primary estate over in Hampshire."

"I see."

Mr. Windham must have heard the cooling in her tone at the mention of a title, because as he and Mr. Lindsey sipped cold cider on Ellen's back porch, he quizzed her on the tenants, the neighbors, the availability of various services in the area, and the likelihood of finding competent laborers in the immediate future, keeping well away from any remotely social topic.

"You'll have to wait until the hay is in," Ellen said as the shadows lengthened across her yard. "There's help to be had for coin. Tomorrow is market day, so you can start getting the word out among the locals, and they'll spread it quickly enough. How are you fixed for provisions?"

"For provisions?" Mr. Lindsey echoed. "We rode out from Town with saddlebags bulging, but that's about it."

"I can keep you in butter, milk, cheese, and eggs. Mable presented me with a little heifer calf not a month past. I was giving the extra to Bathsheba, since she's nursing eight piglets, but she can make shift without cream and eggs every day. I've also been working on a smoke-cured ham but not making much progress."

"You were feeding your sow cream and eggs?"

"Eight piglets, Mr. Lindsey, would take a lot out of any lady. It was either that or much of it would go to waste."

"We'll be happy to enjoy your surplus," Mr. Windham cut in, "but you have to let us compensate you somehow."

"I will not take coin for being neighborly."

"I didn't mean to offend, merely to suggest when the opportunity presents itself, I would like to be neighborly, as well. I'm sure there's some effort a pair of strong-backed fellows might turn themselves to that would be useful to you, Mrs. FitzEngle."

His voice was a melody of good breeding and better intentions, an aural embodiment of kindness and politesse. Just to hear him speaking left Ellen a little dazed, a little…wanting.

"We'll see," she said briskly. "For now, enjoy your cider. Moonrise will be early this evening, and if you're staying in town for now, you'll want to get back to The Tired Rooster before the darts start flying."

"Tame gentlemen such as ourselves will need to be up early tomorrow," Mr. Windham said, rising. "We'll be on our way, but thank you for the cider and the hospitality."

"Until tomorrow, then." Ellen rose, as well, pretending to ignore the hand Mr. Windham extended toward her.

"Tomorrow?" Mr. Lindsey frowned. "Here I was hoping to malinger at the Rooster for a couple weeks waiting for building materials to come in from London, or darkest Peru."

"Lazy sot." Mr. Windham smiled at his friend. "I think the lady meant she'd be in town for market day, and we might be fortunate enough to see her then."

"Until tomorrow." Mr. Lindsey bowed over her hand and went to collect the horses, leaving Ellen standing in the gathering darkness with Valentine Windham.

"I am glad to have renewed our acquaintance," Mr. Windham said, his gaze traveling around the colorful borders of her yard. "Your flowers make an impression."

"I am glad to see you again, as well." Ellen used the most cordially unremarkable tones she could muster. "One is always pleased to know one's gardening efforts are memorable."

"Until tomorrow." Mr. Windham took her hand and bowed over it, but he also kissed her knuckles—a soft, fleeting contact of his mouth on the back of her hand, accompanied by a slight squeeze of his fingers around hers. And then he was swinging up on a big chestnut, saluting with his crop, and cantering off into the darkness, Mr. Lindsey at his side.

Ellen sat, her left hand closed over the knuckles of her right, and tried to think whether it was a good thing her flowers had left an impression on Mr. Windham.

It was a bad thing, she decided, for Mr. Windham was a scamp, and a scamp as a neighbor was trouble enough, particularly when she liked him, and his every touch and glance had her insides in a complete muddle. And while he might recall her flowers, she recalled quite clearly their one, very thorough and far beyond neighborly kiss.

꒰ঌ

"You are going to trifle with the widow," Darius predicted as the horses ambled through the moonlight toward Little Weldon. The night was pleasant, the worst heat of the day fading to a soft, summery warmth made fragrant by mown hay and wildflowers.

"She is a widow," Val said, "but I don't think she's that kind of widow."

"What kind of widow would that be?"

Val ignored the question, more intent on a sweet recollection. "I was out here last spring on an errand for David Worthington, supposedly looking at rural properties that might be for sale. I accompanied Vicar Banks on a courtesy call to what I thought was an elderly widow who'd missed the previous week's services. I saw a floppy straw hat, an untidy cinnamon-colored braid, and bare feet before I saw anything else of her. I concluded she was an old dear becoming vague, as they say."

"Vague does not apply to Mrs. FitzEngle. Just the opposite."

"Not vague," Val agreed. He'd kissed the woman before taking his leave of her on that long-ago afternoon, an impulse—a sweet, stolen moment with a woman whose every feature left a man with a sense of warmth. She had warm brown eyes, a warm sprinkling of freckles across the bridge of her nose, and hair a warm shade exactly midway between auburn and blond—cinnamon came to mind rather than chestnut. "She isn't dreamy or given to flights but there is something…"

"Yes?"

"Unconventional," Val said, though that term wasn't quite right either. Her hands on his body would be warm too, though how he knew this, he could not say. "Ellen could be considered eccentric, but I prefer to think of her as…unique."

Darius said nothing, finding it sufficiently *unique* that Valentine Windham, son of a duke, wealthy merchant, virtuoso pianist, and favorite of the ladies, would think of Mrs. FitzEngle as *Ellen*.

❦

Val peered over the soffit as several slate tiles slid down from the roof on the newly constructed slide and bumped safely against the cloth padding the bottom of the chute.

"It works," he said, grinning over at Darius, the only other occupant of the house's roof.

"Of course it works." Darius sat back on his heels, using his forearm to wipe the sweat from his brow. "I designed it. I don't recall you ordering another entire wagonload of goods from town."

Val followed Darius's gaze down to the yard, where a farm wagon pulled by two exceptionally sturdy horses came to a halt before the house. A handsome black saddle horse was tethered behind, not one Val

recognized. Val and Darius both availed themselves
of the slide to get from roof to yard, causing the lead
horses' ears to flick and the occupants of the wagon to
start whooping with glee.

"Settle down, you two," barked the driver. "Lord
Valentine will think he's set upon by savages." The
man hopped down, along with the two lanky adoles-
cents who'd been so enthusiastically cheering the sight
of grown men sliding to the ground.

"Axel Belmont at your service." The driver grinned,
swiped back his blond hair with one hand, and stuck
out the other. "Though you might not think so when
I warn you my sons Dayton and Phillip have invaded
your undefended borders with me."

Val extended a hand, recognizing the tall blond
fellow from his friend Nick's wedding to Darius's
sister Leah just a few weeks past.

"Good to see you, Professor," Val said, "and may
I make known to you the Honorable Darius Lindsey,
late of the roof, but whom you might have met at
Leah and Nick's wedding. How fares your dear wife?"

Belmont's smile softened. "She's much better,
particularly now that I've taken the heathen off the
property. Nick wrote that you were working on a
project not an hour's drive from Candlewick, and I
have come to inspect progress."

"We're still very much in the planning stages,"
Val said, though this further evidence of Nick
Haddonfield's friendly meddling was mentally noted.
"We're also glad for some company. Darius fears we're
going to be kidnapped by elves."

"Boys!" Belmont's offspring stopped in midpelt

toward the house. "Get this wagon unloaded, and mind you put the contents in the carriage bay where they'll stay dry. The first son of mine on that roof without Lord Valentine's permission gets his backside walloped and has to learn how to tat lace."

Loud groans, followed by reluctant grins, saw the boys reversing direction and heading for the wagon at a decorous pace.

"Spare them no sympathy," Belmont warned. "Not by word, deed, or expression. Abby is teaching them how to charm, and between that and their natural guile, they are shamelessly manipulative."

"They're also at an age where they can eat entire horses, tack and all," Val mused. "But run all day, as well."

"In the opposite direction of their parents, unless it's meal time," Belmont said, eyeing the house again. "Come along, Professor. I'll give you the tour. Dare, you want to come?"

Darius shuddered dramatically. "I've had the privilege. I can work on calculations while you lie to your guest about the potential of the place. Mr. Belmont, a pleasure to see you again."

"Axel," the blond corrected him. "Philip and Dayton are underfoot, and formalities are futile. A surrender of all but the barest civilities is the only reasonable course."

༄

"Your gutters don't work," Belmont said in patient, magisterial tones, "so the water backs up, sometimes under the eaves. If the squirrels or bats have been busy, that puts water in your walls or attics or both, and water will destroy your house more quickly than wind, snow, or most anything else save fire."

"So I must replace all those gutters and spouts," Val concluded, eyeing the seedlings growing in the gutters.

"You must subdue your jungle, as well," Belmont pointed out gently as he ambled along beside Val in the yard. "I went through this same exercise when I married my first wife. Candlewick was in disrepair, and yet it was all we had. You prioritize and try to put each season to its best use. And you work your bloody arse off."

"That much I am prepared to do, but other than the roof, what would you prioritize?"

They meandered the house, the property, and the outbuildings, exchanging ideas, arguing good-naturedly, and tossing suggestions back and forth. By the time they'd finished a complete circuit of house, outbuildings, and immediate grounds, the sun was directly overhead—as near as could be determined through the trees.

"Now comes the reason you'll be glad we crashed your gate," Belmont said. "Get Mr. Lindsey to set aside his figuring, or the locusts will not leave him any lunch." Belmont retrieved a very large wicker hamper from the back of the wagon and bellowed for his offspring to wash their filthy paws if they wanted even a crust of bread. A picnic fit for a regiment was soon laid out on a blanket spread in the shade.

"Compliments of my wife," Belmont said, "in exchange for getting her menfolk out from underfoot for a few hours."

"Lunch!" Dayton and Phillip gamboled up, every bit as energetic as they'd been hours earlier.

"One of their nine favorite meals of the day. Sit down, you lot, and wait for your elders to snatch a few crumbs before you destroy all in your path."

As food was passed around among the adults, Belmont continued speaking. "Day and Phil concocted a plan for Phillip to start school a year early so all five Belmont cousins could have one year at university together. Abby was enthusiastic about it, since it will give us a little time at Candlewick before the baby arrives and all hell breaks loose once again."

"I didn't realize you were in anticipation of a happy event." Val smiled genially, but ye gods... Val's sister-in-law Anna had just been delivered of a son, while the wife of his other brother, Devlin, was expecting. David and Letty were still adjusting to the arrival of a daughter. Nick's wife would no doubt soon be in a similar condition, and it seemed as if all in Val's world could be measured by the birth—imminent or recent—of a child.

"I find the prospect of parenthood..."—Belmont's expression became pensive—"sweet, an unexpected opportunity to revisit a previous responsibility I took too much for granted."

"He didn't appreciate us," Day translated solemnly then ruined the effect by meeting his brother's gaze and bursting into guffaws.

"I did." Belmont corrected them easily. "But as a very young father might. I am an old hand now and will go about the job differently."

Val rummaged in the hamper, finding the topic

unaccountably unsettling, "I put you at, what? Less than five years my senior?"

"We're surrounded by duffers, Day." Phil rolled his eyes dramatically. "The only saving grace is they've no teeth and can't do justice to the meat."

"You two." Belmont scowled at his sons. "No dessert if you don't make some pretense of domestication immediately."

"Not that." Day rolled to his back, letting his arms and legs twitch in the air. "Phil, he uttered the Worst Curse, and we've hardly done anything yet."

"May I finish your sandwich?" Phillip reached for his brother's uneaten portion.

"Touch it"—Day sat up immediately—"and it's pistols, swords, or bare-knuckle rules."

Darius accepted the pie Val withdrew from the hamper. "And to think, Valentine," Darius drawled, "your mother raised five of these, what are they? Boys?"

"Demons," Belmont muttered. "Spawn of Satan, imps from hell."

"Beloved offspring," Dayton and Phillip chorused together.

"Hush," Belmont reproved. "I haven't sprung Nick's plan on Lord Val yet, so you've made a complete hash of my strategy."

"Oops." Dayton glanced at Phillip. "Let's go check on the horses, Phil. You swear you'll let us have a piece of pie?" He drilled his father with a very adult look.

"Honor of a Belmont. Now scat."

They went at a run that nonetheless included

elbows shoved into ribs and laughter tossed into the building heat. The sense of silence and stillness left in their wake was slightly disorienting.

"And you've another on the way," Val reminded him. "I suppose you want to leave your beloved offspring with me for a bit?"

"How did you guess?"

"He's canny like that," Darius said, munching on a chicken leg. "And desperately in need of free labor."

"Don't kid yourself." Belmont examined his hands while he spoke. "They will eat every bit as much as you would spend to hire such as them, but they do work hard, and Nick thought you might not mind some company."

"Nick." Val heaved a sigh. "He sent poor Lindsey here to be my duenna. He ought to be too busy with his new wife to meddle like this."

Val understood Axel Belmont was being polite, offering a way for Val to accept help—and dear Nicholas's spies in his camp—without losing face. Well…there were worse things than taking on a pair of adolescent brothers.

"I will be pleased to have the company of your sons," Val said, opening his eyes and sitting up, "but we'd better cut that pie before they come charging back here, arguing over how to cut the thing in five exactly equal pieces."

"Better make that six," Darius murmured as his gaze went to the path through the woods.

"Six is easy," Val replied, but then he followed Darius's line of vision to see Ellen FitzEngle emerging from the trees. "Six is the easiest thing in world," he concluded, helpless to prevent a smile from spreading across his face.

❧

Ellen was wearing one of her comfortable old dresses and a straw hat. She was also wearing shoes, which Val found mildly disappointing. Since the day he'd first met her—barefoot, a floppy hat on her abundant, chestnut hair—he'd pictured her that way in his imagination. And though she was shod, today her hair was again down, confined in a single thick braid.

"You were drawn by the noise." Val rose to his feet and greeted his newest guest. "Ellen FitzEngle, may I present to you Mr. Axel Belmont of Candlewick."

"Mrs. Fitz." Belmont bowed over her hand, smiling openly. "We're acquainted. I am a botanist, and Mrs. FitzEngle has the most impressive flower gardens in the shire."

"You flatter, Professor," Ellen said, "but I'll allow it. I came to see the massacre, or what surely sounded like one."

"You heard my sons," Belmont concluded dryly. "As soon as we cut the pie, you'll have the pleasure, or the burden, of meeting them."

"Won't you join us?" Val gestured toward the hamper. "Mrs. Belmont sent a picnic as a peace offering in exchange for suffering the company of her familiars."

"How is your dear wife, Mr. Belmont?" Ellen asked, sinking onto a corner of the blanket.

"Probably blissfully asleep as we speak. She will be eternally indebted to your neighbor here when I return without the boys."

Ellen smiled at Val. "You're acquiring your own herd of boys. A sound strategy when the local variety could use some good influences. That looks like a delicious pie."

"Strawberries are good, no matter the setting," Belmont rejoined. He drew Ellen into a conversation about her flowers, and Val was interested to see that while she conversed easily and knowledgeably about her craft, there was still a reserved quality in her speech and manners with Belmont. The professor was all that was gentlemanly, though he treated Ellen as an intellectual equal on matters pertaining to plants, but still, she would not be charmed past a certain point.

And this pleased Val inordinately.

Dayton galloped up, Phil beside him. "Did you see the springhouse? It is the keenest! You could practically live in there."

"Keenest isn't a word," Phil said. "It has pipes and conduits and baths and windows and all manner of accommodations—the springhouse, that is."

"And it's spotless," Day added, ignoring the grammar lesson. "You could eat off the floors in there. Hey! You cut the pie." Belmont handed them each a slice, which—once they'd made hasty bows in Ellen's direction—they took off with them, eating directly from their own hands, still jabbering about the springhouse.

Ellen met Val's gaze. "You do have an impressive springhouse. I confess I've made use of it myself."

"Impressive, how?"

"Come." Ellen rose to her feet unassisted, causing all three men to rise, as well. "I'll show you. Gentlemen, you need not have gotten up. I know all too well that on the menu for every summer picnic worth the name, a nap follows dessert."

While Belmont and Darius exchanged a smile, Val offered his arm. He set off with Ellen in the direction of the springhouse, inordinately gratified that she would initiate this private ramble with him.

A few minutes later, Val's appreciative gaze traveled over the most elaborate springhouse he'd ever beheld. "This is fascinating. It's as much laundry and bathhouse as springhouse, and I've never seen so much glazed yellow tile."

"Light keeps the moss and mould from growing," Ellen said. "And what good is a laundry or a bathhouse that isn't clean?"

The structure itself was stone. Water entered it halfway up one wall, falling into a tiled conduit divided up into a holding pool, then several lower pools, the last of which exited the downstream end of the building near the floor. Pipes allowed the water to be diverted into and out of copper tubs, one of which sat in sturdy hinged brackets over a tiled fire pit.

"So you heat water here and use this for the laundry tub," Val said, pointing to one of two enormous copper tubs. "This other tub, without a fire under it, would be the bathing tub."

"Hence, my use of your facility." As she spoke, Ellen's gaze was focused on the blue fleur-de-lis pattern decorating a row of tiles at waist height. "I wash my clothes here and use the other tub on occasion, as well."

"You're welcome to, of course." Val glanced

around at the pipes lest he be caught staring at her. "I suppose it's you who's kept the place so clean."

"I use the farm pond in warm weather," Ellen said, coloring slightly, "but when it's cold, this little springhouse is a godsend. I never dread laundry day."

"And you must not now." Val shoved himself back to sit on the worktable beside the only door—the door he had left wide open in deference to the lady's sensibilities. "What day is laundry day?"

"Thursday or Friday. Wednesday is market; Sunday is services. Little market is Saturday, if need be."

"I ask, lest we attempt to use this facility on the same day. One wouldn't want to intrude on a lady at her bath."

"Or a gentleman," Ellen agreed, this blush more apparent.

"I hadn't considered the issue of our laundry. Working on the house, Darius and I will pile up a deal of dirty clothes."

"It will be no trouble to toss in a few more shirts and socks when I do my own," Ellen suggested, still not meeting his eyes.

"I will not allow you to do my laundry, Ellen." Val shoved off the table and crossed the space to frown down at her.

"I will not allow you to use my given name without permission," she retorted, her gaze meeting his then dropping. His arched an eyebrow but held his ground, peering down at her.

"Show me where this pond is," he said abruptly, taking her hand and placing it on his forearm. "I love nothing at the end of a hot summer day so much as a good swim, and that will be equally true when I'm not playing…idling my days away indoors."

"I did not mean to bark at you," Ellen said as they walked into the woods. "I am used to my solitude here."

"I have intruded," Val guessed. "You hear us over here, like you did this morning. You heard the hammers and the sawing. The birds are quiet, and we are not. You sense movement beyond your woods, and it isn't little beasts or even local boys. It's change, and you can't control it."

And what was he going on about, as if he could divine her thoughts?

"And because I can control who calls me what, up to a point," Ellen said with a slow smile, "you must ask permission to call me Ellen."

"My name is Valentine," he said quietly. "I beg you to use it and ask your leave to adopt comparably informal address when private with you."

"Valentine," she said, enunciating each syllable as they moved toward a break in the trees. "It's a lovely name. It shall be my privilege to use it. And you must call me Ellen when we are not in the churchyard."

"Thank you," Val said, releasing a breath. "So this is your pond?"

"Yours, actually." Ellen dropped his arm and hopped up on the dock that extended a good forty feet out over the pond. "I use it after dark, and the local boys use it whenever they please."

"A pond should be used." Val stepped onto the boards, as well, watching Ellen move to the end of the dock, her features obscured by the floppy brim of her hat. While she surveyed the tranquil surface of the water, he sat about ten feet from her and started tugging off his boots.

Ellen's gaze lit on him where he sat. "You are going to soak your feet?"

"And invite you to do likewise." Val tugged off his second boot. "Ellen."

She surprised him by nimbly slipping off her shoes and taking a seat beside him. Their bodies did not touch, and yet Val caught a whiff of the lovely honeysuckle and lavender scent of her. She carefully hiked her skirts just a little and let her toes dangle in the water.

"My feet are going to love this pond." Val cuffed his breeches to just under the knees and slipped his feet into the cool water. "All of me will love it, in fact."

"You are a good swimmer? The far end is quite deep."

"I am a very good swimmer. You?" He swirled his toes in the water, unabashedly letting her fix her gaze on his feet. They were big feet, of course, in keeping with the rest of him, and long, with high arches.

"I am competent," Ellen replied, "in a pond. I would not take on the ocean."

"Nor I. Who are these boys you despair of?"

He distracted her with questions for about the next twenty minutes, regarding it as time well spent in his efforts to set her at ease. They were going to be neighbors at the very least, and a man was hardly a man if he didn't take a little opportunity to appreciate a pair of bare, very pretty female feet.

"You have guests," Ellen reminded him. "I should not monopolize your time, Mr. Windham."

"Valentine. And they are uninvited guests."

"Good manners do not distinguish." She lifted her feet from the water and looked around as if searching for her shoes.

"Here." Val took his feet out, as well, and spun to sit facing her, cross-legged. He pulled his shirt over his head and held it over his lap. "Give me your foot."

"My foot?" Ellen's eyes were glued to the expanse of his chest. Val knew it was a chest that boasted an abundance of nicely arranged male muscle—mostly courtesy of years at the keyboard—and for a widow, it could hardly be considered a shocking sight.

"I'll dry you off." Val gestured with his makeshift towel, holding her gaze as if to imply he exposed himself like this to women every day, when in fact, he was by nature fairly modest. Cautiously, she leaned back on her hands and extended a foot toward him.

He seized the foot gently and buffed it with the linen shirt. He dried first one foot then the other, then tarried over his own feet before finally putting the somewhat damp shirt back on.

"Shall we?" Val had put his boots on and risen to extend a hand down to her. He'd left her no choice but to accept that hand and allow him to assist her to her feet. She didn't protest when he kept hold of her hand as he led her off the dock.

A year ago, Ellen had taken him by the hand to show him the wood, a casual gesture on her part—Val was sure of it. She could hardly object that he was turning the tables now, lacing his fingers through hers and setting a sedate pace back toward the house.

"Belmont's boys will be staying for a while," he

said as they gained the shade of the woods. "They're good boys, but I think the professor wants to test out being separated from them before he must send them to university."

"I'm ten years away from my parents' house, and I still miss them both desperately. But I'm also relieved they're gone in another sense."

"Relieved?" Val stopped walking to peer at her. "Was there illness?"

"My father was quite a bit older than my mother," she replied, frowning down at some ferns trying to encroach on the path. "He was probably failing, but I was a child, and his death seemed sudden to me. My mother wasn't young when I was born, so I was their treasured miracle."

"Of course you were."

"And were you somebody's treasured miracle?" Ellen asked, bending to tug at the ferns.

"I was one of ten such miracles," Val said. "But I do not doubt my parents' regard for me." He fell silent on that thought, a little disconcerted to realize it was the truth. He had never doubted their regard for him, though he'd also never felt he had their understanding. He was pondering this realization when Ellen shifted her hand so her fingers gripped his arm near the elbow, which was probably prudent. They would soon be out of the trees, and he had no desire to rush his fences.

Though what fences those would be, he would have to puzzle out later.

Three

"THANK YOU FOR SHOWING ME THE POND," VAL SAID as they approached the picnic blanket.

"My pleasure. It appears the fairies have been here, casting the post-picnic sleeping spell on your companions."

"We're not asleep." Darius opened his eyes and sat up. "Well, Belmont might be, but he had two helpings of cobbler, so allowances must be made. It's too quiet. Where do you think the savages have got off to?"

Belmont sat up and yawned. "They'll be putting up their tent. It's a sturdy business, that tent. If they use some of the lumber I brought to build a proper platform, it will keep them snug and dry and out of your hair."

"Savages with their own accommodations," Val remarked. "Decent of you."

"My brother Matthew and I put a tent to good use on many a summer night," Belmont said. "You might want to help the boys pick out a spot for a tree house, as well, but I'd set them to clearing all these damned saplings, were I you. Then Mrs. Fitz here can draft them as assistant gardeners. Pardon the language, Mrs. Fitz."

Val arched a brow at Ellen. "Gardeners?"

"Good heavens, Windham." Belmont got to his feet. "You can't be thinking your work is limited to the house? If you're to have a proper manor, you need to landscape it. The jungle will just take over again, if you don't. The oaks need to be pruned so they don't continue to litter your roof with acorns and leaves. You'll want flowers near the house, an herb garden for your kitchen, a medicinal garden, a vegetable garden near your home farm."

Val scrubbed a hand over his face. "So many gardens as all that?"

"And ornamental gardens, as well," Belmont went on blithely. "Some scent gardens, cutting gardens for early spring through fall, color gardens. As it's already nigh summer, you'd best get busy, or you'll waste the entire season. You'll take pity on him, won't you, Mrs. Fitz? You can't expect a city boy like Windham to comprehend the task involved."

"I suppose," Darius spoke up as he got to his feet, "the boys could be set to work turning beds and transplanting seedlings. One should think the offspring of a botanist might have a few skills in that regard."

"They've both spent long hours with me in the conservatory and the propagation house," Belmont assured them. "And I'll be happy to send over seedlings, as will my wife. We've all manner of new varieties gleaned from her estates in Kent." Belmont speared Val with a look. "If you're to keep my savages here with you. I promise I'll come back with a wagonload of seeds and sprouts for you and Mrs. FitzEngle."

Well done, Val wanted to shout, because the look of longing that crossed Ellen's face let him know her assistance had just been bribed right into his lap. "Such generosity will be much appreciated, Professor."

"Well, I'm off then." Belmont dusted off his breeches. "The leader is Nelson, and the off gelding is Wellie."

"Gelding?" Val asked.

"I'm loaning you my wagon and team," Belmont explained. "If all else fails, you can slaughter the horses and feed them to my sons. The boys can also ride these two, though we didn't pack saddles for them. Their gaits are smooth enough, provided you don't try to canter—or trot very far. My hay is in, and this is not my best pair, though they're good fellows."

"Most generous of you," Darius cut in, shooting Val a to-hell-with-your-pride look. "A wagon and team will save us a great deal of time and logistical complications, and the stables, at least, are sound and in good repair."

"Well, that's settled," Belmont looked around, his gaze traveling in the direction of noise most likely made by his children. "I will deliver a few paternal words of guidance, not because they will be heeded, but because Abby will expect it of me."

"I'll see to your horse," Darius volunteered.

Val started after Belmont, only to find Ellen's hand on his arm.

"Leave them some privacy," she suggested. "Good-byes are hard enough without an audience."

"And young men have surprising reserves of dignity."

"I was more concerned for their father," Ellen rejoined, smiling. "Perhaps you might suggest a visit to Candlewick in the near future?"

"I'd like to see the place. Belmont claimed it was in bad shape when he took it on."

"And I am sure Mrs. Belmont would like to see the boys," Ellen said. "But if we're to keep them busy, you must tell me what exactly you'd like them to accomplish."

They created a list, starting with the vegetable garden and including the transplanting of some young fruit trees from Ellen's back yard to Valentine's home farm. That property began with the meadow boasting the farm pond and ran along the lane toward more buildings and pastures in the direction of town. As he tried not to blatantly admire the curve of Ellen FitzEngle's lips or the way her neck joined her shoulders, Val instead heard the melody of her voice.

It would take woodwinds—strong, supple, and light, with low strings for balance—to convey the grace of that voice. Or possibly just the piano alone, a quiet, lyrical adagio.

He pulled his thoughts back to the conversation. "Who works the home farm?" he asked as they watched Darius leading Belmont's gelding from the stables.

"The Bragdolls. Or they work the land. The vegetable gardens, chicken coop, dairy, and so forth are not used. The manor has been unoccupied since before the previous Baron Roxbury owned the place."

"I am not inclined to set all that to rights just yet. Your surplus is adequate for my present needs, and I won't be hiring staff for months." *Assuming he even kept ownership of the place.*

"Get in as big a plot of vegetables as you can, anyway," Ellen said. "Children can weed it for you cheaply, and you can sell the excess, if any there is. And if you hire staff even as late as next spring, you'll still need a cellar full of food to feed them until next summer."

"Establishing a working manor with home farm is decidedly more complicated than I'd envisioned."

"You thought simply to restore the house," Ellen reminded him. "That is a substantial project in itself."

Val shrugged self-consciously. "I liked the place when first I saw it. I still like it, and I like all the ideas I have for restoring it to health." It reminded him in a curious way of creating...music. Part craft, part art; part discovery, part invention.

"So what will you name your acquisition?" Ellen asked, looking past Val's shoulder.

"What?" Val followed her gaze to see Belmont shamelessly hugging his half-grown children. "He'll miss them."

He wondered if his father ever missed him, but dismissed the thought. Victor and Bart were dead, and Val had never heard His Grace admit to missing either son. A mere youngest son off to Oxfordshire was hardly going to cause the Duke of Moreland to fret or worry or pine for the lack of him—any more than Val was going to permit himself to pine for his piano.

"It's Monday." Ellen leaned in to lower her voice.

"Suggest you'll bring them to visit at Candlewick on the weekend, and that way, you can dodge services in Little Weldon." She sauntered off, pausing to bid Belmont goodbye. From where Val stood, it looked like a punctiliously polite leave-taking on both their parts. When Belmont crossed the yard to join him, Val was still watching Ellen's retreat with a less than casual eye.

After Belmont had taken his leave and a wagonload of goods from town had been properly stored, Val sat beside Darius in the afternoon shadows and listened and calculated and listened some more. In the back of his mind, he heard the slow movement to Beethoven's Sixth Symphony, a sweet, lyrical little piece of musical comfort that had nothing to do with nails, lumber, sagging porches, and broken windows.

Herr Beethoven, Val concluded, knew little of the realities of country life.

"What say we round up the heathen and finish the day at the pond," Val suggested, alighting from their perch on the lumber. "I don't think they'll last much past dark, and I'm not sure I will either."

"Swimming." Darius affected an expression of concentration then hopped down beside Val. "That's the business where you get wet and hope not to accommodate any leeches in the process. Wouldn't miss it."

With the older males following at a sedate pace and the younger pair pelting through the wood, all four were soon shucking clothes and diving off the dock into the pond. To Val, the scene was reminiscent of many summer evenings spent with his brothers. He set himself to swimming laps around the pond, searching for a sense of peace in the soothing rhythm of water and mild exertion.

"We're heading back to start dinner," Darius called from the dock. He was dressed only in breeches, his dark hair wet and slicked back, the boys similarly attired.

"Leave me my soap. I'll follow shortly."

"Soap?" Dayton hollered. "What about meat pie? What about cobbler? What about cold potato salad and biscuits with butter?" His brother lit out, leaving Dayton to give chase and Darius to smile and bring up the rear. When they'd left, Val swam over to the dock and pulled himself up onto it, content just to sit and appreciate the quiet as he dried off in the warm evening air.

Who would ever have thought the absence of music could have any redeeming quality to it at all? God above, Belmont's offspring were loud. Val couldn't recall himself ever being that loud, but then, he'd been the baby boy. The youngest and then the musical artist, the one most likely to be watching and worrying while his older brothers leapt bellowing from rope swings into swimming holes or tore off across frozen ponds heedless of weak ice or protruding rocks. They had yelled and carried on enough without Val adding to the din.

And now the loudest of them—Victor and Bart— were dead. Val brought his knees up, wrapped his arms around his legs, and lowered his forehead to his knees. The night was growing beautiful as the air mellowed, the shadows lengthened, and soft, summery scents floated on gentle breezes.

Grief was so tenacious a companion he wanted to scream it out into the silence. At least when he could play the piano, there had been a way to express such emotions, to air them audibly without something so ugly as a scream. He sat up, then stood, and dove off the dock into the water and washed every inch of his skin and scalp.

When he was as clean as soap, water, and effort could make him, he sat naked on the dock for a long time watching the shadows lengthen. Evenings were difficult, and he'd frequently survived them only by playing his finger exercises for hours on end. Mindless, technically demanding, aurally homely, they'd soothed him in a way nothing else did.

When darkness threatened to obscure the path home, Val rose and pulled on his breeches. It occurred to him as he gathered up shirt, socks, boots, and towel, that in his own way, he'd grown used to making every bit as much useless noise as the Belmont brothers.

❧

Mr. Valentine Windham had troubles.

Ellen concluded this from her place in the shadowed woods and debated whether she should reveal herself or leave him to wander home in solitude. Coward that she was, she opted to guard her own privacy, lest he see from the look in her eyes she'd been spying for quite some time.

He had troubles, as evidenced by the hunch of his back muscles when he dropped his face to his knees. Troubles, as demonstrated by the long, long silence he held while evening deepened around him and he sat naked and utterly still on the dock. Troubles, as outlined by the leanness of his flanks and belly, the way his ribs and hips were too clearly delineated under his skin.

But God above, troubled or not, he was a breathtakingly beautiful man. Francis had been trim and capable of sitting a horse, but he'd never sported the kind of muscle Valentine Windham did. He'd also lacked Windham's height and the sense of coiled, nimble power Windham's body conveyed when it arched and dove cleanly into the water.

Those images, of Valentine Windham naked and still, naked and hoisting himself out of the water, naked and gathering his clothes at the end of the dock... They made a hot night hotter and made Ellen's clothes feel clingy and damp next to her skin. As full darkness fell, she stripped down and slipped into the water, circling the pond many times, just as Valentine had.

And just as unable to find relief from the guilt and grief troubling her.

❧

"The boys will be all right in their tent?" Val asked as he poured two cups of tea from the pot on the stove while a few drops of rain spattered the roof of the carriage house.

"They're waterproof," Darius replied, accepting his cup. "Rain or shine, this whole summer is a lark to them, as it should be."

"They've gotten a lot done this week. There's not a sapling standing in the yard, the beds are dug and planted, the vegetables are in, and the drive is looking better."

Darius regarded Val by the flickering light of a single candle. "But you are not satisfied."

"With them? Of course I am. They're good boys, and they work hard. I'm lucky to have them."

"With them, maybe, not with yourself."

"And you are such a paragon of self-satisfaction?" The last thing Val wanted at the end of yet another grueling day was Darius Lindsey peering into his soul.

"You will take the boys and Mrs. Fitz to Candlewick tomorrow," Darius replied. "Get some decent cooking into you, play Belmont's grand piano for a few hours, and set yourself to rights."

Val was silent a long time, until he expelled a hard breath and set his mug down on the bricks under the stove. "I will not be playing Belmont's piano or any other, and I will thank you not to raise the matter before others." He crossed the room in two strides and sat on his bunk, hauling off his boots and tossing them hard against the opposite wall.

"So that's what all the gloves are about?" Darius asked, reclining on his cot. "Your left hand is still buggered up?"

"How did you know?"

"I have eyes, Valentine. It took me about two days to figure out you own the world's largest collection of gloves, because you've bought them ready-made in two different sizes. From there, I observed your left hand is swollen, the thumb, index, and middle fingers noticeably red and painful-looking. You make every effort not to favor the hand for fine tasks but beat it to death on manual labor. One has to wonder if your actions are well advised."

"Fairly forbid me the piano," Val bit out. "So I don't play the bloody piano."

"And does your hand improve?"

"Not much." Val tried to match his companion's casual tone. "At first, there was some improvement, but lately, it's no better. I might as well use it for what I can, while I can."

"You say that like you are angry at your hand," Darius mused, "though you do every kind of rough work there is to do with it, and you certainly make me look like I'm barely pulling my weight most days."

"I do every kind of work the common laborers do," Val corrected him. He rose and crossed the room to where his boots lay against the far wall and set them tidily next to the door. "I just can't do the kind of work I was born to do."

"And that would be?"

"Play the piano. My art is how I go on, Darius, and the only thing I know how to do well enough to matter."

"Doing it a bit dramatic, don't you think?" Darius crossed his arms behind his head and regarded Val where he once again sat on his cot.

"No, I don't think. Were I going to be dramatic, I'd slit my wrists, hang myself, or jump into the Thames when the tide was leaving."

"Valentine." Darius sat up. "That is not funny."

"How funny do you think it feels not to be able to play the piano when it's all I've done of worth in the past twenty-some years? I did not excel at school, and I can't point to an illustrious career like my brother, the former cavalry officer. I haven't Westhaven's head for business. I wasn't a jolly good time like Bart or a charmer like Vic. *But, by God, I could play the piano.*"

"And you can build stone walls and referee between Day and Phil and keep an eye on Nick Haddonfield when he hares all over the Home Counties," Darius retorted. "Do you think one activity defines you?"

"I'm like a whore, Darius, in that, yes, the one activity, in my case playing the piano, defines me." Val heard weariness in his own voice. "When Dev was driven mad by nightmares, I played for him so he couldn't hear the battles anymore. When his little Winnie was scared witless by all the changes in her life, I played for her and taught her a few things to play for herself. When Victor was so sick, I'd play for him, and he'd stop coughing for a little while. It's how I let people know they matter to me, Darius, and now…"

Darius got up and crossed the room, then lowered himself to sit beside Val in the shifting candlelight. "Now all this playing for others has left you one-handed, angry, and beating yourself up."

Not beating himself up, precisely, but *feeling* beaten up. "The piano is the way I have a soul, Dare. It's always there for me, always able to say the things I can't, always worth somebody's notice, even if they don't know they notice. It has never let me down, never ridiculed me before others, never taken a sudden notion not to know who I am or what I want. As mistresses go, the piano has been loyal, predictable, and lovely."

"You talk about an instrument as if it's animate," Darius said, hunching forward. "I know you are grieving the inability to exercise a considerable talent, but you are too old—and far too dear a man—to be relying on an imaginary friend. You deserve more than to think of yourself as merely the slave of your muse."

Val shot off the bed and crossed to the door, pausing only long enough to tug on his boots.

"I'm sorry." Darius rose and might have stopped him, but Val turned his back and got his hand on the door latch first. "I don't like seeing you suffer, but were you really happy spending your entire life on the piano bench?"

"You think I'm happy now?" Val asked without turning.

He was down the stairs and out into the night without any sense of where he was headed or why movement might help. Darius was too damned perceptive by half, but really—an imaginary friend?

It was the kind of devastating observation older brothers might make of a younger sibling and then laugh about. Maybe, Val thought as his steps took him along a bridle path in the moonlit woods, this was why the artistic temperament was so unsteady. People not afflicted with the need to create could not understand what frustration of the urge felt like.

The weekend at Belmont's loomed like an obstacle course in Val's mind.

No finger exercises, no visiting friendly old repertoire to limber up, no reading open score to keep abreast of the symphonic literature, no letting themes and melodies wander around in his hands just to see what became of them. No glancing up and realizing he'd spent three hours on a single musical question and still gotten no closer to a satisfactory answer.

All of that, Val thought as he emerged from the darkened woods, was apparently never to be again. His hand was not getting better, though it wasn't getting worse, either. It merely hurt and looked ugly and managed only activities requiring brute strength of the arm and not much real grip.

He found himself at the foot of Ellen FitzEngle's garden and wondered if he could have navigated his way there on purpose. Her cottage was dark, but her back yard was redolent with all manner of enticing floral scents in the dewy evening air. If her gardens were pretty to the eye by day, they were gorgeous to the nose at night. Silently, Val wandered the rows until his steps took him to the back porch, where a fat orange cat strolled down the moonlit steps to strop itself against Val's legs.

"He's shameless." Ellen's voice floated through the shadows. "Can't abide having to catch mice and never saw a cream bowl he couldn't lick spotless in a minute."

"What's his name?" Val asked, not even questioning why Ellen would be alone on her porch after dark.

"Marmalade. Not very original."

"Because he's orange?" Val bent to pick the cat up and lowered himself to the top porch step.

"And sweet," Ellen added, shifting from her porch swing to sit beside Val. "I take it you were too hot to sleep?"

"Too bothered. You?"

"Restless. You were right; change is unsettling to me."

"I am unsettled, as well," Val said, humor in his voice. "I seem to have a penchant for it."

"Sometimes we can't help what befalls us. What has you unsettled?"

Val was silent, realizing he was sitting beside one of very few people familiar with him who had never heard him play the piano. A woman who, in fact, didn't even know he could play, much less that he was Moreland's musical son.

"My hand hurts. It has been plaguing me for some time, and I'm out of patience with it."

"Which hand?" Ellen asked, her voice conveying some surprise. Whatever trouble she might have expected Valentine Windham to admit, it apparently hadn't been a simple physical ailment.

"This very hand here." Val waved his left hand in the night air, going still when Ellen caught it in her own.

"Have you seen a physician?" she asked, tracing the bones on the back of his hand with her fingers.

"I did." Val closed his eyes and gave himself up to the pleasure of her touch. Her fingers were cool and her exploration careful. "He assured me of nothing, save that I should treat it as an inflammation."

"Which meant what?" Ellen's fingers slipped over his palm. "That you should tote roofing slates about by the dozen? Carry buckets of mortar for your masons? I can feel some heat in it, now that you draw my attention to it." She held his hand up to her cheek and cradled it against her jaw.

"It means I am to drink willow bark tea, which is vile stuff. I am to rest the hand, which I do by avoiding fine tasks with it. I am to use cold soaks, massage, and arnica, if it helps, and I am not to use laudanum, as that only masks symptoms, regardless of how much it still allows me to function."

"I have considerable stores of willow bark tea." Ellen drew her fingers down each of Val's in turn. "And it sounds to me as if you're generally ignoring sound medical advice."

"I rub it. I rest it, compared to what I usually do with it. I don't think it's getting worse."

"Stay here." Ellen patted his hand and rose. She floated off into the cottage, leaving Val to marvel that if he weren't mistaken, he was sitting in the darkness, more or less holding hands with a woman clad only in a summer nightgown and wrapper. Her hair was once again down, the single braid tidy for once where it hung along her spine.

Summer, even in the surrounds of Little Weldon, even with a half-useless sore hand, had its charms.

"Give me your hand," Ellen said when she resumed her seat beside him. He passed over the requested appendage as he might have passed along a dish of overcooked asparagus. She rested the back of his hand against her thigh, and Val heard the sound of a tin being opened.

"You are going to quack me?"

"I am going to use some comfrey salve to help you comply with doctor's orders. There's probably arnica in it too."

Val felt her spread something cool and moist over his hand, and then her fingers were working it into his skin. She was patient and thorough, smoothing her salve over his knuckles and fingers, into his palms, up over his wrist, and back down each finger. As she worked, he felt tension, frustration, and anger slipping down his arm and out the ends of his fingers, almost as if he were playing—

"You aren't swearing," Ellen said after she'd worked for some minutes in silence. "I have to hope I'm not hurting you."

"You're not." Val's tired brain took a moment to find even simple words. "It's helping, or I think it is. Sometimes I go to bed believing I've had a good day with it; then I wake up the next day, and my hand is more sore than ever."

"You should keep a journal," Ellen suggested, slathering more salve on his hand. "That's how I finally realized I'm prone to certain cyclical fluctuations in mood."

He understood her allusion and considered were she not a widow—and were it not dark—she would not have ventured even that much.

"What did you say was in that salve?"

"Comfrey," Ellen said, sounding relieved at the shift in topic. "Likely mint, as well, rosemary, and maybe some lavender, arnica if memory serves, a few other herbs, some for scent, some for comfort."

"I like the scent," Val said, wondering how long she'd hold his hand. It was childish of him, but he suspected the contact was soothing him as much as the specific ingredients.

"Is it helping?" Ellen asked, her fingers slowing again.

"It helps. I think the heat of your touch is as therapeutic as your salve."

"It might well be." Ellen sandwiched his larger

hand between her smaller ones. "I do not hold myself out as any kind of herbalist. There's too much guess-work and room for error involved."

"But you made this salve."

"For my own use." Ellen kept his hand between hers. "I will sell scents, soaps, and sachets but not any product that could be mistaken for a medicine, tincture, or tisane."

"Suppose it's wise to know one's limits." Ellen was just holding Val's hand in hers, and he was glad for the darkness, as his gratitude for the simple contact was probably plain on his face. "Ellen…"

She waited, holding his hand, and Val had to corral the words about to spill impulsively over his lips.

"You will accompany us to Candlewick tomorrow?" he asked instead.

"I will. I've made the acquaintance of the present Mrs. Belmont, and Mr. Belmont assured me she would welcome some female company."

"And you, Ellen? Are you lonely for female company?"

"I am." Val suspected it was an admission for her. "My mother was my closest friend, but she died shortly after my marriage. There is an ease in the companionship of one's own gender, don't you think?"

"Up to a point. One can be direct among one's familiars, in any case, but you've brought me ease tonight, Ellen FitzEngle, and you are decidedly not the same gender as I."

"We need not state the obvious." Her voice was just a trifle frosty even as she kept her hands around Val's.

"Do we need to talk about my kissing you a year ago? I've behaved myself for two weeks, Ellen, and hope by action I have reassured you where words would not."

Silence or the summer evening equivalent of it, with crickets chirping, the occasional squeal of a passing bat, and the breeze riffling through the woods nearby.

"Ellen?"

Val withdrew his hand, which Ellen had been holding for some minutes, and slid his arm around her waist, urging her closer. "A woman gone silent unnerves a man. Talk to me, sweetheart. I would not offend you, but neither will I fare well continuing the pretense we are strangers."

He felt the tension in her, the stiffness against his side, and regretted it. In the past two weeks, he'd all but convinced himself he was recalling a dream of her not a real kiss, and then he'd catch her smiling at Day and Phil or joking with Darius, and the clench in his vitals would assure him that kiss had been very, very real.

At least for him. For him, that kiss had been a work of sheer *art*.

"My husband seldom used my name. I was my dear, or my lady, or occasionally, dear wife. I was not Ellen, and I was most assuredly not his sweetheart. And to you I am the next thing to a stranger."

Val's left hand, the one she'd just held for such long, lovely moments between her own, drifted up to trace slow patterns on her back. "We're strangers who kissed. Passionately, if memory serves."

"But on only one occasion and that nearly a year ago."

"Should I have written? I did not think to see you again, nor you me, I'm guessing." Now he wished he'd written, though it would hardly have been proper, even to a widow.

That hand Valentine considered so damaged continued its easy caresses on Ellen's back, intent on stealing the starch from her spine and the resolve from her best intentions. And she must have liked his touch, because the longer he stroked his hand over her back, the more she relaxed and leaned against him.

"I did not think to see you again," Ellen admitted. "It would have been much easier had you kept to your place in my memory and imagination. But here you are."

"Here we are." Haunting a woman's imagination had to be a good thing for a man whose own dreams had turned to nightmares. "Sitting on the porch in the moonlight, trying to sort out a single kiss from months ago."

"I shouldn't have kissed you," Ellen said, her head coming to rest on Val's shoulder as if the weight of truth were a wearying thing. "But I'm lonely and sometimes a little desperate, and it seemed safe, to steal a kiss from a handsome stranger."

"It was safe," Val assured her, seeing the matter from her perspective. In the year since he'd seen Ellen FitzEngle, he'd hardly been celibate. He wasn't a profligate Philistine, but neither was he a monk. There had been an older maid in Nick's household, some professional ladies up in York, the rare trip upstairs at David's brothel, and the frequent occasion of self-gratification.

But he surmised Ellen, despite the privileges of widowhood, had not been kissed or cuddled or swived or flirted with in all those days and weeks and months.

"And now?" Ellen pressed. "You show up on my porch after dark and think perhaps it's still safe, and here I am, doing not one thing to dissuade you."

"You are safe with me, Ellen." He punctuated the sentiment with a kiss to her temple then rested his cheek where his lips had been. "I am a gentleman, if nothing else. I might try to steal a kiss, but you can stop me with a word from even that at any time. The question is, how safe do you want to be?"

"Shame on you," Ellen whispered, turning her face to his shoulder.

"Shame on me is right, for I do not offer you anything, you see, but kisses and illicit pleasures. Those I can give you in abundance, if you want them."

She pulled away, peering at him in the moonlight. "Are you insulting me?"

"I am not. I am commenting on my own unworthiness as a mate to a decent woman. I can bring you pleasure and take some for myself, if you offer it, but that is the extent of my utility."

"You do not intend to stay here," Ellen concluded, pulling her wrapper a little more snugly around her.

"I rarely stay in one place for long." His home had been wherever there was a piano. He had no idea how to define home now. "I am not looking to marry, Ellen. I hazard you are not either, else you would have ended your widowhood some time in these past five years."

Sitting beside her, Val felt a creeping fatalism

...eeping through him. This reckoning between them had sneaked up on him, but now that he was sitting in the dark, making indecent offers to a decent woman, he realized they needed to have this conversation and be done with it.

He could get her rejection of him behind them, and they could set about being cordial neighbors through their shared wood, just as if they'd never kissed. Were his hand not crippled—he hadn't wanted to admit to that word previously—he might at some point be offering for her instead. She was gently bred, a lady to the bone, and sexually attractive to him on a level beyond the superficial easing of lust.

But he *was* a cripple, and the longer he went without playing the piano, the more he experienced his disability as emotional as well as physical. He'd been right to tell Darius the piano was how he'd had a soul. How he'd known himself to possess a soul.

"You are looking to dally," Ellen said softly, bringing Val's thoughts back to the present.

"I am looking to share pleasure," Val replied, hoping it was true. God above, what if he couldn't even please a woman anymore? With his arm around her and her fragrance wafting to his nose among the myriad floral scents, his strongest urge was not to lay her down and bury himself inside her.

It was to hold her close and learn the feel of her under his hands, to offer himself to her for her own stroking and petting and caressing. To take his time and learn how to pay attention to her as carefully as he'd attend a fascinating piece of new music.

"I have not your sophistication," Ellen said, her

head back on his shoulder. "Physically, I was married. I comprehend for men certain acts are more profoundly pleasurable than they are for women. Emotionally…"

"Ah." Val's hand stroked over her spine and rested on her shoulder so his thumb could caress her nape. "I will protect your privacy, Ellen, and your good name." And he would show her when it came to *certain acts*, women could experience more pleasure than any man could endure.

"And if I conceive?"

"I will provide for you and the child." It was the answer required of a gentleman to a lady without a reputation to protect, and it sat ill with him. "If you demanded it, I would marry you."

"I would not demand marriage," Ellen said on a sigh. "I was married for five years and could not give my husband a child." There was such sadness in her voice, such surrender in the way she rested against him, Val knew in her single, quiet sentence she was hiding a story with an unhappy ending.

"You wanted children."

"Desperately. Francis needed an heir, and I was his choice as wife. I could not produce even one son for him."

"Francis was your husband, and you loved him."

"I did." Ellen seemed to grow smaller as she leaned against him. "Not well enough, not soon enough, but I did. I would have done anything to provide him the children it was my duty to give him."

Val stroked her back, feeling his heart constrict painfully—for her. "Sometimes we are denied our fondest wish."

"He was a good man."

"Tell me about him," Val urged, his hand returning to her neck. If there was etiquette involved with a prospective lover asking about a late spouse, he neither knew nor cared about it. Apparently, neither did she.

"As Baron Roxbury, Francis held one of the oldest titles short of the monarchy," Ellen began, "but he wasn't pompous or pretentious. I didn't know him well when we married, but I thought him such a prig at first. He was merely shy and uncertain how to deal with a wife nearly half his age."

Baron Roxbury? Val held still, kept up his easy caresses on Ellen's back, and absorbed the fact that he had propositioned the Baroness Roxbury on her own back steps. *What was she doing rusticating like a tenant farmer's widow when she held such a title?*

"You must have been very young," Val managed.

"Seventeen. I was presented after my marriage, of course, but never had to compete with the other girls for a husband. Francis spared me that, and I went from being my parents' treasured miracle to his treasured wife. I didn't know how lucky I was."

"We often don't." Val forced himself to keep listening, to keep his questions behind his teeth, as he sensed Ellen did not discuss her past often. It wasn't just that she had secrets, it was that she grieved privately. "You miss your Francis."

"I miss…" Ellen's voice dipped. "I miss him bodily, of course. As we became friends, we also became affectionate, and that was a comfort when the children did not arrive. I miss him in other ways, too, though, as my spouse, the person through whom I was afforded social standing and a place in society. That's a trite phrase until you don't have that place anymore."

Val said nothing but turned slightly and looped his other arm around her so she was resting not merely against him but in his embrace. He willed her to cry, but she only laid her forehead to his collarbone and sighed against his neck.

He rested his chin on her crown and gazed out across the moon shadows in her yard. There was peace to be found in holding Ellen FitzEngle like this. Not the kind of peace he'd anticipated, and maybe not a peace he deserved, but he'd take it as long as she allowed it.

"It isn't well done of me," Ellen murmured, trying to draw back, "pining for my husband in your arms."

"Hush. Whose arms have been available to you, hmm? Marmalade's, perhaps?"

"You are a generous man and far too trusting."

From her words, Val knew she wasn't being entirely honest, but he also knew she'd had little comfort for her grief and woes, and trust in such matters was a delicate thing. When he shifted a few minutes later and lifted her against his chest, she did not protest but looped her arms around his neck, and that was a kind of trust too. He carried her to her porch swing and sat at one end so her back was supported by the pillows banking the arm of the swing. He set the swing in motion and gathered her close until she drifted away into sleep.

Val stayed on that swing long after the woman in his arms had fallen asleep, knowing he was stealing a pleasure from her he should not. He'd never been in her cottage, though, and was reluctant to invade her privacy.

Or so he told himself.

In truth, the warm, trusting weight of Ellen FitzEngle in his arms anchored him on a night when he'd been at risk of wandering off, of putting just a little more space between his body and his soul; his intellect and his emotions. Darius had delivered a telling blow when he'd characterized music, and the piano, as an imaginary friend.

And it was enough, Val realized, to admit no creative art could meet the artist's every need or fulfill every wish. Ellen FitzEngle wasn't going to be able to do that either, of course; that wasn't the point.

The point, Val mused as he carefully lifted Ellen against his chest and made his way into her cottage, was that life yet held pleasures and mysteries and interest for him. He would get through the weekend at Belmont's on the strength of that insight. As he tucked a sleeping Ellen into her bed and left a good-night kiss on her cheek, Val silently sent up a prayer of thanks.

By trusting him with her grief, Ellen had relieved a little of his own.

Four

"You look skinny," Axel Belmont observed as he closed the guest room door behind the last of the bucket-laden footmen. "And you've spent a deal of time in the sun."

"Roofs tend to be in the sun," Val said, "if one is fortunate."

"Let me." Belmont snagged Val's sleeve and deftly removed a cuff link. Val let him, thinking back to how long it had taken his left hand to actually get the right cuff link fastened. Darius had taken his inconsiderate self off to London at first light, leaving Val to don proper attire for the first time in days, and make a slow, difficult job of it.

"What's wrong with this hand?" Belmont took Val's left hand in his own and peered at it curiously.

"I've managed to do some damage to it." Val sat to remove his boots, taking his hand from Belmont's inspection. "Manual labor is not without its perils."

"Tell me about it." Belmont took Val's boots and set them outside the door. "I was resetting a pair of shoes on Abby's gelding a few days ago, and he spooked on the cross ties. My toes will probably be purple until Christmas. Good for sympathy, though."

"You're in need of sympathy from your new wife already?" Val asked as he stepped out of his breeches. He eyed the tub with something close to lust and stepped in without another word.

Belmont regarded Val's naked form with frank appraisal. "My wife will want to stuff you like a goose, Windham. Have you no provisions at your campsite?"

"We eat regularly." Val sank into the water on a heartfelt sigh. "I'm not sitting on my arse all day anymore, playing pretty tunes and idling hours away. God in heaven, was there ever a pleasure greater than a hot bath?"

"If you have to ask that, you are not right in the head, or somewhere else."

"I've been accused of same." Val closed his eyes and leaned his head back. "There is a kind of grime farm ponds do not get clean."

"It has been at least a year since I've gone swimming," Belmont replied, gathering up Val's breeches, shirt, and socks. "Now you may soak. I've no doubt my wife is grilling Mrs. Fitz at some length, so take your time. By the way, you seem to be getting on with the lady well enough."

"She is amiable," Val pronounced from his tub. "As am I."

"Amiable." Belmont frowned. "Well, all right. I won't pry, but Abby will get the details out of Mrs. Fitz, so you might want to spill anyway."

Val frowned right back. "What I tell you will get straight back to our mutual friend Nick, who will tell my brother Westhaven, who will tell his wife, who will be interrogated by Her Grace, and so forth. You and your brother are no doubt discreet fellows who do not cut up each other's peace. My borders are not as easily defended as yours."

"Fair enough. So let me leave it at this: If you do want to talk, I can, contrary to your surmise, keep my mouth shut. Ellen is lovely, and had I been a different kind of widower and she a different kind of widow, she and I might have been closer friends."

"What does that mean?" Val scowled, abruptly wishing they were having this discussion when he was dressed and not lounging naked in a tub.

"It means I would not blame either one of you for what you did in private," Belmont said. "Neither would Abby."

Val blinked. "My thanks."

"I'll see your boots cleaned and leave them at the door."

Axel repaired to his library, there to start a letter to Nick Haddonfield, generally regarded to be Val Windham's closest friend. And while Axel would not violate a confidence, something had to be relayed to Nick regarding his brother-in-law Darius and his friend Lord Val, if only placatory generalities. Darius had attached himself to Val at Nick's request, after all, and this little plan to foster Day and Phillip in Windham's camp had been Nick's casual suggestion, as well.

Casual, indeed.

⁓

Ellen unpinned her hat and surveyed the gracious, airy
guestroom. "You weren't joking about a bath, were
you?" Maids were trooping in, each one dumping two
buckets of warm water into a large copper bathing tub.

"Travel in summer is often a dusty, uncomfortable
business," Abby Belmont said as she closed the drapes
to the balcony doors. "And being around Day and
Phillip can leave anybody in need of some peace and
quiet. Shall I send a maid in to assist you?"

"Oh, good heavens, no." Ellen blushed to even
think of it, and Abby regarded her curiously.

"Axel told me you don't use the title. By rights we
should be ladyshipping you and so forth. Let's get you
out of that dress, and you can tell me how the boys
really behaved."

Grateful for the change in topic, Ellen pattered on
cheerfully about Day and Phillip until she was soaked,
shampooed, rinsed, brushed out, dried off, and dressed
for luncheon.

"You didn't love your first husband the way you
love Mr. Belmont, did you?" Ellen asked before they'd
left the privacy of the guest room. The question would
have been unthinkable even an hour ago, but pretty,
dark-haired Abby Belmont—formerly Abby Stoneleigh—
had a comfortable, unpretentious air about her.

"That is a difficult question," Abby replied slowly,
"but no, I was never in love with Gerald and probably never truly loved him, though I was—however
mistakenly—grateful to him. I am in love with my
present husband, but even he, who loved his first
wife dearly, would tell you a second marriage is not
like a first."

Ellen said nothing—the topic was one of idle curiosity only—and let Abby link their arms and lead her
to the family dining room.

In the course of the meal, Ellen watched as Val
consumed a tremendous quantity of good food, all the
while conversing with the Belmonts about plans for
his property, the boys' upcoming matriculation, and
mutual acquaintances. At the conclusion of the meal,
Belmont offered Val and Ellen a tour of the property,
and Abby departed on her husband's arm to take her
afternoon nap.

"May I offer you a turn through the back gardens
while we wait for our host?" Val asked Ellen when the
Belmonts had repaired abovestairs. "There's plenty of
shade, and I need to move lest I turn into a sculpture
of ham and potatoes."

He soon had her out the back door, her straw hat
on her head. She wrapped her fingers around Val's arm
and pitched her voice conspiratorially low. "Find us
some shade and a bench."

He led her through gardens that were obviously
the pride and joy of a man with a particular interest in
flora, to a little gazebo under a spreading oak.

"Did we bore you at lunch with all of our talk of
third parties and family ties?" he asked as he seated her
inside the gazebo.

"Not at all, but you unnerved me with your familiar address."

Val grimaced. "I hadn't noticed. Suppose it's best to
go on as I've begun, though, unless you object? They
aren't formal people."

"They are lovely people. Now sit you down, Mr.

Windham, and take your medicine." She withdrew her tin of comfrey salve, and Val frowned.

"You don't have to do this." He settled beside her on the bench that circled five interior sides of the hexagonal gazebo.

"Because you'll be so conscientious about it yourself?" She'd positioned herself to his left and held out her right hand with an imperious wave. Taking Val's left hand in her right, she studied it carefully.

"I didn't get to see this the other night. It looks like it hurts."

"Only when I use it. But if you'll just hand me the tin, I can see to myself."

"Stop being stubborn." She dipped her fingers into the salve. "It's only a hand, and only a little red and swollen. Maybe you shouldn't be using it at all." She began to spread salve over his knuckles while Val closed his eyes. "You have no idea why this has befallen you?"

"I might have overused it. Or it might be a combination of overuse and a childhood injury, or it might be just nerves."

"Nerves?" Ellen peered over at him while she stroked her fingers over his palm. "One doesn't usually attribute nerves to such hearty fellows as you."

"It started the day I buried my second brother," Val said on a sigh. He turned his head as if gazing out over the gardens or toward the manor house that sat so serenely on a small rise.

"You didn't tell me you'd lost a brother." She switched her grip so Val's hand was between both of hers and her thumbs were circling on his broad and slightly callused palm.

"Two, actually. One on the Peninsula under less than heroic circumstances, though we don't bruit that about, the other to consumption." His voice could not have been more casual, but Ellen was holding his hand and felt the tension radiating from him.

"Valentine, I am so very sorry."

❧

"How did your husband die?" Val asked, desperately wanting to change the subject if not snatch his hand away and tear across the fields until he was out of sight.

"Fall from a horse," Ellen said, though she did not turn loose of Val's hand. "He lingered for two weeks, put his affairs in order—not that Francis's affairs were ever out of order—then slipped away. I thought..."

"You thought?"

"I thought he was recovering." She sighed, her fingers going still, though she kept his hand cradled in both of hers. "There was no outward injury, you see. He took a bump on the head, and there was some bruising around his middle, but no bleeding, no infection, nothing you'd think would kill a man."

"He might have been bleeding inside. Or that bump on the head might have been what got him."

"He was upset with himself to be incapacitated," Ellen said softly. "The Markhams have bad hearts, you see. Their menfolk don't often live past fifty, and some don't live half that long. They are particularly careful of their succession, and so my failure to provide a son stood out in great relief. Francis was upset with himself for not seeing to his duty, not upset with me. His first wife had done no better than I, though, and that was some comfort."

"I didn't know you were a second wife," Val said as Ellen shifted her ministrations to his wrist and forearm.

"She died of typhus. They were also married for five years, and I know Francis was very fond of her."

"Fond." Val wrinkled his nose at the term. "I suppose that's genteel, but I can't see myself spending the rest of my life with somebody of whom I am merely fond. I am fond of Ezekiel."

"Your horse." Ellen smiled at him. "He is fond of you, as well, but when you have nobody and nothing to be even fond of, then fond can loom like a great boon."

"Nobody?" Val cocked his head, addressing her directly. "No cousins, no uncles or aunts, no old granny knitting in some kitchen?"

Ellen shook her head. "I was the only child of only children and born to them late in life. The present generation of Markhams was not prolific either. There's Frederick, of course, and some theoretical cousin who enjoys the status of Frederick's heir, but I do not relish Frederick's company, and I've never met the cousin."

"What is a theoretical cousin?"

"Francis called him that," Ellen said, switching to long, slow strokes along Val's forearm. It was a peculiarly soothing way to be touched, though Val had the sense she'd all but forgotten what her hands were doing. "I gather Mr. Grey might be joined so far back to the family tree as to make the connection suspect, or he might have been born to his mother long after she'd separated from Mr. Grey."

"May I ask you a question?"

"Of course." Ellen smiled at him again, the smile reaching her eyes this time. "We are holding hands in a location likely chosen to shield us from the prying eyes of our host and hostess."

Val smiled back. "I am found out, though since when does it take an hour to escort one's wife abovestairs?"

"I don't begrudge them their marital bliss, or a lady in an interesting condition her rest."

"If rest is what she's getting."

"Your question?"

"Why don't you use the Markham name? You go by Ellen FitzEngle, when in fact you are Baroness Roxbury, and not even the dowager baroness, since Frederick hasn't remarried."

"FitzEngle was my mother's maiden name," Ellen said, her grip shifting back down to his palm and knuckles. "I wanted no associations with the Roxbury barony when I moved to Little Weldon, and there are few who know exactly to whom I was married."

"Why? Were you ashamed of the connection?"

"I was ashamed of myself. I failed my husband in the one duty a wife is expected to perform. I did not want anybody's pity or their scorn. My privacy means a lot to me."

"But you dissemble," Val said gently. "You are entitled to the respect of your position, and yet you labor all day in those gardens as if you have no portion, no connections, no place in society."

Val tightened his fingers around hers when she would have drawn away. "You haven't any portion, have you? No dower property. Why, Ellen? You speak of your husband as if he were some kind of saint, and yet even when he had time to put his affairs in order, he did not provide for you."

"You will not speak ill of my husband. He provided for me."

Secrets had a particular scent all their own, an unpleasant, cloying sweetness from being held too closely and carrying more power than they should. Val admitted he himself was keeping secrets from the woman beside him—the secret of his father's ducal title, the secret of his musical ability—his *former* musical ability. Ellen wasn't simply hiding her own title, however. She was hiding an entire past from an entire village.

"I did not mean to impugn Francis," Val said carefully, turning his hand over to stroke his thumb over Ellen's wrist. "I am concerned for you."

"My situation is adequate for the present. Your concern is misplaced."

His concern was *not* misplaced, though neither was it appreciated. A change of topic was in order. "Are you done with my hand, or might I convince you to hold on to it as we admire Axel's gardens?"

"You might." Ellen rose, and Val escorted her along a shady, winding path. He counted himself lucky, because she did indeed keep hold of his hand as she turned the topic. "Does this place give you ideas about your own grounds?"

"It does." Val understood the conversation must not stray back to the personal until Ellen had her emotional balance. "The first such idea is that my estate needs a name. It will be the old Markham place until fifty years after I hang something else on the gateposts."

"What comes to mind?"

"Nothing. And I don't want to force a name on the place when names and labels have a way of becoming permanent."

"What does the estate signify to you?" Ellen asked, keeping his fingers loosely linked with her own.

Val pursed his lips in thought. "Hard work. A summer project, an escape." A *dalliance*.

He didn't say that, of course. He wasn't sure it was true. When he'd risen that morning and seen Darius departing on his piebald gelding, Val had felt a measure of relief to think the weekend would be spent in company. Somehow, sitting on Ellen's porch in the evening darkness, he'd opened the topic of a different relationship with Ellen—a dalliance.

He'd meant to apologize for a year-old kiss, maybe, or to kiss her again. He wasn't sure which, but he certainly hadn't intended to baldly proposition the lady.

The matter had arisen unbidden, without Val planning to broach it. In his view, women as intimate partners were lovely creatures, like birds or pets or pretty houseplants. They graced his life but were hardly necessary to it. When the occasional urge arose, he often felt it as a distraction from his music, indulging his sexual proclivities as an afterthought or an aside between the more fascinating business to be transacted at his keyboard.

He liked sex—he liked it a lot—but he seldom went in search of it.

And thus, he mused, he was probably no damned good at comprehending when he needed what Nick called a friendly poke, or how to arrange it with a minimum of fuss.

"You are quiet," Ellen said. "Do you think of your brothers?"

"Every day," Val said on a resigned sigh. It appeared they were going to brush up against this most uncomfortable topic again.

"It will get better," Ellen assured him. "If it hasn't already. You don't just think of the loss, you also think of the good times and the gifts they left you with. You see the whole picture on your good days, and the ache fades."

"Maybe. But it felt like I was just getting to that place with Bart's death, which was stupid and avoidable, when Victor's decline became impossible to ignore. And Victor and I had grown closer when Bart and Dev went off to war."

She was silent for a moment as they strolled along. "I have pouted because I was an only child, but I never did consider what an affront it would be to lose siblings, particularly siblings in their prime, and siblings I was close to. I am sorry, Valentine, for your losses."

He stopped walking, the emotional breath knocked out of him for reasons he could not consider. He'd heard the same platitude a thousand times before— two thousand—and knew the polite replies, but now Ellen's arms went around his waist, and the polite replies choked him. Slowly, tentatively, he wrapped an arm, then two, around her shoulders, closed his eyes, and rested his cheek against her hair.

❧

Frederick Markham was angry, and when he was angry his digestion became dyspeptic, which made him angrier still. A fellow needed the comforts of good food and fine spirits to soothe him when aggravations such as petty debts plagued him.

God damn Cousin Francis. With each passing quarter, the indignity of the late baron's scheme became harder to bear. If it weren't for the rents Ellen had passed along from Little Weldon, there would have been no hunting in the shires the previous winter. Even with burdensome economies, the Season itself had been cramped. Now, Frederick had tarried too long in Town, and there was no convenient house party to entertain him as summer got underway.

And because he'd gambled his last unentailed property away, there would not be as much rental income. What on earth had he been thinking?

The old place out near Little Weldon had been a ruin, true, but it had been, to some extent, *his* ruin. Frederick had gotten the deed from the solicitors so he might study it, not toss it aside in a damned card game. And study it he had, while Windham—Lord Valentine, rather—apparently had not.

Else why would the man be pouring time and money into the place? Ellen was a young woman and technically entitled to live there for the rest of her days. She wasn't a fool, of course—the income wouldn't be hers regardless of what any deed said, but Windham might get to sniffing around the legalities and wondering what exactly was afoot.

Frederick's hand absently rubbed at his chest, where heartburn was making him almost as miserable as the summer's heat. Creditors would hound a gentleman to death. He scowled, eyeing a pile of duns on his desk. Perhaps it was time for a respite at Roxbury Hall, and perhaps it was time Frederick reminded dear Ellen of her priorities too.

It was Saturday, the skies were clear, and the roads would be deserted outside of Town. He bellowed for his curricle, bellowed for his valet to toss a few things into an overnight bag, then bellowed for his medicinal flask. If he was tooling out to Oxfordshire in this heat, he'd have to settle his stomach first.

❧

"I've come to kidnap your hand again." Ellen waved her little tin under Val's nose. She'd knocked on his door very boldly about an hour after the household had risen from another very fine evening meal. It was full dark, the crickets were chirping, and Val had been resisting the pull of Axel's music room with every fiber of his being.

"You may have my hand," he said, stepping into the hallway. "Shall you drag me terrified into the night, or will you turn Axel's library into a temporary prison?"

"Let's go out. It's a lovely night, and I am not used to such rich fare. Then too, I miss my gardens."

Val offered his right hand, she laced her fingers through his, and within minutes, they were back at the gazebo, watching a three-quarter moon drift up over the flowers.

"You must tell me if I hurt you," Ellen cautioned him. "I literally cannot see what I'm doing in this darkness."

Val smiled at the thought. "I doubt you could hurt me, but do your worst."

She bent to her task, her touch now familiar, the smell of the salve oddly reassuring.

"What can I do to repay your kindness?" Val asked as the soothing pleasure of her touch worked its magic. "You've given me surplus food that makes the difference between starving and maintaining one's spirits, you look after my hand, and you've broken Belmont's savages to the bridle. You really must let me do something for you, Ellen FitzEngle. I am as afflicted with pride as the next man."

"Probably more so," she observed, turning his hand over and starting on his knuckles. "But you must allow it does me good to be of use to someone else. For five years, I've puttered in my gardens, being not more than cordial with my neighbors and not quite included in with the local community. I like my privacy, but I realize it comes at a cost."

"What cost would that be?" Val asked, wishing he could see her expression.

"I am expendable." She said the words easily—too easily, maybe. "Widows occupy a niche in most villages. They look after children when others can't. They attend confinements; they nurse the sick; they are involved in charitable endeavors if they have the means. Relax your arm, sir, or I will take stern measures."

Val complied, trying to focus on her words without losing awareness of her touch.

"You don't think you contribute as a widow should?"

"I know I don't." She shifted to stroke Val's wrist and forearm. "I might be more involved, had I children, but I don't. I am purely a widow, not a mother, a sister, a sister-in-law, a close neighbor, a shopkeeper."

Val closed his eyes and leaned his head back. "Do you think you are more inclined or less than other widows to take a lover?" He sat forward abruptly and opened his eyes. "Forget I asked that and forgive me."

What on earth was plaguing him, that such a thing would come out of his mouth?

"That isn't a question one easily forgets," Ellen replied, and Val was relieved to hear humor in her voice. "If it's an oblique way of asking if I'm lonely, then you needn't mince around the issue: I am lonely, and I miss my husband's attentions. Perhaps I'm a snob, but I can't see loneliness being assuaged by casual affiliations."

Val shot her a frown and blew out a breath. She'd just articulated something he himself had long tried to put into words: Casual sex was only mildly appealing because in his experience, it might ease lust, but it only heightened loneliness.

Well, hell.

Hell and the devil.

"I think there's something wrong with me," Val said slowly, "because I am a man, and I agree with you."

"You agree with me, how?" Ellen clasped his hand between both of hers, the warmth of her palms seeping into Val's sore and aching bones.

"Loneliness and lust are two different things. I still want to kiss you."

"I did not come out here for that." She carefully set Val's hand on his own thigh and sat up.

"Neither did I." And he wasn't pleased to admit it. "But you'll have to be the one to stop me, as I think we need to get this taken care of."

As introductions to dalliance went, that had to be the worst tone of voice and the worst line of speech Val had ever heard himself compose. He gave her all the time in the world to call him on it and laugh or slap his face or make an abrupt, indignant run for the house. She simply held his gaze, and when he lifted his right hand to brush her hair back, she closed her eyes.

So Val started there, setting his lips on her eyelid, letting the floral scent of her hair tease his nose, then drawing back to kiss the other eye. When he heard her sigh, he shifted to graze his mouth over her cheek and brow and temple, taking his time, learning the contour of each feature with his lips.

When he'd inventoried her face, he paused and switched tactics, bringing the fingers of his right hand up to caress her neck then her jaw. He closed his eyes and traced her bones with his index and middle fingers, reveling in the softness of her skin. It occurred to him he was doing as he'd thought he might when he'd been close to her in the darkness before: He was learning her by touch.

"Valentine," Ellen whispered, "kiss me, please."

"Hush." He bussed her cheek. "I am kissing you." But he wasn't done orienting himself with his fingers or nuzzling at her neck or burying his hand in her hair. She moved toward him, her hands slipping up his chest to link at his nape.

"*Please*."

She sounded as if she'd put five years of longing and loneliness in that one word, and Val gathered his focus to bring his mouth to hers. He paused again, his lips a quarter inch from hers, then closed his eyes and joined their mouths. Ellen's mouth clung to his, her hands winnowed through his hair, and her body arched closer to his.

Oh God, he hadn't dreamed this. In his mind, Val had referred repeatedly to their sharing one kiss as if it had been some polite little gesture stolen in a moment under the rose arbor.

In truth, a year ago, in the waning light of the overgrown woods, he'd kissed her forever, like he was kissing her now. Lips were just the start of it, as Ellen's fingers drifted through his hair, around his neck, over his ears—his surprisingly sensitive *ears*—and down along his chest. She pressed forward, her very body burrowing closer to him, and she conveyed both eagerness and a kind of shy wonder in her touch and posture.

And her mouth, Jesus in the manger, her *mouth*...

"Sweetheart," Val whispered, "slow down, easy..."

But Ellen took advantage of his lapse to seam his lips with her tongue and cradle his jaw with her hands. He tasted her in return and she groaned, a soft, sweet sound of longing and encouragement.

Val shifted and hoisted her to straddle his lap. He hadn't planned to do such a thing, but when Ellen looked down at him, dazed, her lips glistening in the moonlight, he had to approve of the impulse.

"You kiss me," he urged, his hand running down her arm and back up to her collarbone. "Please."

She framed his face with her hands and bent to the task, tasting him first with her tongue then sealing her mouth to his. Val's palm moved to the base of her spine, to urge her down, down onto the rising ridge of flesh at his groin. His left hand remained at his side and never had it felt more useless.

"Give me your weight," he whispered between kisses. "Let me feel your body over mine."

When he pressed down this time, she let him guide her into his lap. She stopped abruptly when she met his erection then cautiously continued her descent until Val had the gratification of her weight resting on his cock.

"Better," he murmured, laying his cheek against her sternum. His hand found her calf next, and Ellen went still.

Around them, the sounds and scents of the summer night went into high relief: The pause between breezes and the lift in the air when the lightest wind resumed, the subtle shift in the moon shadows as the air stirred, the blending of fragrances in the warm night.

Val knew what came next. He'd ease her skirts up, diddle her until she either came or was begging him to make her come, then he'd penetrate that sweet heat of hers, and spend—or, if he were going to be a gentleman, he'd withdraw before he spent, cuddle her for a bit, lend her his hankie, and see her back to the house.

It didn't seem like enough. Not with her.

"Just let me hold you," he murmured, leaving his hand on the firm muscle of her calf. She relaxed against him, and he felt her lips against his neck. He shifted, enjoying the rub of his cock against her weight but for some reason not repeating the movement. His hand settled on her back, and she relaxed further.

For long moments, she stayed draped over him, letting him rub her back, smooth his hand over her hair, and just pet her. His erection subsided some, but the desire to hold her and touch her did not.

It occurred to him the weakness in his hand might be spreading to his cock, but it was just a passing, insecure thought. It felt right to hold her, and while it didn't feel wrong to desire her, it didn't feel desperately necessary to have her sexually, either.

Not just yet.

∾

"Let me have the reins," Ellen said quietly. They'd made their goodbyes to the Belmonts, the savages were asleep in the back of the wagon, and yet she'd waited only until to the foot of Candlewick lane to state her demand.

Val glanced over at her in consternation. "You?"

"Me." She reached for the reins, and Val saw she was wearing riding gloves. They weren't as heavy as the driving gloves he sported, but they'd do.

He passed her the reins. "Why?"

"Because these are very sweet beasts and well trained," Ellen said, shifting a little closer to Val, "and yet they are big fellows and will pull on that hand of yours."

Amusement fled, leaving Val to frown at his gloved hand then at his companion.

"Did resting it and taking care of it this weekend help?" she asked.

"Maybe. A little. It certainly didn't hurt."

"Well, then." Ellen nodded, apparently feeling her point had been made.

"Ellen, I've been resting it for weeks now, and sometimes it's better and sometimes it's worse, but it never heals."

"Take off your glove." She gestured with her chin. "The left one."

He complied and inspected his hand. He tried not to look at it, usually—the results were invariably disappointing. Besides, he could feel the differences, between the good days and the other days. Friday had been a bad day.

"See." Ellen nodded at his hand. "Your third finger is losing its redness, and even your thumb and first finger look a little better. Rest helps, Valentine, real rest."

"How am I to rebuild an entire estate and rest my hand, Ellen?" Even to his own ears, Val's voice was petulant. He was surprised she answered him.

"You admit you need to, for starters," she chided softly. "Of course you will have to use it some, but you hardly give yourself any consideration at all. I see you, sir, up on that roof, tossing slates, or on the lane hacking at the weeds, or hefting stones the size of a five-gallon bucket. Even were you completely hale, you'd be sorely trying that hand."

She didn't know the half of it, so Val kept his silence, feeling resentment and frustration build in the soft morning air.

"I didn't play a single note this weekend," he said at length, but he said it so quietly, Ellen cocked her head and leaned a little closer.

"On the piano," Val clarified. "I peeked, though, and it's a lovely instrument. Belmont plays the violin, and Abby is a passable pianist, or she must be. She has a deal of Beethoven, and you don't merely dabble, if he's to your taste."

"You are musical?"

Val exhaled a world of loss. "Until this summer, I was nothing but musical. Now I am forbidden to play."

Ellen glanced at his hand. "So you work?"

"So I work." He scowled at his hand, wanting to hide it. "I keep hoping that one day I'll wake up and it will be better."

"Like I used to hope I'd wake up one day and realize my husband was alive and I'd merely dreamed his death. Bloody unfair, but I'm not dreaming."

Val smiled at her language, finding commiseration in it from an unlikely source. "Bloody unfair. You drive well."

"And you rebuild estates like you were born to it. But it's still bloody unfair, isn't it?"

"Bloody blazingly unfair."

He hadn't kissed her again after their interlude in the gazebo, and when she had dragooned him onto a bench with her tin of salve twice on Sunday, they'd stayed more or less in plain sight while she worked on his hand. It meant somebody might see his infirmity, but that was a price Val had been willing to pay for the corresponding assistance with his self-control.

That kiss had taken him aback, the intensity of it and the *rightness*. More disconcerting still was the way Ellen had felt in his arms, the way he'd been content to hold her and caress her and she'd been content to be held.

Whatever was growing between them, Val sensed it wasn't just a sexual itch that wanted scratching and then forgetting. It wasn't just about his cock, but about his hands, and his mouth, and so much more. He hadn't thought it through to his satisfaction and wasn't sure he even could.

"What does this week hold for you?" he asked his driver.

Ellen's smile was knowing, as if she realized he was taking refuge in small talk. "Weeding, of course, and some transplanting. We have to get the professor's little plants taken care of too, though, so you'll need to tell me where you want them."

"You must take your pick first. And you cannot keep donating your time and effort to me, Ellen."

"I will not allow you to pay me," she shot back, spine straightening. "The boys do most of the labor, anyway, and I just order them around."

"Order them—and me—to do something for you," Val insisted. "Wouldn't you like a glass house, for example, a place to start your seedlings early or conserve your tender plants over the winter?"

Ellen's brows rose. "I've never considered such a thing."

"I could build a little conservatory onto that cottage of yours," Val said, his imagination getting hold of the project. "You already have a window on your southern exposure, and we could simply cut that into a door."

"Cottages do not sport conservatories."

Val waved a hand and used one of his father's favorite expressions. "*Bah*. If I made you a separate hothouse, you'd have to go outside in the winter months to tend it, and it would need a separate fire and so on. Your cottage will already have some heat to lend it, and we could elevate it a few steps, or I could make the addition the same height as your cottage and put the glass in the roof."

"A skylight," Ellen murmured. "They're called skylights."

"Pretty name. I'm going to ask Dare to come up with some sketches, and you are going to let me do this."

"It will bring in the damp."

Val rolled his eyes. "This is England. The damp comes in, but we'll bring in the sun too, and ventilate the thing properly."

"You mustn't."

"Ellen, I went the entire weekend without playing a single note."

"And the significance of this?"

"I don't know how many more such weekends I can bear." He wasn't complaining now, he was being brutally, unbecomingly honest. "The only thing that helps is staying busy, and a little addition to your cottage will keep me busy."

"You are busy enough."

"I am not." He met her eyes and let her see the misery in them. She wouldn't understand all of it, but she'd see it. "I need to be busier." So busy he dropped from exhaustion even if he had to ruin his hand to do it, which made no sense at all.

"All right." Ellen's gaze shifted to the broad rumps of the horses. "But you will allow me to tend your hand, and you will keep the boys occupied with your house and your grounds."

"Under your supervision."

"I won't stand over them every minute."

"Certainly not." Val grinned at her, wondering when he'd developed a penchant for arguing with ladies. "They require frequent dunking in the pond to retain any semblance of cleanliness, and your modesty would be offended."

"As would theirs."

He let her have the last word, content to conjure up plans for her addition as the wagon rolled toward the old... His estate.

Five

"WHAT?" DARIUS APPROACHED THE STALL WHERE HIS piebald gelding stood, a mulish expression on the beast's long face. "I groomed your hairy arse and scratched your withers. I picked out your feet and scratched your withers again. Go play."

Skunk, for that was the horse's name, sniffed along the wall of his stall then glared at Darius. As Darius eyed his horse, the vague sense of something being out of place grew until he stepped closer and surveyed the stall.

No water bucket.

"My apologies," Darius muttered to his horse. Of course the animal would be thirsty, but when Darius had left Saturday morning, he distinctly recalled there being a full bucket of water in Skunk's stall. Val had taken the draft horses to Axel's, leaving Ezekiel to fend for himself in a grassy paddock that boasted shade and a running stream.

So where had the water bucket walked off to?

He found it out in the stable yard, empty and tossed on its side. When Skunk had had his fill, Darius topped off the bucket at the cistern and hung it in the horse's stall.

Resolved to find sustenance now that he'd tended to his horse, Darius left the stables, intent on raiding the stores in the springhouse.

"What ho!" Val sang out from the back terrace. "It's our Darius, wandered back from Londontowne." He hopped to his feet and extended a hand in welcome. Darius shook it, regarding him curiously.

"You thought I'd abandon you just when the place is actually becoming habitable?"

"We're a good ways from habitable." Val eyed his half-replaced roof. "I thought you might be seduced by the comforts of civilization. Particularly as I was not very good company by the end of the week."

Darius offered a slight smile. "You are seldom good company, though you do entertain. Where are my favorite Visigoths, and can I eat them for lunch?"

"Come." Val slung an arm around Darius's shoulders. "Mrs. Belmont fears for my boyish figure, and we're well provisioned until market on Wednesday."

"So where are the heathen?" Darius asked when they gained the springhouse and Val had tossed him a towel.

"Mrs. Fitz has set them to transplanting some stock provided by Professor Belmont. Ah, there it is." He took the soap from a dish on the hearth and plunged his hands into the water in the shallow end of the conduit. "Christ, that is cold." He pulled his shirt over his head, bathed everything north of his waist, toweled off and replaced the shirt, then started rummaging in the hamper.

"We've ham," Val reported, "and cheese, and bread baked this morning, and an embarrassment of cherry cobbler, as well as a stash of marzipan, and..."—he fell silent for a moment, head down in the hamper—"cider and cold tea, which should have gone in the stream, and bacon already cooked to a crisp, and something that looks like..."—he held up a ceramic dish as if it were the holy grail—"strawberry tarts. Now, which do we hide from the boys, and which do we serve for dinner?"

"We hide all of it. Let them eat trout, charred haunch of bunny, or pigeon. But let's get out of here before they fall upon us."

The boys having made a habit of eating in the springhouse, Val and Darius took their hamper up to the carriage house.

"For what we are about to receive," Val intoned, "we are pathetically damned grateful, and please let us eat it in peace. Amen. How good are you at designing greenhouses with windows in the roof?"

"Could be tricky," Darius said, piling bread, meat, and cheese into a stack, "but interesting. I'm surprised Ellen will let you do this."

"She probably thinks I'll forget." Val accepted a thick sandwich from Darius. "I won't. Between her butter and her cheese and supervision of the boys and her...I don't know, her neighborliness, I am in her debt."

"I was wondering if her neighborliness was responsible for reviving your spirits this past weekend," Darius said, tipping the cider jug to his lips.

"She went with us to Candlewick," Val began, but then Darius caught his eye. "Bugger off, Dare."

Darius passed him the jug. "I see the improve
ment in your mood was temporary. I did hear young
Roxbury eloped for his country seat. Seems our boy
did not take his reprieve to heart but has been running
up debts apace."

Val shrugged. "He's a lord. Some of them do that."

"I dropped in on my brother Trent." Darius passed
over the cider jug. "He mentioned Roxbury is an
object of pity in the clubs."

"Pity?" Val wiped his mouth on his sleeve. "His
title is older than the Flood, the Roxbury estate is
legendarily well run, and he's yet to be snabbled by
the matchmakers. What's to pity?"

"He has no income to speak of." Darius withdrew
a cobbler from the hamper. "If he remains at Roxbury
Hall, he can enjoy every luxury imaginable because
the estate funds can be spent at the estate, on the
estate without limit. His own portion is quite modest,
though, and the previous baron tied most of the rest
up in trusts and codicils and conditional bequests.
Seems all that good management is a function of the
late baron's hard work and the present army of conscientious solicitors."

"That would put a crimp in a young man's stride."
Val frowned at the last bit of his sandwich. "How
fortunate we are, not to be burdened with peerage,
though such a sentiment sounds appallingly like something His Grace would say."

"Are you being sarcastic?" Darius took another pull
from the jug.

"I am not. I see what Westhaven has to go through,
now that he has financial control of the duchy, his life

hardly his own for all the commerce and land he must oversee. It's a wonder he had the time to tend the succession, much less the requisite privacy. And now St. Just is saddled with an earldom, and I begin to see why my father has said being the youngest son is a position of good fortune."

"I've wondered if Trent shares His Grace's point of view." Darius said, relinquishing the jug again. "How soon do you want to get busy on Mrs. FitzEngle's addition?"

"As soon as the roof is done. Probably another two weeks or so, and I will prevail on the Belmonts to invite her for a weeklong visit. If the weather cooperates and we plan well in advance, we should be able to get it done in a few days."

Val repacked the hampers and left Darius muttering numbers under his breath, his pencil scratching across the page nineteen to the dozen.

The hamper in Val's right hand he lifted without difficulty. His left hand, however, protested its burden vociferously all the way down the stairs. A morning spent laying the terrace slates had left the appendage sore, the redness and swelling spread back to the third finger, and Val's temper ratchetting up, as well.

Ellen, blast the woman, had been right: resting the hand *completely* apparently had a salubrious effect. Working it, no matter how mundane the task, aggravated the condition. Val eyed the manor house, deciding to forego his plan to spend the afternoon with the masons on the roof, and turned to make his way through the home wood.

He emerged from the woods at the back of Ellen's property and scanned her yard. In the heat of the day she was toiling over her beds, her floppy hat the only part of her visible as she knelt among her flowers. Val stood at the edge of the trees, watching silently, letting the peace and quiet of the scene seep into his bones. Through the trees he could still hear the occasional shout from workers on the roof of the manor, the swing of a hammer, the clatter of a board being dropped into place.

In Ellen's gardens, the sounds were a distant, mundane chorus, detached, from another sphere entirely. The scent of honeysuckle was more real than those sounds or the industry producing them.

She looked up, like a grazing animal looks up when sensing a possible intruder to its meadow. Val walked forward out of the shadows, knowing without being told she'd hate being spied on. Fear it and resent it.

"Good day." He smiled at her as she rose, seeing she was once again barefoot and back in one of her old dresses. Her hair was in its customary braid, and old gloves covered both hands.

She returned his smile and Val let himself enjoy the sensation of physical warmth it bestowed on him. "Mr. Windham. I hope you've had a pleasant morning."

"I most assuredly have not." Val's smile faded slightly. "Soames was, as usual, late with his deliveries, Darius is in a brown study about something to do with his brother, the Visigoths discovered the cobbler, and my hand hurts."

"Come along." She pulled off her gloves and held out a hand to him.

"I am to be taken to the woodshed for a thrashing?" Val asked as he linked his fingers with hers.

"You should be. You no doubt spent the morning mending stone walls, laying slate, unloading wagons, and entirely undoing all the benefit you gained resting over the weekend. You are stubborn, sir, but I did not take you for stupid."

"That smarts a bit, Ellen." Val peered at her, trying to ascertain if she were truly angry.

"Oh, don't mind me." Ellen sighed gustily. "I shouldn't complain. Your excesses give me an excuse to get out of the sun and to hold hands with a handsome fellow, don't they?"

She retrieved her tin of salve from a pocket and tugged him back across the yard to where the stream at the edge of her property ran next to a single willow. Pausing to part the hanging fronds of green, she led Val to a bench in the shade, one sporting both pillows and an old blanket.

"Come, naughty man." She sat on the bench. "Lend a hand." Val complied, bracing himself for a lecture when she saw the damage he'd done in a single morning.

"You must be in a desperate tear to finish your house," she remarked, opening her tin and frowning at his hand. "You should be ashamed of yourself."

"Ellen?"

"Hmm?"

"Could we just now not take too seriously to task one Valentine Forsythe Windham?" He leaned his head back and closed his eyes. "It's a pretty day, the morning was…disappointing, and I would enjoy this respite with you."

She fell silent, and he let out a sigh of relief. Her hands on him were gentle but thorough, working all over his palm, fingers, and knuckles, up his wrist and forearm, and then simply clasping his hand between her two. The stream gurgled, the breeze soughed, a faint buzz of insects came from the gardens, and Val felt a pleasant lassitude replacing his earlier ire.

"You've worked magic," he said, opening his eyes. Beside him, Ellen's expression was grave, uncharacteristically devoid of the special lightness he associated with her. "What's on your mind, Ellen FitzEngle? You look most serious."

"I get in these moods." She smiled at him, though there was a forced quality to it.

"Broody." Val nodded. "All the Windham men are prone to it. Maybe you are tired? We were up early this morning, and I know I could use a nap. Shall we?" He stood and grabbed the blanket folded over the back of the bench. "If we spread it here, nobody will know Val Windham, Slave Driver and Scourge of the Huns, has caught forty winks with his pretty neighbor." He flipped the blanket out before Ellen could argue then extended a hand to her.

"Just forty winks," she allowed, glancing around as if to make sure of their privacy then lowering herself to the blanket.

"Twenty apiece," Val replied solemnly then lowered himself to the blanket and began unlacing his boots. "Getting up at first light and abusing my hand all morning is tiring work. I can't imagine taming your own jungle is exactly restful, either."

"It is, actually." Ellen regarded him as he popped up

and retrieved a pillow from the bench to stuff behind his head. He stretched out on her blanket and smiled up at her where she sat beside him.

"This is a friendly forty winks, Mrs. FitzEngle." He snagged her wrist. "Join me."

She regarded him where he lay.

"Ellen." The teasing tone in Val's voice faded. "I will not ravish you in broad daylight unless you ask it of me, though I would hold you."

She nodded uncertainly and gingerly lowered herself beside him, flat on her back.

"You're out of practice," Val observed, rolling to his side. "We must correct this state of affairs if we're to get our winks." Before she could protest, he arranged her so she was on her side as well, his body curved around hers, her head resting on his bicep, his arm tucking her back against him.

"The benefit of this position," his said, speaking very close to her ear, "is that I cannot behold your lovely face if you want to confide secrets, you see? I am close enough to hear you whisper, but you have a little privacy, as well. So confide away, and I'll just cuddle up and perhaps even drift off."

"You would drift off while I'm confiding?"

"I would allow you the fiction. It's one of the rules of gentlemanly conduct owed on summer days to napping companions." His arm was loosely draped over her middle so he could sense the tension in her. "I can hear your thoughts turning like a mill wheel. Let your mind rest too, Ellen."

"I am unused to this friendly napping."

"You and your baron never stole off for an

afternoon nap?" Val asked, his fingers tracing the length of her arm. "Never kidnapped each other for a picnic on a pretty day?"

"We did not." Ellen sighed as his fingers stroked over her arm again. "He occasionally took tea with me, though, and we often visited at the end of the day."

But, Val concluded with some satisfaction, they did not visit in bed or on blankets or with their clothes off. Ellen had much to learn about napping. His right hand drifted up to her shoulder, where he experimentally squeezed at the muscles joining her neck to her back.

"Blazes," he whispered, "you are strong. Relax, Ellen." His right hand was more than competent to knead at her tense muscles, and when he heard her sigh and felt her relax, he realized he'd found the way to stop her mill wheel from spinning so relentlessly.

"Close your eyes, Ellen," he instructed softly. "Close your eyes and rest." In minutes, her breathing evened out, her body went slack, and sleep claimed her. Gathering her a little more closely, he planted a kiss on her nape and closed his eyes. His hand wasn't throbbing anymore, his belly was full, and he was stealing a few private moments with a pretty lady on a pretty day.

God was in His heaven, and enough was right with the world that Val's own busy mill wheel slipped its cogs, and dreams rose up to claim him.

❧

Val sensed when Ellen woke, sensed the change in her breathing, the wariness in her body as she sorted through impressions and regained her wits. He'd probably provoked her by shifting his hips back ever so slightly so his growing erection wouldn't disturb her dreams.

He wasn't particularly surprised to awaken aroused—Nature imposed a certain agenda on the slumbering healthy male of the species—but he was surprised at the pleasure it gave him simply to lie on a blanket with the inspiration for his lust. The feel of Ellen's flank under his hand, the soft curve of her hip, the contour of her spine, for Val, they all became more alluring for being covered in the thinnest of cotton rather than revealed immediately to his eyes or his touch. The old blanket beneath them, the faint scent of lavender coming from the pillow under his head, the shift and sway of the willow branches, combined to imbue the moment with a precious languor.

He levered up slightly, tucked Ellen a little closer, and pressed a kiss to her temple. She made no protest, so he kissed her again, letting his lips cruise over her cheek, inhaling the rosy scent of her, drifting his hand along the flat of her stomach.

Was there any greater pleasure than seducing a willing woman on a lovely summer day?

Beneath him, Ellen opened her eyes and then closed them. In the brief glimpse he'd gotten of her mood, Val saw the dawning of pleasure, but something else, something a little sad or forlorn.

Gently, he shifted her to her back and maneuvered his body over hers. He kept most of his weight from her but put his forearms and knees close to her body, not quite trapping her but sheltering her. She lay passive beneath him, and he almost smiled at the challenge that presented.

"Touch me," Val whispered, pressing a soft kiss to the side of her neck. "Put your hands on me, Ellen, wherever you please."

He ambushed her impulse to argue by settling his mouth over hers and seaming her lips with his tongue. When she offered no resistance, he invited himself into the plush heat of her mouth, exploring the contours and textures to be had there and inviting her to do likewise.

She was slow to respond, and he liked that too. Liked the savoring and the need to pay attention to her. She was shy but moved her tongue over his and took his lower lip between hers. Val felt his shirt being tugged from his waistband and had all he could do not to rear back and tear it off. Her mouth carefully exploring his kept him in place.

That and the desire to press his body more closely to hers, to find that exact spot where he could wedge his cock against her sex and push, gently at first, to test her arousal and increase his own.

She understood, bless the woman, for she raised and spread her knees so her dress dragged up her legs and the cradle of her pelvis accommodated him more closely. The fit was good—too good—and Val knew a moment's consternation as his body suggested that coming—right *now*, in his breeches, merely by thrusting a few times against the woman—would suit famously.

He silenced that thought and raised up enough to see Ellen's face. She met his gaze and brushed his hair back from his forehead, her expression a little dazed and bewildered.

He couldn't merely use her like that. Couldn't live with himself if he did, couldn't find any pleasure in it. None. He shifted to lie on his side beside her but kept a leg across her knees.

"Don't…" Ellen frowned and caught his right hand, bringing it to her stomach.

"Don't?" Val kissed her mouth then rested his forehead on her sternum.

"Don't stop touching me," Ellen said, her hand tangling in his hair. "Please." She held his hand over that place in her body where Val suspected the emptiness gathered most intensely, where a child should grow but hadn't. Where life should start but where, for her, it had stubbornly refused to.

He stared down at her, trying to fathom what exactly she was requesting—and what she wasn't.

"I'll touch you," he said softly, "however you want, for as long as you want."

But she wasn't going to give him any more clues, so he began where he was, by stroking gently over her stomach. She closed her eyes and let her hand drift to the blanket, a small gesture Val took for a sign of submission.

Trust, even.

Through the thin cotton of her dress, he traced the crests of her pelvis, the contours of her navel, and the undersides of her ribs. She sighed, her fingers twitching on the blanket.

Lower, he surmised. She wanted him to touch her sex, and he was happy to oblige. His hand drifted to her thighs, and Ellen opened her eyes long enough to meet his gaze. He saw acceptance there and knew he'd guessed right. She wanted him to touch her intimately, and yet she couldn't ask for it overtly.

He held her gaze as he gradually slid the material of her dress up, until it lay across her thighs, shielding her sex from his view but not from his touch. He leaned in and kissed her, not a polite, teasing kiss that invited and dallied and flirted. This was a kiss of possession and arousal and challenge, informing her in no uncertain terms where he intended to take her and demanding she acknowledge the destination.

She tugged at his shirt again, her body coming slowly alive under his. He broke the kiss only long enough to let her pull his shirt over his head, and then he was back, his chest arched over hers, his mouth sealed to hers. She wrapped her arms around him and pulled him closer, her grip surprisingly strong when he resisted slightly.

"Valentine," she chided, physically urging him to give her some of his weight.

"Behave," he growled back, angling his body only partly over hers. His hand covered her breast, and she went still, a shiver going through her body. Carefully, he closed his hand over the soft fullness, and she turned her face into his shoulder.

"Tell me." He repeated the caress, watching her carefully. She was so quiet, so focused, he honestly could not determine if she was enjoying it, until she arched her back, pressing herself into his hand, and he had his answer. As he shaped and stroked and teased, he wondered if her precious baron had ever thought to pleasure his wife, or if Ellen had been deprived of the most basic accommodation between spouses for the entire five years of her marriage.

She made a soft sound in the back of her throat, and her hand closed over his, asking him to touch her more assertively. Gently, Val disentangled their fingers and untied the bows at her bodice. It was the work of a moment to loosen the front of her dress and ease the décolletage and chemise down, so the fullness of her breasts was exposed to the soft summer air.

No stays. God bless the woman; in this heat, toiling in her garden, she'd not worn stays.

"Valentine." Ellen's voice was faintly questioning but not scolding, and Val looked up to see her watching him soberly as he beheld her naked breasts.

"You are beautiful." He leaned in and kissed the slope of one pale treasure. "Lovely." He slid his mouth down to nuzzle the underside. "Breathtaking." He grazed his mouth along the furled pink flesh of her nipple. "Beyond glorious." He settled his mouth over her and felt her whole body gather itself toward the sensation as he drew on her softly.

She arched up and pressed his hand to her other breast, hard, beseechingly, and Val understood that at least five years of sexual solitude was driving this surrender on her part. She was in a torment of longing and asking him for relief.

It humbled him and gave him the determination to ignore the feel of her hand slipping down his back to dive into the waistband of his breeches, pulling him closer, begging him to cover her with his weight.

He'd be lost if he allowed that. Beyond control, hopelessly cast to the winds of his own pleasures. He eased his hand from her breast and stroked down her body, provoking an undulation of Ellen's torso that turned into a subtle, rhythmic press of her body against his.

"Part your legs for me," he whispered against her heart. "Just a little. Let me touch you."

He had to nudge at her thighs with his hand before his words bore fruit, but then she complied, her legs falling open in a boneless, welcoming sprawl. God in heaven, what he wouldn't give to settle himself between those thighs and start...

He would *not* trade her satisfaction for his own. Would not, so he let his hand stroke up Ellen's thigh by slow degrees, ready for her to stop him, as wanting and allowing oneself to have were two different things. His mouth at her breast no doubt quelled some of the last-minute clamorings of her conscience, and perhaps the feel of his erection pressed against her hip obliterated the rest.

Ellen's hand stroking his face went still as Val's fingers brushed over her curls. Soft, springy, he wished with all his heart he could see what he was touching, what he was parting and caressing and tactilely treasuring.

"Lovely," he whispered again, drawing a finger up the crease of her sex. She involuntarily drew her legs together, not to shut him out, he knew, but to brace herself against the pleasure.

"Let me," he murmured, repeating the caress. "Let me give you this."

Her gaze when he met it this time was clouded with desire, though bewilderment was there, as well. Her legs eased apart, and Val knew a spike of possessiveness and a sense he'd breached the last of her defenses. He tucked her tightly against him and resettled his hand over her sex.

"Hold on to me." He kissed her palm and set it on the back of his neck then cradled her sex firmly, so she'd have no illusions. He could not hold out much longer, but he was damned if he'd leave her hanging, so he eased his fingers up to the apex of her sex and found the seat of her pleasure.

"Hold tight," he reminded her, drifting his fingers over her. She shivered and clutched at him reflexively then clung as he set up a rhythm. When he felt her body beginning to hum with arousal, he eased off, teasing her with shallow penetrations of first one then two fingers.

"Valentine." It came out as a moan, burdened with frustration and desire and such pure longing, Val's own arousal spiked again.

He leaned in, took her nipple in his mouth, and drew hard, letting his hand work her firmly in the same rhythm. In moments, she bowed up, pleasure wracking her then drawing her more tightly still. Val drove her relentlessly higher, giving quarter with neither hand nor mouth nor body. Before her pleasure waned, her tears were wet on his chest, her nails had scored his back, and her leg had snaked tightly around his hips.

She'd stunned him, blown to pieces his notions of what pleasing a woman meant, and torn at his composure. He shifted off her and cursed his clumsy left hand, but somehow managed to get one side of his falls and three buttons on the second side undone. Ellen burrowed into his embrace, hiding her face against his chest when Val wanted desperately to see her expression. She seemed upset, but a lack of familiarity with his partner, her shyness, and his own pounding, unsatisfied lust conspired to render Val incapable of frustrating himself further.

But given that she'd been celibate for five years, neither could he merely heave himself over her and start rutting.

Self-gratification for Val had always tidily restored the balance of his bodily humors. It left him feeling relaxed, in charity with life, and best of all, it took only a few minutes.

As his hand closed around his swollen cock, he sensed dimly there would be nothing *tidy* about it this time, not with Ellen panting and sated beside him, and lust igniting at the base of his spine like a lightning strike.

Just brushing his hand over the glans of his erection was enough to make his breath seize in his chest. Four strokes along the length of his shaft, and his ears roared, his vision dimmed, and his entire awareness converged on cataclysmic spasms of pleasure radiating from his cock to his balls, and outward to every particle of his being. His body shook with it, until he comprehended for the first time in his life why an orgasm could be called a little death.

When it was over, he lay dazed, very indelicately *untidy*, and heaving like a racehorse. Ellen was wrapped against his left side, her face pressed against his shoulder, and Val knew only that he had to hold her soon. Had to.

He fished in his right pocket for his handkerchief and tried to clean up the mess he'd created on his belly and chest. Gently extricating himself from Ellen, he crawled down the blanket until he could dip his handkerchief in the stream then tried again to put himself to rights. He rinsed, dipped, and squeezed out the hankie, and sat back on his heels, head nearly spinning from that simple exertion.

Ellen's feet, dusty, elegant, and bare, came into his view, and he had to stifle the urge to kiss them. He sat there, his body humming, until he realized Ellen was propped on her elbows, bodice loosely drawn over her breasts, watching him curiously.

"Valentine, what are you doing?" Her tone was so rife with affection and befuddlement, Val almost blushed.

"I don't know."

"Let me hold you." She smiled at him, stole his pillow, and lay back, clearly confident he would comply.

He rinsed his handkerchief again then crawled back up to her side and slid an arm under her neck. She scooted closer and wrapped her arms around him, urging him down until his cheek was pillowed on her breast.

"Are you all right?" he asked, lacing their hands and resting them on her stomach.

She tucked her face against his temple and shook her head.

"Well, neither am I," Val confessed, his tone conveying both pleasure and confusion. He was...torn. Wracked between profound contentment and a need to be closer to her; between feeling utterly drained and perfectly satisfied. Between confusion that he should have experienced such intensity of sensation when not even having intercourse and the certain knowledge that with Ellen, intensity would be the norm.

"I will be all right," Ellen said softly, "but you have quite, quite knocked me off my pins in a manner that puts new meaning in the term."

"Quite, quite," Val murmured, nuzzling her breast. "I am off my pins, as well, then; in fact, my pins are scattered from here to blazing Halifax."

"You're well rid of them." Ellen kissed his cheek.

Val levered up onto his elbow and peered down at her. "Are you all right? You cried."

She ran her fingers over his jawbone. "Sometimes one cries for relief and for sheer...wonderment."

Val nodded, somewhat reassured—he was suffering a case of wonderment himself. "I did not come over here today thinking to seduce you."

"And for that, I can be grateful. Your spontaneous efforts were impressive enough." Val felt her sigh against his cheek.

"It wasn't enough." This bothered him exceedingly. "I didn't even make love to you properly, and you deserve at least that."

"You are not the judge of what I deserve," Ellen said, sounding smug and replete. "I was married for five years, Valentine, and did not merit the kind of pleasure you just visited upon me."

"Five years?" Val grimaced, not knowing if he should thank old Francis for his ineptitude or castigate the lazy bugger.

"I will not discuss it," Ellen warned him.

"Of course not." But five *years*? "You inspire me, Ellen. That is a warning, by the way."

"I am too content to be alarmed by it," Ellen said, but then she fell silent.

Val traced a finger down her nose. "Your mill wheel is back in motion."

"Spinning freely," she agreed, turning her face into his palm. "So this is your idea of forty winks?"

"Twenty apiece. But having had my twenty, I now want to stay and poach another forty."

"You shall not." She framed his face with her hands and leaned up to kiss him soundly on the mouth. "I might want you to, but we've borrowed enough time and privacy from fate, and the afternoon is advancing."

"I am devastated." Val rolled to his back, taking her with him against his side. "To think mere moments after I've pleasured you, you can hop up, slip on your hat and gloves, and go back to weeding your lilies of the field."

"You mustn't be." Ellen propped herself on her elbow to regard him solemnly. "Think of it as running away to someplace where I can regain my balance, Valentine, and catch my breath. You really have... disconcerted me."

He smiled at her, understanding all too well what she meant. Oh, he wanted to kiss and cuddle and swive her silly, but he wanted to make sense of what had passed between them, as well. Or try to.

"If you insist on driving me away, could you at least help me with my falls first? I'm not as dexterous as I'd like with the buttons."

"Hold still." Ellen sat up and gazed down at him. His genitals were exposed to her view, which he'd known damned well when he'd made the request. Her gaze flew to his, and he gave her his best slumberous, heavy-lidded expression.

"How does one…?" She waved a hand at his groin, a blush creeping up her neck.

"You just tuck me up, Ellen. Then do up the buttons." He waited, realizing however much Ellen Markham had loved her husband, they'd had a very restrained passion between them, at best. Tentatively, her fingers encircled his flaccid length.

"It's unassumingly soft now," she murmured. "Wilted." She stretched him gently and glanced at him for further permission.

"You keep that up," Val warned her, "and I'll regain my starch in very short order. Your touch feels lovely."

That prompted her to shift to a brisk, businesslike organizing of his parts in his smalls, then a deft buttoning of his falls.

"There." She gave him an incongruously self-satisfied pat on the cock through his breeches, and Val realized just touching his wilted self in the broad light of day had taken all of Ellen's considerable courage.

Ye bloody blazing gods, he would *adore* being her lover. *Adore her.*

"And now I will put you to rights," Val said, sitting up and stealing a kiss before she could protest. "Hold still."

He took his time, letting the backs of his hands brush against her nipples often and intentionally, until she batted his hands away and finished tying her own bodice laces.

"You are a naughty, ruthless man," she accused, tossing the pillow back up onto the bench. "Help me shake out this blanket."

Val rose first and helped her to her feet, resisting the temptation to draw her into his arms. If he yielded to his impulses, he'd hold her until winter descended and drove them inside, then hold her by the blazing hearth. The notion surprised him but wasn't as alarming as it should have been.

Before she could don her wide-brimmed hat and leave the sanctuary of their willow bower, Val did wrap his arms around her again, this time positioning his body behind hers.

"I will come back after dark," he whispered, "if you'll allow it."

She went still, and he knew a moment's panic. "Talk to me, Ellen." He kissed her cheek. "Just be honest."

"My...tonight might not be a good time."

"Sweetheart..." Val let her go and turned her to face him. "I will not force myself on you, I just want...I want to see you."

To make sure she was all right, whatever that meant in the odd, new context in which he was trying to define the term. She must have sensed his bewilderment, because she turned away and spoke to him from over her shoulder.

"My courses are due."

Val cocked his head. "So you become unfit company? Do you have the megrims and cramps and melancholy? Eat chocolates by the tin? Take to your bed?"

"Sometimes." Ellen peered at him, her expression guarded.

"Then I will comfort you. I'll cuddle you up and bring you tisanes and rub your back and your feet. I'll read to you and beat you at cards and bring you hot-water bottles for your aches."

Ellen's brows knit. "I truly am poor company at such times and usually before such times, as well."

"You are poor company for people who expect you to play on without missing a note, perhaps," Val replied, holding her gaze. "May we sit a moment?"

She nodded but had gone too shy even to meet his eyes.

"My Uncle Tony's wife," Val said, wrapping an arm around Ellen's shoulders, "is blunt to a fault. She told me relations with Tony were the best way to ease her cramps."

"Valentine!" Ellen hid her face against his shoulder. "Surely you wouldn't want to…?"

"What I want makes little difference. If *you* wanted, though, I'd be pleased to be with you. My point is I enjoy your company, Ellen. You are more than a willing and lovely body to me, and just because I appear on your back porch, that doesn't mean I expect you to be sexually available to me."

Ellen lifted her face to regard him closely. "But what is a dalliance if not…physically intimate?"

"It's what we make of it. I likely have less experience with these things than you think I do, but I will not engage in a liaison with you that is not first and last a friendship. If your priorities are different, you had best tell me now before matters progress."

Ellen peered at him, frowning, and he could positively hear her gears whizzing. "If matters between us…proceed"—she looked at their hands—"*if* they do, I will not trifle with you. I will not share my affections with you and then offer them to others while we are yet intimate. I will not betray your confidences."

"You honor me," Val said softly, his hand cradling her cheek. "I will try to be worthy of that honor, though I know I don't deserve it. And since you have been so brave as to put into words the promises I would never, ever seek aloud, I will screw up my courage and give them back to you. I will not trifle with you, Ellen FitzEngle Markham, Baroness Roxbury. I will not share my affections with you then offer them to others while we are yet intimate. I will do my best not to betray your confidences or your trust."

When Val rose, kissed her cheek, and slipped away through the trees, Ellen remained on the bench, recalling as many precious details of this first, new happy memory as she could. Hope notwithstanding, the memory might have to last her a long, long time.

Her peace was destroyed not ten minutes later when Val's warning shout sliced through the woods like a rifle shot, followed by the unmistakable sound of something very heavy shattering into a thousand pieces.

Six

"DARE! ABOVE YOU!"

Darius barely had time to glance up in reaction to Val's warning bellow before grabbing each Belmont brother by the collar and hauling them back beneath the overhang of the eaves.

Four heavy pieces of slate hit the terrace, followed by a rain of fieldstone plummeting four stories from the roof. An eerie silence followed, broken by Val's voice raised in alarm.

"Bloody, blazing Jesus!" He was across the terrace in four strides. "Tell me you're unharmed, the lot of you." He grabbed first Day then Phillip, perusing them frantically for signs of injury.

"They're all right, Val," Darius said, gaze trained upward.

"Whoever's on the roof," Val called, "secure your tools and get yourselves down here, *now*!"

"You saw the slates coming down?" Darius asked, still glancing up warily.

"I did. Talk to me, lads. Now is no time to stop your infernal chatter."

"We're fine," Day said, though his complexion had gone sheet white, while Phillip was flushing a bright red. "Phil?"

"Right as rain." Phillip nodded just before sinking to the ground. "A bit woozy, though." Day's gaze strayed to the terrace a few feet from the eaves, where the slates had broken into myriad small pieces, and fieldstone lay scattered about.

"Believe I'll join you," Day muttered, sliding down the wall beside his brother. "That was perilously close."

"Too close," Darius muttered, eyes narrowing. "Let's take note of who is coming down that ladder, shall we?" In response to Val's command, the roof crew was making its way to the ground and crossing the yard to peer at Day and Phillip.

"Be the lads a'right?" Hancock, the foreman, asked.

"They're fine," Val said. "A bit shook up. Hancock, who built that scaffolding?"

"The scaffold what holds the chimbly stone?" Hancock asked. "Built it m'self, just afore we broke on Saturday past. Spent this morning piling up that old chimbly onto it so it could be rebuilt proper."

"You built it on loose slates," Val said between clenched teeth.

"Beg pardon." Hancock widened his stance and met Val's gaze. "I did not."

"Explain yourself."

"I been working high masonry for nigh thirty years, Mr. Windham." Hancock put massive fists on his hips and leaned forward to make his point. "If the chimbly is in poor shape, the whole roof is suspect. I checked them slates and they were solid tight to the roof on Friday."

"I seen him do it, Mr. Windham," another man volunteered. "Nobody wants to work on a rotten roof, particularly not with heavy stone. The slate on the north side is coming loose, but the south side is tight as a tick."

Val blew out a breath and exchanged a look with Darius. "Then I spoke in haste and apologize, which leaves us with a mystery."

Hancock nodded, his expression grim. "We had no wind nor rain atween Friday and today, and yet the slates is got somehow loose."

"They did. Nobody up on the roof until I've checked it over. Your crew can finish out the day cleaning up the terrace and laying slate down here. Boys, I need to borrow Darius for a moment, but you're free to take a swim, or repair to your tent, if you'd rather."

"Swim," Day said. "But we'd best check the pond for monsters first."

Val and Darius found nothing to indicate the damage went beyond the four loose slates, but before descending, Val sat on the peak of the roof and frowned at Little Weldon visible on the horizon.

"The only logical conclusion is somebody was here over the weekend and thought it might be fun to loosen a few roof tiles," Val said. "That is a level of mischief bordering on criminal."

"Not bordering." Darius's voice held banked violence. "That's trespassing, at least; malicious mischief, destruction of property, certainly; attempted murder, possibly. If this is what the local boys consider fun, then you might not want to move in. And I am almost certain you had trespassers here while you were at Belmont's."

"How can you know that?"

Darius explained about his gelding's water bucket, and Val's expression became thoughtful. "What would a bunch of boys want with a water bucket? And how would they have the expertise to loosen slate tiles?"

"You have a half-dozen masons working on your roof. All it would take is a son or cousin or nephew of one of those men, and the boy would undoubtedly know enough to loosen tiles."

"But why? Somebody—you, Day, Phil—could have been killed, and I would have been responsible, and it's not as if most of the local families aren't benefiting from our work here."

"You're right. Who would want to sabotage this project?"

"I don't know." Val scanned the bucolic view. "But the scaffold to hold the old chimney stones was built on Friday, and the slates were tight then. Anybody with any powers of observation could see the next step in the task was to pile the fieldstone up on the scaffolding. They loosened the slates, knowing the load on them would increase dramatically as soon as work on the chimney began."

"Causing the slates to fall and the piled rock to come down with them." Darius blew out a breath. "Nasty, nasty business."

"Dangerous." Val straightened to stand on the peak of the roof. "I'm wondering if we should send Day and Phil back to the professor."

"They won't want to go," Darius said, pursing his lips. "Why don't you send a note along to Belmont, and he can make the decision. It's possible Hancock was mistaken and the slates were looser than he thought. It's also possible this was an isolated incident of mischief by children who could not foresee the dire consequences."

"I might be overreacting," Val allowed. "You don't think so; neither do I."

"So what now?"

"We take precautions." Val gave Darius a hand up. "Not the least of which should be a guard here on weekends when the place is deserted."

"I can stay here. Or we can take turns, or you can hire somebody."

"I appreciate your willingness to remain, but whoever stays here alone will be at risk and I can't ask that of you. The locals will be less inclined to hurt one of their own."

"We can argue about this all week." Darius began a careful progress toward the ladder. "Right now it appears your neighbor is coming to see what's amiss." He nodded in the direction of the wood, and Val saw Ellen emerging from the trees into the yard below.

"God almighty." Val followed Dare toward the ladder. "And what if she'd been coming to call fifteen minutes ago? Let's go down. I'd rather she hear it from us, and I'd rather she see for herself we're unharmed."

Val presented the situation to Ellen as a mishap with no real harm resulting, but his words were for the benefit of their audience. When he had her to himself, he'd explain the matter more completely and hopefully talk her into staying with the Belmonts until the manor house was restored. Not that he wanted her several miles distant... But he would be visiting on weekends at Candlewick.

Religiously, if she bided there.

❧

Ellen was unwilling to impede the afternoon's work further with her fretting, but she was determined to grill Val thoroughly about the "slight mishap" when they were next private. She'd taken the lane rather than the bridle path to her property, and thus she approached her cottage from the front. As a consequence, she spied for the first time the little pot of pennyroyal on her front steps.

As she yanked the plant from its pot and tossed it on her compost heap, outrage warred with panic. The plant's presence suggested to her just who might have caused the slates to fall from Valentine Windham's roof.

Surely she was jumping to an unwarranted conclusion. Not even Freddy would be so stupid as to create havoc like that and leave his damned pennyroyal on her front step like a calling card.

Or would he?

❧

"I notice Mrs. FitzEngle does a brisk business." Val peered at his mug of summer ale as if it held the answers to imponderable mysteries. "Is she really so dependent on her sales? The property seems prosperous, at least her little corner of it."

"If you want to know about your tenants' finances," Rafe, the bartender and coproprietor of The Tired Rooster said, "you'd best be looking in on Mr. Cheatham. He was the late baron's solicitor, up in Great Weldon. He'd likely know who's up to date on the rents, since he handles the banking for most around this part of the shire."

"Cheatham. Good to know." Val watched for a moment as Rafe, apron tied over his potbelly, continued to scrub at the gleaming wood.

"I'll tell you something else good to know." Rafe's rag stopped its polishing of the scarred bar. "Them Bragdolls are hard workers, make no mistake, but they work your home farm, and I don't think they quite have Mrs. Fitz's permission to do that."

"Mrs. Fitz?" Val raised an eyebrow and let the silence grow.

"Cheatham comes in for his pint now and again. I know how to keep my mouth shut, contrary to what you might think. Talk to Cheatham."

"Believe I will," Val said, finishing his ale. "Save me an entire fruit pie, and I don't care what you charge me for it."

"A whole entire pie." Rafe nodded, good cheer abruptly wreathing his cherubic countenance. "For growing boys and strappin' lads."

Val walked out of the tavern into the hurly-burly of a small town on a pretty market day, trying to puzzle out what Rafe had been telling him. Clearly, a visit to Cheatham was in order, but Rafe had almost admitted Ellen had some sort of claim on the land as well.

"I see your goods are disappearing quickly," Val

remarked as he approached Ellen's wagon where it was parked on the green. "Can you take a break? I'll have Rafe pull you a lady's pint."

"We can manage," Dayton volunteered. "Can't we, Phil?"

"We'll guard your flowers with our lives," Phil assured her. "Now that Sir Dewey has fortified us with raspberry scones."

"Sir Dewey?" Val asked.

"John Dewey Fanning. He's over there." Ellen gestured with her chin. "Playing chess with Tilden between Rafe's interruptions. Why?"

"He might have served with my oldest brother. You'll introduce us?"

"I can." Though she did not sound enthusiastic about it.

By the time they retrieved a pint for Ellen, Sir Dewey was alone at the chessboard.

"Valentine Windham." Val introduced himself, though in all propriety, Ellen or even Tilden should have made the introductions. "At your service and overdue to make your acquaintance. I believe we are neighbors."

Sir Dewey's smile took in both Val and Ellen. "My good fortune, then. Axel Belmont warned me the Markham place was being refurbished. Here." Sir Dewey appropriated a spare chair and set it down between the other two. "Shall we sit while you tell me how your progress fares at the Markham estate?"

Fanning was probably five years Val's senior, tall, blond, and a little weathered, which made his blue eyes look brilliant. He was genial enough, but beneath his country-squire manners, he had a certain watchful reserve, even when he turned to address Ellen.

"Your late husband would have been pleased to see the progress on the estate, I believe." In the beat of silence following Sir Dewey's pronouncement, Ellen wasn't quick enough to hide her surprise from Val.

"You knew my late husband?"

"His term at university overlapped my cousin Denham's by a year, and Denham and I are very cordial, as were Denham and the baron. By the time I returned from India, Baron Roxbury had gone to his reward. I am remiss for not calling on you." He shifted his gaze to Val. "Heard you had a bit of mishap on Monday."

"If you gentlemen will excuse me." Ellen smiled at them briefly before passing Val her half-empty mug. "I see the boys are in need of assistance and will return to my post."

"You are fortunate in your immediate neighbors," Sir Dewey remarked as both men rose to watch Ellen's retreat. "She's as pretty as the flowers she grows."

"Gallantly said," Val allowed, resuming his seat. "Though I gather you hadn't previously mentioned her marriage to Roxbury."

Sir Dewey continued to watch Ellen across the way. "Had she indicated she wanted it acknowledged, I might have taken that for a social overture, but she hasn't."

Val watched her as well. "You knew Roxbury?"

"I did, years ago, and not that well. The last baron, that is. The current holder of the title does no credit to his ancestry."

"I won the place from him in a card game." Val forced himself to take his gaze from the sight of Ellen laughing at something Day said. "He struck me as a typical young lord, more time on his hands than sense, and ready for any stimulation to distract him from his boredom."

Sir Dewey cocked his head. "An odd assessment, coming from Moreland's musical dilettante."

Val looked over at his companion sharply, only to find guileless blue eyes regarding him steadily. "How is it you come to know of Monday's mishap?"

Sir Dewey's attention fell to the pieces on the chessboard, and he was quiet for a long moment before once again meeting Val's gaze.

"As it happens, the local excuse for a magistrate, Squire Rutland, is off to Brighton with his lady, leaving my humble self to hold the reins in his absence. Mr. Belmont served his turn earlier in the year and is disinclined to serve again. Then too, in the common opinion, I am a retired officer and thus suited to the role of magistrate."

"Then you have reason to know of our mishap. No doubt you will want to investigate the matter, but I'm going to ask a favor of you."

"A favor?"

"While I am gaining my foothold here in Oxfordshire," Val said, "I do not use my courtesy title or bruit about my antecedents. I am plain, simple Mr. Valentine Windham, who owns some furniture manufactories and does modestly well as a result." He picked up a queen, the black one, and studied her. Keyboards were black and white, and if

Val were going to accompany this tête-à-tête with Fanning, it would be a piping little piece for fife and drum designed to keep an entire army moving smartly along.

"I own one of your pieces of furniture," Fanning said, frowning. "Why dissemble when the truth will eventually come out?"

"Have you ever wished you might not be known as the Sir Dewey Fanning who averted wars in India?"

"So you are well informed, too." Sir Dewey's gaze went to the chess piece in Val's hand. "Your brother is Colonel St. Just, correct?"

"I am privileged to answer in the affirmative."

"I ran into your brother shortly after Waterloo," Sir Dewey said quietly. "One worried for him."

Val cocked his head to consider Sir Dewey's expression and found the soft words bore the stamp of one soldier's concern for another. "He still has bad days when it rains and thunders, but he's happily wed now and his countess is expecting a child."

"That is good news," Sir Dewey said, smiling at the chessboard. It was a sweet, genuine smile, and as Val put the black queen back down on her home square, he wondered where that smile had been hiding when Ellen was at the table.

"So what do you make of my mishap?"

"Tell me about it, and I'll share what I know of the local penchant for mischief." They were more than an hour at it, with Sir Dewey asking thoughtful questions regarding everything from Val's business competitors to the terms upon which Roxbury had conveyed the property.

"Would you mind if I came over and had a look around?"

"I would not." Val rose and extended a hand. "Just don't expect tea and crumpets in the formal parlor, as we've no formal parlor worth the name, much less crumpets, much less china to serve them on."

They parted, and Val went in search of his tenants.

He found five out of the six enjoying a midday meal at the Rooster, the Bragdolls not having come into town for market. The picture Val derived from his interviews with his tenants was not encouraging, and he couldn't escape the sense they were all talking past him, exchanging glances that suggested he was being humored.

The visit to Cheatham loomed as something Val would see to sooner, not later.

"So what did you learn from the tenants?" Ellen asked, clucking the horses to a sedate trot when they finally headed home.

"My estate is a mess," Val said. "The rents are collected, but I don't gather much is done with them. The six farms ought to be run cooperatively, so they all shear together, hay together, and so forth, but I gather it's pretty much every man for himself. And because improvements and repairs are not the tenants' job, they don't marl; they don't clean out the irrigation ditches; they don't trade bulls, stallions, or rams; they don't fallow on any particular schedule; they don't mend wall on any schedule; and it's a wonder the land has held up as well as it has."

"How does a furniture maker know about marling

and irrigation and so forth?" Ellen asked, her gaze on the horses' rumps.

"My father holds a great deal of land." Val glanced over at her, gauging the impact of his disclosure. "I don't consider myself sophisticated when it comes to husbanding the land, but I comprehend the basics, and if I don't step in and do something, I will soon have several thousand acres of tired, unkempt property."

"You didn't need this too in addition to all the work to be done on the house."

Val peeked behind him to make sure Day and Phillip had nodded off. "I can't help but think your late husband would not have left the place in poor repair."

"He didn't," Ellen said, swatting a fly buzzing near the brim of her straw hat. "But he died five years ago, and in five years, land can suffer considerable neglect."

"So Frederick kept the rents and did nothing for his tenants?"

"Less than nothing. When they get sufficiently fed up, they'll all move on."

They traveled the rest of the way in silence, but when they trotted up the lane, Val saw an order of crushed shells had been delivered and the back terrace all but finished.

"Day and Phil can put the horses up," Val told Darius. "I'll walk Ellen back to her cottage, then I can update you on our exciting day in town."

"Looks like a tiring day in town," Darius remarked as Day and Phillip yawned and stretched. He swung Ellen down from her perch on the bench and eyed her critically. "Even the indomitable Mrs. Fitz is looking done in, Val. You've taken your slave driving a little too seriously today."

"Have a piece of the raspberry pie I brought home; then pass judgment on me. Ellen?" Val offered her his arm, which she took without protest, and headed with her toward the woods.

"You really ought to be cleaning this wood up," Ellen observed as they gained the shade of the bridle path.

"I don't want to." Val matched his steps to her leisurely pace. "I'm afraid I'll offend the piskies."

"It is beautiful, but if you don't at least cut up some deadwood, these paths will become useless, and the piskies will be the only ones keeping warm in winter. Then too, there are a couple of old pensioners in here who need to be cut down before they topple, and they're big enough to land on your outbuildings or mine."

Val stopped and regarded her in the late afternoon light. "I don't want to disturb the wood because it's the first place I kissed you. It's...magical for me, and I don't want it to change."

It was an unplanned disclosure, a truth Val himself hadn't been aware of until he heard the words coming out of his own mouth.

"Magical." Ellen's expression shifted between amusement, sadness, and...wistfulness?

"Silly." Val glanced around self-consciously. "But there it is." He could still see in his mind's eye the way two butterflies had danced around in a sunbeam the day he'd first kissed her, not far from where they stood now. At the time, he'd thought the butterflies absurd.

Ellen shook her head. "Not silly. Sentimental, though."

"I'm going to kiss you again." He took her hand in his. "Now, in fact."

He settled his lips over hers gently, just as he'd done a year ago. And now, as then, he took his time deepening the kiss, tasting her, breathing in her fragrance, letting his hands wander over her arms and shoulders and neck, until she was leaning into him and kissing him back.

"All day today," Val said as he wrapped his arms around her, "I watched you being so brisk, efficient, and businesslike. You have the knack of the friendly transaction, and you part with your produce willingly enough. But your flowers." He paused to kiss the side of her neck, a spot she seemed to particularly enjoy. "When you sold your posies," Val went on, kissing his way out to her shoulder, "each time, you didn't want to let them go. Your heart broke a little, sending them off that way, for coin."

"Hush. Flowers aren't kisses to be given away..." She buried her face against his shoulder.

"What?" He slid a hand to her nape and began massaging gently. "Your moods are hard to read today, love."

"I'm just tired," Ellen said, offering him a smile. "And cranky and probably in need of my bed."

"I can understand fatigue." He stepped back and took her hand as they started toward her gardens. "It has been a long and challenging day."

"You made progress, though. You met with Sir Dewey, whom Phil says is standing in for Squire Rutland as magistrate, and you met with your tenants.

You were also a considerable help to me, so I expect you to behave with docile submission when I declare it time to treat your hand again."

"Docile submission?" Val shot her a puzzled look. "You'll have to explain this term to me, or better still, demonstrate its meaning."

She gave him an amused smile that put Val in mind of the smiles Her Grace often bestowed on Val's father, then disappeared into her cottage. When she emerged, she handed him a tall glass of cider and took a seat on her swing. Val lowered himself beside her, setting the thing to swaying gently with his foot. While Ellen worked salve into Val's hand, they discussed Sir Dewey Fanning and Val's physician friend, Viscount Fairly, and his good friend Lord Nick—Darius's brother-in-law—who was also a mutual friend of the Belmonts.

"You did not do this hand any favors today." Ellen frowned at the offending appendage. "But you did let me drive out from town."

"I rested my hand as well as I could."

"But you tormented the poor thing yesterday and the day before," Ellen chided as she spread salve over his knuckles. "You are not going to heal quickly at this rate."

"I'm not getting worse," Val replied, closing his eyes. "And if you'll attend me like this, I have an incentive for making only the slowest of recoveries. With respect to the estate, though, I feel daunted. It feels like a quagmire, one that will consume every resource I throw at it and still demand more."

"Like a jealous mistress," Ellen murmured, kissing his knuckles.

"You, though I can't say I've experienced one of those in person—at least not recently. The farms are nearing disgrace, the house is a ruin, somebody is bent on criminal mischief, and my own health isn't one hundred percent."

"Your hand will get better if you rest it."

"You're going to send me off now," Val predicted. "We visit and we hold hands and we even cuddle, Ellen, but you're still shy of me, and I can't tell whether I should be flattered or frustrated."

"Valentine." She set his hand on his thigh. "I am not… I am indisposed."

"Ah, well." Val brushed his hand down her braid. "That explains it, then. As I myself am never indisposed, except perhaps when my seed is all over my belly and chest, I'm sweating with spent lust on a blanket beneath the willow, and my wits are abegging too."

"You are shameless." A blush rose up her neck and suffused her cheeks.

Val looped his arm around her shoulders and pulled her against his side. "And you are very dear. Shall we go swimming tonight?"

"You are being outrageous. Trying to shock me."

"Trying to seduce you," Val corrected her, pulling her in so he could kiss her temple. "Without apparent success, but I'm the patient sort and you won't be indisposed much longer, will you?"

She shook her head.

He stayed with her for a long while after that, rocking the swing gently, holding her, and watching darkness fall over the garden. When she began to doze against him, he carried her through the darkened cottage to her bed and tucked her in.

Leaving Ellen to wonder as she drifted off to sleep how it was her furniture-merchant neighbor rubbed elbows with not one title but several, and, were she a different kind of widow in a different life, if he'd be courting her—and if she'd be allowing him to.

Val retrieved his horse from the Great Weldon livery, feeling as if his interview with Cheatham had been just the kick in the arse he needed to be completely out of charity with life. He was still disgruntled and puzzled when he returned to the estate at midday.

Darius greeted him on the driveway. "Just in time for lunch."

Val quirked an eyebrow at his friend, who had foregone cravat and waistcoat in deference to the building heat. "You're in dishabille."

"And soon I'll be romping the day away at the pond in all my naked glory, like our pet savages. What did you learn in that beehive of commercial activity known as Great Weldon?"

"Nothing positive," Val said, leading Ezekiel to the stables. "The lane looks good."

"The Ostrogoths about bloodied their paws getting the shells raked out for you. Make it a point to compliment them."

"I take it they've had their meal?" Val put his horse in the cross ties and heaved the saddle off its back. He ignored the familiar pain shooting up his left arm and put the saddle down on its customary rack.

Darius took a seat on the only bench in the barn aisle. "Hand bothering you?"

"Hurts like blazes," Val said easily, but what he'd learned in town hurt worse. "It was pointed out to me today by the estimable William Cheatham, Esquire, that Ellen FitzEngle has a life estate on that property known as, et cetera, until such time as she dies, remarries, or loses privileges of citizenship, whichever shall first occur, et cetera."

Darius frowned. "A life estate?"

"Life estate, as in the right to dwell unmolested and undisturbed, free of any interference and so forth, right here, for the rest of her life, with all the blessings attendant thereto."

"All the blessings?" Darius asked as Val groomed his horse briskly, the brush held firmly in his right hand. "As in the rents?"

"Rents, crops, and benefits not including the right to sell fixtures. This was to be her dower property, Dare. I don't understand it."

"What don't you understand?"

"Ellen has been collecting the rents here through Cheatham for the past five years, but she has Cheatham put the money into one of the Markham accounts in a London bank. Not a penny of it has gone into the estate."

"That doesn't seem in character with a woman who dotes on her own land. Your horse is about to pass out with the pleasure of your efforts."

Val glanced at Ezekiel, who was indeed giving a heavy-lidded, horsey impression of bliss.

"Hopeless." Val scratched the horse behind the ears

with his right hand. "At least Zeke doesn't prevaricate on estate matters."

"Did you ever ask the lady where the money is going?"

"I did not," Val said, tucking Zeke into a stall. "But you put your finger on the contradiction I couldn't quite name: Ellen treasures her ground and takes better care of it than some women do their newborn children. It doesn't make sense she'd let the rest of the estate go to ruin."

"No sense at all. Maybe she doesn't have a choice."

Val fetched a rag to wipe off his bridle and boots. "The deed is clear. I now own the place in fee simple, but she has a life estate. Freddy didn't lie exactly, he just implied title was held in fee simple absolute when it wasn't—quite."

"Ellen's tenancy, or life estate, is probably a detail to him in the vast whirlwind of empty pleasures consti- tuting his life." Darius got off his bench and extended a hand to Skunk in the stall next to Ezekiel. "One has to wonder if this is what the previous baron intended."

Val hung his bridle on a peg and laced the throat- latch around the headstall and reins. "No, one doesn't. Ellen is to have those rents, the use of the hall, and so forth, but she's to make improvements, alterations during her life as she sees fit. She wasn't intended to toil away in a simple cottage, getting her hands literally dirty to earn her daily bread."

"This bothers you, not just because the place is a wreck but because she isn't getting her due."

"It bothers me." Val took the bench Darius had vacated. "For those reasons but also because she hasn't told me any of this. I am the new owner and I've been here several weeks. If Freddy has Ellen on some sort of reduced stipend, I can certainly set that to rights."

"And if he has her on no stipend at all?" Darius wondered aloud.

Val sighed, closed his eyes, and leaned his head back while Darius came down beside him. "She's lied to me, Dare."

"Not outright. Family situations are complicated, as we both know. She might have her reasons, and things might not be as they seem. Maybe she's hoarding her rents because she doesn't trust Freddy, and you can't blame her for that. Have a talk with her, discuss how matters will go on from here, and clear the air."

"You're like her." Val rose as he spoke. "You have this direct, brisk way of thinking things through that yields simple answers to complicated problems."

"Maybe the problem isn't so complicated. Maybe you just need to eat some decent food, talk to the widow, and come to an understanding."

And Darius, damn the man's skinny, handsome, genteelly impoverished ass, had been right. With a full belly, Val's sense of upset had faded to something more manageable, until it occurred to him sabotaging his efforts at the manor might not have been aimed at victimizing him.

In some convoluted way, scaring off the new owner, with his deep pockets, London connections, and titled family, could be a way to further erode what little financial security the widowed baroness had attained at Little Weldon.

In other words, Ellen FitzEngle Markham might

have enemies willing to go through Val to bring her harm.

He kept that alarming thought silent and lectured himself sternly about jumping to conclusions, over-reacting, and leaping to the worst case. Though his mental lecture lasted the entire time it took him to assist with glazing the new windows on the north side of the house, he was still pondering the possibility when the crews left, dinner with Dare and the boys was a noisy memory, and evening shadows stretched over the terrace.

"Don't stay out too late," Darius warned as they stowed the hamper in the springhouse. "The boys have remarked on your late-night wanderings. And your wretched ugly self and your wretched ugly hand are in need of beauty sleep."

"Yes, Mother." Val sauntered off toward the woods. "Don't wait up."

Val took his time ambling along the bridle path, not sure what he wanted to accomplish on this visit with his neighbor. He wasn't ready to broach the subject of the rents and her life estate, but he wanted to see her.

Blazing hell, he wanted to bury himself in her body and forget all about rents and life estates—and sore left hands and glaziers and roofing slates and all of it.

But she wasn't on her porch when he emerged from the trees, and so Val was left with a quandary: Did he knock on her door or take her absence for an indica-tion he wasn't to impose? Did he come back in half an hour? Lie down on her bed and close his eyes among the pillows and linens that bore the scent of her?

And where was she, anyway?

"Valentine?"

Ellen's voice came from the yard behind him, and as his eyes scanned the darkening tree line, he saw a pale patch that hadn't been there previously. He crossed the gardens, the flowery fragrances teasing at his nose, until he could make out a hammock slung between two sturdy hemlocks.

"Good evening." He gazed down at her lying in her hammock and realized she had already changed into her bedclothes.

Well, well, well...

"Is there room for two in that hammock?" he asked, still not quite sure of his welcome.

"I don't know, but let's try it, and if we end up on the ground, we'll know there isn't."

Not exactly a rousing cheer, but the boys had said she was in a mood today. Val hopped around, pulling off his boots and stockings, and surveyed the challenge before him. "You roll up that way and hold to the edge, and I'll climb aboard."

The hammock dipped significantly, and it took some nimbleness on Val's part, but he was soon ensconced wonderfully close to Ellen, the hammock pitching them together by design.

"We need a rope," Val murmured into Ellen's ear, "attached to one of the trees, so I can set this thing to swinging for you."

"There's a breeze tonight." She turned so her cheek rested on Val's arm. "I wasn't sure you were coming."

"Why wouldn't I?" Val nuzzled her hair, loving the scent and softness of it. "Because the boys are still making a racket at the pond?"

"I hoped it was our boys and not those other rotten little brats. You shoo them away, and they're like flies. They just come buzzing back."

"Are they truly rotten?" He worked an arm under her neck, drawing her closer. "I was a boy once. I hesitate to think all regarded me as an insect merely on the strength of my puerile status."

"You were a good boy." Ellen's voice held the first hint of a smile. "They are not good boys. They are little thugs and worse. I've been trying to think up a name for your estate, and I keep thinking it should have to do with the lilies of the field."

"The lilies of the field?" Val cast back over his dim command of scripture.

"It's about what seems useless to us being worth the Almighty's most tender regard."

"I thought it was about flowers being pretty," Val said, nuzzling at Ellen's ear. "Roll over on your side. I would like to cuddle up with someone who is exceedingly pretty and worth some tender regard."

"So I might be inspired to whisper confidences to you?" Ellen asked, shifting carefully in the hammock. Val waited for her to get situated then rolled to his side and began stroking his hand over her shoulders, neck, and back.

"The boys said you were not your most sanguine today." Val felt the tension particularly across her shoulders, exactly where his own usually ached when he'd finished a good round of Beethoven. "Have you confidences to share?"

"I do not. You will put me to sleep if you keep that up."

"Then you can dream of me, and I will dream of you—and vegetables."

"Vegetables?" Ellen quirked a glance at him over her shoulder.

"Green beans, tomatoes, peppers, you know the kind." Val kissed her nape. "Fruit helps, but I am beside myself with longing for vegetables. I could write a little rhapsody to the buttered green bean, so great is my torment."

"I understand this torment." Ellen rolled her shoulders. "By the end of June, I am practically sleeping in my vegetable patch, so desperately do I want that first bowl of crisp, ripe beans. Mine are almost ready."

"And what about you?" Val kissed her nape again. "Are you ready?"

His cock had risen in his breeches to subtly nudge at her derriere, and she didn't pretend to misunderstand the question. Rather than answer him, she reached behind her and tugged his hand around her middle.

"I'll take that for a maybe," Val whispered in her ear then rested his cheek over hers. "Are you afraid of something, Ellen? Afraid I'll hurt you?"

"Hurt me?" She scooted around a little. "Of course you'll hurt me."

"Blazes." Val went still behind her. "That answer doesn't encourage a fellow, love. Whatever do you mean?"

"You will offer me the sort of oblivion widows can discreetly enjoy, Valentine, and some sweet memories, but we both know nothing can come of it. When you are no longer interested, or you sell the property, you'll move along with your life, selling your furniture, maybe restoring another estate, and I'll still be here weeding my bed. My beds."

He was silent, letting the slip of the tongue pass and considering himself responsible for her conclusion that nothing could come of their dealings. He'd all but assured her such was the case, and as his left hand throbbed mercilessly, he couldn't really rescind his statement. He was aware, though, some part of him was unhappy with her brutal evaluation of the situation.

"Would you want more if I could offer it?" he asked, stroking his hand up to brush over her breast.

"I cannot want more." She closed her hand over his and pressed his fingers more snugly around her breast.

It wasn't an answer, but Val was too absorbed with the balance needed to shift her body over his in the swaying hammock to argue with her. When she was straddling him, he levered up to brush a kiss over her mouth.

"Your mood is distant. Where have you gone, Ellen?"

"Hold me." She twined her arms around his neck and pressed her face to his shoulder. He complied, cradling her head in his palm, resting his cheek against her temple, but wondering how a woman could be clinging to him so tightly and yet be so far away at the same time.

"Are you looking forward to visiting Candlewick this weekend?" Val asked, his hands stroking slowly over her back. "I think Day and Phil are counting the hours."

"I worked them without mercy at market yesterday." Ellen tucked her nose against Val's throat.

"How is it you smell so good when you've been working all day?"

"We towel off in the springhouse before every meal," Val replied, content to let Ellen's conversation hop around like a pair of breeding hares at sunset. "Dare and I do. Day and Phil are becoming otters, and if Axel hasn't a pond for swimming, he'd better dig one soon."

"He does. Abby and I went for a stroll, and she showed it to me."

"You didn't answer my question. Are you looking forward to the weekend?" Val purposely maintained the easy rhythm of his caresses, but he felt Ellen's breathing pause nonetheless.

"I am and I'm not."

"Tell me."

"I am because they are dear people and very gracious to their guests. I gather they've been through a lot, and it has made them sensible, easy to be with."

"But?"

"But they are so happy with each other," Ellen said softly. "It destroys some of my illusions, and that is hard."

"Which illusions, love?"

"I have several illusions," she said, shifting so she more closely straddled his hips. "I tell myself I was happy with Francis, and I was."

"But Axel and Abby are happier," Val guessed. "They were each married before, and it makes them appreciate each other."

"Maybe." Ellen's tone was skeptical. "Francis was married before, and he didn't look at me or touch me or talk about me the way Axel Belmont regards his Abby."

"So you and Francis were miserable? What a relief to know he wasn't actually canonized in the pantheon of saintly husbands."

"We weren't miserable." Ellen found his nipple and bit him through the fabric of his shirt. "But we weren't close, not like the Belmonts are."

"I think few couples are, but you said they disabused you of several illusions." Val made no move to dissuade her from her explorations—for that's what they were. "The first being they reminded you your marriage was not perfect."

"The second being that I am happy here in my gardens with no social life, no real friends, and only a trip to market or church to mark the passing of my days and weeks and years."

"You are lonely."

"Lonely." Ellen sighed against his throat. "Also just…inconsequential."

"We're all inconsequential. The Regent himself can drop over dead, and the world will keep spinning in the very same direction, but I know something of what you mean."

"You can't know what I mean," Ellen muttered, unbuttoning enough of his shirt that she could lay her cheek on his bare chest. "You have employees at your manufactories, you've mentioned brothers, Mr. Lindsey is attached to you, and the Belmonts are your friends. You talk about this Nick fellow, and your viscount physician friend and his wife. You have people, Valentine, lots and lots of people."

"I'm from a very large family. Lots and lots of people feels natural to me." But as he reflected on her words, Val realized he hadn't been quite honest. For all he did have a lot of people, he still felt as Ellen did, isolated and marginal. While he pondered that paradox, he felt Ellen's fingers undoing his shirt further, until her thumb brushed over his nipple and her cheek lay over his heart.

"Ellen FitzEngle Markham, you are too young and too lovely not to have some pleasures in your life. Your entire existence can't be about flowers and beans and waving off the nasty boys with your broom."

"And your entire existence can't be about slates and shells and bills of lading."

"Which is why"—Val hugged her close—"we will be pleased to accept the Belmonts' hospitality this weekend, right?"

"Right." Ellen capitulated with only a hint of truculence in her tone. But then she drew back, peering at Val's features in the moonlight. "How did your visit to Great Weldon go today?"

"Oh, that." Val closed his eyes. "Cheatham wasn't in, and I'm not sure what he'd have to tell me of any use, as his loyalties will clearly lie with Freddy and the Roxbury estate."

Ellen said nothing but subsided into his embrace. Val gradually drifted off to sleep, leaving Ellen to ponder his answer as the crickets chirped and the breeze stirred gently through the trees. She'd dreaded asking the question and feared to hear his answer. Depending on Cheatham's discretion, she might have been revealed in the very worst possible light.

But her fears had been for naught. Val had learned nothing, and so she had a reprieve. Maybe in the little time fate had given her, she'd somehow find the courage to tell the man the truth, for surely somebody in the shire—the tenants, the local boys, the well-meaning gossips at the Rooster, *somebody*—would tell him the woman in his arms was a liar, a cheat, and a thief intent on stealing from him until she had no other choice.

Seven

"WHERE'S YOUR KIT?" AXEL ASKED AS HE AND VAL repaired to the airy, high-ceilinged guest chamber across the hallway from Ellen's room.

"Here." Val tossed a rolled-up shaving kit to Axel as a procession of footmen trooped in carrying the tub, Val's traveling gear, and steaming buckets of water.

"Shirt off." Axel stropped a straight razor against a small whetstone. "And sit you here." He smacked the back of a dressing stool. "I got your note regarding mischief on your roof."

"I don't think it was an accident." Val sat without even trying to put up a fuss about Axel acting as his valet. "Darius has remained behind, essentially to stand guard. And your sons could have been killed."

"Or you." Axel dipped a shaving brush into the half-full tub and worked up a lather with Val's shaving soap. He sniffed the soap and dabbed lather onto Val's cheeks. "Lovely scent. How do you conclude somebody tampered with your roof?"

"We know there were trespassers." Val craned

his chin up so Axel could lather his throat. "We also know the slates were tight on Friday."

"You know your roofing crew claims they were tight on Friday," Axel corrected as he began to scrape the razor along Val's jaw. "From what you described, it took at least a half ton of fieldstone piled on that scaffolding to loosen the slates. Correct?"

"You don't think it was mischief," Val said when Axel swiped the razor clean on a towel.

"I do not. It was too random. Anybody could have been hurt by those stones, or nobody. The weight might have been enough to loosen the slates, and then again it might not. Somebody who really wanted to cause you harm would have taken more predictably troublesome measures to do it—if they had any sense. Hold still."

Val considered Axel's reasoning and found it sound. Axel, like his brother, Matthew Belmont, in Sussex, occasionally served as local magistrate. He had experience investigating crimes, and more to the point, he was Day and Phillip's father. He would not put them at avoidable risk of harm; of that Val was certain.

Axel tossed a clean towel directly at Val's shaven face. "I think you've dropped some weight. Your face is thinner."

Val shrugged as he stood. "Darius claims the rest of me is thinner, as well. I confess to being indifferent on the matter but not the least indifferent to the thought of that tub of hot water."

"Cuff links." Axel waggled his fingers, and Val held out his left hand.

"Ye gods, Windham." Axel frowned at Val's

swollen joints and reddened flesh. "Did you hit this thing with a hammer? It has to hurt."

"It flares up," Val muttered, snatching his hand back as soon as Axel had the cuff link out. "I think I can manage from here."

"Like hell you can. You either let me unbutton your falls, or I'll stand here and watch while you attempt it yourself."

"Axel." Val scowled at him in earnest.

"What?" He grabbed Val's breeches by the waistband and scowled right back. "Do you have them made this loose?" He deftly unfastened the buttons while Val stood and suffered the assistance.

"I don't like them tight." Val shoved breeches and smalls over his hips. "If you must know, they are a little looser than when they were made."

"Abby can probably take them in for you." Axel picked up Val's discarded clothing and kept further comments on his guest's leanness to himself.

"Might I have the soap?" Val asked, sinking down into the water with a grateful sigh.

"You might." Axel rummaged in the satchel brought up with the last of the hot water, fetched a sliver of milled soap, and laid out a complete change of clothes on the bed. "Dunk, and I'll do the honors."

In truth, it felt good to let Axel fuss over him just a little, although being scolded for the state of his hand was grating in the extreme. Axel would no doubt alert Val's family—and dear Nicholas, as well—but they weren't likely to come haring out to Oxfordshire to pester him personally, not when there were no real accommodations, no social life, and only the barest of provisions. Then too, Val hadn't sent either of his brothers the exact direction to his latest folly, and they were both busy men.

Westhaven's letters were full of the wonder—and drivel—that probably characterized all new papas. Devlin's letters read more like dispatches. They were terse, factual, and few in number. The Rosecroft estate up in Yorkshire hadn't been in much better shape than Val's own acquisition, and Devlin was newly married, newly blessed with a stepdaughter, and shortly expecting his own firstborn.

And if Val regretted that his oldest brother was a week's journey away, at least it was an improvement over the years when the man was leading cavalry charges against the damned French.

But Val rose from the tub, admitting just how much he'd missed his brother Devlin since coming down from the north two months previously. It had been a pleasant winter in Yorkshire with Dev, little Winnie, and Emmie—cozy, almost, and were it not for the condition of Val's hand...

He looked down at that hand and let out a low oath, as its condition was almost as bad as when David Worthington had examined it. Two things were now certain, though: rest improved it, albeit at an excruciatingly slow pace; and using the hand for anything like a normal level of activity caused it to deteriorate with appalling swiftness.

Val struggled into his shirt then fumbled at length to get his clean breeches fastened as he realized Ellen had not treated his hand for more than two days. After lunch, he promised himself he would seek her out and beg her assistance. If he had to suffer Axel's dressing him like a fidgety toddler, it really would send him round the bend.

He was toweling his hair dry when he heard the door to his room open and close. A servant would have knocked, and Ellen was supposed to be at her own bath.

"Axel," Val muttered from the depths of his towel, "if you've come to do me up like a little fellow newly breeched, you can bugger the hell off."

"Now that's a fine way to address your host," growled a deep and familiar baritone. "I'm sure Her Grace will be pleased to know my baby brother's impeccable manners are serving him in good stead."

Val tossed the towel aside, and as if his thoughts had conjured the man, there stood Devlin St. Just, Colonel Lord Rosecroft, Valentine's oldest brother, in the bronzed, healthy, and grinning flesh.

"Dev?" Val was in his brother's crushing embrace in the next instant, his back being heartily pounded, and his throat suspiciously tight. Val pulled back and assured himself that his eyes had not lied. "What in the hell are you doing away from Emmie and Winnie?"

"I was banished." St. Just's grin became sheepish. "Emmie isn't due for a few more weeks, and she accused me of hovering. I missed those members of the family who were not kind enough to winter with us, so here I am on a lightning raid, as it were."

"And damned glad I am to see you. Damned glad. How long can you stay?"

"I'll depart for York by the end of the week, but Oxford is nominally north of Town, so you were on my way." St. Just stepped back, and Val was treated to the critical appraisal of the brother who was half Irish and all former soldier.

"And Belmont knew you were coming?" Val pressed. "He said not one word to me, and I've had his boys underfoot for the past several weeks."

"Belmont knew I was coming but not exactly when, as he and I have business to transact of a sort, and our wives are connected."

"Your wives..." Val frowned and recalled that Abby Stoneleigh—now Abby Belmont—had mentioned being related to the late Earl of Helmsley and his surviving sisters.

"I thought the army was the world's largest village," St. Just said, "but the English peerage takes that honor. If you're done with that tub, I'd like to hop in before the water is done cooling."

"Help yourself, but I'm sure Axel will send up clean water, if you'd prefer."

"Compared to what was available in Spain"—St. Just was already out of his shirt—"this is sparkling. Smells good too."

"I'll leave you some privacy, then." Val moved toward the door.

"The hell you will." St. Just shucked out of his breeches. "We'll have to make polite conversation at table, so stay and take your interrogation like a man. For starters, I've seen prisoners of war in better weight than you, Valentine Windham. What has you off your feed?"

Val smiled at the directness, even as he resented his brother's assumption that answers would be

forthcoming—or he should resent it. He watched St.
Just settle himself in the tub and noted the signs of
good care that married life had left.

"You aren't answering my question, Valentine,"
St. Just chided, soaping a large foot and then dunking
it. "Don't think I won't leave this tub and beat it out
of you."

"You won't. I'm busy lately trying to put my property to rights, and provisions are limited."

"You need a camp cook." The second foot disappeared beneath the water. "An army marches on its
belly, as the saying goes, and cook pots are as important as cannon. Is this your soap?"

"It is," Val answered, sitting on the bed and watching as St. Just dunked to wet his hair.

"Do the honors. I am going smell like a bordello
when I get out of this bath."

"You will smell like a gentleman." Val hunkered
behind the tub. "This is my only clean shirt until
Belmont's laundresses take pity on me, so splash me
at your peril."

"I'm trembling," St. Just retorted, only to have Val
smack a soapy palm against the back of his head with a
firm wallop before working up a fragrant lather.

"How are your womenfolk?" Val asked, feeling a
tug at his heartstrings at just the thought of Emmie St.
Just so near her confinement.

"Em thinks she's big as a house. The heat isn't
so bad up north, and that's a blessing, as she sleeps
poorly. This makes me fret, which makes me sleep
poorly, and so forth. Winnie is watching closely but
doing as well as can be expected. She said to tell

you she practices the piano *a lot*, and while I cannot vouch for the quality of her practicing, I can vouch unequivocally for its volume."

"Stand," Val instructed. "We'll finish you off." Val sluiced a pitcher of rinse water over St. Just's tall frame and then passed him a bath sheet.

"I do adore a bath." St. Just sighed. "One takes them for granted until they're no longer available. Now, tell me about this monstrosity you've acquired in Little Cow Pie. Belmont says it was a disgrace several years ago, albeit salvageable."

"He would know," Val said, amazed at how quickly his personal business had been disseminated over the family gossip vine—and amazed at how quickly St. Just was getting back into his clothes. "It needs a lot of work and will likely take me all summer just to make habitable."

"And what is this I hear about a friendly widow, little brother?" St. Just tugged on his boots and straightened. "Did she convey with the property, rather like a certain daughter of mine?" He settled a fraternal arm over Val's shoulders and sauntered with him toward the door.

"You must 'fess up," St. Just teased. "I am the soul of discretion, except that Emmie has all my confidences, and Winnie overhears an appalling amount, and then Emmie corresponds with Anna, and Winnie writes to her cousin Rose, and I am forever getting letters from Her Grace."

"So do I answer your question or not?"

St. Just opened the door before he replied and stopped in his tracks.

"Little brother." St. Just's arm slid off Val's shoulders. "You had better be glad I am besotted with my dear Emmie, else I'd be tempted to inform you I now behold the physiognomy of my next countess. My lady." St. Just picked up Ellen's hand and bowed over it. "Devlin St. Just, the Earl of Rosecroft, your most obedient servant."

"Valentine." Ellen glanced at him in cool puzzlement. "How is it you never told me your brother is an earl?"

St. Just kept Ellen's hand in his. "You mustn't blame my brother for respecting my modesty." He tucked her hand over his arm while Val mentally tried to form a more suitable answer. "I am a freshly baked earl, having just arrived to my honors in the last year and under something less than cheering circumstances. I hardly think of myself as Rosecroft, much less demand that my brother do so. Will you allow me to escort you in to luncheon?"

As St. Just continued to flirt and charm his way to the table, Val was left to watch and simply appreciate. Ellen was blushing, but she was also slowly letting St. Just's Irish wit and charm draw her in and tempt her into flirting back.

It was lovely and dear and sad in a way. Axel and Abby took up the slack in the conversation and left Val time to regard his host and hostess a little more closely. Ellen had been right—they had a closeness between them that put Val in mind of St. Just and Emmie, Gayle and his Anna.

David and Letty.

Nick and Leah.

Blazing hell.

"You're quiet." St. Just turned piercing green eyes on his brother. "This has never boded well with you. It means you are hatching up mischief."

"If I'm hatching up mischief, it's because Belmont's scamps have led me astray. Do you suppose I might ask for seconds on the green beans?"

"The ones swimming in chicken broth and slivered almonds?" Axel passed him the bowl. "Noticed yours disappeared in record time, and you aren't even setting a good example for Day and Phillip."

"He needs a hothouse." Abby smiled at her guest as he dug into his vegetables. "I'm sure you have some plans around for something modest, don't you, Axel?"

"I have plans." Axel grinned at his wife. "Modest, immodest, and everything in between."

Abby rolled her eyes at Ellen. "See what I put up with? Let's leave these reprobates to discuss the state of the realm, Ellen, and take our dessert on the terrace."

"Splendid notion." Ellen rose, bringing the men to their feet, as well.

"Abandoned." Axel sighed. "Well, let them eat cake."

"The last person reported to say that lost her head rather violently," Val pointed out.

"I've quite lost my head, as well." Axel leered at his wife's retreating figure.

Val rolled his eyes. "Open a window. I need some air." Or perhaps he just needed some privacy with Ellen.

❧

For reasons of his own, Darius Lindsey had made an agreement with himself that he could spend the summer, riding Val Windham's coattails, hiding here in the wilds of Oxfordshire. He expected there would be an element of penance about the whole thing, even if there was also a much greater element of benefit to him.

To his surprise and chagrin, he was enjoying himself immensely. In some ways, it was turning out to be the most pleasurable summer of his adult life. He swung out of his hammock and stretched slowly, seeing Val's army of workmen and cleaning ladies were knocking off for luncheon.

No. It was Saturday, so they'd be heading home for the day no later than one of the clock, leaving the premises unoccupied.

By the time Darius had demolished a serving of raspberry pancakes with butter and preserves—Val had taught him how to prepare this meal earlier in the week—each and every laborer had departed for home. The afternoon stretched, perfect for lazing by the pond with a book and dozing in the wonderful silence of a hot summer day.

God bless Axel Belmont, Darius thought as he gathered towels, soap, clean linen, shaving kit, and a jug of cold mint tea.

"Hullo, the house!"

Well, hell. Darius stepped from the springhouse and spied a man on a handsome chestnut gelding. The rider was blond, blue-eyed, sat his horse like he knew what he was about, and wore the kind of ensemble that was comfortable because of its exquisite tailoring and fine fabric.

"Greetings," Darius answered evenly, towel over his shoulder, shaving kit in his hand. "Darius Lindsey. Welcome to Mr. Windham's property. And you might be?"

"Just in time for a swim, it appears. Or a bath." The man swung down uninvited and extended a hand. "Sir Dewey Fanning, at your service, Mr. Lindsey. I believe Mr. Windham might be expecting me. We discussed a call when we met at market on Wednesday."

"He mentioned it," Darius said, taking his guest's hand briefly. "And my swim can wait. Val said you're serving as magistrate?"

"I have that honor." They stabled Sir Dewey's horse and were shortly up the ladder. "So from whence fell your stones?"

Darius showed him around then obliged further inquiries by giving Sir Dewey a tour of the house.

"Francis would be pleased," Sir Dewey remarked as they reached the kitchen. The counters were being redesigned to accommodate a huge cookstove that sat squat and black in the middle of the room. Glass fronts had already been installed on the upper cabinets, and a new pump graced one end of a long, glazed porcelain sink.

"You knew the late baron?"

"In little more than passing," Sir Dewey said, running a hand over the smooth surface of the sink. "He'd approve of the restoration of the place and would never have let it get to this state, much less let the farms be mismanaged."

"Val will set it to rights." Darius watched as Sir Dewey frowned at the tile floors. They might be replaced once the heavier work was done. For now, sawdust, wood shavings, and the occasional screw or nail littered the floor.

"Are your crews in the habit of working in bare feet?" Sir Dewey asked, squatting by a door leading to the cellars.

"Assuredly not. One rusty nail in the foot and a man's life might be over."

"Then you'd better have a look at this," Sir Dewey muttered. "It's not good. Not good at all."

❧

Sir Dewey Fanning presented himself at Candlewick just as Abby Belmont was preparing to preside over tea with her guests. Ellen had disappeared abovestairs, leaving Val with such a sense of untethered restlessness he was almost grateful for Sir Dewey's arrival.

Until he heard the man explain that he and Darius had found two bonfires laid in Val's manor house, one in the attics, one in the basement, both surrounded by the dusty imprints of small bare feet, and both with a can of lamp oil tidily stowed nearby.

"So what do you make of it?" St. Just asked the magistrate. "Is somebody recruiting children to do this mischief, or are we dealing with children wandering the property in addition to arsonists and would-be murderers?"

"Hard to say," Sir Dewey replied. "Belmont, any insights?"

"God above." Axel ran a hand over his hair. "My only suggestion is that we adjourn to the library and switch to something besides tea. It seems to me the situation is complicated with neither motive nor suspect very clear."

"The motive," Val reflected when Axel had put a drink in his hand, "seems to be to discourage me from my project, at least."

"If not to discourage you all the way to the Pearly Gates," St. Just groused.

"Probably not quite." Val took a considering sip of his drink. "As Sir Dewey has pointed out, the fires were laid but not set. The slates that fell from the roof didn't hit a single person, and the likelihood they'd actually strike me wasn't great."

"Could children have loosened those tiles?" Axel asked.

Sir Dewey nodded. "Half-grown boys could easily with the right tools. They could have piled up those scraps of lumber, sneaked about of a night or a Sunday afternoon, and because they frequent your pond, Mr. Windham, nobody would think a thing about it did they see a pack of boys heading up your lane or across your fields."

"I can't help but wonder"—Val's gaze met his brother's—"if whoever doesn't want me to proceed also discouraged Ellen FitzEngle from maintaining the place."

St. Just scowled at his drink. "Interesting point. Why don't we just get the lady down here and ask her a few very direct questions?"

"Because she's a suspect," Sir Dewey said, his voice damnably gentle while his blue eyes pinned Val with piercing clarity. "Isn't she?"

"Ellen?" Val blew out a breath, trying to balance

his heart's leanings with the facts. "In my opinion, no. She has neither this kind of meanness in her, nor would she hurt others."

"But using your head?" Axel prompted when no one else spoke up. "What does logic tell you?"

"Logic?" Val pursed his lips, studied his drink, and looked anywhere but at his brother.

St. Just spoke up in the ensuing silence. "Logic says she has a life estate on the property that she neither disclosed nor took care of. Logic says she's hiding something; logic says if she hasn't taken an interest in the house so far, what does she care if it burns to the ground or if renovations stop well before they're completed?"

"That doesn't tell us her motive," Sir Dewey pointed out. "It tells us questioning her directly would likely be of little use."

"So question her indirectly," St. Just shot back. "Snoop about, get the solicitors talking, and circle around behind her fortifications; exonerate her or see her charged."

"It seems to me," Val said, "we've convicted the lady of serious crimes without identifying either her motive or her opportunity. She's been with Day and Phil for most of each day except for when she's been with me here. She might have stolen about in the dead of night and piled up all that wood, but it's far-fetched to assume so. It's equally far-fetched to think she'd collude with the local boys, when she neither trusts nor likes the ones from the village."

"Good points," St. Just agreed—which was something. "But somebody means you or your property harm, Val, and she stands to gain if you vacate the premises."

Val rose and put his empty glass on the sideboard. "She stands to gain more by letting me toil away for months and sink a fortune into that house. By law, she can then waltz in and enjoy all the fruits of my efforts until the day she dies, and I can neither charge her rent nor evict her. The worst I could do is move in with her."

"This is true." The idea that Val could spike his brother's formidable guns was some relief, but St. Just wasn't finished. "I don't like it—having somebody to suspect is much easier—but you're right. Ellen FitzEngle's interests are not served by torching the house."

"And we're forgetting something else." Val turned to face the other three. "Ellen is the one who is most clearly entitled to live in that house and collect the rents on the tenant farms. I have other places to live, other sources of income, but she likely does not. It could very well be that whoever is up to no good could care less about me; rather, it's Ellen's interest they seek to harm."

Axel eyed the decanter narrowly. "Complicated, indeed."

"And more complicated still." Val sighed as he headed for the door. "What do I tell the lady, if anything? And when?"

He left, and silence spread behind him among the other three men.

"Emmie's confinement waits for no husband," St. Just said. "Val needs reinforcements, and Westhaven can't leave his post."

"I agree," Axel said, "but Val won't like it.

He won't like questions about his property or his affairs."

"I don't like bonfires laid in my brother's very house," St. Just countered. "Send off a few notes and see what reinforcements are available."

~⁓

Ellen had dodged tea, pleading fatigue, but she hadn't been able to lie on her big, fluffy bed and drift away. She was tired, of course—she'd slept little and badly lately—but she was troubled too, and there, sitting so handsome and calm in the breezy shade of the trees, was the cause of her troubles.

No, she remonstrated herself, Valentine Windham had not caused her troubles, though he was certainly catalyzing them, and she needed to clear the air with him. He might be angry—he would certainly cease his attentions to her—but that was better than this growing deception between them. She changed direction and met his gaze, approaching his perch with as much resolve as the roiling in her stomach would allow.

Fear was an old, familiar enemy, and since Francis's death, she'd never really been free of it. It ebbed and flowed, sometimes bad, sometimes worse, and now it had shifted, expanded to include fear for the man she was about to confront. Bad enough she had made such a conscienceless enemy, but at least she could protect this very decent man from harm before he gained an enemy, as well.

"Hello." She greeted Val and waited for his acknowledgement. He'd been affectionate company when they were private, but almost as if he sensed she'd withheld information from him, he'd also shown her a certain indefinable reserve.

"Hello." He took her wrist in his hand to tug her down beside him on the bench under Belmont's spreading oaks. "You are playing truant?"

"It was too hot to nap and I have much on my mind." Two truths. Ellen told herself it was a good start.

"You look burdened with weighty thoughts, perhaps." A neutral enough greeting, but Ellen heard reservations in it. Best get the discussion over with.

"You are going to be disappointed in me."

"Why is that?" He did not slip an arm around her shoulders.

"I have not been…forthcoming," Ellen said, wishing she had the courage to take his left hand between her two as she had many times in the past.

"I have never raised my hand to a woman, Ellen," Val said, allaying her fears not at all. Of course he wouldn't strike her. "I can't recall even raising my voice to a woman, not even to my sisters, and there are five of them."

It was as much reassurance as he'd give her, and Ellen realized that somehow Val must have indeed suspected she'd been prevaricating.

He reached for her hand, and all she could do was watch as he held it between both of his. "I know you've been troubled by something in recent days, and I am vain enough to believe it's not my intimate attentions about which you're having second thoughts, at least not directly. But if there's something you need to tell me, Ellen, just say it. We're rather at a standstill otherwise."

She risked a glance at him and saw no censure, but rather, a grave, resolved seriousness. He had warned her he wanted more than a romp and a fond farewell, warned her they would be friends if they were to be lovers.

"How is your hand?" she asked, apropos of nothing, but she could hardly think over the pounding of her heart.

"It hurts," he said simply. "Constantly, but not as badly it did in the spring. Talk to me, Ellen. Please."

Please.

She was going to miss him, miss him with a sharp, low-down ache that might never fade, and she'd never really had him.

"It's my fault your estate is in such disgrace." She stared straight ahead as she spoke. "It was neglected five years ago but salvageable, then we had some big storms and...I let it go."

Val nodded as if he'd expected this. "And how were you supposed to pay for repairs when you were not the owner and you have no portion, no dower property?"

"It is my dower property," Ellen said, the words bringing an inconvenient lump to her throat. "Francis knew I liked it because it was quiet and unpretentious and the farms were in better shape than the house. It isn't entailed, but I hold the life estate, while Freddy had the title in fee simple. He's younger than me, so it likely would have reverted to the Markham estate if I never remarried."

"You chose not to put it to rights," Val summarized. "But what have you done with the rents, Ellen?"

His voice wasn't angry, it was gentle, almost resigned.

"The rents go in the bank," Ellen said, reaching the limit of the half truth she was willing to disclose. "If there's something critical on one of the farms, I've told myself I'll see to it, but I don't know enough about farming to understand what matters and what is just the tenants' endless grousing."

"I see," Val said, holding her hand passively between his. "Well."

❧

Beside him, Ellen was still and quiet, as if waiting for him to rain down contumely and criticism upon her.

What Val felt was a vast, sad relief that she'd confessed her mismanagement of the funds. He couldn't blame her for not putting her fate in Freddy's hands or for being ignorant of proper land management.

"Well?" Ellen glanced over, and the way she veiled emotion from her eyes tore at him. He dropped her hand, and she bowed her head until he slid his arm around her shoulders.

"Well," Val said, kissing her temple. "You are being honest and I have to appreciate that. The question becomes, where do we go from here?"

"How can you want to spend time with a woman who has lied to you?" she bit out miserably. "I hate myself for it, and you must hate me too."

"Must I?" He rubbed his chin on her crown. "Because your trust has been abused by the present baron and you were slow to confide in a stranger trying to get into your bed?"

"You're not like that."

Val snorted softly. "All men are like that. I haven't been exactly honest either, Ellen." The words were out, a little surprisingly and a little relieving too.

"You haven't?" She raised her head to peer at him. "Can you be now?"

He could; he wasn't going to be, not entirely.

"I did see Cheatham. He told me you had kept the rents, and the deed itself cites your life estate in the property. I didn't really study the deed until I met with him, though he wasn't willing to tell me much more than I could have inferred from the document itself if I'd only read it carefully."

"I see." Ellen's head returned to his shoulder. "Would you have been...intimate with me, knowing I wasn't being honest?"

Val was silent for a long, thoughtful moment. "I don't know. Maybe, eventually. I desire you profoundly and had already divined your reasoning. I haven't offered you marriage except as a last resort and can't blame you for looking to yourself and your own interests."

"I don't think you would have pursued our dealings with this between us."

"Why not?"

"Because you didn't." Her voice was very quiet. "On that blanket under the willow, you could have. I wouldn't have stopped you. In the hammock, I wouldn't have stopped you had you been determined. You are very...persuasive."

Persuasive.

"We have a larger problem," he said, hauling back hard on the lust thumping through his vitals like a chorus of timpani.

"What sort of problem?" Ellen lifted her head to regard him again. "I will understand if you are done… flirting with me. We will be neighbors when you complete your renovations, at least until you sell the place."

"Flirting." Val frowned. "I am very persuasive, and yet you consider my best efforts at seduction to be worth only the label 'flirting.'"

Ellen's gaze dropped to her lap. "In any case, I will understand."

"Good of you." Val's frown intensified as he tried to puzzle out what exactly was bothering him. "And am I to understand if you've lost interest in me? If you decide a man who seeks some honesty with his lover is a little too much work? If you prefer weeding your daisies to sharing passion in my arms?"

Ellen's gaze swiveled to meet his.

"I have not lost interest, Valentine. I wish I had, because I don't understand how you can tolerate the sight of me, and yet I still crave your embrace. I crave the simple scent of you, all cedar and whatever else it is you wear. I crave the texture of your hair against my fingers and the taste of you on my tongue…" She stopped herself, maybe shocked at her own words and the vehemence of them.

The truth of them.

Val gently pushed her head back to his shoulder. "That's putting it plain enough." Reassuringly plain.

As they sat in silence, he savored her confession, more glad to hear it than he would have admitted. The money she'd kept was troubling, but it was legally hers, and in her shoes he might have done likewise.

Her reticence about it was more troubling still, but in truth he'd been at the estate just about a month.

There were things it had taken his brothers years to confide in him—and he hadn't been hiding his ducal affiliations from them at the time. That was a sobering, lust-inhibiting thought, thank God. It inspired him to an additional exercise in honesty. "We do have another problem."

She remained resting against him, a comfort thrown into higher relief by all their guarded honesties. "What problem is that?"

Val's hand closed over her fingers, and he brought her knuckles to his lips then pressed the back of her hand against his forehead.

"I should say"—he let out a quiet, tired sigh—"I have a greater problem, as it might be me somebody is hoping to kill."

~∞~

Monday morning came around foggy, damp, and chilly. The wagon was again loaded with food, amenities, more food, and a few books, all carefully stowed under tarpaulins.

As were the firearms and ammunition obligingly sent along with the other provisions, the spyglass, and the antique crossbow Day and Phillip's maternal grandfather had willed to them.

Day and Phillip were dozing in the back, and Abby was making her farewells to Ellen at the wagon. St. Just, however, was checking the girth on his gelding.

"Are we too early for your groom?" Val asked Axel as they watched St. Just adjusting stirrup leathers.

"I sent him off Saturday night on some errands. He should be back posthaste."

Val glanced at the wagon to see Abby was hugging Ellen, something that hadn't happened the previous week. "I wish Ellen would stay with you."

"I thought we agreed we'd stick as much to routine as possible, and that means Mrs. FitzEngle goes back to weeding her petunias and you go back to slave driving."

"I don't like it."

"St. Just will watch your back," Axel reminded him. "Sir Dewey will drop by, as well. Then too, I'll be coming around by midweek, and we've got the solicitors on the alert in case anybody's asking questions about the place."

By means of the post, Val had actually gone further than that but would keep the details of his own tactics private for now. "I guess we'll see you next week, then, if not before."

"Before," Axel assured him then glanced at the sky. "Weather permitting."

"Right." Val turned to walk back to the wagon, only to be spun by a hand on his arm—his left arm— and wrapped in a hug.

"Safe journey." Axel smacked Val once between the shoulder blades and let him go. "You might beat the rain."

Val climbed up beside Ellen, took the reins in his gloved hands, signaled to St. Just, and urged the team forward. St. Just went ahead to avoid the wagon's dust, letting the gelding stretch its legs, before also dropping into a relaxed trot. He would have missed the turn up the lane to Val's property if not for Val's shout and wave at the estate gates.

"According to Belmont, you've gotten a lot done," St. Just remarked, peering around assessingly as they gained the stable yard. "And in a short time. Best be hiring some staff."

Val shook his head as he climbed down. "Not yet. The interior has a long way to go, as do the grounds and farms."

"And he insists," Ellen said, "on doing most of it himself." She turned and spoke over her shoulder. "Wake up, boys. Your palace awaits."

"Is it lunchtime?" Day asked, sitting up and peering around.

"It's unload-the-wagon-and-put-up-the-team time," Val replied, "and we need to hurry if we're not to get soaked."

"Come, me hearties." St. Just winked at Day and Phil. "We'd best unload our contraband before the excise men come around."

Val reached up to swing Ellen to the ground. "I'll be seeing you safely home, and my first priority is installing some locks on your doors." Ellen merely nodded, retrieving a wicker basket and falling in step beside Val. "What is in that little basket, Mrs. FitzEngle?"

"Apple tarts. Your brother was showing Mrs. Stoneleigh how to make them, and she insisted on sending some home with me, as did your brother."

"One can never have too many apple tarts in one's larder," Val said as they ambled through the wood. "At least if St. Just made them. I hurried through breakfast, so perhaps you'll save me one when I'm done fitting locks on your doors?"

"Of course."

Val glanced over at her, wishing he had a hand free to hold hers, but he was toting both her traveling satchel and a toolbox. "I feel as if for all we've been plotting and planning this weekend, for all that you and I have cleared the air regarding the rents, we're still left with a distance between us."

"Knowing somebody is contemplating arson, at least, and more likely murder, leaves me preoccupied. Mr. Windham."

"I am sorry," Val said as they reached her back porch.

"Sorry?"

"I've brought this trouble to you," he said, pushing the door open for her. "You were safe and content here, then I go tearing up your peace, and now you are afraid for your own safety. When we find out who's behind this, I will hold him accountable for that more than anything."

"Come in," Ellen said, stepping back into her kitchen, "and welcome. I don't believe you've been inside before."

"Except to put Sleeping Beauty to bed in the dark of night." Val smiled slightly, glancing around. "This is like you. Pretty, tidy, organized, and yet not quite the expected."

The dominant feature was the large fieldstone hearth, raised to allow feet to be propped on it, socks dried, or water heated. Two insets in the stonework sat ready for dutch ovens or warming pans, and a sturdy potswing held a cast-iron cook pot. For those times of year when the fireplace would not be used, a small cast-iron stove stood in a corner of the kitchen opposite the sink. The fireplace opened on two sides, both on the kitchen cum sitting room, and on the bedroom behind it.

There were sachets and scent bowls in corners and on end tables, giving the whole cottage a fresh, floral air.

Ellen stood in her kitchen, arms crossed. "Well?"

"May I peek at your bedroom?"

The room was light and airy with only sheer curtains over the window, and a breeze coming in to flutter those. A shelf built over the bed held books, a wardrobe contained Ellen's dresses and shoes, and a chest of cedar at the foot of the bed likely her more delicate apparel. The bed, wardrobe, and shelf were pine, a pedestrian wood, but light in color and pretty to the eye.

And the bed… It was probably intended to be a canopy, but stood without the hangings, covered by a worn white quilt gone soft and thin with age. Val entered the room only far enough to stroke a hand over the quilt and inhale the lavender scent of the bed linens.

"Lovely."

"Humble," Ellen countered, standing beside him and gazing down at her bed. "It was a guest room set that was being moved up to the servant's wing at Roxbury. I appropriated it and did not ask permission."

"It's pretty and sensible." Val left off inspecting her personal space and met her gaze. "Like you, and if we don't leave this room right now, Ellen FitzEngle, I'm going to want you in that bed, naked and panting my name while I make you come so hard you can't see."

Eight

ELLEN SAT ON THE BED, DROPPED ONTO IT, MORE LIKE, her expression thunderstruck.

"Ellen?" Val knelt to peer up at her where she sat. "Shall I leave?" He put a hand on her knee then slid it up to her hip, holding her gaze as he did. She laid her fingers over the back of his debilitated left hand. They'd been heading for this moment for weeks, but now that it was upon her, she looked not just surprised but stunned.

"I'll leave," Val said, settling back onto his heels and resting his cheek against her thigh. "If you ask it of me, I'll get up and see about your locks, share a cup of cider and an apple tart, ask you your plans for the week, and understand."

"Understand?"

He brought his other hand around her waist and held on, knee-walking in close to hug her middle on a sigh.

"Now isn't the time," Val suggested. "You don't feel ready, you're having second thoughts, or you don't particularly relish getting involved with a man who's the target of impending mayhem."

Much less, he thought, one who had only one reliably functional hand, even after more than a month of abstaining from his music. He was pushing her, but he wanted out from under the uncertainty of his reception in her arms. It had been almost a week since they'd been what he could call intimate, and in the intervening days his desire for her had only grown.

"Now is the time," Ellen said softly. "But if you let me think about it, I'll lose my nerve and make excuses, and I don't want…"

He pulled back to survey her velvety brown eyes, finding them so somber as to unnerve him. He wanted this joining to be pleasurable for her, joyous even.

"You don't want?"

"To never have known what it's like," she finished the thought, "to be with you like that. To be your lover."

Warnings went off in Val's head, as her words could mean she wanted only a single experience of him, wanted a taste, a sample, nothing more. *He* wanted more, he wanted more than he deserved of her; he wanted to devour her, to make a feast of her, and to offer himself for her delectation too.

Ah, well.

A man worked with what life gave him, and life was giving him this opportunity with Ellen. He folded himself back down against her lap in gratitude and felt her hand stroking the back of his head. The moment was made complete and more memorable by the sudden gentle tattoo of rain on her roof, a showery patter that presaged a good, soaking rain, not merely a passing cloudburst.

"Valentine?" Ellen's hand went still against his nape. "I don't know what to do."

He did not sit up. "About?"

"How do we go on?" she asked, curling down over him to press her nose against his back. "I've never... not in daylight, not here."

"It's better in daylight," he assured her. "I can see your beautiful face and your lovely body and let you look your fill of me."

"Will you undress?"

"Of course," he replied, smiling with pleasure, approval, and anticipation when he sat back on his heels. "With your help." He rose and sat beside her on the bed, settling a hand on her lap so she could remove first one cuff link then the other.

"Now what?"

"Unbutton my shirt?" He could have pulled it over his head, of course, but he wanted to communicate very clearly that they were in no hurry. So one by one, he had her remove each article of his clothing until he was standing without a stitch in her bedroom.

"Let's get you comfortable, as well." Though comfortable was going to be a stretch, he surmised. Her blushes suggested she could barely tolerate his nudity, much less her own.

"Don't you want to get under the covers?" Her tone was almost hopeful, while her gaze was glued to his chest. She reached up a hand toward his sternum then dropped it back to her side.

Val picked up her hand in his own. "I would *adore* for you to touch me." Carefully, he laid her palm over his heart then left it there so she could feel the steady, reassuring life-beat.

"I want to touch your heart too," Val said, stepping in to kiss her cheek. "Clothes off, Ellen, hmm?"

She didn't comply immediately but stroked her hand over his chest, his biceps, his belly, his shoulders. She was touching him with such *wonder*, he could barely stand still for it. When her hands fell to her sides, he kissed her cheek, let his hands settle gently on her hips, and waited.

And while he waited, he couldn't help but kiss her. The way she fitted her curves and hollows to his was enough to send lust singing through his veins. When she sighed into his mouth and cautiously met his tongue with her own, he gathered the fabric of her dress in his hands. By slow, stealthy degrees, he drew her into the kiss even as he drew the worn cotton up around her hips. She gave a little gasp when the sensation of air on her legs must have registered, but Val held her hips still when she would have stepped back.

"Steady," he whispered against her neck. She nodded, and he drew the dress and chemise up the rest of the way, leaving Ellen blushing in her shoes and stockings.

And even today, no stays. Val almost cried with gratitude at that discovery.

"There you are," he whispered, running his hands down her sides and up her back. He wanted to look—wanted badly, badly to look—but he could feel the heat of Ellen's blush where her face was planted against his collarbone.

"Under the covers now?"

"Let me get you out of your shoes and stockings."

He'd been careful to keep his erection away from her midriff—he was more than ready for what followed. She'd not seen him erect, not the way she might now, and he wasn't about to frighten her.

Impress, God, yes; frighten, no. Never.

He pushed her back with one hand on her sternum so she again sat on the bed, and then knelt to remove her shoes and stockings. On impulse, he leaned in and again embraced her around the waist, pressing his face to her thighs.

"It's different," Ellen said softly, her hand running down the bare plane of his back. "We touched, just this way, only moments ago, but it's different."

"It's better," Val murmured, cheek against her leg. "Closer."

"Your back…" Ellen touched him again, a slow, smooth skim of her hand up the long muscles beside his spine, then over his shoulder blades and onto his shoulders. "I think I can see every muscle God put in here, as if you're a perfect specimen."

It was on the tip of his tongue to explain all that muscular articulation came from playing the piano, but that would have admitted a shadow to the bedroom, and the only shadows he wanted were those cast by the soft gray light filtering in from the rainy day outside.

"I want to see your back," Val countered, straightening, "and for that, we can get into your bed."

"Now?" Ellen's hand lingered on his shoulder. "You'll let me touch you more, later?"

"I'll let you touch me any way you please, forever and ever, but in your bed, love."

He knew she was stalling, nervous and uncertain, but she'd warned him that had she too much time to think, she'd deny them their pleasures. That, he would not allow. Could not.

Holding his gaze, Ellen shifted back, careful to keep her legs together when she turned on her seat and scooted across the bed. Val joined her in one movement, lifting the old worn quilt and the sheet beneath it to drape over her legs.

"We need rules of surrender here," Val said, sitting cross-legged on his side of the bed. He wasn't bothering with the covers, and Ellen had to notice his erection, enormously swollen where it arced up against his belly.

"Rules of surrender?" Ellen repeated, her gaze taking him in with an expression of trepidation.

"Ellen." Val's smile disappeared. "I won't hurt you."

Her gaze dipped to his groin then back up to his face, and he prayed he hadn't lied. She'd been without a man for five damned years, and Val was…he was well endowed, and he knew this for a fact. Tagging along with Nick on this or that debauch, having four older brothers, spending a couple years at public school then several more at university… Val had seen enough to know his equipment was in proportion to the rest of him.

"I won't hurt you," he said again, holding her gaze. "Because our first rule is you tell me if you don't like something. Promise?"

She nodded once, but her gaze drifted back to his groin.

"If you can't find your voice, then pinch me," Val went on. "Pinch me hard, understand?"

"Pinch you," Ellen repeated. "Hard."

"Hard enough to bruise," Val clarified. "And my arse doesn't count, because when I'm in a certain mood, I like that."

"Dear heavens."

He smiled at her blush. "Rule number two." He reached over and stroked a finger down her jaw. "We avoid conception by every reasonable means, but if there's a child, you must tell me." She grimaced, and Val wanted to curse, because at least one shadow had found them.

"I'll tell you," she said slowly, "but..."

"But?" Val waited patiently, because to him, to Ellen, to anyone, this should be important.

"It's hard for me to conceive. If I do, I won't do anything to harm the child. You promise you won't ask it of me. Nothing to harm the child, no matter what."

"I promise I will not ask you to do anything to harm our child." The words were unhesitating and firm, the easiest promise he'd ever given. "I promise I will take such good care of you, no possible harm could come to our child."

Ellen shook her head and pressed two fingers to his lips. "Don't say such things."

"I mean them," Val rejoined, drawing her fingers from his lips. "I am not in this bed for a casual romp, Ellen. You matter to me, and any child of ours would matter to me very much."

"That's...good." Ellen nodded, heaving a deep breath. "To me, as well."

Val regarded her at some length, sitting beside him with the sheet tucked primly under her arms, her cinnamon hair down her back in a tidy braid. This discussion of children had to touch sensitive nerves for her, for she'd quite plainly considered the lack of a Markham heir her failing. He'd love to give her a child, to prove to her the shortcoming had not been hers.

But children deserved legitimacy, and that meant asking Ellen to tie herself not just to a man with a disability but to a man who came with a parent who thought nothing of bribing mistresses to conceive or footmen to spy on their masters. The Duke of Moreland considered such measures excused by his need to protect and control his children—not in that order. And His Grace considered grandchildren more than reason enough to force marriages where they ought not to be forced, no matter how much Val might wish to have Ellen for his own.

So, there would be no children. Another shadow, but one that haunted every coupling outside a marriage bed and probably many within one, as well.

"Any more rules?" Ellen asked, drawing her knees up to her chest.

Val shot her a bemused smile. "One."

"And that would be?"

"You tell me what you *do* like. I can read your body to some extent, and will delight in doing so, but I cannot read your mind."

"What I like?" Ellen's brow furrowed. "I don't think I understand this rule."

"Do you want to be on the bottom, or would you rather ride me? Do you want my mouth or my hand,

and would you ever want to use your mouth on me? Are your nipples more sensitive, or your lovely derriere? And what of toys, bindings, spanking?"

The look she gave him was such a combination of confusion, fascination, and bewilderment, Val realized if she didn't have the vocabulary, she likely lacked the experience, as well.

"I see."

"What do you see?" Ellen asked, uncertainty in her voice.

"How did you and Francis typically join?" Val asked, sliding down and crossing his arms behind his head.

"In the dark." She glanced over at him, her gaze going to the soft down at his armpits. "In bed, at night. Without removing our nightclothes. We certainly did not *discuss* it, and I am not comfortable discussing this with you."

"What did you like most about being with your husband?" Val asked, reaching out a hand to stroke her arm. "What do you miss most?"

She shot an unreadable glance at him over her shoulder, though Val could see longing in her eyes and…loneliness?

"He'd hold me," she said very quietly, "afterward. At first, he'd just kiss my cheek and go back to his bedroom, but I asked him to stay, and it became… comforting. I had to make up excuses—I was cold, I had something to discuss, but eventually, he'd stay for a few moments of his own accord."

Val kept his expression bland but surmised that dear Francis had left his wife hanging, and holding her was the only comfort she could ask for. Of course she'd want cuddling and comforting if her every experience was one of vague frustration.

"Let's start there. Let me hold you. But, Ellen?"

"What?" She was regarding him warily, as if his rules had provided not the sense of control and safety he'd intended for her, but just the opposite.

"You can recall your husband with all the love you ever bore him," Val said, holding her gaze. "You can be grateful for the years you shared, the affection and the memories, but in this bed today, you are with *me*."

"I am with you." Her reply was gratifyingly swift and certain. "Only with you, and you are with me."

"Just so. Now come cuddle up with me on this beautiful rainy day, and be my love."

She curled up against his side with a sigh that bespoke five years of fatigue and loneliness, five years of coping, managing, and wishing for more, even when more could never be.

Val heard that sigh and propped his chin on her crown. "What does an enterprising gardener do on a rainy Monday?"

"I can start seedlings or get some baking done. Tally my books, work on my mending or sewing or embroidery. I can clean this cottage, particularly the windows—they get dusty easily this time of year."

"I see," Val murmured, drawing a slow pattern on her arm with his index finger.

"What do you see?" Ellen closed her eyes, and Val felt her begin to relax.

"I see you are as bad as I am."

"In what regard?" In imitation of her lover, Ellen

began to sketch on his chest with her third finger, though she probably wasn't aware of her own actions.

"I am accused of being too serious. If you were to ask me what I will do with this rainy day, I would mention correspondence with both family and business associates, the accounts, perhaps plastering, glazing the kitchen cabinets, laying new tile in the foyer, moving pots of flowers to the terraces, hanging hammocks, ordering this and that from London, tending to my horse, and a whole list of activities that fall sadly outside the ambit of fun or even pleasure."

Though a month ago, his list of activities would have been much shorter: He would have been at his piano. For the first time in his recollection, that state of affairs struck him as…sad.

"You don't play," Ellen observed succinctly, and Val started a little at her word choice.

"Well put." Val kissed her temple. "I no longer *play*."

"Is this play to you?" she asked, waving her hand at the bed in general.

"It is pleasurable, and it can be playful—I'd like to see you playful in bed, Ellen—but it isn't a mere frolic."

"Folly but not frolic. So what do you like?" She completely spoiled the boldness of the question by burying her face against Val's shoulder so he could feel her blush.

"I am easy to please," Val replied, hugging her to him. "I like to share pleasure, to give it and receive it from a willing partner. Beyond that, I am fairly flexible and accommodating."

In truth, he was what plenty of grateful ladies had called "a generous lover," and ironically, he attributed the ease with which he pleased his partners to the same skills he'd honed at the keyboard: He listened—to the pillow talk, to the sighs, to the silences, to the urgent, inarticulate sounds, and to the occasional tears. He was willing to take small risks, to care a little more than he should, to expose his vulnerabilities a little more than he should, to experiment beyond what might be strictly expected. In other words, he was willing to put a little feeling into even his casual liaisons.

And then too, there was the simple matter of virtuosic manual dexterity.

But with Ellen, there was going to be nothing of the casual. He knew that as he held her naked beside him in bed, discussing seedlings and ledgers and—God bless her—his own preferences.

"You know," Val went on, "I haven't been asked before what pleases me."

"Valentine…" Ellen's voice was repressive, and he smiled at her truculence.

"I don't mean in bed," he added, though it was true there, too. "I mean in the larger scheme. You know you love to garden and put up your jams. I can see you enjoy embroidery, and you dote on that lazy beast who lumbers around your gardens ignoring the mice. I'm not sure I've given much thought to what I enjoy."

Besides—would the thought never leave his head?—playing the piano.

"You ride very well and you dote on your beast, too."

"I've always liked horses, and my father taught us to take care of our stock. As boys, we rode everywhere and often."

"Do you enjoy horses, though?" Ellen's cheek was pillowed on Val's shoulder while she lazily spelled out words of a lascivious nature on his chest: w-a-n-t, k-i-s-s, t-o-u-c-h... *Did she think he couldn't feel the letters she was burning into his skin?*

"I did," Val answered her, "but St. Just became the family horseman, and one wouldn't want to steal his thunder."

"What about your manufactories, then?" D-e-s-i-r-e. M-o-u-t-h.

"I run them." Val shrugged, suffering her spelling practice manfully. "They make a scandalous profit, but one can't expect that to last. I know something I do like," Val said just as Ellen stroked a finger across one of his nipples, perhaps crossing a *t*.

"What?" Her finger paused, and it was both relief and frustration for that finger to stop stroking over his skin.

"Kissing you." Val shifted slowly, carefully, so he was poised above her on his knees and forearms. "I really like kissing you, Ellen FitzEngle Markham, but I've found that practice can make the enjoyable nigh sublime. Assiduous, unrelenting practice."

He started with the softest, most fleeting hint of what was to come, just whispering his lips across hers. She sighed and brushed her lips over his just as lightly.

"I like kissing you too, Valentine Windham." She repeated the gesture, and he settled in a little more closely to her—on her—preparing to besiege her mouth.

"I like it exceedingly," Ellen said, closing her

eyes as Val's lips went cruising over her features. He
inhaled the fragrance of her hair, nuzzled her ear,
pressed his cheek to hers, and ran his tongue up the
side of her neck.

He wanted every sense—scent, touch, taste, sight,
and hearing—involved before he'd proceed further.

"Valentine Windham, you are," Ellen whispered in
his ear, "the most *sumptuous* man." On his back, her
finger traced out the letters m-o-r-e.

That little, breathy compliment settled into Val's
heart, just like her willingness to use his name, and
lit a small steady flame of determination. This had to
be perfect for her. He could not give her marriage or
permanence or much of his future, but he could and
would give her this day and as many others as she
would permit.

"You are my feast," Val whispered to her. "I hardly
know where to start, you present me with so much
to enjoy."

"Kiss me more," she suggested, pressing her lips to
his cheek. "I want to kiss you everywhere."

Blazes. Val seized her mouth with his own, angling
his body up and over hers, the better to engulf her lips
and teeth and tongue and mind. His hands found hers
where they lay on either side of her head, and he laced
his fingers through hers. She closed her fingers around
his and arched up, offering more than kisses and asking
for more than kisses.

By degrees, he let her have some of his weight,
pressing his chest to hers. She seemed to need it,
pushing herself up against him, asking him to anchor
not just her hands to the pillow but her body with his.

Her mouth was open under his, her tongue seeking and exploring. Val gave her his tongue in a slow, sinuous rhythm, one she unknowingly began to mimic with her hips.

She was catching fire beneath him, and Val battled the temptation to merely slip himself inside her body. She would more than allow it. She would welcome him and let him worship her as intimately as a man could.

But not yet.

He was not going to leave her hanging, not like her sainted husband had time after misguided, inept time.

"Easy," Val murmured, shifting up farther to rest his cheek against her temple. "We've all day and then some."

She said nothing, but turned her face and closed her lips over his nipple. Above her, Val went still, tensing momentarily then relaxing. He shifted just a little to the side, so Ellen could be more comfortable while she tasted and suckled and tongued him.

And *bit* him, with just the right hint of sting, before soothing him with her tongue and feathering a sigh over his wet flesh.

"I like that," Val whispered, sliding a hand under the back of her head. "Don't stop."

She didn't stop; she hiked her knees, though, and pushed her pelvis against his, shamelessly seeking his weight. He let her push and retreat against him, resisting mightily the urge to synchronize his own undulations with hers, while he enjoyed the draw and slide of her mouth.

"Both," Ellen muttered, pushing at Val with her hands. He shifted to the other side, understanding she wanted to work at his other nipple.

And work at him, she did. God, what a mouth...

While her free hand came up to rub at the wet, exposed flesh she'd just abandoned, each caress sending a riot of pleasurable sensation to Val's groin. He had to slow her down, as much as he didn't want to disturb what had to be the boldest overtures Ellen had ever made to a man in her bed.

"My turn," Val warned, wrapping an arm around her shoulders and rolling them both so he was on his back beneath her.

"Valentine." Ellen blinked at him from her perch straddling him. "I want..."

"I know." He leaned up and kissed her swiftly, hard, to shut her up before she could finish that thought. "And you'll have it. Soon. But I get a turn, too." He hooked his hands under her arms and lifted her bodily, thinking to position her breasts for his mouth. Needing to, in fact.

But her sex dragged along the rigid length of his cock, and they both froze at the contact.

"Oh, yes." Ellen closed her eyes and let her upper body go limp, hanging on Val's hands. "Again, please."

She wasn't waiting for him to reposition her; she was searching with her hips for him, and he was all too readily in evidence. Slowly, she drew her sex over him again and again.

Distraction, Val admonished himself desperately. If he didn't distract her, he was going to finish before they'd started; damned if he wouldn't. He lifted Ellen slightly, so her breasts were closer to his mouth, and captured one rosy nipple between his lips.

"Ah, God…" Ellen's prayer was hissed through clenched teeth as Val began to play with her.

"Turnabout," Val murmured against her soft skin. "Put your hands on my shoulders, love."

She opened her eyes as if to locate these shoulders he'd mentioned, and complied by sliding her hands over his chest, particularly over his nipples, back over his nipples. She might have had every intention of repeating that caress until her fingertips were sizzling with the pleasure of it, but Val's mouth prevented her.

He made love to her breasts. When she braced her weight above him, he used his hands to capture her breast and position it—by fondling, stroking, petting, and kissing—at his mouth. When he finally drew on her nipple, she groaned relief.

"Ride me," Val whispered as he shifted to torment her other breast. His hands slipped down to her hips, where he applied enough pressure to show her what he meant. Firmly, he pushed her hips down and held her, so her sex was snugged down to his cock. Val rocked her slowly along the length of him, and Ellen whimpered.

"Make yourself feel better," Val murmured. "Find relief. Use me."

She made a few tentative passes over him, and Val sensed she was torn between relief and increased arousal.

"Trust me." He urged her along him again. "You feel so good to me, Ellen. Just move on me a little."

He bit her nipple, lightly, then bit and suckled at

the same time, and Ellen's body began to move with its own momentum. She arched, and he nipped her again so her nipple stayed in his mouth as her chest heaved up, and she let out a half groan, half sigh. There was frustration in that sound, and Val heard it.

"Let me help you." Val anchored her to him, his arm a tight band low on her back to keep her close to him as she moved more and more strongly. And then, just *there*, where all the sensations of pleasure and torment should focus for her, Val worked a hand between them and brushed a thumb across her wet flesh.

"No." She tried to shrink away, but Val's arm trapped her against him, and his hips arched up to increase the pressure against her sex.

"Valentine," she whispered. "Oh, God, Valentine…"

He could feel her body seizing, and bucked up hard against her, holding her tightly to him and aching with his own need to spend. He stroked over her again and again, until she was shaking and clinging to him, then crying softly against his neck.

"It's too much," she finally murmured dazedly. "It's so much too much, and I never knew…"

It had been too much, Val silently agreed. He hadn't intended that her orgasm be so…*violent*, but she'd resisted the pleasure, and he'd forced it on her, and he wanted nothing so much as to do it again and again until they were both sore and spent and mindless with it.

Until she'd been compensated for five years of marital frustration and five years of wasted widowhood.

"Just let me hold you. Take a moment to gather your wits."

"I will never have wits again," Ellen muttered, curling up more closely on his chest. "I don't even believe wits exist at this point. What on earth did you do to me, Valentine Windham? That was different from what happened at the stream. You are an awful, awful man."

There was such affection in her tone, such pleased, bewildered exasperation, that Val felt the very opposite of awful. "I didn't mean to be so rough with you. You are a lady."

"I was rough with you," Ellen countered. "I became a beast."

"An awful beast."

"God above." Ellen's sigh breezed over Val's heart. "I was awful, wasn't I?"

She sounded so proud, Val hugged her tightly, odd feelings coursing up from his chest. "A tigress pouncing on her prey could not have produced more awe in me than you did." He nuzzled her neck. "You have got such a mouth on you."

Her tongue flicked out and Val flinched away.

"For shame," he scolded. But when she merely nuzzled lazily at his neck, he stroked his hand over the back of her head in an easy rhythm. "Insatiable tigress."

"Mmm."

He let her find simple comfort in his arms for long minutes, because it appeased some need he had as well, to hold her, pet her, and stay close even as his own arousal still hummed through his body. He couldn't go at her like that again, not so soon, and maybe not ever.

No matter she was pleased as punch with herself and he with her. On a sigh, she turned her head so her ear was above his heart.

"Does this mean I'm wicked?" she asked, appallingly serious.

"It means you are passionate," Val corrected her, tipping her chin up and holding her gaze. "Passionate is a good thing, Ellen. It is the antithesis of being asleep in the midst of life."

"Asleep." She sounded as if she understood his use of the term and frowned at him. "I was falling asleep, you know, before you came. It hurt too much to stay awake."

"And right now," Val observed with dry humor, "not much of anything hurts, does it? And a nap sounds just the thing?"

"Hmm." Ellen curled down again so he couldn't see her face. "Is that why men like swiving so much? It puts one in charity with the universe?"

"Or one's little corner of it. But there's much to like about it."

"Really?" Ellen stacked her hands and rested her chin on the back of them to survey him like the feline he'd compared her to. "Like what?"

"To see you overcome with pleasure. I have never beheld anything as lovely."

He saw the wind drop abruptly from her sails.

"It felt lovely," she admitted, closing her eyes. "You made me feel lovely."

"No," Val said firmly. "You *are* lovely, and you

allowed yourself to see it and feel it and *know* it for a few moments." He believed that with every fiber of his being.

"I want to be under you again," she announced. "Please."

She wanted sheltering and comforting, and Val could not have denied her one thing at that moment. If she'd asked for his right hand, he would have passed it along to her without a word.

"Are you going to cry?" Val asked quietly as he rolled them and obligingly crouched over her. She scooted down until her cheek was against his heart and she could wrap both arms and legs around him.

"I might. I don't understand it."

He held her tighter without being asked, and she clung to him more closely. "I am your friend, Ellen," Val murmured, stroking her hair.

"And my lover," Ellen reminded him, stretching up to kiss his throat. She reached around to stroke his nape, and beneath him, Val felt their sheer bodily intimacy calming her. She shifted and caressed him with her sex, and he didn't for an instant mistake the invitation.

"You're sure? I can see to myself, if you're not."

"I want you inside me. Please."

"I want to be inside you, but you have to trust me on this, Ellen."

"Trust you?" She licked his chest as if it were smeared with the brandy glaze from a hot apple tart.

"No dragging me back to your cave by my hair, hungry tigress," Val teased, but his tone was serious. "I could hurt you if I'm not careful, and I will not be responsible for that."

"I'll try to behave, but you won't hurt me."

"Depend upon it," he growled, shifting down to meet her eyes. "But recall you are to pinch me if you think I'm even getting close to the near occasion, right?"

"And on your...arse"—she managed the word—"doesn't count, because in certain moods, you *like* that."

"You were paying attention."

She smoothed her hands up his chest. "And I expect in certain other moods you like to be pinched here." She tested his nipples gently and was rewarded with a groan and closed eyes.

"Love it." Which was a small revelation to him. "Adore it, but you said you'd behave."

"I am behaving." Ellen blinked up at him and pushed his hair back from his forehead. "You are stalling, though, Valentine. Make love to me, please."

"Yes, love." He lowered his forehead to hers, and the enormity of the moment threatened to overwhelm him. He wanted her desperately, and she was willing and even eager.

"Valentine..." Ellen singsonged his name as she lifted her hips, just grazing the tip of his cock with her sex. He didn't flinch away but pressed minutely forward.

"Kiss me, Ellen," he instructed sternly. "Now."

Oh, ye bloody blue blazes... He teased and nibbled and flirted with her mouth as his hips teased and flirted his cock against her sex. She twined her arms around his neck, her legs around his waist, and let him manage as she rubbed her tongue over his and her breasts against his chest.

"Valentine, please..."

"Patience." But to his own ears, his voice had a hoarse, distracted note to it, as if he were concentrating just as hard as she was.

And then, like an answer to a craving, the broad head of his erection was more than just teasing her, it was gently, so gently, pushing against her wet heat. Ellen shifted restlessly, maybe trying to impale herself on him, but Val went still and lifted his face from hers.

"You gave your word," he reminded her, stroking her hair back from her cheek. "This is important, my love, and you promised."

She nodded, meeting his gaze and drawing in a steadying breath. "For the love of God, please hurry."

He had to smile, for she was flat out begging. "We will make haste slowly," he assured her, dipping his head to kiss her cheek. "Hold on to me."

She wrapped him closely and closed her eyes. He didn't kiss her now, didn't distract her with any other caresses or words or sensations, but let her concentrate on the lovely sense of being filled, joined, and physically loved by a man who treasured the privilege.

Treasured *her*.

He wasn't quite thrusting, but rather pushing carefully then holding his position, retreating only minutely, and then pushing even more carefully. There was progress, but it was maddeningly slow.

"I want to move," Ellen whispered.

"Not yet," Val muttered, his teeth clenched with the effort of his restraint.

"You won't hurt me," she assured him, but on the next tentative shift of his hips, she fell silent.

"Close yourself around me. Inside, as if you'd draw me into you a little or hold me still."

She made an effort to comply.

"God, yes." Val drew in a slow breath. "Now let me go."

Her body eased, and he pushed one small increment farther into her heat.

"Again," Val ordered. She slowly caught his rhythm and slowly, push and squeeze by push and squeeze, he was filling her, joining with her, and sharing with her the most incredible depth of pleasure. Her second orgasm welled up without warning, barreling out of the quiet around them just as she was constricting her muscles around him.

"Valentine…"

"*Yes.*" His voice was a satisfied growl as he moved more strongly inside her, intensifying the orgasm even as he manacled his own lust in self-discipline. He was excruciatingly careful with his timing, and already he'd shown her how not to struggle against the pleasure, to go with it, to embrace the drowning glory of it, and even seek its greater depths.

As he let her catch her breath, Valentine waited above her, his hips moving in a slow, relaxed undulation. Her body could accommodate him now, easily and eagerly, because he'd been patient and careful. His fingers brushed her hair back from her forehead in a slow, tender caress, and then, sensing her emotions welling, he cradled her head against his shoulder as he kissed her temple.

"All right, then?"

"Undone. Hold me."

"Bossy," Val tucked her closer and hiked one of her legs higher on his hip. "I'll distract you, good sort that I am."

He rocked and petted and teased her from one orgasm to the next, balancing his caresses to both soothe and arouse. Then he shifted rhythm and angle and hooked one of her knees in the crook of his elbow, startling her into another orgasm. After another pause for Ellen to catch her breath, he went still, just studying her face for long moments as he traced her features with his fingers while his cock was hilted in her depths.

He gathered her close and twined his fingers with hers on the pillow. Knowing he'd already asked much of her, Val shifted to firm, measured thrusts. Beneath him, Ellen began to pant as her hips rose and fell in counterpoint to his.

"You too," she got out, not yet having the sophistication to hold her pleasure at bay. She turned her face into his shoulder, and Val felt her teeth, not biting but pressed to his flesh in a hungry, silent scream.

"Ah, God… Ellen…" Val hilted himself against her and pushed hard repeatedly, spending in the depths of her body as his ears roared, his body shook, and his soul sang. The relief of it was tremendous, to not merely dally but to *join*. He thrust on and on, swamped by a transcending pleasure of not just the body but the heart, as well. And God bless the woman, she held him tightly through it all, even as his movements ceased and his world gradually righted itself.

"You won't be able to breathe unless you let me go, love." He kissed her temple. "I won't go far, but you need a little room."

Her hands unclenched, her legs slid down his flanks, and her body eased from his. He shifted up, maybe an inch, and immediately felt her cling more tightly.

"Not yet," she said, pressing her face to his sternum.

Val went still and realized the unjoining was going to take as much forbearance and finesse as the joining had, particularly as he wanted nothing so much as to flop to his side, drag Ellen over him, and stay in that bed until Judgment Day.

Joinings, he corrected himself. Where he'd found the stamina to go on as he had was a mystery, as he'd never in all his years of dallying and swiving and carrying on been quite *that* virtuosic before. After weeks of abstinence, he should have been on a murderously short fuse, but with Ellen, the sheer pleasure of being inside her had been tremendous, and the pleasure of bringing her to fulfillment even greater.

Val's own orgasm had come along as a rousing cadenza, a flourish at the end to dazzle and delight, but completely beside the point of the larger composition.

Ellen had been the point, and she still was.

"I'll be back," Val assured her, "but we're going to leave a mess if I don't bestir myself for a moment now."

She went pliant in some indefinable way, letting him ease himself from her then from the bed. As he crossed her bedroom to a basin and pitcher on her hearth, his body felt looser, his skin more comfortable to be in than it had in weeks. He dipped a flannel, wrung it out, tended to himself, and dipped it again.

He sat on the edge of the bed, holding the dampened cloth in one hand as he tossed back the covers with the other. "Knees up, love."

She lifted her knees, drawing in her breath as Val gently pushed them open and held the cloth against her most intimate parts. He watched as he did it, staring at her in frank appreciation as he first held the cloth against her then swiped at her in slow, careful strokes.

"You're going to be sore. A soaking bath might help, but I do apologize."

"Sore how?" Ellen asked, her gaze on his face as he refolded the cloth and placed it against her again.

"Here." He reached over with his free hand and ruffled her pubic hair. "I am a greedy pig, and I belong in your hog wallow."

"You are a tiger," Ellen corrected him, pulling him down against her midriff. "Lovely, fierce, and not afraid to take what bounty you find before you. You belong in my bed."

Her hands stroked through his hair, calming him, helping him adjust from passion to reality. But the leap was long and fraught, in part because Ellen had taken to lovemaking with stunning enthusiasm.

Lovemaking, with *him*. Val smiled against her stomach and crawled up her body to rest his cheek against her breast.

"Hold me," he murmured against her breast. Her arms came around him, tentatively, as if she were just now considering he might feel the same need for comfort and cuddling she did.

She settled in to the embrace, spelling on his back again, and Val closed his eyes to picture the letters she made. Earlier, she'd been bold and naughty with her vocabulary. Now, she spelled his name, which pleased him. She spelled the whole thing, not just the conveniently brief "Val." He let his mind drift toward slumber until he realized she was repeating a pattern on his back in the soft gray light of the rainy morning.

Like a finger exercise or a scale.

He focused, resisting the pull of sleep, and felt her fingers start the pattern over again: I-l-o-v-e-V-a-l-e-n-t-i-n-e-W-i-n-d-h-a-m.

He wanted to weep but held perfectly still, listening to her practice over and over again, until the rain on the roof, the gentle caress of her fingers, and the aftermath of passion conspired to lull him to sleep.

&c&

For the first time in her life, Ellen awoke in the arms of an intimate.

In the arms of her lover, she corrected herself, keeping her eyes closed the better to savor the sensations. Val's chest was ranged along her back, his right arm draped casually over her waist, his legs tangled with hers. His left arm was tucked under her neck and splayed along the pillows.

She opened her eyes and peered at his left hand. "It looks improved to me," she said, looking more closely. The thumb and index finger were still visibly discolored but not as swollen. The third finger looked almost normal.

Val flexed his fingers without moving any other body part. "It feels a little better, but then it should. Between wasting much of Thursday at Great Weldon and spending the weekend at Candlewick, that hand has seen a great deal of rest in the past five days. But perhaps"—Val's voice dropped half an octave—"if you kiss it regularly, it might heal more quickly still."

"Scandalous man." Ellen wrapped her hand over his right forearm. "So tell me how we go about this."

"About this?" Val placed a kiss on her nape and nuzzled her neck.

"This getting up, getting dressed, and going about our day, as if…" She trailed off, frowning at his hand.

"As if?"

When Ellen remained silent, he gently pushed her onto her back and peered down into her face. "As if?"

"As if we haven't just misbehaved intimately."

He cocked his head, his beautiful green eyes shuttering. "Are you going to castigate yourself and resent me now?"

"I am not ashamed. I am *shy*."

His dark brows flew up and then down as his lips curved in a smile. "Shy. I am shy too, you know."

"Shy you might be." Ellen tried to roll back to her side. "You are not plagued by a great deal of modesty, though."

"I am modest, for a man raised with four brothers. What are you really asking me?"

"I don't know." She subsided beneath him, not truly bothered by his show of…curiosity? Caring? With men, the two could be related. "I just don't want…awkwardness. I find it amazing we're here in this bed, not a stitch between us, and I can even look at your face without burning alive with mortification."

"You amaze me too, in many ways. But tell me, do you think Axel and Abby Belmont don't romp away the occasional morning? She's expecting, and it's no secret the child will not be born nine months after the wedding."

"They anticipated their vows." Ellen reached up to trace one of his perfectly arched dark brows with her finger. "It happens." Then she had a disconcerting thought. "You said we'd take every reasonable precaution, Valentine. What precautions did we take?"

"You are not fertile for another few days." He turned his cheek into her palm, so she felt the slight rasp of his beard. "Your menses started on Thursday, and thus you will likely not come in season for another few days. I would not have risked making love to you beyond tomorrow."

She eyed him curiously. "How do you know this?"

"St. Just explained it to me when I was twelve, among other things. You are also not likely to conceive the week before your courses start, but there are those many women whose patterns do not fit the usual. There's a name for them, in fact."

Ellen's lips pinched with disapproval. "What is this name?"

"Mothers." Val grinned at her. "Or brides. Now, are you going to waste this entire day trying to locate your misgivings, or will you share an apple tart with a hungry tiger?"

Ellen smiled as he bit her neck playfully. "I do have misgivings."

"I know, dear heart." Val growled and teethed her shoulder this time. "But I've put them out in the springhouse where they will not trouble you as much. Did you know tigers are fond of apple tarts, particularly when consumed naked in bed?"

"I prefer my apple tarts properly clad," Ellen rejoined, reaching around to pinch Val's bottom.

"She pinched me." Val sighed dramatically. "If I didn't adore her before, I am thoroughly smitten now."

"You are ridiculous," Ellen said, though the sheer ease of his humor was marvelous to her. "I appreciate the effort."

"What effort?"

"To tease and distract me, though I have to say I like the feel of you draped around me too. You are trying to preserve me from awkwardness."

Val closed his eyes. "Is it working?"

Ellen laced her fingers through his. "It is, a little anyway, but you mentioned apple tarts for the tiger. Posthaste." He let her shift out from under him this time, sitting back as she reached the point where she'd have to drop the sheet to rise from the bed.

"I love to watch you, Ellen. Clothed, naked, waking, sleeping. Love it, adore it, thrive on it. It's better than apple tarts, just watching you."

She nodded, grateful for the encouragement and willing to believe him, because she was similarly afflicted where he was concerned—God help her.

While it lasted, this business of being a tigress was going to be much more challenging than she'd anticipated. Thank goodness there was at least one very handsome male tiger in her personal jungle to make it worth her while.

Nine

HE WAS AN AWFUL MAN, VAL CHIDED HIMSELF AS HE ambled home through the rainy woods. Ellen Markham wasn't suited to dallying and trifling away the summer in each other's arms. She was too decent for that, too good and innocent and dear. And yet, as Val wandered in the woods, he knew he wasn't going to give her up.

Not yet. Not when he'd just coaxed her into sharing a bed, and ye gods… Val would never have an uncharitable thought about St. Francis Markham again, because the poor blighter, with his dying breath, had to have known he was leaving Ellen and universes of pleasure with her yet unexplored.

When Val was with Ellen, time was easy and sweet and somehow significant in ways it hadn't been since Victor died. She soothed something in him and tempted him to offer confidences and assurances and all manner of words he shouldn't even be considering, much less longing to give her.

So he was awful. Virtuosically awful. A cad, a bounder, and everything he'd ever despised in his confreres among the spoiled offspring of the aristocracy

and the flighty artists in their music rooms and studios.
He was going to break her heart. The only consolation
he could offer himself was the absolute certainty she'd
break his, as well.

But not yet.

He continued his meandering in the rain, an awful,
very wet man, but for some reason, the dampness felt
good, and he wasn't in a hurry to get dry. On a whim,
or because he didn't really want to face anybody
else, he detoured to the pond, where he took off his
clothes, stuffed them under the overhang of the dock,
and dove in.

The pond felt curiously warm compared to the rain
on his skin, and so he set out on laps, trying not to
think.

In his head, where nothing should have been, he
heard a tune. It was a simple, sweet, wistful melody,
but it wanted something sturdy beneath it, so he
added some accompaniment in the baritone register.
Then, the entire little composition was residing in the
middle register of the keyboard, and that didn't feel
expansive enough. As Val sliced through the water,
he added an occasional note of true bass, just enough
to anchor the piece, not enough to overshadow its
essential lightness.

But that affected the balance, so he began to experiment with crossing the left hand over the right, to
sprinkle a little sunshine and laughter above the tender
melody.

Around and around the pond he went; around and
around in his head went the melody, the accompaniment, the descant, the harmonies.

He stopped eventually, because he wasn't sure what to do with his composition. He was used to having music in his head and used to having a keyboard to work out all the questions and possibilities on. Even then, he'd play with an idea until it needed a rest, then put it aside and let time work its magic. He pulled himself up on the dock and realized it wasn't even raining anymore.

And he'd been in the water a fair while, if his protesting muscles and growling stomach were any indication.

Though he hardly felt like eating when there was such lovely music distracting him.

∽

"Who's for a sortie over to the neighbors?" Val put the question casually while dinner plates were being scraped clean and Day and Phil were haring off for their evening swim.

"I'll come," Darius said. "The alternative is to stay here with the Furies."

"I'm thinking we should all go," St. Just said, passing Darius his empty plate. "It will leave the boys a responsibility they're ready for, create a show of force before the locals, and—most significantly—allow me to walk off my second helping of pie."

Darius stuffed the plates and silverware into a bucket of water and rose. "What exactly is it we're trying to accomplish?"

Val finished his ale and put his mug into the bucket. "Fair question. One must consider motive when trying to assign blame for a nasty deed. I have to ask who among all my neighbors and associates has a motive for scaring me off?" Val cast his gaze from St. Just to Darius.

"All my tenants," Val answered himself. "They've been unsupervised for five years, and they've grown increasingly shortsighted regarding their care for the land."

"You think your tenants have turned their children loose on you?" St. Just asked.

"I don't know about that, but my tenants have a substantial motive for wanting to get rid of me, and they have access to those children."

St. Just grimaced. "You make a good point. One Sir Dewey should be apprised of."

"He should. Shall we be off?"

Over a surprisingly good bottle of whiskey, Val established with Mortimus Bragdoll that the home farm would be reverting to the estate's use, though no rent would be charged for Mort's appropriation of the land previously. In exchange, Bragdoll agreed to set his hand to cleaning up the buildings, scything down the weeds, repairing the fences, and otherwise restoring the property to good condition. Bragdoll was built on the proportions of a plough horse, with four sons growing into the same physique, leaving Val no doubt the home farm would be adequately tended to.

And at Darius's prompting, Bragdoll started making a list of improvements—beginning with the roof on the hay barn—the present Lord Roxbury had declined to see to.

All in all, Val thought the gathering on the Bragdolls'

porch productive, though it failed entirely to illumi-
nate the question of whether his own tenants were
attempting to burn him out and possibly bring harm
to Ellen as well.

"I'll be back tomorrow evening," Darius said,
folding a list into his pocket as Bragdoll put up the
whiskey bottle. "If you have the other tenants here,
we can decide what comes next after the hay barn has
been seen to."

"Aye." Bragdoll pulled on his ear. "And my Ina will
join us, too. She's the smartest among us, and she'll tell
you exactly what needs doing."

He looked like he might say more, but marital
loyalty apparently trumped an urge to commiserate
with his own gender. Val, Darius, and St. Just took
their leave, unaware Hawthorne Bragdoll, youngest of
the four sons, sat with his mother on the second-floor
porch and watched their departure.

"Think he means it when he says he'll make the
improvements?" Thorn asked.

"Mr. Windham?" Ina pursed her lips in thought.
"Yes, I think he means to do right, but as to whether
he knows what he's about, I've no clue, young Thorn.
The man is a stranger to us, and to hear Deemus tell
it, he wears gloves no matter what he's about, like
a dandy. Works hard, though, if you can believe
Deemus or Soames."

Thorn nodded. Neither Deemus nor Soames was
much given to exaggeration when sober, and that
was too bad. It meant Mr. Windham was likely
a decent sort, pouring a great deal of time and
money into a dilapidated estate. If Thorn's instincts

were accurate—and they very often were—poor Mr.
Windham was in for one hell of a hiding.

And Thorn knew what it was like to get one hell of
a hiding a fellow had done nothing to deserve.

✧

"Go back to sleep," Val whispered. For the past three
nights, he'd slipped into Ellen's bed after she'd retired
then slipped out again in the dead of night. He'd made
it a point to cross paths with her during the day as
well, but with people around, so she might get used
to being near her lover in relative public.

This, however, this quiet closeness in the night, it
drew him. He didn't make love to her—not when
pregnancy was a greater risk—and he hadn't found
a way to explain to her about sponges and vinegar.
Those were not entirely reliable, in any case, and he
wasn't about to go purchasing what he needed in
Little Weldon's apothecary and herbal shop. He could
have withdrawn, of course, but that bore risks, as well,
and with Ellen, he found he'd rather just damned wait
a couple weeks than settle for half measures.

Then too, waiting meant he did not give his conscience yet more ammunition with which to assail him.

So he held her and cuddled and whispered in the
darkness, sometimes falling asleep for a while, sometimes holding Ellen while she slept.

"I wasn't quite asleep." Ellen stirred and rolled
to face him, slipping one arm under his neck and
hiking a leg over his hips. She located his lips with
her fingers then leaned in to kiss him on the mouth.
"I've missed you."

"Since luncheon, you've missed me? I've missed you too," Val said, grazing one palm over her breast. "I've missed particular parts of you intensely."

"Is that why you haven't made love to me since Monday?"

"You're blushing." In the dark he could not see her blush, but when he laid the back of his hand against her cheek, he felt it.

"I am. I'm also asking you a question."

Val dropped his hand and went back to thumbing her nipple gently. "I have left you in peace for a variety of reasons, the first of which is consideration for your tender person."

"Oh." It clearly hadn't occurred to Ellen her person might merit such consideration. "My thanks. Do men get sore?"

"Not as easily as women, or I don't think we do, but you inspired me to a prolonged and lengthy performance. Blazing hell, that feels good."

Ellen had one hand on his cock and used her free hand to rake his nipples with her nails. "What were your other reasons?"

"For what?"

"Abandoning me."

"Ellen?" Val caught her hand, stilling it wrapped around his member. "Abandoning you?"

"You make passionate love to me," she said, all teasing gone, "and then you essentially avoid me, unless we're among your fellows or it's the dark of night. You hold me tenderly in the dark then depart with a kiss to my cheek, Valentine. I would not have you reporting to my bed out of guilt or the sense you've embarked on a course you cannot gracefully depart from."

"Blue blazing… You think I could stay away? From you?"

"You have. You've stayed away from me in one sense, at least."

"Dear heart." Val shifted to crouch over her. "You are so wrong. If I join with you now, I can get you with child. I've kept a respectful distance during the day so you might have some privacy and a chance to tend your flowers. I am hesitant to disturb your sleep because I know how hard you work and I do not want to impose."

"So I was…adequate?" She buried her face against his neck.

"No." He shifted up and she let him go.

She held her tongue while Val got out of bed and lit an oil lamp using a taper and the embers in the hearth. He turned the wick up to let her see not only his naked body but his features as well.

"Look at me, Ellen Markham." Val sat at her hip and reached for her hand. "I want you to see my face when I tell you this, so you'll know I'm not flirting or prevaricating or being what you call sophisticated and what I would call false.

"You were not adequate," he went on. "You were every wish and prayer I've ever articulated or dreamed made flesh. You were my most generous fantasies brought to life; you were an experience I could not have conjured from my wildest, most selfish and creative artistic imagination. I hunger for you."

Hunger. He'd chosen the word advisedly. It was

an order of magnitude more compelling, even than *adore*.

"You can blow out the lamp," Ellen said, dropping her gaze.

"Do you believe me?" Val scooted closer and looped his arms around her shoulders.

"I believe you." But she kept her forehead against his shoulder.

"Let me hold you." Val blew out the lamp and climbed under the covers. How in the blazing hell could he have been so remiss? Women needed reassurances; he knew this, and he wasn't usually so unforthcoming. There was always something he could tell a woman—she had smooth skin even if her figure was less than average. She kissed enthusiastically if not with much skill. She was restful if not inspiring.

And he realized why he'd had no pretty words for Ellen.

She was beyond the little consolation compliments Val might have come up with for his usual fare. She was beyond flirtation and banter and superficial kindnesses.

And she was well beyond his silly duplicity regarding his station in life.

"Why the sigh?" Ellen stretched up and kissed his jaw. He'd put her on her back while he'd kept to his side. Her leg was again hiked over his hip, her cheek against his chest.

"You won't be safe again for another week at least. That looms as an eternity."

"It does seem like a rather long time."

"We can settle for half measures," Val suggested,

not liking the idea they had options he would keep from her.

"Like on the blanket under the willow?"

They did not indulge in those half measures Val alluded to, but Ellen was giggling and blushing far into the night, and for Val, that was just as enjoyable, if not more. He explained to her all the taunts and insults and naughty terms she'd heard on darts night and not understood. He listed not less than a dozen terms, all referring to his member, and stopped only when Ellen was laughing so hard she cried.

❧

Summer in London stank, literally.

Summer at Roxbury Hall stank literally and figuratively, but thank all the gods Freddy's third-quarter allowance had arrived with the first of July and he was free to leave for Town.

Freddy took himself to the stables where his handsome bay gelding had been kept walking the better part of an hour. It was just as well, as Freddy's mood was not suited to a fresh horse with spunk and sport on its mind. He swung up from the mounting block, thinking the ladies' block might have been the better choice, as his blasted breeches were far tighter than the expense of having them tailored merited.

By the time he reached Great Weldon, Freddy's breeches were fitting a little more comfortably, and his mood was improving. He needed more coin if he was to be ready for hunt season in the fall and Portugal in the winter, hence the necessity to tend his schemes and detour through the rural provinces of Oxfordshire.

He rapped on the polished bar of The Hung Sheep.
"Whiskey, my good man."

He detested the place, particularly the image of
the cheerfully leering ram that swung over the main
entrance. Nonetheless, a certain kind of business could
be transacted here, and so here he would bide at least
for a few minutes.

When his whiskey appeared, Lord Roxbury leaned
across to catch the bartender's eye. "Be a good fellow
and tell Louise to attend me in the snug."

The bartender barely nodded before disappearing
into the kitchen. A young lady emerged a few minutes
later sporting a smile Freddy knew was as false as her
truly impressive breasts were genuine.

"Milord." She beamed at Freddy where he sat
frankly ogling her breasts. "May I fetch you another?"

Freddy wrinkled his nose. "It's a pathetic brew, but
I've miles to go yet, so yes."

Her smile slipped a bit, though Freddy wasn't about
to admit the drink was both decent and inexpensive.

"So there ye be." She set the drink down a moment
later, not spilling a drop. "What else can Louise get
for ye?"

"Answers." Freddy scowled at the drink. "It's been
two weeks, my girl. What news have you for me?"

"Plenty of news." Louise smiled broadly. "What
coin have ye for me?"

Freddy's scowl became as calculating as Louise's
smile. For God's sake, she took his coin, and all he
asked of her—almost all—was that she pass along to
him a few bits of gossip and keep her younger relations' eyes sharp in the same cause.

"I have something for you, Louise," Freddy said, "but it will have to wait until we can be private. But then, as I recall, the stables are private enough for a woman of your refined tastes, aren't they?" He slid his hand over her wrist and pulled her down to sit beside him. "Talk, Louise, and then you'll walk me to my horse."

He laced his fingers with hers and squeezed tightly. She didn't wince—peasant stock was tough.

"From what Neal's pa says, Mr. Windham is improving up a storm at the old Markham place. The roof is almost done, the floors and windows are all in, the plastering and painting is thundering along, and even the grounds are looking tidy and spruce."

"How charming," Freddy drawled. "What about the estate itself?"

"Mr. Windham met with Neal's pa and says he'll look after the place, now he owns it. Mort and Neal and the boys are to clean up the home farm, since Mr. Windham will be setting that to rights too. The hay barn is to get a new roof, but quick-like, as there's already hay in it."

"Did your cousins set up the kindling where I showed them?"

"They did." She made another effort to withdraw her hand, which gave Freddy another opportunity to exert his superior strength.

"And the lamp oil?"

"It's there."

"Where can I find your cousin Dervid now?"

"He'll be in the livery." Something in her tone suggested the boy might be anywhere but in the livery.

"Then he might want to watch us, hmm?" He was hurting her, but for his coin, she'd endure the hurt and afford him the pleasure of her wide, clever mouth. "Come along, Louise." Freddy rose to his feet, tossing coins on the table. "And best be loosening that bodice of yours. I wouldn't want to rip it when you earn your coin, would I?"

He'd rip it anyway. Breasts like that begged for a man's attention. Begged for it.

And he was nothing if not a man, after all.

Val was smiling when he walked into the Rooster, mentally challenging himself to come up with another twenty terms for the male member. Ellen had laughed so hard the sound had actually filled his ears with music. Light, scampering melodies that would require lightning-quick fingers with unerring accuracy—and be great fun to play.

He paid for a pint and some purchases at the Rooster, posted his letters to family, picked up a few for himself, and stopped by the livery, letting the grooms know he'd one more errand before he'd need Ezekiel for his trip back to the estate.

He owed Ellen, and in a way that didn't feel exactly comfortable. She worked on his sore hand diligently at least once per day, usually more. Val himself had been increasingly conservative about using his hand, not quite willing to admit he had grown more hopeful in the past week.

It was never going to be as good as it had been. Never.

But it was better when he didn't use it, better when Ellen worked with it. Better if he was careful not to fall asleep with that hand tucked in its customary spot under his pillow. So Val took himself to the apothecary, there to attempt compliance with more of the medical wisdom David Worthington had dispensed weeks ago.

"Good morning, fine sir," came a cheery voice from the back of the shop. It was a tidy little place but crammed to the gills with jars and bins and trays and sachets. "Thaddeus Crannock." A little wizened man appeared to go with the voice. "Pleased to make your acquaintance. You'd be Mr. Windham, now, wouldn't you?"

"I have that pleasure." Val smiled slightly, while Mr. Crannock produced a pair of wire-rimmed spectacles and fitted them over his ears—which were not pointed but perhaps should have been.

"What might I do for you, Mr. Windham?" Mr. Crannock peered at his customer, looking like a turtle in bright sunshine. His neck was a leathery brisket, but his clothes were immaculate, if twenty years behind fashion.

"I'm looking for a particular tea," Val said, glancing around the shop.

"Teas and tisanes are right here." Mr. Crannock bustled across the room. "We've dozens of teas, and I can mix them for you in any proportion. The mints are very popular now, as is the chamomile, particularly with the ladies."

"And willow bark tea? Do you have a quantity of that?"

"Oh, aye." Mr. Crannock began peering at his glass jars. "When the fevers come in summer, everybody needs their willow bark tea. Bitter stuff, though it does the job."

"If you mixed the willow bark with this stuff'"—Val lifted the lid of a jar at random and took a sniff—"would the willow bark still be effective?"

"Why, yes." Mr. Crannock looked pleased with his customer. "It would provided you let it steep. And that pennyroyal will soothe a bilious stomach."

"This is pennyroyal?" Val took another sniff. "It's rather like spearmint, isn't it?"

Mr. Crannock nodded. "Aye, 'tis, but we have the spearmint itself, and peppermint and catmint, as well. Shall I blend some for you?"

"Why don't I take some of each," Val suggested. "The willow bark and the pennyroyal, and some of this…" He sniffed the jar labeled peppermint. "And some chamomile."

"We've lemon verbena sachets, as well," Mr. Crannock offered. "I expect you can procure those from Mrs. Fitz, since she provides the sachets to me."

"What else does she sell to you?" Val asked, still ambling around, sniffing a jar here and a sachet there.

"Only sachets and soaps," Mr. Crannock said, weighing out Val's purchases. "I've asked her to grow me some herbs or grind me up some simples and tisanes. She won't do it. Says it's too easy to make an error."

"Is there really so much danger of making an error?"

"Oh, my." Mr. Crannock's expression was horror-stricken. "You can kill a man with the wrong potion,

Mr. Windham. The digitalis aids the heart, but too much and the patient expires. Arsenic is just as dangerous. And if you don't know your plants— the belladonna and nightshade, the mushrooms and toadstools—you can do the same again, and it's not a pleasant way to go."

"So you're sure you've sold me only harmless teas?" Val teased good-naturedly.

"Don't leave the pennyroyal around the women-folk unless they understand what it is," Mr. Crannock said. "It can solve certain female problems but cause others."

Val put his coin on the counter and picked up his purchases. "As I do not suffer female problems, I will not inquire further. Good day to you, and my thanks."

Mr. Crannock beamed. "Good day. My regards to Mrs. Fitz, if you see her."

Val left, wondering if that last happy aside was intended as a fishing expedition, a polite nothing, or a reflection of local speculation regarding Val's dealings with Ellen. People, His Grace, the Duke of Moreland, always said, were going to do at least two things with unfailing regularity, and one of those things was talk. Val had been nine before St. Just had taken pity on him and explained what the second activity was, though the disclosure had seemed nonsense to a boy enthralled with his piano and his pony.

Val repaired to the livery, finding Zeke tacked up and sporting a small keg trussed behind the saddle. When Val was in the saddle, the groom handed him a covered pie plate, a burden which required that Zeke be kept to a moderate pace.

As Val made his way back to the estate, he found himself considering what the Duke of Moreland might say about Ellen Markham. Much to Val's surprise, the duke had welcomed Anna James into the family on Westhaven's arm, without a peep of protest or bluster.

And what in the bloody, blazing, stinking *hell*, Val wondered as he approached his own lane, was he doing considering Ellen Markham as a marriage prospect? The improvement in his hand was encouraging, yes, but he'd known the woman only a few weeks, and she'd shown no inclination to seek a more permanent union. He'd swived her once—thoroughly and gloriously, true, but only the once. They were a long and difficult way from considering each other as potential spouses.

Which nonetheless didn't put the notion out of his head entirely. He was still pondering possibilities when St. Just met him in the stable yard.

"If we cut this now," St. Just said, taking the pie from Val before Zeke was even halted, "we can destroy all the evidence before the infidels come back from the home farm. Sir Dewey and Darius are making an inspection of the pond and can help us dispose of the evidence. Ale goes with pie. Put up your pony, Valentine, and we'll save you a little slice."

"I will tattle to Her Grace," Val said, swinging down. "I traveled six miles in a sweltering heat, paid good coin, and carried that pie back with my own two hands."

"Traveling uphill both ways," St. Just added solemnly, "with a scalding headwind. Last one to the pond is a virgin with a little pizzle."

"Pizzle," Val muttered, loosening his horse's girth. "I forgot pizzle. That makes thirteen."

"You're daft, Valentine. A man doesn't forget his pizzle." St. Just spun on his heel and headed for the trail to the pond.

When Val—bearing the small cask and some tin cups—joined his brother on the dock, Sir Dewey was sitting on the planks, boots neatly to the side, feet immersed.

"So to what do we owe the pleasure?" Val asked as he started to work on his own boots.

Sir Dewey shrugged. "Thought the king's man ought to see and be seen. The local lads aren't talking, and Vicar hasn't heard anything of note either."

They both watched as St. Just set down the pie, straightened, and began to unfasten his breeches. "Tap that keg, why don't you, baby brother? It's hot out here, and we'll need to wash down our pie." His shirt followed, and he was soon standing naked at the end of the dock. "You have the prettiest pond, Valentine."

He executed a clean, arcing dive into the water, the movement combining grace and strength.

Darius quickly followed suit, while Val merely swizzled his feet in the wonderfully cool water.

"Are you always so quiet?" Sir Dewey asked.

"I'm hearing a song in my head," Val mused. "A sort of rollicking, triple meter that men might sing in German."

"A drinking song?"

"To the Germans, if it's triple meter and rollicking, then of course it's a drinking song. Even if it isn't, enough schnapps and beer, and it will do whether the piano's in tune or not."

"There's a decent piano in the assembly rooms over the shops," Sir Dewey said. "The damned thing is sorely in need of tuning, not that anybody seems to care. It would serve for pounding out a drinking song and I'm sure you'd be welcome to use it."

"Why not get it tuned?"

"Hire a tuner to come work on one instrument?" Sir Dewey scoffed. "Even in the enchanted confines of Little Weldon, the concept of economy is practiced to an art. Each year, I think they'll simply inflict a pair of violins on us at the summer assembly, as the humidity afflicts the instrument badly."

"Who tunes your piano?" Val asked, swirling his feet thoughtfully. He was grateful, he realized, for the particular pleasure of simply soaking his feet on a lovely summer day while a merry little oom-pah-pah tootled along in his head.

"I've had my piano only a few months, and because you so generously provide that it gets tuned before your delivery crews depart, it still sounds lovely."

Val looked out over the water. "Why aren't we in the water, earning our pie?"

"You're not going to tune that piano for us, are you?" Sir Dewey observed softly. "Belmont said you hadn't set foot in his music room, either, which is puzzling. You are Lord Valentine Windham, and if there's one epithet attributed to you, it's 'the virtuoso.' Your musical artistry precedes you even in the rustic circles I frequent."

Val eyed the pie. Lovely summer day, indeed.

"Since when does the cavalry teach reading tea leaves and tramping around in a man's head for a pastime, Fanning?"

"I've heard you play," Sir Dewey said. "It was at a private gathering at Lord and Lady Barringer's last year. There were the usual diligent offerings and even competent entertainments, but then there was you, and the true art of a genius. I ordered one of your instruments the next day. You have a gift, Windham, and you likely deny yourself as much as you deny those around you when you don't use it."

"Oh, likely." Val started working at the cork on the small keg. "We artists are a complicated lot. Are you going in for a swim or not?"

Sir Dewey drew his feet from the water. "When you're willing to play for us, I'll join you all for a swim, how's that?"

Val scowled, watching as Sir Dewey rose and gathered up his boots. There were implications there, about exposing one's vulnerabilities, and trust and self-acceptance, but it was a pleasant afternoon; there was plenty of ale to drink, and Val wasn't the least bit interested in tramping around in his own head, thank you very much.

Particularly not when there was a very charming German drinking song rollicking about there already.

~

"How are things coming?" Abby asked as she turned Ellen around to undo the hooks on her dress. "And how did you get this thing on?"

"You fasten it most of the way then drop it over

your head, then contort yourself in a learned maneuver that takes years to perfect."

"I know that maneuver, and I know the tendency to choose practical clothing over the pretty. Shall I brush out your hair?"

Ellen intended to politely refuse. Abby Belmont had a busy household to run, her stepsons would no doubt want to greet her, and there was a meal to get on the table.

"Would you mind?"

"Of course not." Abby hung Ellen's dress in the wardrobe and fetched a brush from the vanity, while Ellen took the low-backed chair before it. "When I was married to That Man, he thought I should not have a lady's maid, claiming it set an example of sloth and dependence on one's inferiors. The Colonel was so full of nonsense. You have beautiful hair."

"How do you reconcile that?" Ellen asked, closing her eyes. "How do you put up with knowing you were married to Stoneleigh for years, and in some senses those years were wasted?"

"Like five years of widowhood might feel wasted?" Abby asked softly. "With regard to my first marriage, it was the only marriage I knew, and the Colonel wasn't overtly cruel. But I am convinced, as well, years in his household gave me a particular independence of spirit and resilience."

"Independence of spirit is no comfort on a cold winter night," Ellen said, her smile sheepish.

"I didn't know what all I was missing," Abby reminded her. "I think sometimes, what if I lost Axel now, especially with the baby coming and the boys

not yet off to school? God above, I'd go mad with
grief and rage."

"You do," Ellen said quietly. "A little bit, you do
go mad, but the world does not take heed of your
madness, and you must get up, don your clothes, tidy
your hair, and put sustenance in your body all the
same."

Abby leaned down and hugged Ellen's shoulders for
a long, silent minute, and Ellen found tears welling.
She swallowed and blinked them into submission, but
the intensity of the emotion and the relief of Abby's
silent understanding surprised her.

Abby straightened and resumed brushing Ellen's
hair. "Axel says it's like this: He loved his Caroline
and so did the boys. In some ways, they all still love
her, and that's as it should be. He keeps some of her
clothing in a trunk in the attic because they carry her
scent."

As Abby spoke, Ellen realized abruptly that part
of her misgivings regarding Valentine Windham
stemmed not from her own duplicity with the man,
or even fear of entangling him in her past, but simply
from a widow's guilt.

Like sun bursting through rain clouds, it hit her that
loving Valentine Windham, being intimate with him,
did not betray Francis. Francis would *want* her to find
another love, to be happy and to be loved.

Love?

Abby looked a little concerned at Ellen's expression.
"Perhaps I should not have been quite so personal on
the topic of grief."

"Of course you should." Ellen met Abby's gaze in

the mirror. "I am glad you were. It's a topic nobody wants to bring up, and you can't very well stroll up to the neighbors and tell them: I'm missing my spouse who has been gone for years, would you mind if I had a good cry on your shoulder?"

"We should be able to, but we don't, do we?"

"I didn't." Ellen closed her eyes as Abby drew her hair in a slow sweep over both shoulders.

"Maybe you did, a little, just now. Let's put you in the tub and wash this hair. As hot as the weather is, it will dry in no time."

Ellen let Abby attend her, let her wash her hair, pour her a glass of wine while she soaked, and wrap her in a bath sheet when she was done. She hadn't permitted herself this luxury—an attended bath—since Francis had died.

Punishing herself, perhaps? Or maybe just that much in need of bodily privacy.

"We can sit on the balcony and I'll brush out your hair," Abby said when Ellen was in her dressing gown, her hair hanging in damp curls.

And Abby went one better, having a tray of cheese and fruit brought up to go with the wine. They spent the time conversing about mutual neighbors, gardens, pie recipes, and the boys.

"They are splendid young men," Ellen said after her second glass of wine—or was it her third? "And I think having them around makes us all less lonely."

"Lonely," Abby spat. "I got damned sick of being lonely. I'm not lonely now."

"Because of Mr. Belmont. He is an impressive specimen."

Abby grinned at her wineglass. "Quite, but so is your Mr. Windham."

Ellen shook her head, and the countryside beyond the balcony swished around in her vision. "He isn't my Mr. Windham." It really was an interesting effect. "I think I'm getting tipsy."

Abby nodded slowly. "One should, from time to time. Why isn't he your Mr. Windham?"

"He's far above my touch. I'm a gardener, for pity's sake, and he's a wealthy young fellow who will no doubt want children."

Abby cocked her head. "You can still have children. You aren't at your last prayers, *Baroness*."

"I never carried a child to term for Francis," Ellen said, some of the pleasant haze evaporating, "and I am…not fit for one of Mr. Windham's station."

Abby set her wine glass down. "What nonsense is this?"

Ellen should have remained silent; she should have let the moment pass with some unremarkable platitude, but five years of platitudes and silence—or perhaps half a bottle of wine—overwhelmed good sense.

"Oh, Abby, I've done things to be ashamed of, and they are such things as will not allow me to remarry. Ever."

"Did you murder your husband?" Abby asked, her tone indignant. "Did you hold up stagecoaches on the high toby? Perhaps you sold secrets to the Corsican?"

"I did not murder my h-husband," Ellen said, tears welling up *again*. "Oh, damn it all." It was her worst, most scathing curse, and it hardly served to express one tenth of her misery. "What I did was worse than that, and I won't speak of it. I'd like to be alone."

Abby rose and put her arms around Ellen, enveloping her in a cloud of sweet, flowery fragrance. "Whatever you think you did, it can be forgiven by those who love you. I *know* this, Ellen."

"I am not you," Ellen said, her voice resolute. "I am me, and if I care for Mr. Windham, I will not involve him in my past."

"You're involving him in your present, though." Abby sat back, regarding Ellen levelly. "And likely in your future, as well, I hope."

"I should not," Ellen said softly. "I should not, but you're right, I have, and for the present I probably can't help myself. He'll tire of our dalliance, though, and then I'll let him go, and all will be as it should be again."

"You are not making sense. I don't want to leave you here alone."

"But you should," Ellen said. "The gentlemen will be done with their baths and hungry for their luncheon. I'll take a tray here, if you don't mind."

"I'll leave you the cheese and fruit for now." Abby got to her feet, her expression unconvinced. "Perhaps you're done with the wine?"

"I think some tea is in order. You mustn't take my dramatics too seriously."

"I won't. I'll make your excuses to the fellows and send you up some reading with your luncheon."

"My thanks." Ellen let herself be hugged again. All three times she'd been pregnant, Ellen had felt the same wonderful, expansive affection for everyone in her world—well, almost everyone, as there was no genuine affection to be had for Freddy or some of his friends.

"Perhaps I'll take a nap," Ellen suggested.

"I never realized how invigorating a nap could be," Abby replied, drawing back and picking up the wine bottle. "Not *that* kind of nap, though those are delightful, but simple rest. My first husband frowned upon it, unless one was sickening for something or suffering a migraine."

"What a disappointing man he must have been, and what a lovely contrast Mr. Belmont must make."

"Mr. Belmont encourages me to nap when I'm tired." Abby's smile was feline.

"Out." Ellen pointed to the door, smiling back. "Out, out, out, and thank you for the visit, the wine, and the privacy."

Though when Abby had left her alone, Ellen did not nap. Indeed, it took her some time to cease weeping.

Ten

"YOU HAD THAT LOOK AT LUNCHEON YOU USED TO GET when you'd been away from the piano too long," St. Just remarked as he and Val grabbed the cribbage board, a blanket, and a small hamper.

"I am preoccupied," Val said, "but not with a melody." He wished he might be, rather than the disturbing things he'd overheard between Abby and Ellen as they'd visited on their balcony just the other side of the rose trellis adorning his own. What on earth could the Baroness Roxbury have done that was worse than murdering her husband?

"What's the worst offense you could commit?" Val asked his brother as they rooted through Axel's library cabinets for a deck of cards.

"Worst in the sense of violating my honor?" St. Just eyed Val curiously. "I suppose it would be betraying Winnie, who as a child is more helpless and dependent on me than is my countess."

"They are both your property," Val pointed out, spying a deck of cards. "Or as good as."

"True, but Winnie is helpless, entrusted to me

by no less than The Almighty in every regard. Her health, her happiness, her education, her spiritual well-being…"

"Daunting?" Val smiled in understanding.

"I have Emmie and Winnie to lean on. We shall contrive."

"If you don't have a son, what happens to the title?"

"Goes to Winnie's eldest son, even if I do have a son with Emmie."

Val met his brother's eyes, not sure if the man were teasing. "Are you joking?"

"Dead serious," St. Just replied as he waved his brother through the door of the library. "His Grace saw to the drafting of the letters patent and knew I didn't want the earldom in the first place. As it stands, I will have the title for my lifetime, then my adopted daughter—our dear Bronwyn, who is in fact the former title holder's offspring—will inherit on behalf of her heirs."

"What did you have to give up to get this concession from Moreland?" Val asked as they gained the kitchen.

"I didn't give up anything." St. Just piled their booty on the counter and went to the breadbox, extracting two fat muffins. "His Grace knew I never wanted an earldom—despite Her Grace's insistence that one be imposed on me—and came up with this on his own. It's a few words in the letters patent about my firstborn of any description rather than firstborn legitimate natural male son, and so on. Why do you find it so hard to believe the duke might act on decent notions?"

"He can." Val made the admission easily. "He's been more than decent to Anna, but his own ends are usually the ones he's most inclined to serve."

"His Grace becomes fixed on his goals." St. Just wrapped the muffins in a clean dishcloth and tucked them in the hamper. "He's a man who pursues 'ais aims with an untiring fixity of purpose, regardless of the price it exacts from him in bodily comfort or personal ease. You hold this against him with a great deal of determination, I note."

There was something irritatingly older-brother in St. Just's observation, as if Val were missing some obvious point.

"I wouldn't say I hold it against him so much." Val frowned at the hamper. What was St. Just getting at? "The way he is just...frustrates. He's more human since his heart seizure, and he's made his peace with you and Gayle, but he and I have never had much in common."

St. Just cocked his head, a curious smile on his lips. "Dear heart, what do you allow yourself to have in common with anybody? You stopped riding horses with me when you were little more than a boy; you've kept your businesses scrupulously away from Gayle's eye; you seldom went out socializing with Bart or Victor, though you'll escort our sisters all over creation; and you've chained yourself to that piano for most of your adult life."

"I believe we've had this discussion. Would you be very offended if I begged off our cribbage match?" There was only so much fraternal cross-examination a man could politely bear, after all.

"Of course I don't mind. I'll trounce Belmont instead, or the grooms, or maybe just cadge a nap under some obliging tree. Go to your lady. It's clear you were pining for her all through lunch."

Val scrubbed a hand over his face. "Was I that obvious?"

"A brother far from home suspects these things. There's cake in the breadbox. You might take her some."

"One piece and one fork."

"Well done. And Val?"

Val turned, cake knife in hand, and waited.

"I'll be leaving on Monday, once I've seen you returned to Little Weldon," St. Just said. "I won't stop worrying about you, though. And because I will be absent and Gayle is up to his eyes in nappies, you might consider letting His Grace know where things stand here. You need someone at your back."

Val drew in a slow breath, nodded, and departed.

He made his way through the house, unsettled by his exchange with St. Just but unable to put his finger on the exact source. The Duke of Moreland was an old-style aristocrat—bossy, self-indulgent, and much concerned with his own consequence. To say he was high-handed was comparable to calling the Atlantic wet.

Val put the puzzle of his father's machinations away as his steps took him to Ellen's bedroom, and he debated at the last minute whether he should intrude. What could he say: What crime did you commit that prevents me from courting you?

Did he want to court her?

Ellen stared at the same page she'd been staring at for half an hour then put the book aside in disgust. Catullus and Sappho, indeed. What had Abby been about? Romance was little comfort to an impoverished, widowed baroness who ought to know better. So why had she even allowed herself to think, to acknowledge in her own mind she could be falling in love with Val Windham?

The answer came to her as another insight: because it was the *truth*. She loved the man, despite short acquaintance, despite the difference in their present stations. She found a certain backhanded relief in simply acknowledging the uncomfortable, unwise truth, rather like confession to a trusted confidante. She loved Val Windham, and as such, wanted only good for him. When the time came, she'd slip from his life quietly, gracefully, and as gratefully as she could.

Love did that. Love did the right thing, and because love was the motivation, the right thing became the only thing to do. Not hard, not costly, not too much. Right.

A soft tap on her door interrupted her musings, and she had only made it to the edge of the bed before the door opened, revealing the object of her contemplation.

"You are awake." Val smiled at her, and her heart turned over at his sheer, luscious, masculine pulchritude. Just gazing at her, there was a tenderness and a welcome in his eyes that made her heart speed up.

"I napped a little. Abby and I got to visiting over a lovely bottle of white wine, and I am not used to even that."

"And in the heat, one can imbibe more than one should and more quickly than is wise." He lowered himself to sit beside her. "I missed you at lunch."

"I missed lunch," Ellen replied, though the compliment had her blushing at her hands. "And do I see cake on your plate?"

"You might." Val set the plate on the night table. "Are you done napping, and can I talk you into joining me on a blanket down by the pond?"

"You may." She'd enjoy her time with him and then have the memories and enjoy those too. "Let's eat our cake before we venture forth so we'll have less to carry."

Val nodded solemnly. "Always an important consideration. I thought of some more words." He took the plate in one hand and Ellen's wrist in the other and tugged her toward the balcony.

"What kind of words?" Ellen went willingly. The balcony was cool and shady—and safer than the bed.

"Pizzle," Val said, setting the cake down on a wicker table. "Putz, which I think is a German word, as is schlange. In German it means snake, but the connotation is clear."

Ellen grinned and did not meet his eyes. "You've put thought into this?"

"No," Val admitted, seating himself beside her on a chaise. "The words keep occurring to me, so I'm passing them along. What have you been thinking about, Mrs. FitzEngle?"

Her past, Ellen wanted to say, but honesty was not going to win this day, not if there were to be happy memories from it.

"Vegetables," Ellen improvised. "Do you have a favorite?"

He held a forkful of cake before Ellen's mouth. "At lunch, my favorite was the asparagus with hollandaise sauce, but the peppers stuffed with potatoes and sausage were also quite good."

"Naughty man." Ellen's mouth watered at the thought of such fare even while Val put a bite of cake on her tongue.

"Very." He passed her the fork and met her gaze.

He wanted her to feed him. A bolt of heat leapt through Ellen's middle, and abruptly the cake in her mouth tasted richer, sweeter, and more pleasing to her palate. She took the fork and offered him a small bite. He slipped his lips over the fork and closed his eyes as Ellen withdrew it.

"Delectable."

"How do you do that?" she asked, passing him back the fork.

"Do what?" Val asked, lashes lowering. "Eat cake?"

"You take a simple moment, something completely mundane, and imbue it with…passion. With subtleties and complexities and unspoken feelings. One feels like one was wading in the shallows, and suddenly, the bottom isn't there and isn't anywhere to be found, either."

"I like the analogy." Val fed her another piece, sliding the fork very slowly from her mouth, pausing, then removing it entirely. "But I can't say it's conscious on my part. Rather like making love or making music—a function of an artistic temperament, I suppose. Let's fetch a blanket, take these books, and find a quiet, shady spot out of sight of the house."

She didn't even think of refusing him but let him lead her at a meandering pace to a spot along a rushing stream where the air was a little cooler and the stream bed a fine, sandy gravel perfect for wading.

He read an Austen novel to her, which was more entertaining than Ellen wanted to admit, and he dozed beside her on the blanket, and he fed her more kisses. The afternoon was turning out to be sweet, lazy, and altogether enjoyable, when Ellen heard Val's voice in her ear.

"You, my love"—he kissed her neck—"are not wearing drawers."

"It's too hot," Ellen said, smiling at his wicked tone of voice.

"Perhaps." Val's hand slid up her leg, hiking her dress along with it. "Perhaps it's too hot for even the clothing you have on."

"Valentine." Ellen opened her eyes. "It is broad, sunny daylight. Will you behave?"

"Misbehaving is always more fun in broad, sunny daylight, and I'm not asking you to take your clothes off, just let me move them aside."

"Has this been your objective since you came to my room?" Ellen asked, trying to peek over her shoulder to read his expression.

"Honestly?" Val met her gaze. "It became my objective the moment I first kissed you, and yes, I do mean that first kiss, a year or so ago. Lie back, Ellen."

Val's voice dropped, and his touch became silken. "Let me pleasure you."

"You will not...spend inside of me?" She was proud of her ability to use such language, though with Val, it wasn't naughty, it was somehow simply intimate. Wonderfully intimate.

"I will not, though not for lack of wanting to." His eyes followed his hand where it caressed her knee. "It has been a long week, sweetheart, and though I love holding you and talking with you, I want to pleasure you now while we have the time and the privacy."

What did he have in mind? Ellen could not guess, though she tried to read his intent in the way his gaze dropped to where his hand now stroked her hip. He looked at her as if he could see through her skirts, as if his eyes could touch where his hand rested.

What he had in mind turned out to involve his mouth, his beautiful, luscious, naughty, knowing mouth, and Ellen's most intimate person. She was scandalized and shocked and most of all, she was *pleasured*.

⤳

Long moments later, with Ellen's clothing still in disarray, Val gave her some time to compose herself. He rummaged in the hamper, poured himself a drink, took a sip, and passed the mug to her.

"Cider," he said. "Sweet, like you."

"God in heaven." Ellen raised her head enough to take a sip from the mug he held for her. "Merciful, everlasting God... Where does a man learn to do such things?"

Val took that as proof dear Francis had not done such things, at least not with Ellen. The man was a fool, a blazing, benighted fool, and to be pitied for his waste of a wonderfully passionate and generous wife.

Wife. The thought landed like a flaming arrow in the dry tinder of Val's imagination, but he pulled it out and ruthlessly doused it in common sense for later consideration. Again.

Val smiled down at her where she sprawled in boneless, satisfied splendor. "Let me cuddle you up, and no, you are not to put yourself to rights. I'll do it, when needs must."

Instead of tidying her up, he drew her down to curl on her side, then spooned himself behind her. "Go to sleep," he urged, his hand finding her breast and cupping it gently.

She subsided, no doubt hearing in his voice how pleased he was.

Leaving Val to hold her in the sheltering curve of his body and wonder again what crime such an innocent could have committed that was worse than murder.

❧

Dinner on Saturday night was a lively affair, with Phillip and Dayton providing much of the entertainment as they regaled their parents with stories of the mishaps and altercations of the week past.

Abby rose at the conclusion of the meal. "Ellen, would you join me on the back terrace for a cup of tea?"

"It would be my pleasure." Ellen smiled, meaning

it. The day had had a few dips and bumps, but the afternoon and evening had been lovely. A cup of tea with good company would finish it pleasantly indeed. The gentlemen rose and repaired to the library, leaving the ladies whispering, arm in arm as they left the house.

"You didn't eat much at dinner," Ellen observed. "Is it the baby?"

"I get a little queasy." Abby linked her arm with Ellen's. "It passes, and then an hour later, I am stalking through the kitchen like a hungry wolf."

"Peppermint tea sometimes helps, or it did me."

"I wasn't aware you'd carried. Will it offend you if I order peppermint tea for us now?"

"Of course not." Ellen sank onto a wicker rocking chair. "After such a rich meal, I could use some too."

Abby took a second rocker and smoothed a hand over her skirts. "So you lost your baby?"

Ellen did not meet Abby's eyes in the silence that followed. She could mutter some polite inanity—she had on many occasions: It was a long time ago. It wasn't meant to be. The Lord makes these decisions.

Except the Lord hadn't made the decisions.

"Three," Ellen said in low, bitter tones. "I lost three babies, all in the first half of my terms. I was miserable with the pregnancies—couldn't keep much of anything down, and I survived on mint tea." On what she'd thought was mint tea, God help her.

"Oh, my dear." Abby reached over and took Ellen's hand. "I am so, so sorry."

"I shouldn't be telling you such things. Your disposition cannot benefit from such a tale."

"But it's part of life," Abby countered. "Axel's first wife lost two babies, and he said that, more than anything else they faced, daunted her spirit. He did not know how to comfort her, but it's why in seven years of marriage they only had the two boys. Axel would have loved a daughter, though."

Ellen met her gaze in the waning light. "And all you want is a healthy child who grows into some kind of happy adulthood."

"Desperately," Abby said, and they shared a silent moment of absolute female communion. "I pray without ceasing for it, and I know Axel does too. But let me order our tea, and we can watch the moonrise while we discuss more pleasant things."

A deft signal the topic was to shift, and Ellen was relieved. She hadn't spoken of the babies to anyone, but Abby was becoming a friend, and five years was long enough to live in silence without a single friend.

❧

"You'll need it." Axel held out a snifter of brandy to his guest.

"I'll not refuse it," Val said. "Nick has vouched for your kitchen, your cellars, and your hospitality."

"We are going to have an uncomfortable discussion." Axel poured himself a drink as he spoke. "I will impugn, or possibly impugn, a lady's honor."

"We're not going to discuss Abby, are we?" Val said, slowly lowering his drink.

"Move over." Axel settled beside him on the couch facing the hearth and bent to take off his boots. "Feel free to do likewise. You had a bath today, and I have sons." He fell silent for a moment, staring at his drink. "Abby and Ellen shared a bottle of wine earlier today and certain confidences were parted with. Abby brought them to me."

"I happened to overhear some of the same conversation, since the ladies were on the balcony adjoining my room," Val said, watching as Axel set his boots aside. "It gets worse. Ellen has the local solicitor collect the rents then puts every penny into a London account. As the holder of the life estate, she is the landlord and liable for all improvements, and she has made none."

"What is she doing with the money?" Axel asked, settling in with a sigh. "Hoarding it for eventual flight to the Continent?"

"Could be, or it could be she's being blackmailed."

Axel nodded, obviously more than willing to consider this possibility. "For her terrible crime, worse than killing her own husband, whom she professed to love."

"She did love him, and he loved her, and they should have lived happily ever after. I simply cannot see Ellen as a murderer."

"Neither can I." Axel took a sip of his drink. "I still think you should make some inquiries. Find out if the money remains in that London account, for starters. That will tell you whether somebody's bleeding her or she's hoarding it. Either way, her behavior points to guilt over something, though I can't see her as a murderer, either."

"Why not?" Val let the slow burn of the whiskey take the edge off the need to get away from this conversation and play fast, complicated music far into the night.

"She's a gardener," Axel said, contemplating his feet. "She makes things grow; she isn't a destroyer of life. Every time I see them, her gardens have that look of exuberance. They don't simply grow, they thrive and glory in her care. Everything I've heard of her marriage to Lord Francis suggests he was thriving in her care, as well."

Val really did not want to hear that. "For example?"

"When I ran into the man at my club, he never tarried in Town but professed to be eager to get home to his wife. He did not vote his seat when she was in anticipation of an interesting event. The birth would have been months away, and he remained in the country with her."

"Blazes." *Ellen had carried a child?*

"They never entertained over the holidays," Axel recalled, "and the explanation Roxbury offered was he wanted the time to enjoy being with his wife. He was smitten, and one gets the sense she was pleased to be married to him as well. You know the lady better than I." Axel saluted a little with his drink. "If she loved him, she likely didn't kill him."

"She might have inadvertently caused his death, provided a second dose of laudanum when a first had already been given, something like that."

"A mistake." Axel nodded agreement. "You are hoping it was a mistake, and so am I. The only reason I am telling you this is because I think Ellen could use a friend."

"I am her friend. Maybe her only friend."

"As her friend, you should make those inquiries. Find out what's to do with that money; maybe dig a little regarding the late baron's death."

"I see your point." Though he hated the idea of rummaging around in Ellen's past without her knowledge or consent. "How does one dig past loyal solicitors?"

Axel snorted. "Loyal to whom? Not to the widowed baroness, certainly. But if the solicitors do hold the purse strings, they've likely held on to the late baron's staff, as well. You might talk to them, see what they recall."

"Or send somebody off to talk to them," Val agreed, a certain someone coming to mind. "Before I go tearing around, violating the woman's privacy, hadn't I better stop to ask why I'm going to such an effort?"

"Because you're smitten." Axel slouched down, his drink cradled in his lap. "Even if you weren't smitten, you're constitutionally unable to ignore a damsel in distress."

"I can ignore them. I have five sisters."

"Distress is not a missing hair ribbon. St. Just has told me how careful you were with Winnie last winter, how much time you spent with her. Nicholas reports you dote on little Rose, as well."

Nicholas and his damned *reporting*. "I will concede I have a weakness for the underdog, but ask any man with four older brothers and he'll tell you the same."

"You have honor," Axel said simply. "You do not tolerate injustice, and that is a fine quality in any man—or any man's son."

"Tell that to Moreland," Val muttered before taking a hefty swallow of his drink.

"I think he already knows." Axel yawned. "You'll see what you can do to help Ellen?"

"I will. Have you somebody to take a message to London tonight?"

Axel glanced out the window. "Moon's up. Wheeler will likely be game. You can afford this?"

Val smiled at him, knowing the question wasn't intended as an insult. "You are a good friend, Axel Belmont, and a brave man. Compared to what I've put into the estate, this little investigation will be a pittance, and I can well afford it. I haven't just produced a few pianos for the occasional schoolroom; I've also imported a lot of rare and antique instruments from the Continent. The Corsican left many an old family with little enough coin, so I can buy very, very cheaply and sell very, very dearly."

"Trade." Axel smiled. "One doesn't want to admit it, but it can be fun."

"Fun and profitable. I am seeing to it priceless instruments find a home where they'll be taken care of, appreciated, and even played."

"Shrewd of you," Axel said, his gaze appraising. "St. Just claims your business sense is every bit as astute as Westhaven's."

"Maybe, but only in my very limited field."

"I don't buy that," Axel countered, rising, going to the desk, and rummaging for paper, ink, pen, and sand. "I'll leave you to your correspondence and warn Wheeler somebody had better be saddling up."

"My thanks." Val took the seat behind the desk.

"And Val?" Axel paused by the door. "I can't help but wonder if there isn't a connection we're missing."

"Connecting what?"

"Your estate has been beset with hidden traps, and it's as if Ellen's future has been sabotaged, as well. I can't see the common thread, but I sense there is one."

"As do I. I'll see what I can find out."

But after he jotted off a note to Benjamin Hazlit in London and had it delivered to the stables, Val sat for a long time, pondering Axel's parting words. He knew what it felt like to have one's future sabotaged, and it wasn't a feeling easily tolerated.

❧

Ellen came awake when Val quietly closed her bedroom door, his voice barely above a whisper. "It's going to storm and I wanted to be with you. Go back to sleep."

"I can handle a storm, Valentine," Ellen said, but she heard something brittle in her own voice. Her confidences to Abby earlier in the evening reminded her that she'd handled too many storms, truth be told, and hated each and every one.

"Maybe I can't," Val replied, lifting the covers and slipping in beside her. "Budge over and cuddle up, wench."

"It is blowing something fierce," Ellen admitted, snuggling closer. Snow might pile up, and rain might come down, but the violence and wind of the summer storm intimidated her the most.

"You're safe with me." Val kissed her crown. "Do you believe that?"

"Safe?" Ellen frowned in the darkness as she curled up against him. "Safe how?"

"I will not let harm befall you, Ellen. Now go to sleep."

What an odd declaration, and how lovely to find he was as naked as she. "Can one be safe in the embrace of a tiger?"

"Yes, though perhaps one cannot get a good night's rest in the arms of a tigress."

Ellen considered his words while the wind picked up and the rain slapped down in gusts and torrents just beyond her window. The darkness and the fact that Valentine would seek her out in the middle of the night gave her courage. "May I ask you something, Valentine?"

He left off nuzzling her temple. "You may ask me anything, Ellen. That is part of what it means to be safe in the company of another. You are also safe in my esteem."

She stretched up and put her lips near his ear. "Would you allow me to put my mouth on you?" To elucidate her inquiry, she slid her hand down over the flat, warm plane of his torso to cup him gently and then wrap her fingers around his member. "I've wondered about it since we were by the stream earlier. I've wondered a very great deal."

"Your *mouth*?"

She held him a little more snugly. "Is it wrong to want such a thing with you?"

This was a request she could not have made in daylight. In her hand, Valentine's arousal was literally growing by the moment, and where she was draped along his naked frame, he'd gone still.

"It isn't wrong. There is no bodily intimacy between us that could be wrong, Ellen, but neither is it something a decent man expects of any woman."

She heard hesitance in his voice, which was not the same thing at all as censure, distaste, or shock. "When we were at the stream, Valentine, you surprised me, but I enjoyed it. Why did you use your mouth on me? I'm sure decent women don't expect that, either."

He wrapped one hand around her nape and used the other to cradle her jaw. "You trusted me. You did not let shyness overcome your curiosity, and I wanted to give you pleasure." He fell silent a moment, his fingers moving slowly over her face as if to map her features in the darkness. "It pleased me tremendously to give you that pleasure, Ellen."

In the next silence, she stroked the burgeoning length of him under the covers. Maybe what she wanted was wicked, but she could not reconcile wickedness with the pleasure and closeness he'd shown her earlier in the day, or with the tenderness welling within her for the man who'd come to her bed in the middle of a storm.

He pushed the covers aside and lay there, signaling in one eloquent gesture his willingness to appease her curiosity.

"Thank you, Valentine." She pressed her mouth to his chest, drawing in the scent of him, gathering her courage. He did not offer her instructions or warnings or prose on about rules and pinches. She concluded from his silence and his passivity that in this, he was deciding simply to trust her.

She scooted a little and pillowed her cheek low on

his abdomen. His scent was different here. No less clean but more male. Using her hand, she guided him to her mouth and allowed herself one lapping pass of her tongue over the soft skin of his crown.

Beneath her cheek, his belly tensed, and then she heard and felt him let out a sigh.

Perhaps a few words were not a bad idea. "You'll tell me if I do it wrong?"

"You won't." He brushed his hand over her hair then let it rest at her nape.

When she licked him again, she let herself explore him with her tongue, found the different textures of the male organ, learned the contour of it from a wonderfully intimate and sensitive perspective. With long, slow strokes, she wet his length, then wrapped her fingers around him, and used her hand in concert with her mouth.

To feel him growing more aroused, harder and hotter in her grip and her mouth, was prodding Ellen past curiosity and a need to give him pleasure, on to fueling her own arousal. She took him into her mouth and set up a rhythm like the ones he'd used with her, while desire crested higher in her own veins.

"Ellen, I'll spend." She heard him, though she barely recognized that harsh rasp as her lover's voice. She heard the desperate heat in his words and drew on him gently in the same rhythm that her hand was stroking his length.

"Ellen... *God*..."

He cupped her jaw and carefully disentangled himself from her mouth, then closed his hand over hers. The firmness of his grip was surprising, the feel of his hot seed spurting over their joined fingers a moment later both intimate and shocking.

When he subsided, his hand still around hers, Ellen remained where she was, her head resting on Val's chest for a long moment while his arousal faded. She relaxed against him, feeling the rise and fall of his breathing beneath her cheek, while tenderness for him threatened to overwhelm her.

Was this what *he* felt when he gave her pleasure? Was this sense of trust and communion as precious to him as it was to her?

"I need to hold my tigress." There was a different note in his voice—softer and perhaps slightly awed.

Ellen uncurled herself from him, groped around for her handkerchief on the nightstand, and tended to him as he'd tended to her. "Your tigress needs you to hold her, too." She tossed the hankie away and tucked herself along his side, hiking a leg across his thighs as if she'd protect him with her very body.

"Thank you, tigress." He wrapped an arm around her shoulders, and Ellen felt his lips against her hair. While the storm raged outside, beneath the covers she felt safe and warm, well pleased with her tiger, and pleased with herself, as well.

When Ellen's breathing signaled that she'd drifted into peaceful slumber beside him, Val lay for a long time, gliding his hand over her hair, listening to the storm.

There was a lesson for him here, in Ellen's courage and generosity—in her trust. This intimacy she shared with him came from her heart, and the resulting depth of pleasure was unprecedented in Val's experience.

The best music Val had ever created, the most sublime, had come not from the thrill of playing before a packed salon of educated connoisseurs, not from demonstrating hard-earned technical prowess before fellow students at the conservatory, not even from the polished efforts he'd put before his most learned teachers.

The best, loveliest music he'd ever created had come from the need to give something of value to someone he cared for—reassurance, comfort, consolation, relief from pain or despondency. The best music he'd ever created had come not from his fingers or his musical mind, but from his heart.

⌘

The next day was spent largely cleaning up after the storm. Because neither Axel, Val, St. Just, nor the boys were inclined to attend services, they spent the day cutting, dragging, and cursing fallen trees and trees limbs.

"Where is Nick Haddonfield's considerable brawn when it's needed?" Val asked the sky as he paused to swig some cold cider.

"Probably in bed with his new countess," St. Just muttered.

"You miss your Emmie," Axel observed, a curious smile on his face. "And you are anxious to start your journey north."

"I am, though I am not pleased to be leaving my brother in such unsettled circumstances."

"I'm not unsettled." Val tossed the jug of cider to him. "I am looking forward to moving into my house and living like a human for a change, instead of some forest primate in the tropics. Why is it always the big trees that come down?"

"Not always." St. Just took his drink and passed the cider to Axel. "Your oaks have withstood centuries of storms."

"My oaks?"

"As in the oak trees growing along the lane of the property you own and have still refused to name."

"It isn't that I've refused to name it." Val slipped the reins of the waiting team around his shoulders and under one arm. "A name just hasn't come to me."

"Names." Axel grunted as he took an axe to a sturdy root. "I can't get Abby to name our unborn child."

"She will." St. Just took up a second axe and began to hack away at the root in alternating swings with Axel, while Val used the team to keep tension on the entire tree. They kept a steady chop-chop, chop-chop, until Val began to hear something like a clog dance in his head. Hearty, energetic music that managed to be both buoyant and solidly grounded at the same time.

"Look sharp, Val," St. Just called as he heaved the axe in one mighty, final swing and hacked the root in twain. The team jumped forward but hawed obediently as Val steered them over to the side of the lane, dragging the great weight of the tree trunk with them.

"This one will keep you warm for while," St. Just said, wiping his brow. Val urged the team forward to get the remains of the tree as close to the woodshed as possible.

"That's the last of the big ones." Axel glanced at

the sky, "I'm guessing it's close to teatime. Let's call it a day."

"Amen," St. Just muttered as Axel bellowed instructions to his sons. They waved from where they were sawing branches off another fallen tree and signaled they'd follow by way of the farm pond.

An hour later, the men were scrubbed and presentable for dinner while the boys had yet to be seen.

"We've company, wife," Axel said as he passed Abby a small serving of wine. "The boys should be here in time for dinner on those rare occasions when we allow civilized folk to dine with them."

"It isn't like them to be rude," Abby replied, "we'll just enjoy our drinks and be patient a while longer."

"One hopes," a baritone voice intoned from the door, "there is a drink for my weary little self?"

"Nick!" Val watched as Abby passed her husband her drink and pelted across the room to fling herself against the newcomer. "Oh, Nicholas Haddonfield, you are a sight for sore eyes. Axel, did you do this?"

"I was warned." Axel smiled at his wife where she stood in the careful embrace of a blond, blue-eyed, enormously tall, enormously good-looking man.

"Professor." Nick's smile gleamed with a pirate's sense of mischief. "I see you've been busy, and holy matrimony is agreeing with our Abby. And my little Valentine." Nick beamed at Val. "Gone ruralizing in the wilds of Oxfordshire, leaving me all by my lonesome in Kent. I am desolated without you, Val."

"You are happily married without me," Val chided, but he stepped into Nick's arms anyway, as one just did.

"And who have we here?" Nick turned to Ellen and flashed her a charming smile.

Val performed the introductions. "Ellen, may I make known to you Nick Haddonfield, the biggest scamp in the realm, and since his marriage, the happiest. Nick, Ellen Markham, Baroness Roxbury, my neighbor and friend."

"Baroness." Nick executed a very proper bow but kissed Ellen's hand—a shocking presumption—rather than merely bowing over it.

"Ignore him," Axel warned. "Any attempt to chide, flirt, or comment only encourages him, and this is *after* he has found a woman willing to marry him."

"And bear my children," Nick added, eyes twinkling. Talk from there wandered over mutual acquaintances, family, and various females in confinement.

"Does your countess cry a lot?" Nick asked St. Just as they moved in to dinner. "Poor Leah cries at the sight of a kitten, a puppy, or a foal. Of course, this necessitates that I comfort her, which I am all too willing to do."

"One would think she'd cry at the sight of you," Val said.

"Oh, she does." Nick's teeth gleamed, and his blue eyes sparkled. "With rapture."

"Nicholas," Abby chided, but Nick only grinned more broadly.

"Pass my starving Valentine the peas," Nick suggested. "He's likely to chew my leg off if we don't get him some more food. Aren't you keeping well, Val?"

"I'm working hard," Val said, but he did take another helping of peas. And potatoes and more ham.

"It tends to whittle off the lard. You look to be in good health."

"I am. Leah insists I stay more in one place, and as long as she's in the same place, I am content."

"How did we merit a visit?" Abby asked. "Though I'm delighted to see you."

"Likewise, Abby love." Nick blew her a kiss. "But this one"—Nick tilted his chin at Val—"has abandoned my townhouse for this estate renovation project, and I must see what prompts his desertion. Leah was worried for you, Val, and we cannot have my wife worried when in a delicate condition, for that worries *me*."

"Can't have that," Val remarked between bites, though he couldn't entirely mask the affection from his tone. "So you'll be jaunting out to Little Weldon with us tomorrow?"

"I will if you can tolerate my company."

"I will be delighted to have your company, but the accommodations are rustic at best."

"This," Nick scoffed, "to a man whose height means he must camp half the time rather than be squashed into what passes for a bed at the typical posting inn. We'll manage, Val, and I'm curious to see what has lured you into the shires. But, St. Just, I am also curious to know how you fare up north. Our families are related, I think."

A general round of what-does-that-make-you followed, with cousins and removes and in-laws being bandied about the table, since Nick's wife was distantly related to St. Just's stepdaughter and to Abby, as well.

"Abby." Val addressed his hostess in a break in the

conversation. "I know we've yet to enjoy our choco-
late cake, but I find I could use a little constitutional
before the final course. Would there be objection to
having cake on the back terrace thereafter?"

"Excellent suggestion."

Nick met Abby's gaze. "And I will provide mine
hostess escort, with your permission, Professor?"

"Abby?" Axel cocked his head at his wife.

"A stroll sounds like just the thing." Abby rose and
leaned over to kiss her husband's cheek. "Particularly
if Nick is to depart tomorrow and it might be my only
chance to pry confidences from him."

Axel smiled at Nick. "Take care of her, or I'll kill
you where you stand."

"But of course." Nick bowed graciously and held
his arm out for Abby.

"Ellen." Val raised an eyebrow. "Would you join
me?" She went to him with something that could only
be gratitude in her eyes, and they silently took their
leave.

"Last night was so violent," Val observed as Ellen
strolled silently on his arm, "and tonight is lovely. One
wonders how the creatures and plants are supposed to
cope."

"Some of them don't cope. Axel will put a number
of trees to rest in his woodshed this fall, and I can only
wonder what shape your home wood is in."

"Hadn't thought of that." He hadn't wanted to
think of that, really. "These summer storms are sometimes very localized. So what did you think of Nick?"

"Nick?" Ellen's voice held the slightest chill. "Don't you mean Lord Reston? I met him before, you know, when Francis was alive and we occasionally spent time in Town. He's charming, if a bit too flirtatious, but Francis liked him. What I cannot decipher, Valentine, is why you're trying to keep me from finding out that your friend—for the man clearly is your friend—has a title. You've already mentioned as much, so can you explain your prevarication to me, please?"

Eleven

"YOU HAVE SOMETHING AGAINST TITLES?" VAL KEPT his tone excruciatingly neutral as they strolled along.

"I am titled," Ellen said, "so no, I don't have anything in particular against titles. I do not hold them in any great esteem either, however. When Francis died, I was surrounded by titles at his funeral, and they all said kind things and murmured the appropriate platitudes. They even sent letters of condolence, but I can tell you, Valentine, not a one of those kind, caring titles has bothered with me since."

"That is certainly plain speaking. Nick would agree with you."

"Lord Reston," she said again, very firmly.

"He's the Earl of Bellefonte now. Viscount Reston was his courtesy title. The old earl died only a few weeks ago and the loss is quite fresh. How well do you know Nicholas?"

"Not well." Ellen's tone relented a little. She kicked a pebble out of her path. "We were introduced twice, a couple years apart. I do not believe he recognized me, but he leaves an impression."

Of course he did. Between Nick's great height and his gorgeous, blond, blue-eyed appearance—and his outrageous flirting—Ellen would probably recall meeting Nick Haddonfield when she couldn't recall her own name.

"Nick dropped out of sight for a few years because he did not want to be forced to marry," Val said. "He traveled to Sussex and took a position as a groom, then as stable master on a rural estate."

"He worked with his hands?" There was grudging curiosity in her tone.

"With a muck fork, more likely. That was the time I got to know him. He was just Wee Nick to me, an occasional companion to sport about Town with. If I omitted his title, it was an oversight, but Nick did not correct me."

"He did not," Ellen agreed, and some of the starch seemed to go out of her. She leaned a little more on Val's arm, her weight welcome and even comforting. "And are you in the habit of having him check up on you?"

"He moves around a lot and checks up on most of his friends," Val explained. He did not want to defend Nick—Nick needed no defending—but he wanted Ellen to understand why Val considered the man a friend. "This spring I moved in with him for a few weeks during the Season. I'd come down from the north and was at loose ends and was most assuredly not willing to dwell in one of my parents' residences."

"Hence the appeal of your new acquisition," Ellen concluded. "You are taking more than a passing interest in it."

"I am." Val smiled at the observation. "Home was anywhere there was a decent piano."

"You were that serious?"

"I was; then this happened." He held up his left hand. "One must make a different plan sometimes, and really, spending the rest of my life on a piano bench wasn't much of a plan." To his surprise, he could make this honest observation without any rancor.

"But you make furniture," Ellen protested. "That must take up some of your time."

"I make pianos, Ellen," Val said, feeling a curious relief to have this truth revealed. "Or my employees do. It's very lucrative, at least for the present."

"Pianos?" Ellen stopped in the middle of the path, cocked her head, and regarded him.

Val waited, even as he knew the female gears in her brain were whizzing about, perfectly recalling every God's blessed word he'd ever uttered about making furniture or any other damned thing of the smallest relevance to his latest admission.

"You didn't lie, exactly," she said as she slowly resumed walking, "but you prevaricated. Why?"

"What sort of dashing young man makes pianos? And how does the peace of the realm require pianos? Pianos are frivolous extravagances, unlike chairs and tables. Civilized society needs chairs and tables." To his horror, Val heard echoes of His Grace's reasoning in his voice, though it had been years since his father had even muttered this sort of logic in Val's hearing.

"You don't seriously believe this, do you?" Ellen's voice held consternation and she was again looking at him.

"Many people do, including, I suspect, my own father." Val dropped her hand to slip an arm around her shoulders. "Many more people are willing to part with their coin to get their hands on one of my pianos, so I try not to dwell on it."

"I am still trying to grasp that you make pianos," Ellen said as they approached the back terrace. "It has to be terribly complicated."

"It's wonderful, really." Val assisted her up the steps from the gardens to the terrace. "All that wood and wire and metal, and from it comes the most sublime sound."

"Like brilliant, fragrant flowers from simple dirt," Ellen replied. "There has to be something of divinity in the process. There is no other explanation, really."

"It's exactly that," he said softly, "something of the divine." In the muted moonshine, he settled for running the backs of his fingers over her cheek and taking her hand in his, but this was part of what he had in common with her. They both had the artist's need to create beauty, to nurture it, watch it grow and develop, and see it please the senses and the soul.

As they took their places among the others, Val wanted to pull his oldest brother aside and lecture him at length. St. Just had been of the erroneous opinion Valentine lacked common ground with anyone.

Anyone at all.

⁂

"I had thought to part ways with you in Little Weldon," St. Just said the next morning as they passed through the village, "but given there's more storm damage here than at Candlewick, I think I'll just see you safely home."

"You needn't," Val said from atop the wagon. "I've Wee Nick to babysit me, Darius is guarding the fort, and the heathen are my extra eyes and ears."

"Here, here," Nick said from his perch on his mare. "Heathen?"

"Here," Dayton chirped.

"And here," Phil added.

"It's less than three miles," St. Just said. "By the time we've argued it through, we can be halfway there."

"Suit yourself." Val clucked his team forward. To his relief, the lane to his estate was clear except for considerable leaf litter and the occasional small limb. The house looked to be unscathed, and the outbuildings were all standing.

"Guess you were due for some good luck," St. Just observed. "Heathen, if you'll take the team, I will make my goodbyes to my baby brother."

While Val assisted Ellen from the wagon, St. Just grabbed each boy, rubbed his knuckles hard across their crowns, and then bear-hugged the breath right out of them. Nick offered his arm to Ellen, insisting that she have escort through the woods to the cottage, but offering St. Just a friendly wave and salute.

"At least he didn't hug me," St. Just muttered, smiling at Val. "My final orders to you are to marry the widow, settle down, and get some babies for your as yet unnamed estate. I imparted much the same wisdom to her."

"She isn't interested in marriage." She hadn't ever

said no much, but neither had she pestered Val for his hand, so to speak.

"Change her mind," St. Just shot back. "She's a lady with troubles, Val. I can smell it on her the way I smelled it on Anna and on Emmie. Solve her troubles and put a ring on her finger."

"I still don't think she'd have me."

"You ass." St. Just stepped closer and fisted a hand in the hair at the nape of Val's neck. "Do you really think without a piano bench under your backside you aren't worth the ducal associations? Is that what this subterfuge is about? Denying you're Moreland's legitimate son because you are only a mere mortal, not a god of the keyboard, due to a simple sore hand?"

Val glanced at his hand. "I didn't think you'd noticed."

"You didn't think I'd *noticed*?" St. Just growled and shook him a little, as if he were a naughty puppy. "When I came back from Waterloo, you played for hours and hours just so I could sleep. You fetched me home from certain death then played me a lifeline. When I went haring off to York, you spent the damned winter up there just to make sure I was coping adequately. You are the first friend Winnie has made, and when she can't tell me or Emmie what's wrong, she bangs at that piano until Scout's ears hurt. You tucked us in each night with lullabies, you interceded for me with the biddies, you... Damn you."

"Damn you, too." Val stepped close, and mostly to give himself a moment to swallow back the lump in his throat, hugged his brother. "Sometimes"—he dropped his forehead to St. Just's shoulder—"I wonder if it isn't all just a lot of noise. It's good to know some-body was listening."

"I was listening. I heard every note, Val." St. Just held him a little tighter then let him step back. "Every note."

St. Just shot him a look then, one that allowed Val to see just a hint of the weary soldier St. Just had been, a hint of the despair and bewilderment that had fol-lowed him and so many others home from Waterloo.

"Write," Val said, unwilling to hold that gaze. "I promise to reply within two years at least." He walked with his brother over to where the horse was waiting. "Don't take stupid risks, give Emmie and Winnie all my love, and here." He reached into his waistcoat and drew out a folded piece of paper. "For Winnie."

"A letter?" St. Just tucked it inside his own pocket without unfolding it.

"Something like that." Val smiled a little. "A love letter, maybe. Be off with you, and my thanks for all you've done here."

"My pleasure." St. Just grabbed him by the back of the neck again, kissed his forehead, and swung up on the horse. "Marry the widow, little brother. She makes you smile."

Val nodded, saying nothing, as there was a damned lump in his throat *again* preventing speech. He watched St. Just canter down the lane on his fine chestnut horse and knew the urge to scream at him to turn around, not to go, not to *leave* him all alone. It was an old memory, of the times when St. Just had come home from the Peninsula on winter leave and enjoyed the holidays with family, only to depart again when the campaigns resumed after the New Year. Bart had come home with him, all jolly swagger and loud stories, and then Bart had never come home again.

But Val also wanted to bellow at St. Just to tell him—just one more time—that the music had meant something. That somebody had been listening.

He blew out a breath and forcibly turned his gaze to the manor house, where his crews had started work for the day. The roof would be completed by the end of the week, and the interior work was moving along nicely. It would soon be time to move in furniture and even people.

How had that happened, and then what would he do with himself all day? Val's gaze strayed down the empty lane, and the lump in his throat ached almost as fiercely as his hand might have several weeks ago.

"You're back." Darius strode out of the house. "Wasn't sure the roads would be passable after that damned storm. Did St. Just take off without a farewell for me?"

"I'm sure he meant no offense, and we about fare-welled him to death." Even as he said it, Val was convinced Darius had waited in the house on purpose just to avoid the parting scenes. "How was the weekend?"

"The weekend was quiet except for that damned storm. Your home wood is probably a wreck, but I was too busy at the home farm on Sunday to really inspect. Your father sent you the largest crate of something mysterious, by the way. It arrived Saturday, thank the gods, and you're to keep the team that hauled it in."

"I'm to keep the team?" Westhaven had sent a team

north to St. Just as part of a housewarming. Maybe it
was to be a family tradition, and any team was going
to be a useful addition, since Axel would need his own
back when the boys went home.

"As I live and breathe." Darius exhaled, his gaze
going past Val's shoulder. "Is that my brother-in-law
dragging Mrs. Fitz through the woods?"

"It is." Nick was not the type to hurry needlessly.
"And something is wrong."

"Valentine." Nick wasn't panting, but at his side,
Ellen was. "You'd better take a look at Ellen's property, and you won't like what we found."

"Ellen?" Val held out an arm, and she went to his
side then turned her face into his neck. He kept his
arm around her as they made their way back through
the wood, and he noted plenty of damage. One of
the old pensioners Ellen had warned him about had
crashed to its side, taking down limbs and saplings
with it.

Blazing hell. The enchanted home wood had gone
and changed on him when he'd been unwilling to deal
with the need for change himself.

"Oh, ye gods," Darius said softly behind him. Val
followed his friend's gaze across Ellen's back gardens
to her lovely little cottage.

Her formerly lovely little cottage. Another tree had
toppled, landing mostly in Ellen's side yard, but clip-
ping the south side of her cottage by just enough that
the roof was ruined and the wall sagging dangerously
beneath it.

The sight was ominous, and to Val, somehow
profane, as well.

"We'll fix it," he said, tipping her chin up so he could see her eyes. "Your conservatory was going in on that side, and this will just speed up construction. Dare, get my crews over here to clear this mess. Nick, we'll be needing the team for sure. Day and Phil can go through the outbuildings and find a suite of bedroom furniture, then pick out a room in the house that's close enough to done we can move Ellen into it."

He braced a hand on either side of Ellen's neck. "You are going to let me take care of this and no argument, please. God"—he hugged her to him—"if you'd been home, puttering at your embroidering, putting up jam…"

She nodded, eyes teary, and let him hold her.

"Ah, look there." Val pointed to the base of the fallen tree. "Your greatest treasure is unscathed." Marmalade sat on his fluffy orange backside, washing a front paw as if he hadn't a care in the world.

"I want…" Ellen stretched out a hand toward the cat, who pretended not to notice.

"I'll fetch him for you." Val kissed her nose and made for the cat, who strolled back a few paces closer to what had been the bottom of the tree. Val reached for the beast then froze and looked more closely at the tree. He tucked the cat against his middle and stole another glance around at the surrounding trees before taking Marmalade back to Ellen.

Val handed her the cat. "He says you have abandoned him shamelessly, and for your sins, you must allow him to accompany you up to the manor, where all his friends, the mice, are waiting to welcome him."

"Oh, Val." Ellen managed a watery smile but leaned against him as she clutched her purring cat. "I'm so glad he's unharmed. You're a good kitty, Marmie. A very good, brave kitty."

"He's also a very heavy kitty." Val said, taking him from her grasp. "Let's move him up to the manor, where I'm sure we can find him a dish of cream and you a cup of tea." *Or something stronger.* He certainly needed something stronger—to think she could have been killed, or worse.

The thought gave him pause, for even if she were maimed, Val would be grateful she was alive and no less interested in her company. It flummoxed him, that twist in his thinking, but he set the thought aside on the growing pile of things to consider later when he had peace, quiet, and solitude. He settled Ellen in the kitchen of the manor, putting a mug of brandy in her hand. He also scrounged up paper and pencil and had her make a list of what she wanted immediately from her cottage.

The rest would be moved as needs must into the outbuildings. For the present, getting her settled upstairs was going to take most of the day.

"May I leave you here while you finish your list?"

"You may," Ellen said. "I shouldn't be so dramatic. Trees have fallen all over the shire, and I live among a wood. You are kind to offer me your house."

"Kind." This talk of kindness made him want to bellow and throw fragile objects against the hearth-stones. "There's nothing kind about it, Ellen. If you think…" He caught himself and let out a breath. "We can talk more about that later, my love. For now, steady your nerves, pet your cat, and we'll have your things mov·d in no time." He hugged her tightly, kissed her, and made himself go find Darius and Nick.

Nick was easy to spot, of course, by virtue of his golden hair and striking height. Then too, he was walking the new team—the one sent by Moreland— down the lane toward Ellen's cottage. No matter what had possessed the duke to make such an extravagant gift, the timing was more than fortunate, and Val would have to write and thank the old boy lest Her Grace chide Val for forgetting his manners.

"Nick!" Val hailed him and caught up easily, for the horses were nothing if not deliberate in their paces. "How'd you get them hitched up so fast?"

"They came with a groom," Nick said. "Your papa sent along old Sean, and you're to keep him as long as you can stand his cursing and grumbling."

"Sean's here?" Val's brows rose. Sean was one of the most senior grooms at Morelands.

Nick shrugged. "Sean said foaling is done in Kent, and His Grace didn't think you'd hired talent adequate for these two yet."

"His Grace has spoken and I suppose I'm to make a go of this place."

"Or maybe," Nick suggested gently, "he simply wants to be helpful, Val."

"Maybe." Val nodded, unwilling to waste time arguing. "Let me show you something before you start hauling away next year's firewood."

Nick signaled the horses to stand and followed Val around the side of the cottage.

"Look closely at the stump, Nick."

"Well, bugger all, would you look at that," Nick growled, eyes traveling upward. "That tree fell into its neighbor, there." He pointed to another stout tree in the hedgerow, one sporting a bright, pale gash in its bark several feet long at a height of maybe thirty feet. "And probably caught fairly snugly until someone sawed through what remained of the trunk at the base. Bloody hell, Val. You've got problems."

"And Ellen has, too," Val rejoined. "What if she'd been home, sleeping or working at her books? Baking?"

"We have to hope whoever did this took long enough to comprehend she wasn't home," Nick said. "Sawing green wood, even a few inches of it, makes noise."

"You think I want to risk Ellen's life on a hope?" Val spat bitterly. "The hell of it is, I can't determine if it's her enemies or mine doing this. Axel told you about the bonfires?"

"He did. Which just means we have to be careful, and at the least, you are the target. Burning down the house would not harm Ellen."

"And wrecking her cottage would not harm me. So maybe it's the combination of me and Ellen someone objects to." He paced off a few feet, staring at the ruined cottage. "She loved her little house, Nick. I think it was all she had and the only place she felt really safe. Would you take her to Kent? Or to David and Letty?"

"Of course. Leah would love some civilized company. But let's get this mess cleaned up and put our heads together later. For now, you have a widow to console."

❦

"This is the last of it," Day said as he and Phil came in, arms full of the details Ellen hadn't realized she'd miss until she was in the middle of making her bed: She spied in Phil's arms some embroidered pillows, her old quilt, her favorite mug, and her brush and comb. She took each item from Phil then stopped and drew in a breath when she saw Day holding out a plant to her.

"What is that, Dayton?"

"It was sitting on your counter. I didn't know if you'd want it, but it looked lonely and will need watering."

"You found this weed on my counter?" Ellen took the plant, trying to keep the outrage from her voice.

"I can take it back, Mrs. Fitz," Day offered as she snatched the plant from his hand.

"God damn him to hell," Ellen muttered as she hurled the plant, pot and all, out an open window. "Thank you, gentlemen, I'd like some privacy now." Her back was to them, as thorough a dismissal as she could imagine.

"Mrs. Fitz?" Phil's voice was tentative. "Shall we send Mr. Windham to you?"

"No thank you," Ellen said quickly enough that they both beat a hasty retreat. Ellen waited to make sure they'd gone, closed her door, sat on the bed, and cried.

Again.

Out in the yard, Phil and Day crossed paths with Val and Nick, who were returning from an afternoon hauling, sawing, and patching on Ellen's cottage.

"Are we due for a swim?" Val asked his younger assistants. "Or do we attack the hampers first, and what is this doing in my tidy yard?" He knelt to pick up a badly cracked clay pot, a crumpled plant still housed within.

"We found it on Mrs. Fitz's counter," Day replied. "I thought it might be a houseplant or one she'd like for her room, so I brought it to her. She pitched it out the window and said it was a weed."

Val's brows arched in consternation. "Ellen pitched a *plant* out her window? You saw her do this?"

"We both did," Phil said, "but it isn't a weed; it's pennyroyal. It makes a nice tea and soothes the digestion like peppermint."

Nick reached out a long arm and pinched off a leaf.

"Phil's right," Nick said, bringing the leaf to his nose. "Pennyroyal can be confused with spearmint because the scent and flavor are similar, but it's pennyroyal all right."

Val frowned, trying to recall what the apothecary had said about pennyroyal. "Why don't you repot it? We'll take it to your father on Saturday. He can find a use for it, but meanwhile I'd keep it out of Ellen's sight."

"Right." Day nodded. "So dinner or a swim?"

"I vote dinner," Nick said. "The swim will settle the meal and cool us off before bed." The boys concurred and struck out for the springhouse.

"Which reminds me," Val turned to regard Nick as the boys moved off, "where will we put you, my friend? The cots in the carriage house are too small for me and Dare, but they would torture you."

"I have a bedroll."

"Would you be willing to take a hammock? Ellen has one that is quite sturdy and she won't miss it."

"A hammock would be lovely, but how is it you vouch for the sturdiness of this hammock?"

"Shut up, Nicholas."

"Valentine?"

"What?"

"There is another use for pennyroyal." Nick's tone was thoughtful. "It settles the digestion, true, but women use it to bring on their menses."

"Why would a woman want to do that?" Val asked as they headed toward the carriage house. "Seems to me the ladies are always complaining about the cramps, the mess, and the inconvenience of it all."

"Let me put this less delicately. Women use it to bring on menses that are *late*, sometimes very late."

"To abort?" Val shot a curious glance at his friend. "Lord above, Nick, the wicked things you know will never cease to appall me. Is this an old wives' tale or documented science?"

"I don't know as science had gotten around to considering the subject, but I know of many women who swear by it, if used early in the pregnancy. I also know of one who died from overusing the herb too late in her pregnancy."

"So this plant is a poison. Just what we need."

"What do we need?" Darius asked from the porch of the carriage house, "and where are our pet heathen?"

"Laying out supper," Val replied. "Somebody left a poison plant on Ellen's counter."

"Pennyroyal," Nick added. "And she pitched it out the window while Day and Phil watched."

"Ellen pitched a *plant*? She was offended, I take it? I didn't know the stuff was poison. I thought pennyroyal was for bringing on menses and settling the digestion."

Val rolled his eyes. "Does everybody but me know these things? Let's go get dinner before the locusts devour all in their path. And Nick, I elect you to go fetch Ellen."

"Yes, Your Grace." Nick bowed extravagantly and spun on his heel, while Darius—the lout—guffawed loudly.

Dinner was good, the hampers having been prodigiously full, owing to the addition of Nick to the assemblage. Ellen didn't say much, but she did eat, mostly because Nick pestered and teased and dared her into taking each bite. Val sat back and watched, wishing he could do something besides feed the woman and put a roof over her head. Those were necessities, things Freddy Markham should have been doing out of sheer duty, things Francis had intended Ellen never want for again.

Hoofbeats disturbed the meal, and Val got up and went to the door of the springhouse. A rider was trotting up the lane on a winded, lathered horse. The man swung down and approached Val directly.

"Are you Valentine Windham?" He was a grizzled little gnome, and he looked vaguely familiar.

"I am Windham."

"This be fer you." The man thrust a sealed envelope into Val's hands. "I'm to wait for a reply, but I'll be walking me horse while I do. Poor blighter's about done in with this heat."

"There's water in the stable." Val eyed the envelope—no return address, but he recognized the hand. "We've a groom who can walk the beast. Yell for Sean and then hold your ears while he cusses a blue streak. When you've seen to the horse, come to the springhouse, and we'll find you some tucker."

"Obliged." The man nodded once and led his horse toward the stables.

"We have callers?" Darius asked, emerging from the springhouse.

"A courier from Hazlit." Val eyed the packet dubiously.

"The snoop? I didn't know you used him."

"Needs must." Val tapped the edge of the envelope against his lips. "And he's an investigator, not a snoop. Moreover, he was critical in securing your sister's safety, so have some respect."

"Val?"

He glared at Darius in response.

"Ellen is safe now," Darius said gently. "I know you want to break somebody's head, but how about not mine, at least not until I've updated you on your home farm?"

"This is not good news, I take it?"

"Not good or bad. The storm did us the courtesy of removing most of the roof remaining on the hay barn. The Bragdolls and I spent Sunday morning getting it tarpaulined, but another steady blow and that won't serve."

Val closed his eyes—*would nothing go right this day?*

"We will pull crews from the house to work on the barn."

"Makes sense. You've got an entire wing under roof now here, and the other wing isn't in immediate danger of disintegration."

"Tomorrow I'll look over the hay barn with you first thing, and we can make a more detailed plan. For now, I want to get Ellen off her feet, dunk my stinking carcass in the pond, then find some sleep."

"Long day," Darius said. "Maybe there will be some good news from your *investigator*."

"Fuck you, Lindsey," Val replied with a weary smile.

"So many wish they could." Darius swished his hips a little as he strode off, and Val felt a smile tugging at his mouth. He set the envelope on his cot in the carriage house and returned to the springhouse just as the boys were clearing the table.

"You." Val put a hand on Ellen's shoulder. "Remain seated. Your day has been busy enough. How is your room?"

"Lovely. It's as big as my entire cottage, though."

"So enjoy it. Have you wash water there?"

"Phillip and Dayton made sure I have every possible comfort." She gave him a semblance of a smile, but her eyes were tired, and Val found it just wasn't in him to force small talk on her.

"Come." Val took her by the hand and laced his fingers with hers, not caring who saw, what they thought of it, or what ribbing they might try to give him later. When he and Ellen left the springhouse, he put an arm around her waist and tucked her close

to his body. That she went willingly, despite all the
eyes on them, alarmed Val more than her fatigue or
her quiet.

He dropped his arm to usher her into the house.
"What's really wrong?"

She paused, and if he hadn't been watching her
with close concern, he might have missed the effort
she made to compose her features.

"My cottage was all I had. It was my home, my
refuge, where I grieved, and where I healed. It has
been violated."

He regarded her in silence then led her up the stairs
to her bedroom. In a single day, it had gone from being
an empty chamber to a cozy, inviting nest. Embroidered
pillows from the cottage told Val whose nest it was, and
the fluffy bed tempted him beyond endurance. He led
her out to the balcony, which sported two wooden
rockers padded with embroidered cushions.

"We need to talk," Val said, settling her in one
rocker. It took all his willpower not to scoop her
into his lap and just hold her, but that wouldn't solve
anything, except maybe the vague, relentless anxiety
he'd been feeling since Axel had pulled him into the
library a couple nights ago.

"I am really quite tired," Ellen replied, but Val saw
more than fatigue in her eyes.

"You are really quite sad," he countered, "and
upset. We're going to repair your cottage in no time,
and it will be better than new. What is the real problem, Ellen?"

He wanted her to tell him and before he opened
that packet from Hazlit, or received any others.

She just shook her head.

"You pitched the pennyroyal out the window. You would never harm something growing, much less growing and tender."

"God." She clutched her arms around her middle but shook her head again.

"Ellen..." Val's voice was low, pleading. "I stink like a drover two hundred miles from home, or I'd come hold you, but you have to tell me what's going on."

"I can't." She still wouldn't meet his eyes.

"You won't," Val countered tiredly. "I did not want to tell you this, but if you look closely at the tree that fell on your cottage, you'll see it toppled partway but then was cut at the base—in essence, it was pushed onto your roof. Maybe whoever did it knew you were from home, maybe not. Somebody, it appears, has succeeded in scaring the hell out of you, Ellen, and that scares the hell out of me."

He could not stand one more moment of her silence, so he stood and passed a gentle hand over the back of her head. "The house is entirely secured on the first floor. I'll come check on you later."

She clutched his hand and tucked her forehead against his thigh but said nothing, leaving Val to stroke his hand over her hair once again then depart in silence. He made his way through the darkened house, careful to lock the front door behind him, and then found himself on the path toward the pond. He changed his mind, doubled back, and retrieved Hazlit's packet, taking it to the sleeping porch on the second floor of the carriage house to read by lantern light.

When Nick and Darius returned from their swim, Val was still sitting in the shadows, Hazlit's missive open on his lap.

"Bad news?" Nick asked, sinking down to rest his back against the porch railing.

"Here." Darius waved a bottle before Val's eyes. "This is bad news too, but not until tomorrow morning, and only if Nick and I let you get drunk."

Val took a hefty pull of the bottle and passed it to Nick. Darius lowered himself to the hammock but used it as a seat, keeping his feet on the floor.

"Somebody cut the tree," Darius said, "and that was after they laid bonfires in the very house. There's no telling what other mischief we're going to have to endure. What does Hazlit add to this puzzle?"

"The rents are dutifully deposited in a Markham general account," Val said in a hollow voice. "One that Ellen could withdraw from, but she doesn't."

"So there should be a pile of money there," Nick concluded, passing the bottle to Darius.

"There's nothing but a token amount. Frederick Markham has withdrawn every cent in the account regularly for the past five years."

"So the good baron is bleeding his widowed cousin dry." Nick frowned into the gathering darkness. "Bad form. You might have to call the blighter out."

Val nodded agreement. "I might. Ellen would frown on that. It gets worse."

Darius passed the bottle back to Val. "What could be worse than stealing from your cousin's widow, forcing her to grub in the dirt for necessities and live out here like a social leper?"

"The rents should consist of the amounts due from the six tenant farms," Val said. "But for the past five years, there have been seven individual deposits from seven different sources. Freddy has been charging Ellen rent on her own damned land."

"You going to kill him?" Nick asked. "I know all manner of ways to end a life, Valentine."

"Nick..." Darius chided, "don't put ideas in Val's head he'll come to regret."

"I am not going to kill him," Val said, taking another hefty swig. "I might, though, make him wish he were dead."

Nick accepted the bottle from Val. "What do you have in mind?"

"I'm going to invite him here as my very first guest, to show him what a gift he passed to me when he lost that hand of cards. I'm going to keep my friends close and my enemies closer."

"Never should have let you spend that time in Italy." Nick shook his head and passed Darius the whiskey. "Citing Machiavelli, plotting dark deeds when a simple cudgel to the back of the idiot's head would do the job."

Val smiled thinly. "It may come to that. For now, I want to refine my plans, post a note to His Grace, finish my house, and wash the filth of this day from my person."

"We know." Darius waggled the bottle resignedly. "Don't wait up for you."

⁂

"Did you lock the door?" Ellen murmured, cuddling

closer to the man who'd just joined her in her bed. She'd left only the sheet over her body, and in the evening breeze, she'd taken a slight chill. Val gave off heat like a toasted brick, and reassurance and warmth that had nothing to do with the physical.

"I did." He kissed her cheek. "Rest. We'll talk in the morning."

"Val?"

"Beloved?"

Beloved? Oh, ye gods and little fishes, that was more than adored, desired…

"You shouldn't say such things, but I want you to know something," Ellen said, glad for the darkness.

"It can wait until morning."

"I'll lose my nerve." Her voice broke as she wrapped an arm around his lean waist. "And you'll hate me."

"I'll never hate you," Val said, tucking her face to his shoulder. "Talk to me."

"It's Freddy. All the attempts to sabotage your work here. It's him."

"I won't ask how you know, but I agree with you. It's Freddy."

"So what will you do?" Ellen let her grip on him slacken.

"Don't run off." Val gathered her back against him. "For now, I'm going to hold you and rest and consider options. You are not to worry about this, Ellen."

"I do worry. You don't know what he's capable of."

"Arson? Destruction of property, attempted murder?"

"He must have known I was from home," Ellen

said, though Freddy was absolutely capable of taking
a life—of taking three lives or even four. "Freddy is
an opportunist. He probably stopped by to plague you
or see how your progress was coming and realized the
storm had left him a way to further torment me."

"He's been tormenting you for a while now, hasn't
he?"

"Since the accursed day I met him." She couldn't
keep the bitterness from her tone. "You'll be careful?"

"With you?" Val kissed her temple. "Very. With him,
even more so. Now sleep, and let me do the fretting."

As she dropped off, Val lay beside her, staring at the
ceiling and then at Ellen's face in the moonlight pouring through the curtains. She slept, finally, lulled by his
caresses and his warmth. She'd offered him something,
at least, and he was encouraged by that but also wary:
Why would she offer only part of the story, unless she
intended to take the rest of it with her when she left?

Twelve

"WHAT A BLOODY PERISHING MESS," NICK OBSERVED, looking up at the roof of the hay barn. "And the damned thing would be half full."

"We have more hay," Val said. "It's stored elsewhere, under tarpaulins, in sheds, and so forth. The good news is it looks like we're in for a stretch of decent weather, and the supplies are on hand. Tell the men to bring in the rest of the hay now, and we'll shift them to the roof this afternoon. If they work quickly we'll have the hay here and the roof on by week's end."

"That's ambitious," Darius cautioned.

"But not impossible. The first hay crop is off the fields; the foals and calves and lambs are on the ground; the vegetable plots are producing. This is the lull in midsummer, when the rest of the corn is ripening and there's no land to be worked daily. I'll get the word to my tenants. You manage the crews."

"And I?" Nick arched an eyebrow. "I'm to scamper back to Kent and take your dear Ellen with me?"

"Not yet," Val said, not sure why he was hesitating. "You and Dare know more about estate management than I, and if you can spare another few days, I'd appreciate it."

"I can stay." Nick went back to studying the roof. "As you say, the land is quiet this time of year, and it's easy to travel. Besides, I like seeing what you're up to."

Val's smile was sardonic. "So you can report it to my family."

"Speaking of which." Darius pulled an envelope from his pocket. "Devlin gave this to the boys to give to you after he'd left. They were too busy yesterday, and last night…"

"Right. I told you not to wait up for me."

Val took the missive with him back through the trees, reading while he walked. Nick was silent at his side, while Darius departed for the Bragdolls' farmstead to start rounding up the labor needed to move the rest of the hay crop to the barn.

"What does he say?" Nick inquired as they reached the pond.

Val stopped and looked out across the water. "He says it took him two years to sleep through the night after Waterloo, and I've given my hand only a couple months. I am not to…despair."

"Your hand?" Nick peered at Val's right hand, which was holding the letter.

"This one." Val held up his left hand.

"It appears to have all its parts." Nick took Val's hand in his and examined it. "Unfashionably tan, maybe a little callused, but quite functional."

Val looked at his hand in surprise then flexed it. "It was sore. It's been so sore I couldn't play."

Nick dropped his hand. "It doesn't look sore, but not all hurts are visible."

"No." Val stared at his hand. "They aren't. But this one was, quite visible, and now it's...not."

"Does it feel better?" Nick asked, puzzlement in his expression.

"It does," Val said softly. "It finally does. I've still got twinges, and it will hurt worse by day's end, but the mending seems to be progressing."

"Country life agrees with a man." Nick slung an arm around Val's shoulders. "So does a certain aspect of nature best enjoyed on blankets by the side of streams."

"What?" Val stopped and glared at his friend.

"St. Just and Axel both saw you on Saturday, enjoying the shade with your Ellen," Nick said, grinning. "What a lusty little beast you are, Val. I am pleased to think I've set a good example for you."

"Blazing hell." Val dropped his eyes, a reluctant smile blooming. "I suppose I ought to be grateful they didn't come running over the hill, bellowing for the watch."

"Suppose you should, but really, I think there's a lot to be said for the healing power of some friendly, uncomplicated swiving."

"You think there's a lot to be said for any kind of swiving."

"I do." Nick's expression was dead serious. "More to the point, you were overdue, Valentine, and not just for some romping."

"Maybe." Val resumed walking, and Nick dropped his arm. "I was, probably. But one doesn't always find what one needs when one needs it."

"One doesn't, but you're doing a fine job improvising."

Val glanced at him, seeking hidden meaning in Nick's use of a musical term, but Nick's handsome face was schooled to innocence.

By Tuesday afternoon Val had informed all of his tenants of the plans for the week and put both teams to work moving hay. The crews on the barn roof started to replace worn trusses and move material from the manor to the hay barn.

Val found Ellen at midday, arranging a bouquet in what would likely be his bedroom. She'd chosen red roses and bright orange daylilies.

"Interesting combination," Val murmured, coming up behind her and inhaling her floral scent. "I like seeing you in this house, Ellen." She went still, and Val knew a gnawing sense of stealing moments before time ran out.

"Hold me." She leaned back against him. "I shouldn't like being here so much, but I do."

"Here in my arms"—Val tightened his embrace—"or here in my house?"

"Both." She turned and slipped her arms around his waist. "And you shouldn't be sleeping with me, either."

"I'm protecting you." Val dipped his head to kiss the side of her neck.

Ellen angled her chin. "As if locks won't do that job."

"They won't, entirely." He stepped back and took her hand. "Mama Nick has demanded our presence in the springhouse. What Nick demands, Nick gets."

"He's an odd man, but I like him."

"His size sets him apart," Val said as they moved through the house, "and I think he's just used to being his own man as a result. I'm glad you like him—he can be overwhelming."

Ellen shot him another look, and Val stopped and met her gaze. "What?"

"That man…" Ellen waved a hand toward the springhouse. "The one who so blithely hitched a team to the tree on my house, he's an *earl*, Valentine. Your brother is an *earl*, and your friend Dare is an earl's spare. What is the nature of your family that you associate so closely with so many titles, and your brother, of all the men who served long and loyally against the Corsican, was given an earldom for his bravery? Sir Dewey stopped entire wars, and he was only knighted, for pity's sake."

"What are you asking?" Val dodged behind a question, ignoring the insistent voice in the back of his head: Tell her your papa is a duke, tell her your other brother is an earl, as well, tell her, *tell her the truth.*

"I hardly know you," Ellen said in low, miserable tones. "I don't know who your people are, where you've lived, how you come to be a builder of pianos, what you want next in life."

"My name is Valentine Forsythe Windham." He stepped closer, unwilling to hear Ellen talk herself out of him. "My family is large and settled mostly in Kent. You've met my oldest brother, and I will gladly describe each and every sibling and cousin to you. I learned to build pianos while studying in Italy and thought it made business sense to start such an endeavor here. What I want next in life, Ellen Markham, is you." He drew her against him, daring her to argue with that.

"FitzEngle," she whispered against his shoulder. "Ellen FitzEngle."

"Why not Markham?" *Hell, why not Ellen Windham?*

She would run, fast and far, that's why, so he kept his mouth shut and held her on the porch of the carriage house for a brief, stolen moment. "We've been summoned." Val smiled down at her, trying not to let a nameless anxiety show on his face. "But, Ellen, please promise me something?"

"What?"

"If you have questions, you'll ask me, and I'll answer. When we've caught our culprit, I want to talk with you. Really talk."

"If you are honest with me, you will expect me to be honest with you," she said. "I want to be, I wish I could be, but I just…I can't."

"You won't," Val reiterated softly, "but when you're ready to be, I will be too, and I promise to listen and listen well."

She nodded, and just like that, they had a truce of sorts. Val cursed himself for his own hypocrisy but took consolation in the idea Ellen might someday be ready to tell him her secrets. It was a start, and she'd already warned him about Freddy.

That was encouraging, Val told himself—over and over again. And if a truce sometimes preceded a surrender and departure from the field, well, he ignored that over and over again, too.

The next day, Ellen took the boys to market with her,

leaving Val, Darius, and Nick to assist with the roof to the hay barn. At noon, Darius called for the midday break, and the crews moved off toward the pond, there to take their meals.

"Shall we join them?" Darius asked.

"Let's stay here with the horses," Nick suggested. "Doesn't seem fair everybody else gets to take a break and the beasts must stay in the traces."

"Wearing a feed bag," Val said. "It's cooler inside the barn, and I could use some cool."

"I'll second that," Darius said, "and a feed bag for my own face."

They took their picnic into the lower floor of the barn, the space set aside for animals. At Val's direction, it had recently been scrubbed, whitewashed, and the floors recobbled to the point where it was as clean as many a dwelling—for the present.

"I like this barn." Nick looked around approvingly. "The ceiling isn't too low. What's for lunch?"

Darius passed each man a sandwich and watched while Nick took a long pull from the whiskey bottle.

"Save me a taste, if you please." Darius snatched the bottle back, leaving Nick to wipe his mouth and grin.

"Damned good," Nick allowed, leaning back to rest against a stout support beam running from floor to ceiling.

The beam shifted, and that small sound was followed by an instant's silence. Nick's quietly urgent "You two get the hell out" collided with Val's equally insistent "Dare, get the team."

Val darted to Nick's side and added his weight to Nick's, holding the beam in place.

Dare got the team into the barn and wrapped a stout chain around the upper portion of the beam. While the horses held it in place—no mean feat, given the delicate balance required—Val and Nick fetched trusses to provide the needed support.

When they were all outside the barn, the horses once again munching their oats, Val turned to frown at the structure.

"Somebody was very busy with a saw on Sunday," Val murmured. "I thought you were over here much of Sunday, Dare?"

"Sunday morning." Darius scrubbed a hand over his chin while he eyed the barn. "Sunday afternoon I accompanied Bragdoll's sons to help clear some trees off the other tenant farms."

"So the hay barn became an accessible target. Who knew we'd be restoring the roof so soon?"

"Bragdolls for sure," Nick said. "What they didn't know was you'd be stuffing all the rest of the first cutting into the barn this week, as well. Without that added weight, the center beam might have held until some unsuspecting bullock tried to give itself a good scratch."

"More sabotage," Val muttered, grimacing. "I wasn't planning on moving animals in here until fall."

"So perhaps," Darius said slowly, "the idea was to let the thing collapse once the new roof was on, thus imperiling your entire hay crop and the lives of the animals inside the barn."

"Another bad hay year," Nick said, "and you'd lose your tenants."

"If our culprit is Freddy Markham," Val said, and

there was little *if* about it, "then he has no more sense of the hay crop than he does of the roster at Almack's. A collapsed barn is simply trouble, requiring coin to repair, as far as he's concerned. He wouldn't think about the loss of a few peasant lives or driving people off their land."

"A treasure," Nick said. "A real treasure, and you think he's been plaguing you all along?"

"I do, though I want to know why. He was hardly likely to invest anything in this estate, and he walked away with half a sizeable kitty instead."

"All this drama has worked up my appetite." Nick sauntered back into the barn, retrieved the food and the bottle, and passed it to Darius. "Let's take this to some safe, shady tree and finish our meal in peace. But where do you go from here, Val?"

"I've already sent an invitation to Freddy to join me as my first houseguest at my country retreat." They settled in the grass, Val's back resting against the tree. "I've warned Sir Dewey what I'm about, and he doesn't endorse it, but neither can he stop me."

"Did you tell him what happened to Ellen's cottage?" Darius asked.

"Sent the note yesterday, and we should expect Freddy to call next Wednesday."

"When Ellen's at market," Darius said. "You won't tell her he's visiting? Are you going to tell her the bastard almost dropped a barn on the three of us and two splendid horses?"

"Here, here," Nick chimed in around a bite of sandwich.

"I will tell her about the barn, and I think we need

to tell the heathen, as well," Val said, "but she isn't to know Freddy's coming."

"I can take her to Kent," Nick reminded Val, "or to the London town house, or even to Candlewick."

"She'll know something's afoot," Val countered. "And if she bolts, that might tip my hand to Freddy. The gossip mill in Little Weldon turns on a greased wheel, and I'm convinced somebody is feeding Freddy information."

"And they may not even know they're passing along anything of merit," Darius said, taking a bite of his sandwich.

"I'll tell you something of merit." Nick lay back and rested his head on Val's thigh. "A nap is very meritorious right now, but maybe another medicinal tot of that bottle first, Dare." He waggled long fingers, closed his eyes, and took a swig.

"Right." Darius stretched out, using the food sack as his pillow. "A nap is just the thing."

Val sat between them, Nick's head weighting his thigh, an odd warmth blooming in his chest. They'd just risked their *lives* for him, these two. And now, like loyal dogs, they were stretched out around him, dozing lazily until the next threat loomed. It was a peculiar silver lining, when the threat of death brought with it the unequivocal assurance one was well loved.

❧

Hawthorne Bragdoll sat in his favorite thinking tree and considered the scene he'd just witnessed at the hay barn. The damned building had all but collapsed, held up only by the blond giant—a bloody earl, that

one—and Mr. Windham. Windham was big, and
gone all ropey and lean with muscle, but that blond
fellow—he was something out of a traveling circus, a
strong man or a giant, maybe. He put Thorn in mind
of Vikings, for all the man did smile.

Especially at women.

Neal had been in a swivet when that tart of his,
Louise, had smiled back at the giant. Poor Neal didn't
know Louise Hackett's mouth did much worse than
smile at the occasional handsome, well-heeled fellow,
but Thorn didn't begrudge her the extra coin. Times
were hard, and for serving maids and yeomen, they
were always going to be hard. Still, coin for services
was a long way from this bloody-minded mischief.

Intent on avoiding all the clearing work to be
done on Sunday, Thorn had repaired to his second-
favorite thinking tree in the home wood, only to
see a gangling, pot-gutted, nattering dandy strutting
around a half-fallen tree right beside Mrs. FitzEngle's
cottage. While Thorn watched in horrified amaze-
ment, the dandy had ordered Hiram Hackett and his
dim-witted brother Dervid to saw the tree so it fell on
the widow's cottage.

A few weeks earlier, Thorn had seen Hiram and
Dervid making trip after trip into the manor house,
each time carrying a load of lumber scraps and other
tinder. They'd hauled in a couple cans of lamp oil too,
and Thorn had been sure he was about to be treated
to the sight of the biggest bonfire since the burning
of London.

He'd kept his peace, as the house was empty,
and Windham was not his friend or his family. But

purposely crashing a tree into the widow's only home…

That, Thorn concluded, was just rotten, even by his very tolerant standards. Mrs. Fitz was an outcast, like Thorn, and he sensed she was a cut above her neighbors, something that won her Thorn's limited sympathy. Thorn had no sisters, but he had a mother, and someday, given his pa's fondness for the bottle, his mother would likely be widowed.

And if anybody had dropped a damned tree on his mother's house… Thorn clenched his fists in imagined rage and then settled back into his tree to do some more thinking.

❧

"Now this is interesting." Freddy Markham picked up the sole epistle gracing the salver in the breakfast parlor of his London town house. The bills and duns were carefully separated out before he came down each morning, leaving the invitations, or invitation, as the case was, for his perusal over tea, while the less-appetizing correspondence awaited his eventual displeasure in the library.

"My lord?" Stanwick's tone was deferential, though his eyes were full of a long-suffering, probably related to the tardiness of his wages. The man had no grasp of the strictures of a gentlemanly existence.

"I am invited to be the luncheon guest of Lord Valentine Windham that I might see what progress he's made with the old estate out by Little Weldon." Freddy kept the glee from his voice—it didn't do to show emotion before the lower orders.

"And will you be going, my lord?" Stanwick politely inquired as he prepared Freddy's cup of tea.

"Wouldn't miss it. I'll be taking the curricle, weather permitting, because I don't want to malinger there. I'll just tip my hat, wish the man well, and spend a couple nights in Oxford." With the scholars on summer holiday, the usual bevy of willing women would be more than happy for his custom, come to think of it.

"When shall I have you packed, my lord?"

"The invite is for Wednesday next, so I'll depart Monday." Freddy tapped the invitation against his lips. "I say, Stanwick, since when did we stop serving biscuits with our tea? A man could get more than a bit peckish, and me a lord of the realm."

"I'll see what the kitchen has to offer, my lord."

Freddy watched him go, confident some sustenance would be forthcoming despite the deplorable impatience of the trades regarding payment of their bills. Good servants understood that a lord of the realm was above such things, and so food would continue to materialize on his table.

He was almost sure of it.

❧

Given the last weekend's mischief, Val decided he would remain on his estate that weekend. He urged Ellen, Nick, Darius, and the boys to vacate, and offered to hire the Bragdolls to patrol the grounds, but only Darius agreed to go.

And what errands he saw to in London, neither Nick nor Val wanted to ask.

To Val's surprise, Axel and Abby Belmont decided to come for a visit on Saturday, the stated purpose being for Axel to lend his eye and hand to the addition on Ellen's cottage—the unstated purpose no doubt being for the man simply to see his sons.

Val woke Saturday morning as he had every morning for the past five, in Ellen's bed and in her arms. There were other bedrooms ready, enough that Val could offer the Belmonts some genuine hospitality should they be inclined to stay the night, but Val couldn't bring himself to give up his nights with Ellen.

She was going to bolt. Val could feel it. His two oldest brothers had bolted for the cavalry rather than face Moreland's insufferable high-handedness. He himself had bolted for Italy. His brother Gayle had bolted into the commercial complexities of a ducal estate in sore financial disarray. When Dev had come home from war, he'd bolted first into the bottle, then into the wilds of Yorkshire.

Valentine Windham could sniff an impending departure miles off. Ellen was emotionally packing her bags, and there was not one damned thing he could do to change her mind.

But he was a man, so rather than stew endlessly without result, he eased himself out of Ellen's bed as the first gray light filtered through the curtains, kissed her cheek, and retrieved his clothes from where he'd tossed them on a chair. He had a long list of things to do, and if he couldn't resolve his situation with Ellen, he'd at least see about his list.

He was as bad as his father, thinking that passing

bills in Parliament somehow compensated for being an inept, overbearing excuse for a papa.

"Val?"

"Here, love." He returned to the side of the bed and crouched down half-dressed to meet her sleepy gaze. "Back to sleep with you, since I kept you awake for much of last night."

She leaned out over the edge of the mattress and clamped her arms around his neck.

"What's this?" he murmured, settling at her hip and smoothing her hair back.

Ellen leaned up, hugging his shoulders. "When will you tell me about your family? Really tell me, not just toss out a few placatory details?"

He was silent, his conscience trying to shout down his sense the time was not right. How would she react? *My papa is one of the most powerful men in the kingdom, as well as one of the most determined and the most devoted to his lady. He'll want legitimate children of us, so let's make our farewells sooner rather than later.*

"When will you tell me what's really amiss between you and Freddy?" Val said quietly. He took her hand and kissed her knuckles, trying to convey he wanted merely to listen, not to judge, but such desolation came into Ellen's eyes, he regretted his question.

"I'll tell you. Soon, and when I do, you will wish I hadn't."

"Did you betray Francis, then?" Val asked softly, bringing her hand to his cheek.

"Yes," Ellen said on an unsteady breath, "but not... not the way you mean. I wasn't unfaithful, though that hardly matters."

The room was gradually, inexorably growing lighter, but Ellen remained silent.

"We'll talk when you're ready," he promised, pressing another kiss to her neck.

"And you'll tell me about your family?"

Val smiled sadly. "When I do, I will wish I hadn't—and you might too."

❦

"All is in readiness," Darius confirmed as they watched the farm wagon jingle down the lane toward the village early the next Wednesday morning. "Though I can't like this idea of yours, Val, simply confronting the man, no magistrate about, no one but Wee Nick on hand to enforce the king's peace."

"Wee Nick," said the man himself, "outranks the pusillanimous buffoon, has double his weight, double his reach, and at least five times his brain power. And should my charming presence fail to inspire him to good conduct, you will be waiting in the wings, ready to rescue us."

"Rescue Val. What will you tell Freddy about Ellen?"

"As little as possible," Val said. "She should be none of his concern, nor he any of hers. The entire purpose of this meeting is to see that's the case."

"At least you're doing something about him," Nick pointed out charitably, "though as to that, you've gotten a great deal done here in a short time."

"Good crews," Val said, glancing around. "Though I have to confess, it makes me nervous, the quiet. I can hear them banging away over at Ellen's, but not to see scaffolding all over my north wing, not to hear the constant ring of curses and shouts and hammers, it's unnerving."

"You never heard much of anything before," Nick said, "except all the notes in your head. You hear things now."

"Possibly." Val considered the notion. It was one thing not to listen, but Nick was accusing him of not *hearing*. His Grace was the one who never even heard others.

"You don't get that gone-away look in your eyes as often as you did a couple months ago," Darius added, "and you don't make a fat, unhappy fist of your left hand a hundred times an hour."

"I fisted my hand?" Val asked, staring at the hand in question as he spoke.

"I noticed it, because at first I thought it meant you were angry and ready to plant somebody a facer, perhaps even my charming self. Then I realized you didn't even know you were doing it."

Val's gaze moved from one friend to the other. "It has begun to amaze me that I managed to walk upright and speak English on occasion, such a stranger have I apparently been to myself."

"Not a stranger to yourself," Nick corrected him, frowning down the drive, "more a visiting dignitary to those who care about you."

Val fell silent, wondering what else his friends might have wanted to tell him, but for this tendency he'd displayed to become absorbed in his own artistic world, even while in the company of others. He realized abruptly he was doing it, again, while his friends exchanged a rueful smile.

"Bugger the both of you." Val shoved them each
on the arm. "I'm going to go through the house one
more time. If you'd take the outbuildings, Dare, and
you the stables, Nick, I'll feel better."

"Of course." Nick strode off, leaving Darius to eye
his friend.

"You've put the house in order this week," Darius
said. "The place looks good, and I assume you'll be
moving into it when Ellen's cottage is done."

"That would make sense," Val replied, unwilling to
voice his reluctance to do just that. Ellen back at her
cottage seemed another step closer to him out of her
life. If she ended their association, he could not bear
to take up residence in the house alone, not with her
toiling away in her gardens, one home wood and three
universes of stubbornness away.

"So when," Darius asked gently, "will you set up
the piano?"

Val slewed around to stare at his friend. "*What
piano?*"

"The one your papa sent along with the team,"
Darius said. "The one that's been sitting in its crate in
the carriage bays for the past week and more."

Val cringed. "We left a piano *in the carriage house?*"

"Freddy will expect you to have a piano," Darius
said, his tone merely bored. "And we've half the
morning to kill before he gets here."

"And Nick's considerable brawn to assist us." He
should *not* even set the damned thing up. What was
His Grace thinking, now of all times, to send Val a
piano? It was so typical of their dealings, that his father
would finally mean well and get the timing so exactly,

ironically *wrong*. Val stared down at his left hand, which looked no different from the right of late. He could always crate up this gift later and send it back from whence it came.

"Let's get this over with," he muttered, telling himself no piano should be housed in a damned carriage house, and certainly not in *his* carriage house.

"If you insist."

"You going to tune the thing?" Nick asked, draping an arm over Val's shoulder when they'd gotten the instrument set up in a first-floor parlor. "I know you have your kit with you."

Val's lips compressed into a thin line, but Nick was right. He did have his tools with him—he always did.

"Ellen might enjoy playing it," Darius suggested with devilish innocence.

"Bugger you both," Val said on a sigh. Except a piano should be kept in tune.

His craftsmen had packed the instrument very carefully—for it was one of his, damned if it wasn't—and the piano was in fine shape, not even needing much tuning. Val closed the lid and looked around the room for the bench that had been delivered with the piano. He positioned it before the piano and noticed a corner of white paper sticking out from under the seat.

A note in his father's slashing, confident hand.

> *Valentine,*
>
> *You play these things better than I have ever done anything, save perhaps love Her Grace. She picked this one out after trying all that were ready for sale*

*at both of your shops. She said it was particularly
lovely in the middle and lower registers, whatever
that means. Her Grace will be sending along some
of your music, though I told her it would be better
for you to come choose what you wanted from
Morelands, as an old fellow might get to see his
youngest (and only bachelor) son that way, but there
is no reasoning with Her Grace on certain points.*

*You are to keep Sean, if you please. Morelands's
stables are too large and busy for one of his years,
but he would not ask for lighter duties. This was
Her Grace's idea; the piano was mine.*

*I hope you are keeping well, as am I—which
you would know had you had the courtesy to correspond with your own papa from time to time. And
polite, chipper little thank you notes to placate your
mother do not count.*

                                        Moreland

Val had to chuckle at the aggravating blend of
what? Officiousness, bashful innuendo, and simple
familiarity in the short note. His Grace was never,
not in a millennium of trying, going to be a subtle or
calming sort of person. He was direct, ruthless, and
devoted to his duchess. Since a heart seizure a year
ago, there had been some softening, but Val still felt
the blatant attempts to manipulate, even in the terse
little epistle.

He was to visit his father.

He was to write to his father.

He was to play the piano, though his father had

railed at him for years that music was a nancy-pants way for a man to go through life when it went beyond drawing-room competence. Never mind the gift of a piano was at complete odds with all those lectures! If His Grace wanted to change *his* tune, then all other tunes simply ceased to exist—past, present, or future. It was an amazing quality, to alter reality at will. The trick of it was probably the first secret passed along from one duke to the next. He'd have to ask Gayle about it when next he saw his brother-the-heir.

He closed the lid of the piano bench, but not before he noticed one other document—a bill of lading marked "paid."

It was a beautiful instrument. Val sighed as he regarded the gleaming finish. A grand, of course. His mother would not content herself with less for him. He lifted the lid and sat, vowing to himself he was just testing the tuning.

To keep his vow, he limited his test to the little lullaby he'd composed for Winnie and sent north with St. Just. Winnie was a busy child. She darted around the estate like a small tornado, poking her nose into adult business at will with the canine mastodon, Scout, panting at her heels.

So he'd written Winnie a cradle song to play when Scout was having trouble settling his doggy nerves or when Winnie wanted something quiet and pretty to end her busy days with. It wasn't the first piece he'd written for her, though it might be the last.

Gently, he laid his hands on the keys, the familiar cool feel of them sending a wave of awareness up his arms and into his body.

"I've missed you, my friend," he told the piano quietly, "but this is just a visit."

The notes came so easily, drifting up into the soft morning air and out across the yard. Simple, tender, lyrical, and sweet, the piece wafted through the trees and flower baskets, through the beams of sunshine, and out over the pond. On the balcony of the carriage house, Nick and Darius exchanged a smile as the final notes died away.

"It's a start," Nick said quietly. "A modest start, but a good one."

Thirteen

WHEN HE FINISHED DRESSING FOR HIS CALLER, VAL had an hour left of his morning, so he crossed to the house and made his way to his library. He sat for long minutes at his desk, wondering what he could write to his father that wouldn't be considered a placatory thank you note—the challenge had been tossed down, and Val wasn't inclined to ignore a challenge. Not from Moreland, and not given the state of Val's life.

To His Grace, Percival, the Duke of Moreland, etc,

It crossed my mind if a short, placatory thank you would not count, perhaps a long, effusive, entirely sincere thank you might. At the risk of self-aggrandizement, the instrument chosen for me is truly lovely, and I do appreciate it.

I am pleased to report I even have a music room for your generous gift, though the estate I found here at the beginning of the summer was in sad disrepair and not habitable by other than rodents, vagrants, and bats. All three have been evicted, and

*the next few weeks will see the manor finished in
all its details. Darius Lindsey, Axel Belmont, and
Axel's sons have been particularly helpful in this
regard, and now no less than Nicholas, the Earl of
Bellefonte, has put his hand to the effort, as well.
This has been an enjoyable project, but daunting,
for the neglect of the house is only one aspect of the
estate's troubles.*

*I believe one Frederick, Baron Roxbury, has
made a great deal of other difficulty for me here,
and I have yet to uncover his motives. As the former
owner of the property, he can have no legal interest
in the place, and yet he seems to bear ill will toward
both me and the late baron's widow. Any insights
Your Grace can offer regarding Roxbury's situation
would be appreciated.*

*My regards to my sisters and Westhaven, should
you see him before I do. We sent St. Just on his way
north roughly ten days ago and hope to hear good
news from him and Emmie in the very near future.*

*You remain in my
thoughts and prayers,
Valentine*

"Beg pardon, Mr. Windham, but your guest is
here."

Val's only officially hired servant, a footman named
Davies, appeared in the doorway. There were women
in the kitchen today, because Val had known he'd
have company coming, but as for the rest…

"Thank you, Davies." Val rose, tugged down his

waistcoat, and shrugged into his morning coat. "Please show my guest into the formal parlor and have the kitchen send up the tea tray. Does Lord Bellefonte know our guest has arrived?"

"He does, my lord, and is arriving from the carriage house as we speak, by way of the kitchen."

Val let his features settle into the expression worn by a duke's youngest son—polite, faintly bored, but benevolently tolerant of his many, many inferiors. When he joined Freddy Markham, Freddy was standing by a window with an upside-down Waterford vase in his lily-white hands.

"Good day, my lord." Val smiled just a little. "Do I take it your journey from Town was pleasant?"

"Windham." Freddy grinned and set the vase down. "Spent last night in Oxford seeing the attractions and appreciating the summer ale. Put me in quite good spirits."

By the slight cooling of his smile, Val let it be known Freddy's failure to use his host's courtesy title was not appreciated.

"How pleasant for you," Val remarked, his tone implying something else entirely. "Shall we be seated?"

"Oh, so we're to do tea and crumpets. Lovely, but I have to say, you've certainly gone to a lot of trouble over the old place."

Val shrugged. "It has good bones. One hates to see something of value allowed to go to waste for simple lack of attention." Freddy's brows rose, but his expression suggested he couldn't quite put his finger on where in that remark the insult to him lay.

"One does," he replied, a little less exuberantly.

"Shall we have a tour? I haven't seen the interior for years and years."

Val lifted one eyebrow. "You've seen the exterior, then?"

"Oh, well…" Freddy shot his cuffs and ran a finger around the inside of his collar. "If I'm in the neighborhood, I occasionally take a spin out this way just to have a look."

"And what would there be to look at? I understand from my tenants their farms were of no interest to you."

"No interest?" Freddy frowned. "What have I got to do with their farms? They're the farmers, right? And here's our tea!"

"Allow me to pour." Val did a creditable job with a teapot. He'd attended any number of his sisters' tea parties as a child, and it was a skill any mincing dandy—real or impersonated—had to perfect. When he passed Freddy his tea, Val had the satisfaction of seeing Freddy's hand trembled slightly.

"I say." Freddy smiled brightly at Val. "Since it's just we fellows, would there be something we might doctor this with to set the day to rights?"

Val silently passed along to Freddy the decanter of very good brandy Freddy had no doubt spied on the sideboard.

"Am I late?" Nick sauntered in without knocking. "I am, and I beg the pardon of the assemblage. Roxbury." Nick met the man's eyes but did not bow, because Nick did, clearly, outrank Freddy.

"You're Reston." Freddy rose, all smiles again, and stuck out a hand.

"Owing to a recent bereavement," Val interjected, "he's Bellefonte now."

Nick inclined his head and pointedly ignored Freddy's hand. From his great height, Nick stared down his nose, blue eyes glacially cool, until Freddy bowed in response.

"Tea, Bellefonte?" Val gestured toward the tray.

"Of course." When Nick spied the brandy, he arched a disbelieving eye. "Lord Valentine, you are not ruining a perfectly good pot of libation with that profane practice of brandying the tea, are you?"

"Of course not," Val replied pleasantly as he poured Nick a cup.

"Bellefonte was visiting friends at Candlewick," Val explained to Freddy, "and deigned to grace us with his presence today. We are acquainted through family."

Val and Nick deftly dropped one titled name after another, until Freddy was all but trying to disappear into his teacup between longing glances at the brandy decanter.

Val rose when the teacups were empty. "We've had our tea, and Lord Roxbury did not come all this way to listen to us reminisce. The point of his sortie was to see the progress made with the property, so let's give him a tour of the house, shall we?"

Val started in the kitchens, and room by room, rattled off the repairs, renovations, and restorations required. He tossed in the work needed on the roof, in the yard, in the outbuildings, and on the grounds. The list was endless, and while it should have made Freddy ashamed, the only visible result was to light a sullen spark of anger in his eyes.

They'd toured all four floors when Lord Roxbury asked for the use of a water closet and was shown to a guest room.

"I'll be happy to meet you gentleman out front, if you'd like to stroll the grounds now we've seen the house?" Lord Freddy offered.

"We'll await you on the front terrace," Val replied, not meeting Nick's eye for even an instant. They walked off, leaving Freddy to ostensibly use the water closet.

"Don't give him too long," Nick murmured as they walked, "it's the work of a moment to nip up the attic stairs and strike a spark on that pile of kindling." Val nodded as they turned the corner of the corridor and found Darius waiting for them.

"What an insufferable little ass," Darius whispered, rolling his eyes. A door opened and closed down the hall, then footsteps sounded on the narrow stairs leading into the attics.

"Let's go." Nick tugged on Val's arm, but Val held still, listening to the pattern of the footfalls.

"Now. We'll leave the door open, Dare."

They climbed the attic steps silently, pausing at the top to listen. Freddy was jiggling a can half full of liquid, swishing it around, presumably to let some slosh over the lip, then swishing it again. The can was set down, and another silence ensued, during which the distinctive scratch of flint on steel came clearly through the stillness of the attics. Val moved; Nick silently followed.

"Why the hell won't you light, damn you?" Freddy was muttering at the pile of tinder.

"Because," Val said, "the wood has been kept quite damp, and you really do not want to swing for arson, Roxbury."

"Windham!" Freddy rose to his feet, his face turning an interesting shade of red. He slipped the flint back into his pocket and glanced around, as if an excuse would come winging to him from the rafters.

"Downstairs." Val gestured through the attic doorway. "Now."

"You can't prove anything," Freddy hissed in a low, mean voice. "It will be your word against mine."

"And mine," Nick added pleasantly from Val's elbow.

"And mine," Darius chirped from Val's shoulder. "I believe you've been invited downstairs, Roxbury?"

Val let Nick and Darius escort an abruptly quiet Freddy back down to the formal parlor. It was a bit of a progress, since they had to cross the house and descend three floors, and in that time, Val wondered why he didn't feel a greater sense of triumph. His instincts had been right. Ellen's warning had been accurate—Freddy had been out to destroy the house, but Val still had to wonder why.

And in the next fifteen minutes, he wanted to find out.

Needed to.

"You have one chance," Nick said when they'd reached the formal parlor, "and one chance only to explain why you just tried to burn Lord Valentine's property to a cinder." He pushed Freddy once on the chest, dropping him into a chair. Freddy looked from Nick to Val and back to Nick again.

"I'd spill," Darius said with a sympathetic shrug. "The man wants the truth, and after all, there was no harm done."

Freddy huffed out a semblance of an indignant sigh. "There is no need for all this drama. You caught me fair and square, and I'll take my lumps and go home."

"Fair and square?" Nick's tone was laden with menace. "You're fool enough to lose an estate on a wager, and you think fair and square served when you're caught trying to torch that same estate, Roxbury? There are servants here, *women and girls*, who wouldn't know the attics were in flames until it was too late. And in a house this age, fire would spread even without the lamp oil you so obligingly provided."

"How did you know it was lamp oil?"

Nick rolled his eyes at Darius, leaving Val to stifle a derisive snort. *How could a man this stupid have come so close to achieving his ends?*

Nick leaned in, letting his size silently speak volumes. "Talk, Roxbury. Now."

"Best heed the man," Darius offered. "He has a devil of a temper, and you've threatened his friend. Then too, if you're thinking of taking your chances in the Lords"—Darius paused and shook his head—"consider that one." He nodded at Val. "Moreland will take it amiss you disrespected his son, and Moreland has the Lords in his ducal pocket." Darius offered Nick a small smile. "Not to denigrate your influence, my lord."

"Of course." Nick returned the smile but let it die when he turned to Val. "We're wasting time, my lord.

Let me have five minutes with this miserable excuse for dog shite, and you'll have your answer."

"Please!" Freddy shot out of his chair as if cued for it in a stage play, only to have Nick's single, meaty hand shove him right back onto his seat. "I can explain, and it isn't complicated. I was simply, well, going to encourage you to sell the place back to me."

"By creating a series of accidents?" Val posited, settling into a comfortable wing chair. "Starting with loose slates on my roof? Including a couple of bonfires in my residence? Continuing on to an attempt to collapse my hay barn while the roof was being restored?"

Freddy's complexion went from ruddy to sheet white in a moment. "How do you know?"

Val snapped his fingers and rose. "And I forgot! You tried to destroy Ellen Markham's cottage by dropping a damned tree on it. Fortunately, the lady wasn't inside, and only her peace of mind, sense of safety, and pitiful savings were obliterated along with her residence."

"How do you know?" Freddy cried again. "I wasn't trying to kill anyone; I merely wanted you gone and happy to sell the property back to me for a pittance."

"Freddy…" Darius shook his head slowly. "If they didn't know before, they certainly do now."

"Leave us." Val spoke to his two friends through clenched teeth.

"Val," Nick muttered, "I don't think that's a good idea."

"Neither do I," Freddy added, glancing nervously all around the room.

"The windows are locked," Val informed him,

"and my friends will be right outside the door. They will not interfere, however, unless I ask them to."

"Val." Darius met his friend's eye, raised his left hand to his waist, and made a tight fist. "Be careful."

Val nodded and let the silence build. Nick merely rolled his eyes and followed Darius from the room.

"So what are we about?" Freddy asked, swallowing audibly when the lock clicked shut on the only door.

"We'll settle this like gentlemen." Val shrugged out of his coat. "And I promise not to kill you, because I understand you've only the one heir, and his claim to Markham blood is quite attenuated. Surprises me I'd care about your miserable succession, but I think it would mean something to Ellen."

"Ellen?" Freddy ran his finger around his neckcloth again. "Is this about her?"

"Coat off, Markham." Val started rolling back his cuffs. "I'll even let you take the first swing, and yes, part of this is about Ellen. You are no kind of man if you think preying on your cousin's widow is acceptable."

"She's managing," Freddy muttered as he struggled to get out of his coat. "She's the kind of female who will always manage, and how was I supposed to squeak by on a bloody damned allowance like some schoolboy!"

"She manages." Val removed the signet ring from his smallest finger. "Why couldn't you?"

"Because a gentleman has needs," Freddy nearly shrieked. "You should know that." He extricated himself from his coat and put his fists up.

"It isn't considered sporting to keep the rings on, old man," Val said, limbering up his fists.

"It wasn't stealing," Freddy retorted, an odd note of genuine relish in his voice. "She owed me, Windham. She will always owe me." With that, Freddy put up his fives and took up a stance reflective of the scientific approach favored by the bloods who frequented Gentleman Jackson's salon.

Val, youngest of five brothers, took one look at his opponent, resisted the urge to thank God for small favors, and laid Lord Roxbury out flat with one right-handed punch.

And as disappointing as it was, Val limited his retribution to that one very effective blow.

❦

Darius resumed his assigned role as the more sympathetic bystander and assisted Freddy to his feet.

"He drew blood!" Freddy stared at his fingers, touched them to his lips, and found more blood.

"You essentially bit yourself," Darius said, handing Freddy a glass of water while Nick and Val looked on dispassionately. "I'd offer you some ice, but that amenity is yet in short supply in these rustic surrounds. You might want to use your handkerchief or cravat on that lip, though."

"But blood leaves an awful stain," Freddy said, his words slightly slurred. "Stanwick would leave, and then where would I be?"

"Can't have that." Darius shook his head. "Have we sent for Lord Roxbury's equipage?"

"His curricle is in the drive," Val said. "Sean is walking his team."

"So that's it, then?" Freddy rose unsteadily, but

Darius did not offer any more support. "You plant me
a facer and we call it even?"

"No." Val let Nick assist him back into his morning
coat. "That was simply to address the requirements of
honor, and damned unsatisfying it was, Roxbury. I'll
be calling on the local magistrate, and you'll be hearing
from me."

Freddy's split lip began to bleed down his chin, but
nobody offered him a handkerchief, so he was compelled to use his own. He blotted the blood daintily,
eyeing Val all the while.

"The Lords won't convict me, and I can have you
charged with assault. Duke's son or not, you're just a
commoner, and I hold one of the oldest titles in the
land."

"I didn't say you'd be charged," Val replied mildly,
"but I will say, before witnesses and men of honor, as
well, if you ever try to extort another farthing from
Ellen Markham, I will hunt you down and wrap your
balls around your scrawny neck until you expire, and
then I will feed your carcass to the pigs."

Freddy's bloody lips compressed, but then a short,
ugly laugh burst from him.

"You won't have me charged." He patted the
handkerchief against his lip. "You know you're holding the low cards now, Windham, so I'll take my leave
of you with a little kindly advice: Ellen Markham is
capable of murder. Family loyalty prevents me from
seeing her tried for the crimes she's committed, but
let me suggest that even if you're besotted with her,
you'd be a fool to trust that woman farther than
you can pitch her, much less with the lives of your

children. She's dangerous, and make no mistake. I keep my distance from her for reasons my late cousin would understand only too well."

He left them on that, and Val went to the window, watching in silence as Sean stepped back from the horses' heads. When Freddy had tooled off down the lane, Val remained at the window.

"Did he tell you anything during your bout of fisticuffs?" Nick asked.

Val smiled slightly. "He told me he can't fight worth a bloody farthing. Jackson has been taking his money for nothing."

"A man must deal as best he sees fit." Darius took a sip from a glass of whiskey, passed a tumbler to Nick and the third one to Val. "You're not satisfied with this outcome?"

"I am not. Still, let's put our statements down for Sir Dewey and see what he makes of it."

"You are glued to that window, Val." Nick came to stand at his shoulder. "Whatever for?"

"I don't want Freddy running into Ellen," Val said. "I told the boys to keep her in town until at least four this afternoon, but she's like my father. When she takes a notion, there's no arguing with her."

"Rather like you," Darius murmured, joining them at the window. "And there is Sean with Ezekiel."

"Gentlemen." Val passed his glass to Nick. "It has been a pleasure, of a sort. You have my eternal gratitude. I'm off to town."

"Of course you are," Darius said. "At a hand gallop, at least."

"Canter," Nick decided, "owing to the heat."

Val left with Darius's final shot ringing in his ears. "Dead gallop," Darius bet Nick. "Owing to the *heat*."

∽

To Val's relief, Ellen was enjoying a lady's pint outside the Rooster when a quick cross-country gallop got him to town. Her wagon had sold out again, but Phil and Day—clever, clever lads—told her they wanted to shop at some of the other vendors' booths and stop in at the lending library.

"Sir Dewey." Val nodded at Ellen's companion. "A pleasure. Ellen, your day has gone well?"

"It has." She smiled at him, and Val felt his heart trip on the next few beats. Good God, she was lovely. Just sitting here outside the Rooster, cradling her mug in her hands. A little dusty, a little tired, but in her warm, earthy dark-eyed way, she was beautiful. "I think Mr. Belmont should be warned his sons are turning into regular charmers," Ellen went on. "The ladies adore buying their posies and sachets from those two."

"Belmont also has a certain charm with the ladies," Sir Dewey said, "but if you will excuse me, Mrs. Fitz, I see the boys approaching and will ask Mr. Windham to accompany me to the livery."

"Oh?" Ellen frowned slightly. "Are you to discuss the situation at the estate?"

"No." Sir Dewey added just the smallest smile to support what Val took for a lie. "I am going to importune him, again, to tune the piano in the assembly rooms before we gather for our summer revelry."

"You can tune pianos?" Ellen asked, cocking her head at Val.

"I can," he admitted, wanting to skewer Sir Dewey. "It isn't that difficult once you have the tools and know what to listen for."

"You really must pitch in, then," Ellen told him. "Even at the end of the evening, when all have appreciated Rafe's special ales at some length, that poor piano is not a welcome addition to the orchestra."

"Two fiddles and a tambourine." Sir Dewey rolled his eyes. "Maybe a guitar, possibly a flute, until Thorn Bragdoll gets bored watching his brothers tromp on women's toes."

"Which one is Thorn?"

"The one who is too smart to get caught where there's hard work to be done," Sir Dewey replied. "The runt, for now, though if he grows into his feet, he'll be the pick of the litter. Mrs. FitzEngle, it has been a true pleasure."

The gentlemen took their leave of Ellen as the Belmonts came bounding up with a few purchases.

"Well, now you've done it," Val groused as they ambled toward the livery.

"Put you into a neat corner," Sir Dewey said, congratulating himself. "You don't really mind?"

"That I have to tune a piano? I guess not. I tuned one earlier today and survived more easily than I'd thought I would."

"And is that all you accomplished?" Sir Dewey asked, stopping in the shade of a venerable oak where they would not be overheard. Val filled him in as succinctly as he could, ending with Freddy's admonition regarding Ellen.

"That is disturbing," Sir Dewey said. "I've already

sent for the reports regarding Francis Markham's death—Belmont suggested I might have need of them—and there is nothing to indicate Ellen was responsible. Her husband was on the mend, and she was observed by all to be devoted to his care and very properly so. Do you know you use her first name in company, by the way?"

"I had not realized."

"She did not seem offended. Perhaps you should be encouraged."

"Not likely. I'll bring over the statements regarding today's doings, and you can let us know if they need revision."

"That will serve." Sir Dewey fished in his pocket. "If you're going to tune that piano, you'll need this key. The assembly rooms are above the shops on that side of the green." He pointed over Val's shoulder. "The door is between the bakery and the apothecary."

"Suppose I have no choice now." Val stuck the key in his pocket without looking at it.

"None at all." Sir Dewey grinned as he spoke. "I'll be waiting for those statements, and when you drop them off, perhaps you might be willing to take a certain juvenile canine back with you?"

Val blinked in confusion.

"A puppy? Mr. Lindsey suggested you might take a puppy off my hands at some point. Favor for favor, don't you think?"

"What favor?"

"I spent the entire day watching every handsome swain in the shire tease and flirt with your lady, and that I consider a substantial favor."

"She doesn't see it." Val watched as Neal Bragdoll paused to pass the time of day with Ellen. He was a handsome man, big, strong, and capable in matters of the land...and still single.

Sir Dewey shifted to watch Ellen as Val did. "What doesn't she see?"

"She doesn't see that she matters here. She thinks she's invisible."

"Or maybe," Sir Dewey suggested, "she wants to believe she is. Talk to her, and come get your puppy. Fair is fair." Sir Dewey left to fetch his horse, and Val started across the green, only to have his blood run cold.

Freddy Markham was steering his curricle around the square, scanning the market-day crowds as his horses walked along. He stopped just outside the Rooster, bringing his vehicle near the outside table where Ellen sat with the Belmont brothers.

"Why if it isn't my dearest cousin-in-law," Freddy declaimed, his attempt at a sneer distorted by his split lip.

"Leave her alone." Val's voice rang out decisively, silencing the crowd gathering at the sight of such a conveyance. "Put your whip to that team, Roxbury, and don't ever show your face here again."

Ellen's head slewed around at his tone and his words. "Valentine?"

"Lord Valentine," Freddy corrected her, "but don't get any ideas, *Lady Roxbury*, he's far above your touch, just as my cousin was. Still, your secrets are safe with me, as I account myself a gentleman, unlike some."

He had the sense to depart on that note, leaving

the crowd to buzz and murmur until Rafe came out, barking they'd best be coming inside to eat or clearing the street so his customers could see his front door. As the onlookers began to disperse, Rafe speared Val with a look.

"I knew it," Rafe muttered. "I told Tilden, I did. Said you was a lord. Always figured Mrs. Fitz for a lady."

As people began to eddy and swirl around them again, Val turned to the boys. "Fetch the team and my horse, if you please." They scampered off, leaving Val seething with a need to do violence—further violence—to Freddy Markham.

"*Lord Valentine?*" Ellen's voice was low, insistent, and unhappy.

"Not here, though we need to talk."

"Yes, I suppose we do."

The trip home passed in silence, with Val on Ezekiel and the boys dozing in the back of the wagon. They took both Zeke and the wagon when Val helped Ellen down, leaving Val and Ellen regarding each other in wary solitude on the front steps.

"I don't want to have this discussion where we can be overheard," Val said, taking Ellen by the wrist. She'd been so silent, and without a word, Val felt her withdrawing, curling into herself, seeking the only safe place she'd found.

"Where, then?"

"Your cottage."

"It will be private," Ellen allowed, but she didn't seem pleased.

Val chose to walk her home through the wood,

which had been gradually cleaned up as time from other tasks allowed. As it had the afternoon he'd met her, sunlight slanted enchantingly through the trees, birds sang, and a breeze sent the sturdy, spicy fragrance of the woods into the nose and the imagination.

"I want to kiss you," Val said, tugging Ellen to a sudden stop. They'd reached the place where he'd kissed her more than a year ago. He wanted to trap her in their woods, shut out the world, shut out the march of time, shut out the impact of the truths bearing down on their future.

To his great relief, Ellen stepped into his arms when he turned to face her.

"You will listen?" Val asked, breathing in the scent of her.

Ellen nodded against his neck. "I promise I will listen."

They completed their journey with their arms around each other's waists, and Val had the impression Ellen didn't relish this truth-telling any more than he did. When they reached her cottage, she sat him on the swing and brought them each a mug of cider.

"I love you," Val began, wondering where in the nine circles of hell that had come from. He sat forward, elbows on his knees, and scrubbed a hand over his face. "I'm sorry; that came out...wrong. Still..." He glanced at her over his shoulder. "It's the truth."

Ellen's fingers settled on his nape, massaging in the small, soothing circles Val had come to expect when her hands were on him.

"If you love me," she said after a long, fraught silence, "you'll tell me the truth."

Val tried to see that response as positive—she hadn't stomped off, railed at him, or tossed his words back in his face. Yet. But neither had she reciprocated.

"My name is Valentine Windham," he said slowly, "but you've asked about my family, and in that regard—and that regard only—I have not been entirely forthcoming."

"Come forth now," she commanded softly, her hand going still.

"My father is the Duke of Moreland. That's all. I'm a commoner, my title only a courtesy, and I'm not even technically the spare anymore, a situation that should improve further, because my brother Gayle is deeply enamored of his wife."

"Improve?" Ellen's voice was soft, preoccupied.

"I don't want the title, Ellen." Val sat up, needing to see her eyes. "I don't ever want it, not for me, not for my son or grandson. I make pianos, and it's a good income. I can provide well for you, if you'll let me."

"As your mistress?"

"Bloody, blazing…no!" Val rose and paced across the porch, turning to face her when he could go no farther. "As my wife, as my beloved, dearest wife."

A few heartbeats of silence went by, and with each one, Val felt the ringing of a death knell over his hopes.

"I would be your mistress. I care for you, too, but I cannot be your wife."

Val frowned at that. It wasn't what he'd been expecting. A conditional rejection, that's what it was. She'd give him time, he supposed, to get over his feelings and move along with his life.

"Why not marry me?" he asked, crossing his arms over his chest.

She crossed her arms too. "What else haven't you told me?"

"Fair enough." Val came back to sit beside her and searched his mind. "I play the piano. I don't just mess about with it for polite entertainment. Playing the piano used to be who I was."

"You were a musician?"

Val snorted. "I was a coward, but yes, I was a musician, a *virtuoso* of the keyboard. Then my hand"—he held up his perfectly unremarkable left hand—"rebelled against all the wear and tear, or came a cropper somehow. I could not play anymore, not without either damaging it beyond all repair or risking a laudanum addiction, maybe both."

"So you came out here?" Ellen guessed. "You took on the monumental task of setting to rights what I had put wrong on this estate and thought that would be…what?"

"A way to feel useful or maybe just a way to get tired enough each day that I didn't miss the music so much, and then…"

"Then?" She took his hand in hers, but Val wasn't reassured. *His mistress, indeed.*

"Then I became enamored of my neighbor. She beguiled me—she's lovely and dear and patient. She's a virtuoso of the flower garden. She cared about my hand and about me without once hearing me play the piano, and this intrigued me."

"You intrigued me," Ellen admitted, pressing the back of his hand to her cheek. "You still do."

"My Ellen loves to make beauty, as do I." Val turned and used his free hand to trace the line of Ellen's jaw. "She is as independent as I am and values her privacy, as I do."

"You are merely lonely, Val." Ellen bent a little over their joined hands but then looked up and frowned slightly. "Lord Valentine."

"Not to you, *Lady Roxbury*."

Her frown became considerably more fierce. "What was Freddy doing in Little Weldon?" she asked, straightening.

"I invited him, ostensibly to see the progress on the estate," Val said, watching a battle light come into Ellen's eye. "He confessed to setting the various traps on the property and did so before witnesses. I also treated myself to landing a single blow on his ugly face and made sure he knew I did so in your name."

"*You did what?*" Ellen shot to her feet, dropping Val's hand as if it were diseased. "You struck Freddy? You confronted him?"

"I did. His mischief was deadly, Ellen. And his only motivation was to regain possession of the estate. He thought he could scare me off by creating accidents and setbacks, then buy the place back for a pittance, probably to sell for considerably more."

Ellen shook her head. "He wants the rents. It's about the money, and with him it will always be about the money."

"What aren't you telling me?" Val rose to stand behind her where she stood looking out over her gardens. "Ellen?" But she shook her head and remained unyielding when Val slipped his arms around her waist. That, more than any words, alarmed him.

"Ellen," Val spoke quietly, "Freddy won't be bothering you anymore. I've seen to it."

"No." She huffed out a breath. "No, you have not, Valentine. You have merely waved a red flag before a very angry and powerful little bull. Freddy will go off, tend his wounds, and plot his moves. He sulks and fumes and skulks about, but he does not learn his lesson."

"You're keeping secrets." Val rested his forehead against her nape. "Why in God's name won't you trust me, Ellen?"

"If I tell you, will you leave?"

It was Val's turn to be silent, to consider, to weigh what was in the balance, and where, if anywhere, lay the path of hope.

"I'm not going anywhere until the house and farms are completely functional," he said. "That will take a few more weeks."

"Weeks." Ellen stood very straight in his arms. "And then you'll go?"

"If that's still what you want and you've told me the reasons why by then," Val said, tossing his entire future into the hands of a fate that hadn't dealt with him very kindly of late. "And until I go?"

"I will be your mistress," Ellen said, her posturing relaxing.

"No." Val turned her in his arms and tucked his chin against her temple. "You will be my love."

❧

What followed for Val was a period of peculiar joy, mixed with acute sorrow. He respected Ellen's choice as one she felt compelled to make, not easy for her, but necessary.

He also hoped when he heard her reasons, he could argue her past them, and the hoping was…awful. Hope and Val Windham were old enemies.

Best enemies.

He'd hoped his brother Victor would recover, but consumption seldom eased its grip once its victims had been chosen.

He'd hoped his hand wasn't truly getting worse, until he couldn't deny that reality without losing use of the hand entirely.

He'd hoped his brother Bart would come home from war safe and sound, not in a damned coffin.

He'd hoped St. Just might escape military service without substantial wound to body or soul, but found even St. Just had left part of his sanity and his spirit at Waterloo.

He'd hoped he might someday do something with his music, but what that silly hope was about, he'd never been quite sure.

And now, he was hoping he and Ellen had a future. The hope sustained him and tortured him and made each second pass too quickly when he was with her. But he couldn't always be with her, because Ellen insisted she have time to tend her gardens and set up her little conservatory.

Val sent Dayton and Phillip back to Candlewick, with hugs and thanks and best wishes all around. He hired a few servants and commissioned the wily

Hazlit to complete a few more errands. He wrote to
his brother Gayle, who controlled both the Windham
family finances and the Moreland exchequer, and he
wrote to David and Letty Worthington, and not just
about bat houses and vegetable plots. He wrote a long
letter to Edward Kirkland and sent missives to several
other musical friends.

He retrieved the damned puppy from Sir Dewey,
dropped off the sworn statements, and spent a long,
pretty afternoon exhorting Sir Dewey over drinks to
look after Ellen's safety in the event Val was unable to.

As Val mounted up later that afternoon, he recalled
his original purpose in departing his estate had been to
tune the piano in the Little Weldon assembly rooms.
How he'd ended up at Sir Dewey's was a mystery
known only to lovelorn fellows at loose ends, among
whom Val would not admit he numbered.

On that sour note, Val turned his attention to the
task he'd set for himself, slipping off Zeke's bridle and
saddle before turning him out in the paddock on the
village green.

To Valentine Windham, each piano developed a
particular personality. It wasn't always possible to tell
as a piano left his shops what the personality might
be, but he could usually make an educated guess by
playing the instrument at length.

So Val approached the assembly rooms, wondering who awaited him abovestairs. He found a little
brown instrument sitting to the side of what passed
for a stage at one end of the room—a piano, but
likely some venerable forerunner to the small upright
pianos growing popular for cottage use. It sat in

shadows and a layer of dust, giving Val the impression of a little old dowager, forgotten in the corner,
her lace cap askew, her fichu stained, and the light in
her eye growing vague.

It took hours. She'd forgotten where most of her
pitches were and wasn't inclined to be reminded too
sternly all at once. Val had to compromise with her
on more than one occasion, for he could break a wire,
strip a screw, or even—heaven help him—crack the
sound board if he demanded too much too abruptly.
So he coaxed and wheedled and badgered and begged,
and eventually, she began to boast something close
to a well-tempered tuning. Her tone quality was as
gracious and merry as Val had suspected it would be,
and he was pleased for her, that she could once again
demonstrate her competence as she deserved.

"You've some music left in you yet." Val patted
the piano before putting away his tools. It was
tempting—so terribly tempting—to try just a few
tunes and see how she liked them, but he resisted.
The entire village would hear him playing this piano,
and it was bad enough they knew he could tune such
an instrument.

So he put away the rags he'd used to clean it, the
felt and tools he'd used to tune it, and carefully closed
the lid over the keys. As he left the assembly rooms,
he looked back and saw the little piano on the empty
stage. No longer dusty, no longer quite so shopworn.
It was the least he could do for a friend.

And to his surprise, leaving the piano to rejoin Ellen
at his home was no more effort than that.

❧

"Valentine?" Ellen's sleepy voice called from her bedroom.

"Of course it's Valentine," he replied, not lighting a lamp. In the past week, he'd learned to navigate her little cottage in pitch darkness, because, while Ellen would not share the manor house with him, he would share the cottage with her. "And as soon as I get this damned thing unknotted, I will be there in that bed with you. I've missed you the livelong day," Val went on as he made quick use of the wash water, "and not just at lunch. God spare me from London solicitors."

"Were they here on your commercial business?"

"There's always plenty of that. I gain more sympathy for my father as I age. Neither he nor I have any patience for the hours of meetings solicitors seem to think make civilization progress."

"Francis abhorred that, as well," Ellen observed on a yawn. "Are you ever coming to bed?"

"I am here." Val climbed into the bed. "So what are you doing over there?" His arms came around her and drew her close. "I love you, Ellen Markham." He kissed her cheek. "When are you going to tell me you love me?"

"How can you be sure I do?"

Val hiked a leg across her thighs. "First, you are sending me away. This is proof positive you love me, for you are trying to protect me from some sort of grave peril only you can perceive."

Ellen's breathing hitched, and Val knew his guess had been right. Gratified by that success, he marched forward.

"Second"—he slipped a hand over her breast—"you

make love with me, Ellen. You hold nothing back, ever, and are so passionate I am nigh mindless with the pleasure of our intimacy." He punctuated this sentiment by dipping his head and suckling gently on her nipple. She groaned and arched up toward him.

"I make my point." Val smiled in the dark and raised his head. "Third, there is the way I make love with you."

"And how is that?" She sounded more breathless than curious.

Val shifted his body over hers. "As if I trust you. I know you are human, and you will do what you think best, but you do it with my interests in mind, Ellen. I don't have to watch myself with you, because you love me, truly. I know it. It isn't the way my siblings love me, though they are dear. It isn't how my parents love me, which is more instinct than insight. It isn't the way my friends love me, though they are both dear and insightful."

"So how is it?" Ellen asked, slipping her legs apart to cradle him intimately.

"It's the way I want and need to be loved," Val said quietly, resting his weight against the soft, curving length of her. "It's perfect."

"But I am sending you away," Ellen reminded him, her fingers at his nape.

Val levered up on his forearms and began to nudge lazily at her sex with his erection. "So you're running out of time to tell me the things that matter, aren't you?"

If she was going to use words to answer, Val forestalled her reply by kissing her within an inch of her soul. Her response was made with her body, and to Val's mind she told him, as emphatically as any woman ever told her man, she did, indeed, unequivocally love him.

And always would.

"What has you sighing?" Val asked as his hand stroked over her hair when they were both sated. "Missing me already?"

"Of course I'm missing you." Ellen hitched herself more closely to him. "I will always miss you."

"You might trust me instead," Val said softly.

She remained silent, and for the hundredth time that day, his heart broke, and he battled back despair. "Ellen?" He kissed her crown. "The assembly is this Saturday. I'll be leaving the next day, as will Dare and Nick."

She nodded, offering neither protest nor argument.

Lying beside her in the darkness, Val heard a slow, mournful dirge in his head. It soared, keened, regretted and lamented, a soul-rending, grief-stricken blend of tenderness, discord, resolution, and heartache. It went on and on, hauntingly sad, and still, neither his musical skill nor his artistic imagination nor all his ducal determination was adequate to bring it to a peaceful, final cadence.

Fourteen

"WHOSE IDEA WAS IT," VAL GROUSED AS NICK knotted his cravat for him, "to leave this benighted place the day after the local version of a party?"

"Some duke's son devised the notion," Nick replied. "An otherwise fairly steady fellow, but one must make allowances. He's dealing with a lot at present. Stickpin?" Val produced the requisite finishing accessory, and Nick frowned in concentration as he shoved gold through linen and lace. He patted the knot approvingly. "You'll do."

When Val merely grimaced, Nick offered him a crooked smile. "Dare and I will get you drunk, and there will be all manner of eager little heifers panting to take a spin with the duke's son. Shoulders back, chin up, duty and honor call, and all that. Darius is also waiting for us in the library, guarding the decanter."

"Suppose we must relieve him." Val sighed, and met Nick's eyes. "Heifers don't pant."

Nick's smile was mischievous. "Maybe not after a duke's youngest son. After a fine new earl like yours truly, turned out in his country finest and sadly lacking his dear countess at his side, they will be panting, or my name isn't Wee Nick."

They collected Ellen, who was looking pretty indeed, in a summery short-sleeved blue muslin dress patterned with little roses in a darker blue. She'd tucked her hair back in a chignon and woven some kind of bright blue flowers into her bun. A white woven shawl and white gloves completed her ensemble, and Val was reminded she was, by any standards, still a young woman.

A beautiful young woman.

And she was nervous. Even as a baroness, she'd likely never had quite the escort she had to the Little Weldon summer assembly, with the son of a duke at her side, an earl's spare, and an earl in train, as well.

Nick handed Ellen into Val's traveling coach—the only one he'd brought out from Town—and rocked the vehicle soundly when he climbed in and lowered himself beside Darius on the backward-facing seat.

Between Nick and Darius, the conversation stayed light, flirtatious, and even humorous, but as far as Val was concerned, they might have been in a hearse, so low were his spirits. He heard again the dirge, violins over cellos, the mournful bassoon adding its misery to the mix.

He looked up to find Ellen watching him as the coach rolled into the village and Sean brought the team to a halt.

"If you give your supper waltz to anyone else, Ellen," Val murmured as he handed her out, "I will spank you on the steps of the church."

"Likewise," she replied, her smile sweet and wistful. "But look, they've set up the dancing outside."

Sure enough, half the green was roped off, the trees hung with lanterns, and a podium set up for the musicians. Val's little dowager friend sat in the center of the podium, three stools behind her. Two violin cases rested on the piano's lid, and a guitar case leaned against one of the stools.

Flowers sat in pots every few feet around the dancing area, and children were shrieking with glee as they darted between adults. Tilden manned a tapped keg across the street outside the Rooster, and young men congregated around him in whatever passed for their evening finery. A punchbowl was set up under a tree, and ladies were gathering there like a bouquet of summer blossoms.

"The assembly itself will be upstairs," Ellen explained. "There will be food there, and a place to stow hats, shawls, canes, and so forth."

"Just like a London ball," Darius quipped. "But with considerably more fresh air."

As the evening progressed, the good humor and energy of the dancers seemed to increase. Rafe's generously distributed summer ale likely had a great deal to do with the level of merriment, and Val was just about to find Ellen and suggest a discreet and early departure, when the musicians announced that the next dance would be a waltz. A buffet at the long tables set up on the other side of the green would follow the waltz, and the party would then move into the Rooster for the annual summer darts tournament.

A cheer went up, and Val ducked through the crowd to find Ellen standing near the stairs leading up to the assembly rooms.

"May I have the honor of this dance?" He bowed to her as formally as he might have bowed to any duchess, and Ellen dipped an elegant curtsey.

"The pleasure is entirely mine," she recited, laying her hand on his knuckles and following him across the street.

He didn't lead her to the dancing area, though, but to the side yard of the livery, which was quiet and heavily shadowed. As the introductory measures drifted out across the summer night, Val was relieved to find it would be an English waltz, the slower, sweeter version of the Viennese dance.

He drew her closer than custom allowed; she tucked against him and rested her cheek against his shoulder.

The little group of musicians made a good job of it, the violins lilting along in close harmony, the piano and guitar accompanying with more sensitivity than Val would have expected. But for once, when there was music played, he didn't focus exclusively on the sounds in his ears, but rather, spent his attention on the woman in his arms.

"Talk to me, Ellen," Val whispered as he turned her slowly around the darkened yard. "I leave tomorrow, you promised me answers, and we're out of time."

"Not now, Valentine, please. We're not out of time yet, and all I want in this moment is to have this dance with you."

He wasn't going to argue with her, but tucked her more closely to him and wished the dance would never end. When the last notes died away, she stayed right where she was, both arms around his waist, her forehead pressed to his chest.

"Ah, damn." Val stroked her hair and pressed a kiss to her temple. "Shall I simply take you home, Ellen? I can send the coach back for Nick and Dare."

She shook her head. "Everybody would remark our departure, and while you leave tomorrow, I have to live with these people."

Val rested his chin on her crown. "It should reassure me you're not planning on haring off somewhere and not telling me."

"Oh, Val…" Ellen's voice held weary reproach.

"Let me take you home," Val tried again. "It will give us a chance to talk, and I think we need that." She *owed* him that was closer to the truth, in Val's mind.

She stepped back then, and Val felt a cold, sinking sensation coil in his gut. "Ellen?"

"I know I told you I would explain," she said, turning her back to him, "but does it have to be now?"

"For God's sake." Val ran a hand through his hair. "If not now, then tell me when, please? I will be on my horse leaving for London at first light, and the sun set an hour ago. We are down to hours, Ellen, and bloody few of those."

"I know, but I don't want to see your eyes when you learn what I have to tell you. I don't want to see what you think of me writ plain on your face."

Val stepped closer to her. "You are being cowardly and asking the impossible of me. You are not a cowardly woman, Ellen Markham."

"Cowardly." Ellen winced and crossed her arms. "I am merely asking you for patience. We're at the local assembly, for pity's sake."

"You've had weeks, Ellen," Val shot back, his temper rising through his frustration and bewilderment. "You want to send me off for what amounts to no reason."

"I can write to you."

"You won't, though. Why in the name of all that's holy can't you just, in the smallest, least significant way, trust me? There's nothing you can say or do or think or imagine that will make me stop loving you. It isn't in me to do that."

She shook her head, and Val saw the glint of fresh tears on her cheeks.

"Blazing hell." He crossed to her and wrapped his arms around her. "I'm sorry, Ellen. I'm sorry I've made you cry, sorry I can't be more patient, sorry you are so frightened. What can I do to make it better?"

She drew in a slow, shuddery breath. "Let me collect myself. The evening has been long, and we are both exhausted. You find Nick and Darius, and I'll be along in a minute."

Dismissed, Val thought darkly. It crossed his mind that the simple truth might be Ellen had tired of him, and out of misguided kindness was allowing him some dramatic fantasy of past bad deeds, skulking relations, and a cruel fate. What did he have to recommend himself, really? His title was a mere courtesy, his wealth garnered in that most unprepossessing of pursuits—*trade*—and his former abilities as a musician completely unknown to her.

By the time Val worked his way back to the green, he was relieved to see the party was moving into the Rooster. Children were still shrieking and larking about, the laughter and revelry around the punch bowl and keg were louder than ever, but near the musician's corner, the violinists were packing up.

Bile rose in Val's stomach as he took in the carnival that had been the summer assembly in Little Weldon. His world was ending, *again*, and The Almighty was seeing to it this misery befell him in the midst of a bloody party.

Movement by the doors to the stairs caught his eye, and when he discerned what was going on, he started over at a determined trot.

"For God's sake, be careful!" It came out more loudly and more angrily than he'd intended, and Neal Bragdoll blinked at him in semidrunken consternation.

"We're movin' the pianna, guv." Neal frowned. "Can't leave it outside all night." Neal's brothers nodded agreeably, as if any damned fool could see what they were about.

"You nigh bumped the legs right off of her," Val shot back. "If you can't be any more careful than that, you might as well leave her out here for the rain and the dewfall to destroy her more gently."

"Her?" Neal set his end of the piano down, and a moment later his brothers did likewise with their end. "This is a pianna, not a her."

"For God's sake," Val nearly shouted, "*I know that*, but it doesn't give you leave to wrestle it around like a damned sack of oats. You neglect her year after year, and still you expect music when you come to do your drunken stomping about, and then you can't be bothered to take the least care of an instrument old enough to be your grandmother. There's music in here"—he smacked the lid of the piano. "There's craftsmanship you can't even conceive of, there's…goodness and beauty." He stopped, and his voice dropped considerably. "There's…something of the divine, and you just can't…you can't take it for granted and endlessly bash it about. You can't do that, much less again and again and again. You just…you can't."

An awkward, very unmerry quiet fell, underscored by the continued sounds of revelry coming from the Rooster. Val looked up from the little piano to see Neal's slack-jawed confusion mirrored on faces all around him.

"Lads." Sir Dewey appeared at Val's side, Nick looming behind him. "Let's try this again and treat this piano like it was your grannie's coffin, shall we?" Neal exchanged a look with his brothers, one of whom shrugged and bent to pick up his corner. Nick took the fourth corner, and the procession carefully moved up the stairs.

"You'll want to see her situated," Sir Dewey said softly, his hand on Val's arm.

What Val *wanted* was for the earth to swallow him up and end this miserable, unbearable day. No music, no Ellen, nothing to fight for but a battered old piano that had been knocked about long before the Bragdoll brothers' drunken buffoonery.

Still, Sir Dewey was looking at Val with a kind of steadying, level gaze, and what else was there to do, really? Val nodded and followed Sir Dewey up the stairs.

"There's an ale for each of you gentlemen," Sir

Dewey said when the piano was back in its place. "Tell Rafe to put it on my tab."

"Thankee." Neal tugged his forelock, shot a glance at the piano once again sitting on the stage, and left with only one puzzled look at Val.

"You'll stay with him?" Sir Dewey directed the question at Nick, who nodded and began moving around the room, blowing out candles. "I must return to the Rooster or there will be hell to pay within the hour. Rafe's special blends are mayhem waiting to happen."

"My thanks," Val got out.

"Sir Dewey." Nick saluted in farewell and went on with his task. Val sank down on the piano bench where it sat along the far wall, facing out so he could watch Nick's perambulations around the room.

"This looks like a metaphor for my life," Val said.

"A bit in need of a tidying?" Nick asked as he picked up the last branch of candles and moved to set it on the piano.

"*Not* on the piano," Val barked then shook his head. "I beg your pardon. Set it wherever you please."

Nick put the candles on the floor and budged up next to Val on the bench. "So why is this room like your life?"

"The party is over, meaning Ellen will not have me." To his own ears, he sounded utterly, absolutely defeated.

"This hurts," Nick observed, a hankie appearing in his large, elegant hands.

"I thought…" Val looked away from that infernal handkerchief. "I thought losing Bart was the worst, and then Victor was worse yet. I am still mad at them for dying, for leaving. Bart especially, because it was so stupid."

"You are grieving," Nick said, folding the hankie into perfect quarters on his thigh. "It hasn't been that long, and each loss reminds you of the others."

"I miss them." Three words, but they held universes of pain and bewilderment. And *anger*.

"I know, lovey." Nick scrunched the handkerchief up in a tight ball. "I know."

"I missed the piano," Val said slowly, "but not as I thought I would." He looked up enough to glance into the gloom where the little piano stood. "I saw myself as talented and having something to offer because I could conjure a few tunes on a keyboard."

"You are talented," Nick said staunchly. "You're bloody brilliant."

Val laughed shortly. "I'm so bloody brilliant I thought if I just played well enough, I might stop…"

"Stop?"

"Stop hurting. Stop missing them," Val said slowly, then fell silent. "I am being pathetic, and you will please shoot me."

"Valentine?"

Nick was a friend, a dear, true friend. He'd neither ridicule nor judge, and Val's dignity had eloped the moment Ellen had made it plain she'd never really intended to confide in him.

What did that leave to lose?

"Being invisible to your father hurts," Val said. He fell silent, wondering where the words had come from. Growing up, he'd been the runt, too young, too dreamy, too artistic to keep up with his brothers or their friends. As a younger man, he'd been disinclined to academic brilliance, social wit, or business acumen, and denied by ducal fiat from buying his colors. For the first time, he wondered if he'd chosen the piano or simply chained himself to it by default.

Nick shot him a curious glance. "Would it be so much better if you'd ended up like Bart and Victor? If Esther and Percy had to bury three sons instead of two, while you were spared the pains of living the life God gave you? I think the more important question now, Val, is are you invisible to yourself?"

"No, Nick." A mirthless laugh. "I am not, but just when I realize what a pit I had fallen into with my slavish devotion to a simple manual skill, just when I can begin to hope there might be more to life than benumbing myself on a piano bench, I find a woman I can love, but she can't love me back."

"I think she does love you," Nick replied, remaining seated as Val rose and crossed the room. "And you certainly do love her."

Val considered Nick's words. They settled something inside him, in his head—where he planned and worked out strategies—and in his heart, where his music and his love for Ellen both resided.

"I do love her." Val lowered himself to sit on the little stage enthroning the piano. "I most assuredly do. It's helpful to be reminded of this."

"Now I am going to cry," Nick said with mock disgust as he crossed the room and once again sat right next to Val. "What will you do about Ellen?"

"About Ellen? I agree with you: We love each

other. She believes her love for me requires us to part. I believe our love requires us to be together for whatever time the good Lord grants."

"So you must convince her," Nick concluded with a nod. "How will you go about this?"

"I have some ideas." Those ideas were like the first stirrings of a musical theme in Val's head. Tenuous, in need of development, but they were taking hold in Val's mind with the same tenacity as a lovely new tune. "God alone knows if my ideas will work."

Val remained sitting side by side with his friend pondering these ideas as the convivial sounds from the green eventually faded, leaving only the occasional burst of voices from the Rooster, until Darius appeared in the door, Ellen at his side.

"The coach is ready to take us home," Darius said, "and I am ready to go."

"You go." Val rose. "I'm not quite ready. Ellen, pleasant dreams. I'll see you in the morning."

❧

There was nothing brittle or dismissive in Val's tone as he bid her good night. He sounded weary and resigned—kind, even. She'd seen him remonstrating the Bragdolls but not been able to hear exactly what was said.

"I'm not quite ready to go either," she said, drawing her white shawl more closely around her.

"We'll send Sean back with the coach, then," Nick offered, eyeing them both.

"No need." Val reached out to tuck the end of the shawl into the crook of Ellen's elbow. "We can walk, if Ellen's agreeable. It's less than three miles, and it's a pleasant night."

"I do." And if all it got her was a few more of those small gestures of caring, she'd count the tears worth the heartache.

"Good night, Ellen." Darius kissed her cheek and touched her arm. Nick went one better, wrapping her in a careful hug. He kissed her forehead for good measure, then hugged Val and slipped an arm through Darius's as he took his leave.

The single candle flickered.

Like my spirit, Ellen thought, eyes searching Val's face for some clue to his mood. He'd been angry after their waltz, and so hurt, and she'd had little to offer him in the way of comfort.

"I have something for you," Val said, extending a hand to her.

"You must not give me one more thing, Valentine." Ellen linked her fingers through his. "You've given me too much."

"Things." Val shrugged. "A few nails and boards, that isn't much, Ellen."

"Not just the conservatory." She used the back of his hand to brush the tears off her cheeks. "You've given me much more than that."

"Barely anything worth mentioning," Val replied, and his voice held a note of true humor. Ellen studied him closely as he tugged her onto the stage. "There's one more small token I would leave with you. Forgot the bench." He smiled at her and hopped down to retrieve a piano bench from against the far wall. His step was light, and Ellen realized the difference now as opposed to earlier in the evening was that he seemed to have gained a measure of peace.

Peace? She hadn't told him the worst of her secrets yet.

He set the bench down by the little piano and patted the bench. "I do better with an appreciative audience."

Ellen's eyes flew to his. "But, Valentine, there are things I promised to tell you, hard, miserable things."

"Yes, I know." Val sat and pushed the cover off the keys. "Things to make me hate you until my dying day and wish vile fates upon you nightly." He patted the bench again and offered her the sweetest smile. "I have made up my mind that I don't need to hear them, Ellen. If you don't want to tell me, I don't need to hear them. If you do want to tell me, then I do need to hear them."

She all but fell onto the piano bench, so taken aback was she by his words.

"You are not arguing," he observed. "This is good, for I don't want to argue. There are other things I must convey—things about myself—but to get them out properly, I will need the assistance of my little friend here. You can sit closer than that, can't you?"

Cautiously, she moved a little closer, close enough that Val could kiss her cheek.

"Now." He laid his fingers on the keyboard. "Where to begin?"

❧

Always before, Val had played for others with some secret, suppressed hope somebody was noticing, that they were impressed with his skill, that they would recall the Windham fellow who did so well at the keyboard. Invariably, they did, until all anybody really recalled about the Windham fellow was that he did so well at the keyboard—until it was all he could recall of himself.

For Ellen, he did not play to *impress*, he played to *express*. He did not care if she noted his technical skill, his proficiency, or his virtuosic ability. He wanted her to hear his soul, to hear his love and his absolute faith in her. He played for her, but he also played for *himself*, for the sheer joy of being so fluent in such a beautiful and challenging language. He opened up his heart, not merely his hands, and played and played and played, giving her every good and noble and honest part of himself he could translate into notes and sounds.

The crowd in the Rooster went quiet, gradually shifting out into the street to hear the enchanting music drifting so delicately through the summer night. In the shade oak near the livery, Thorn Bragdoll sat rapt, his fingers twitching with longing for his flute. The old men sharing a last pint on the steps of the bakery stopped drinking and drew out handkerchiefs, and Rafe and Tilden left their bar to join their customers, staring up at the open windows of the assembly room.

And when Valentine let the last tender melody fade up into the stars, he put his hands in his lap and hoped it was good enough for the woman he loved. He shifted to straddle the piano bench and wrapped his arms around Ellen's waist. She curled up against his chest and held on to him as if she were drowning.

"Damn you, Val Windham," she breathed against his neck. "Damn you, damn you. All summer..." She stopped and drew in a shaking sob.

He listened, his soul calm enough to absorb any reaction, as long as she was in his arms.

"All summer," she went on, "you climbed around on the roofs and in the trees, hanging *bat houses*, mucking stalls, wrecking your hands, when you can... My God, Valentine. My God."

She was shocked, Val got that much, but he wasn't sure what the rest of her reaction was.

"I have listened to you," Ellen said earnestly.

Not, I have listened to you *play*, or I have listened to your music. *I have listened to you*. Val heard the distinction and saw it in the urgency on her face. "I have listened to you," she said again, "and I am grateful for the privilege. More grateful than I can ever say, but now, you must listen to me."

"I'm here, Ellen." Val's arms settled back around her, and he waited until she was again tucked against his chest. "I'm listening."

"My babies," Ellen said in soft, heartbroken tones. "Val, I killed my babies."

"You did not kill your children, Ellen." Val stroked a hand down over her hair, gently disentangling the flowers she'd woven into her bun earlier. "You will never convince me otherwise. You would never knowingly bring harm to any living thing in your care." She went still against him, utterly, unbreathingly still. "Love?"

"Oh, Valentine." She let out her breath. "I do love you. For those few words alone, I love you. Your faith in me warms my soul and brings light to places condemned to shadow. But you're wrong."

"I am not, but tell me why you think otherwise."

"I conceived three times," Ellen said slowly. "Each time, the child did not live to draw breath."

"Many women cannot complete their pregnancies," Val pointed out, his fingers now working on the chignon itself. "It isn't your fault you miscarried."

Ellen shook her head. "I did not miscarry. I aborted those babies, Valentine. My actions were what caused those pregnancies to end."

"You loved your husband. You wanted to give him children, and you loved those children, Ellen. Knowing you, I believe you loved them before they were born." He pressed his cheek to her temple and knew an urge to take her inside his body, to envelope her with the physical protection of his larger, stronger form.

"I did love them, husband and children both." Ellen stopped and drew in an unsteady breath. "I could not protect my children. I did not carry easily and suffered endless upsets of digestion. With every pregnancy, even before my menses were late, I was unable to keep my meals down. Francis was distraught, but everybody said it would pass quickly. It never did."

"You still did not cause those pregnancies to end."

"My love…" She used the endearment for the first time, though Val had never heard anything so sad. "You are wrong. To treat my upset digestion, I drank teas and tisanes by the gallon. I found one Freddy offered me to be the most soothing and the one that stayed down the best. He was so solicitous, and Francis was pleased to see it, as Freddy was not the most promising young man in other regards. I was grateful for the relief, but then I would lose the child. Three times this happened, the last time just a few weeks before Francis came to grief."

Three miscarriages in five years, followed by the death of her husband? Val wanted to howl with the unfairness of it, to shake his fist at God and take a few swings at Francis.

"You needed time to heal." Val began teasing her braid from its coil at her nape. "You should have been given more time to recover."

"I didn't want time to recover," Ellen wailed. "I wanted to provide my husband with his heir, and he accommodated my wishes reluctantly, as it was the only thing I asked of him, and I asked it incessantly."

"So where in all this very sad tale do you accuse yourself of not caring for your children, Ellen?" Val drew his hand down the thick length of her braid in slow, soothing sweeps. "You were young, and God's will prevailed."

"Not God's will, Val," Ellen said tiredly. "Freddy's. That lovely, comforting tea he brought me, the only one that quieted my digestion? It was mostly pennyroyal, though he told me it was a blend of spearmint, and I did not know any better."

"Pennyroyal?" Val's memory stirred, but nothing clear came to mind. "Ah, the little plant you tossed aside. You were not happy to see it."

"Pennyroyal will bring on menses. Ask any midwife or physician. It is an ancient remedy for the unwanted pregnancy, but in a tea or tisane, particularly if it's mixed with other ingredients, it tastes like spearmint. I eagerly swilled the poison that killed all three of my babies, Val, and it's my fault they died."

"But you didn't know. Freddy should be brought to account for this, and it is not your fault."

"It is my fault," Ellen rejoined. "Early in my marriage, Freddy approached me and suggested he and I might be allies of a sort. He was just a boy then, a gangly, spotty, lonely boy, and I found his overture endearing. It soon became clear he wasn't a nice boy. We had trouble keeping maids when he was visiting in the summers, and then when he was sixteen, he came to live with us."

"He's a bully and a sneak and a thoroughgoing scoundrel."

"He suggested I might want to share my pin money with him," Ellen went on, "but I'd overheard the footmen discussing Freddy's gambling losses, and since he was still only a boy, I did not think it wise to indulge him."

"And you were right."

"And I was a fool," Ellen retorted bitterly. "Freddy exploded when I refused him; that's the only word I can use. His reason came undone, and he said awful things. I had not said anything to Francis about Freddy trying to borrow from me, because I didn't want Freddy to suffer in his cousin's esteem. But when Freddy lost his temper like that, I had the first inkling I should have been afraid of him."

"He would have been only a youth. Francis would have dealt with him sternly."

"Francis wanted to see only the best in Freddy. That

cranky, sullen, lazy, manipulative boy was Francis's heir and the only other member of Francis's family I did not want to destroy Francis's respect for him altogether."

"So you made an enemy," Val concluded. "One willing to stoop to sneaking and poison to get what he wanted."

"Exactly, and Freddy could be so charming, so convincing in his apologies. When he came bearing tea and sympathy to my sickroom, offering to play a hand of cards or read to me, I was touched and tried to forget his terrible tantrum. I should have known better."

"When did you learn the truth?" Val asked, now drawing his fingers through Ellen's unbound hair, even as he vowed to kill Freddy by poison and make sure the whelp of Satan knew exactly how he was dying and why.

"After Francis's funeral," Ellen said, her voice taking on a detached quality, as if the words themselves hurt her, "the solicitors read the will, and Freddy maintained his composure beautifully, until he and I were left alone in the formal parlor at Roxbury Hall. Then he had another tantrum, quite as impressive as the first."

"Let me see if I can figure this," Val said, wanting to spare her the rest of the recitation. "Francis had cut him out of the will, more or less, or at least until he was thirty, but you were well provided for. Freddy told you he would be collecting all your income, lest he reveal you had terminated your pregnancies on purpose, and ruin you socially."

"He did better than that." Ellen paused and lifted

her arms from Val's waist to his neck. "He told me my willful behavior—for he would confess I had begged him to procure me that tea, and he just a lad who didn't know any better—amounted to a serious crime, and if I couldn't be convicted for that, he'd demonstrate that a woman who would kill three babies might also kill their father."

"God above. I should have killed the little shite when I had the chance."

"You are not a murderer," Ellen said firmly. "Freddy is, and a murderer of innocents, Val."

"You are not a murderer, either," Val said, tightening his embrace.

"Nonetheless, I can be very convincingly accused of murder…of my unborn children's murder, of my husband's."

Through the haze of rage and protectiveness clouding his brain, Val tried to remember what he'd read of law. "Firstly, your children weren't born, so they could not be murdered, not under civil law as I recall it. Secondly, you've been investigated regarding your husband's death and found innocent."

Ellen dropped her forehead to his throat. "I disobeyed my husband when I terminated those pregnancies, and therein lies a crime. Then too, by virtue of the use of pennyroyal, I am demonstrated to be familiar with poisons, and Freddy will harp on that to have the investigation reopened. He will ruin me *and anybody associated with me*, and enjoy doing it."

"He cannot ruin you if you are my wife, Ellen. I won't allow it, and I flatter myself my family has the influence to send Freddy packing."

"I will not allow you to put it to the test. He has killed babies, Val, and I have every suspicion he killed Francis, as well."

"Was he not investigated?" Val asked, mental wheels turning in all manner of directions.

"He had not yet reached his majority and did a very convincing job of being the bewildered youth bereft of his mentor and his only real relation on this earth. He wailed at great length he wasn't ready to be the baron and did not want to be the baron, and if only one of my children had lived, he would be spared the awful task of filling Francis's shoes."

"Then he turned around and promptly drained the income from all three of your estates."

Ellen's head came up. "You know about the other two?"

"Francis loved you very much," Val said gently, "and you told me he'd had two weeks to set his affairs in order. This estate was hardly habitable, so I concluded there were others. Maybe Francis had some inkling Freddy would not deal well with you, or maybe he just wanted you to have all you were due."

"But you knew." Ellen cocked her head. "And you said nothing?"

"I just found out recently." Val tucked her against him again. "I wouldn't have, except the Markham solicitors were told to keep an eye on you even if you insisted they leave you in peace."

"Told by whom?"

"Your late husband." Val kissed her cheek. "They continue to hold him in great respect. As long as you insisted they keep their noses out of your affairs, they could only watch the income come into Freddy's pockets through the back door. Someday, I'd like to see these estates of yours, Ellen Markham."

"But you cannot, Valentine. If Freddy knew I'd told you all this, he would feel excused in killing you outright."

"Why hasn't he killed you?"

"The life estate here," Ellen explained. "I get the rents here only as long as I am alive, and these rents are substantial enough I am worth more to Freddy alive than dead. Francis set it up so if I die without issue, the other two estates go his distant relative, Mr. Grey, while this one reverts to a trust Freddy can't touch for years."

"Mr. Grey is the theoretical cousin?"

"Unless I remarry and produce children, in which case the properties will pass to them or can be sold by them on my death for equal division—hence Freddy's reluctance to see me married to anyone before my dotage."

"This is a lot to consider, Ellen," Val said, feeling the effects of sitting too long on one hard little piano bench—which was odd. A year ago, he would never have considered any piano bench too hard. "Shall we discuss it further while we make our way home?"

"Yes." She let Val draw her to her feet. He settled her shawl around her and drew her unbound hair over her shoulders, then took her hand and led her down the stairs.

The moon had risen, illuminating the deserted green, while laughter and the sound of a harmonica came from the Rooster.

Val and Ellen passed along the lane through the soft summer night, the air fragrant with the scents of honeysuckle growing along the hedgerows. It wasn't a long walk, not nearly long enough in some regards. When they got to Ellen's cottage, Val unlocked the door and lifted Ellen into his arms, carrying her across the threshold.

She smiled, probably at the gallantry and symbolism of it, but it was a sad smile. When Val laid her down on the bed and moved off to shed his clothes, she made no protest, though. He undressed her, as well, and tugged her to a sitting position so he might assist her with her nighttime ablutions, then tucked her under the sheet and managed his own washing up with swift dispatch.

He wanted to argue with her, wanted to ravish her, wanted to keep her safe and never leave her side.

In what Ellen no doubt believed to be their final hours together, what Val wanted most, though, was to cherish his lady. He put aside his misgivings, doubts, schemes, and arguments, pulled her into his arms, and stroked his hand over her back until at last, sleep claimed them both.

When he next came to awareness, it was to hear the pretty, fluting morning carol of the birds—an incongruously optimistic sound given what the day held. The cottage was still dark, but dawn was just minutes away.

"You're still here." Ellen, sleepy, warm, and precious, burrowed into his embrace.

In the cocoon of drowsiness and trust enveloping them, it occurred to Val to lay his plans before the woman he loved, except she would not agree with the course he'd chosen. They'd argue, and then they'd part in anger.

They'd talked enough, at least for the present, so when Val settled his length over her, he offered her one heartfelt, "I love you," before allowing his hands and mouth and body to express for him what words could only approximate.

"I love you, too," Ellen replied, lifting her hips to receive him and closing her arms around him. "I always will."

He joined them slowly, memorizing every sensation and sound: Ellen's sighs; the way her body welcomed his into sweet, female heat; the feel of her foot gliding up his calf; the hot glow of pleasure simmering in his groin. He kissed her, grazed his mouth over her every feature, and held still while she returned his explorations. When he moved again, it was with less restraint and more desperation.

"Stay with me."

Val heard Ellen's words whispered against his shoulder and understood what she was asking—and what she wasn't. Not, "Don't ride away today," which would have had him singing hallelujahs for the whole shire to hear, but rather, "Share bodily pleasure with me, intimately, completely, one last time."

A gentleman with any sense wouldn't. A smart man, out of consideration for the woman and for his own future, might not. A wise man certainly couldn't even entertain the notion, given the timing of the lady's request.

But Val was her lover, and binding Ellen to him

through any means was entirely consistent with his hopes, his dreams, and his heartfelt needs. Even that might not have allowed him to comply with her plea, but he knew her and took it upon himself to know her dreams and needs, as well.

When Ellen locked her ankles at the small of his back, when she was making an odd little keening sound against his shoulder, when slow, deep strokes into her body had Val's entire being aflame with the pleasure of their joining, he allowed himself to stay with her. He deluged her with pleasure and submerged himself in the same flood, until passion was spent, and the time to part was inexorably upon them.

By the time he rose from the bed, the cottage was growing light, and the birds had gone quiet.

"Valentine?" Ellen struggled up against the pillows banking the headboard.

"Love?"

"Thank you—for everything. And I do love you."

He offered her a smile, realizing that even in giving him the words, she was confirming her belief that they needed to part. He heard the farewell in her words, though he didn't want to. The same farewell had been in her smile when he'd carried her over the threshold; the same farewell had been in her entire story when he'd held her on the piano bench in the assembly room, and in her loving just moments earlier.

So he'd leave her and let her—and Freddy—think the game was over. Lord Valentine Windham, musical artist and virtuoso without portfolio, had things to do if he was going to ensure his lady's peace of mind and safety. If Ellen had to remain here, he'd trust friends,

Almighty God, contingency plans, and the good luck he was long overdue to keep her safe until Val himself was once again at her side.

Fifteen

SEAN TOOK ZEKE'S REINS FROM VAL'S HAND, AND Ellen watched as Val stuffed his riding gloves in his pocket. He was all brisk efficiency this morning, while Ellen felt dazed and aching in every corner of her soul.

"Walk with me, Ellen." He linked his fingers through hers and turned her toward the home wood. "You will listen to me, for the sooner I can get moving, the less heat Zeke will have to deal with between here and Town."

She nodded, heart breaking, while Val—man-fashion—focused on practicalities.

"You are to move to the house," he began, sounding very stern indeed, as stern as a duke. "If Freddy is waiting to strike, you will be safer at the house. The staff is instructed not to admit him and to keep you safe at all times. I understand you will want to continue to pass along your rents to that weasel, and I can't stop you, but I've hired gardeners for this property, and I expect you to put them to work."

"I can't stay in your house," Ellen protested weakly. "I'll be a kept woman."

"Stay in your cottage," Val shot back, "and you could be a dead woman. I'm leaving, Ellen. *Leaving.* You own the life estate here and you have as much right to dwell in that house as I do. I will feel better knowing you are at the manor and not in the cottage where you might have already come to grief. I want your promise on this."

She bit her lip but couldn't deny his logic. "I'll live at the house. I promise."

"Good." He nodded briskly and barreled onward. "You will also receive callers, including but not limited to Sir Dewey, and Axel and Abby Belmont. Abby will want a female friend on hand as her pregnancy progresses, and I think you owe her that much. I understand her sister-in-law will be up with Axel's brother at the start of the Oxford term, and they will likely call on you."

"I can receive them." She didn't know quite how, but for Valentine, she'd make the effort.

"And the vicar and his wife," Val went on, "and Mrs. Bragdoll, if those louts of hers can ever be left unsupervised for a moment. And you will correspond with my sisters-in-law." Ellen merely nodded, too overcome with the looming parting to do more than hear his words.

"Valentine?"

"Yes, love?" His green-eyed gaze held hers as he walked with her past a particular corner on the path through the woods.

"You're really going?" Except it wasn't a question.

"You've asked it of me," Val reminded her gently, "and you are convinced Freddy will pester me literally to death if I don't leave you to continue on with him ~~as you did before~~, and you have forbidden me to call him out."

She nodded and leaned into him, fell into him, because her knees threatened to buckle with the magnitude of the loss she was to endure.

Val embraced her, resting his cheek against her hair. "You're a strong woman, Ellen Markham, and I have every faith in your ability to soldier on. I need to know as I trot out of your life that you will be fine and you will manage here without me. So"—he put a finger under her chin and forced her to meet his gaze—"tell me some pretty lies, won't you? You'll be fine?"

Ellen blinked and obediently recited the requested untruth. "I'll be fine."

"I'll be fine, as well." Val smiled at her sadly. "And I'll manage quite nicely on my own, as I always have. You?"

"Splendidly," Ellen whimpered, closing her eyes as tears coursed hot and fast down her cheeks. "Oh, Val…" She clutched him to her desperately, there being no words to express the pure, undiluted misery of the grief she'd willingly brought on herself.

"My dearest love." Val kissed her wet cheeks. "You really must not take on so, for it tortures me to see it. This is what you want, or do I mistake you at this late hour?"

"You do not." The sigh Ellen heaved as she stepped back should have moved the entire planet. She wanted Val safe from Freddy's infernal and deadly machinations, and this was the only way to achieve that goal. She had the conviction Valentine Windham, a supremely determined and competent man—son of a duke in every regard—would not take Freddy's scheming seriously until it was too late.

It was up to her to protect the man she loved, and that thought alone allowed her to remain true to the only prudent course. "You have not mistaken me, not now—not ever."

"I did not think you'd change your mind." Val led her back toward the house by the hand. "I have left my direction in the library, and in the bottom drawer of the desk you will find some household money. I know you'd prefer to cut all ties, Ellen, but if you need anything—anything at all—you must call upon me. Promise?"

"I promise," she recited, unable to do otherwise.

"And Ellen?" Val paused before they got to the stable yard. "Two things. First, thank you. You gave me more this summer than I could have ever imagined or deserved, and I will keep the memories of the joy we shared with me always. Second, if there should be a child, you will marry me."

"There will not be a child," she murmured, looking back toward the wood. He was thanking her? She'd cost him a fortune and put his well-being in jeopardy, and he was thanking her? "I do not, and never will, deserve you."

"Promise me you'll tell me if there's a child?" Val's green eyes were not gentle or patient. They were positively ducal in their force of will.

"If there is a child, I will tell you."

"Well, then." Val resumed their progress. "I think that's all there is to say, except, once again, I love you."

"I love you, too," Ellen replied, wishing she'd given him the words so much more often and under so many different circumstances.

"Goodbye, my dearest love." Val bent and kissed Ellen's cheek, not taking her in his arms. "Be safe and call upon me if there's need."

A final nod as Val slipped a hankie into Ellen's hand, and then he mounted up and turned his horse, putting Zeke first to the trot then moving the horse up to a brisk canter. Ellen got a final sympathetic glance from Nick, and then he and Darius were off, disappearing down the drive in a clatter of hooves and dust.

And then *silence*.

She'd had a great deal of silence in the past five years, and for the most part, she'd come to treasure it. But this silence was different, as it wasn't just the lack of sound, it was also the lack of Valentine Windham.

❧

"A caller, Lord Val." David Worthington's butler, like every member of the staff at David's townhouse, knew how to give the impression it was his pleasure to serve. Val glanced up from where he was bent over the desk in the music room and blinked.

"Who is it?" Val asked, glancing at the clock. Blazing hell, it was nearly teatime already.

"His Grace, the Duke of Moreland." The butler didn't make a face, but in his voice there were pinched lips and pruney expressions.

"No avoiding him," Val muttered. "Best do the tea and crumpets drill, and he's partial to crème cakes, if I recall aright. Let's use the family parlor, since the formal parlor faces the street."

"Very good, my lord." The butler bowed politely and withdrew, leaving Val to roll down his cuffs and shrug into his coat.

With a longing glance over his shoulder, Val mentally strapped on the familiar armor of indifference and strolled—deliberately—off to the family parlor.

"Your Grace." Val bowed politely. "You are looking well." His father looked ever the same—tall, lean, blue-eyed, with a thick mane of white hair, his ensemble impeccable even in the middle of a wet and chilly fall day.

"I am looking old," the duke shot back, "and tired. I trust you are well?"

"You may tell Her Grace that I thrive," Val said with a small smile. "Shall we sit?"

"Of course." His Grace plopped onto a pretty little chintz sofa, one likely reflective of Letty's influence. "Too deuced miserable to stand around nattering. When will you come see your mother?"

"I did visit Morelands several weeks ago."

"And you haven't since," the duke retorted. "And what kind of visit was that? You spent one night, and then off again to see Bellefonte, and then it's back to London—and in this bloody raw weather, Valentine?"

"Bellefonte is a very good friend," Val said, grateful for the interruption of the tea tray. "Now, there's hot tea, and by purest coincidence, a few crème cakes. I'm not sure how many are on the tray, so I couldn't possibly report to Her Grace how many you ate."

The duke's blue eyes warmed with humor. "Smart lad."

"Tea or something stronger?"

"Tea with lots of sugar and a dash of whiskey, though the whiskey we'll find here is probably too fine to deserve such a fate."

"Fairly's cellars are to be envied, but you didn't brave London in this rain to discuss whiskey."

"I most assuredly did not," His Grace replied, arranging three cakes on a small plate—it would not hold more. "I got your letters."

Val sipped his tea—his undoctored tea—and merely raised an eyebrow.

"Took a while." His Grace demolished a cake in two bites. "Summer, you know, people are rusticating and off to fornicate their way through various house parties. You cannot know how relieved I am Her Grace did not indulge in that folly this year at Morelands."

"I'm surprised she hasn't left for Yorkshire yet. A new granddaughter must have her in alt."

"We are pleased." The duke's eyes twinkled as he appropriated the royal first person plural. "But we are also getting appallingly old, and St. Just, canny fellow, has hinted he might bring Emmie, Winnie, and the baby south for the winter. Her Grace and I would rather see that—so the entire family can then enjoy St. Just's visit—than we would like to make a progress of hundreds of miles."

"I can't blame you. I'd love to see St. Just again, as well as Win and Emmie, but I am not inclined to make that journey now."

The duke shrugged, piling more cakes on his now-empty plate. "St. Just is an old campaigner. He's used to haring about and will probably need to do a fair amount of it for the next few years. His countess comprehends this. Excellent cakes, by the way."

"I'll pass your compliments along to the cook." As long as the sweets held up, it appeared he and his father were going to have a civil visit. "So what do we hear from Gayle and Anna?"

"Not much." The duke smiled fondly. "My heir is running them ragged, of course. He'll have his papa's height, that one. Esther thinks he'll have her green eyes. But back to your letters. Let's have a spot more libation first though, but easy on the tea."

Val got up, crossed to the decanter, and poured his father two neat fingers.

"Jesus in the manger." His Grace closed his eyes. "That is decent. That is damned decent. You should enjoy some before you've a wife about to begrudge you every pleasure a man holds dear." His Grace smiled at his tumbler. "Almost every pleasure. My thanks. I always told Her Grace you were too smart to waste your life on a piano bench."

Val winced—then wanted to wince again because he'd let his appearance of indifference visibly slip. Never well advised, that.

"Oh, for God's sake, boy." His Grace set the tumbler down hard. "I pay you a compliment, and you cringe as if I meant it as an insult." His lips pursed, and he regarded his youngest son while Val stood, half-facing the window overlooking the gardens. "My lack of enthusiasm for your devotion to music was based on

reasons, young man, though I don't suppose much of
that matters now. If we're to have a tête à tête over
your situation with Roxbury, can't you at least ring for
a little more sustenance?"

Val went to the door and spoke to the footmen.
The cakes arrived, along with a selection of chocolates, some marzipan, and some candied violets, and
all before His Grace could resurrect the familiar lament
over Valentine's devotion to musical endeavors.

"This is what your mother would call hospitality."
His Grace's eyes lit up at the sight of the tray. "Now,
where were we?"

Val resumed his seat. "Try the violets; they're St.
Just's favorite."

"Ah, yes!" His Grace paused in midreach. "That
reminds me, as St. Just was most concerned for you
in his recent letter. A girl—can you believe it?" His
Grace was smiling beatifically. "But as to *your* letter,
here's what we've got."

He popped some violets into his mouth before
going on.

"Bad piece of work." The duke shook his head.
"This Markham fellow is a veritable bird-dropping on
the family escutcheon, not at all like his cousin. I knew
the previous baron, and he was young but sensible
and could be trusted to vote his party's position unless
he had a damned good and well-stated reason to the
contrary. Everybody respects that."

"But the present baron?" Val pressed, forcing himself to attend this topic and not the question His Grace
had left dangling in Val's mind.

His Grace sat back, his expression no longer jovial

or paternal in the least. "In the last session, the dirty little rodent sold his vote at least six times."

"This is not good?"

"This is not good," the duke said patiently. "The vote is a sacred trust, rather the petite version of the divine right of kings, something given to a man from a much greater power, call it God or the realm or what you will. You trade your vote, of course, judiciously, to gain something of value by giving away something of lesser value, but you do not accept money for your vote."

"Bad *ton*?" Val hazarded, as the distinction seemed pretty fine to him.

"Criminally bad *ton*," His Grace clarified, "if blatant enough. It implicates both the one selling his vote and the one buying it. Of course, there will be layers of intermediaries in most cases, but Roxbury got himself indebted with the very worst sorts of people, so he was sloppy, and thus left an easy trail to uncover. Corrupt and stupid, never a pretty combination."

"You have signed statements?"

"Oh, of course." The duke's eyes lit up with enthusiasm. "And not just from the usual unsavory characters but from the bankers and other MPs Roxbury approached about selling their votes, as well."

"Members of Parliament would testify against him?" Val sat back, relieved beyond telling. *And Ellen thought the man was so damned powerful.*

"Of course." The duke cocked his head. "One always wants to appear to be on the side of crusading justice. Shall I explain the documents to you?"

"If you would." Val nodded, for the first time feeling justified in his hopes.

What followed was something Val could think of only as an etude in parliamentary politics. His Grace patiently elucidated the particulars of six different bills, their strengths and weaknesses, the reasons various factions were in support of them and various other factions were not. The duke described convoluted committee structures and the channels through which Freddy had approached various MPs and committee chairs. While Val tried to concentrate on the ramifications of Freddy's behavior, His Grace casually enumerated the consequences of each bill being passed or not passed into law, being amended in this or that detail, being sent back to committee for further drafting, or being otherwise modified to suit some particular interest or industry.

The information flowed from His Grace's fertile brain in a tidy, well-orchestrated presentation, not a note out of place, not a phrase out of balance.

As the candied violets met the same fate as the crème cakes and chocolates, insight struck Valentine Windham with the force of a particularly well-aimed mule kick: his father was a parliamentary prodigy, a political virtuoso whose composition of choice was nothing less than a substantial influence on British affairs in the present age.

The attributes of virtuosity were all there: A towering commitment to the subject of choice; a fluency gained through long, dedicated years of study; and a generosity about sharing the wisdom gained in those years, that came across as nothing less than art.

"There is another favor I would ask of you, Your Grace," Val heard himself say when the duke's exposition was complete.

His Grace sat back and grinned at Val over the remains of the tray of sweets. "This is my lucky day. Say on, my boy." Val explained, the duke laughed softly, nodded, and rose to take his leave.

"Your Grace." Val paused with his hand on the parlor door. "Why did you object to my interest in music?"

"Beg pardon?"

"You said you had reasons for objecting to my obsession with the piano," Val reminded him. "Might I know why?"

His Grace frowned mightily. "I could not help you."

"Could not help me?" What was this? "You made sure I had the best instructors, the best instruments, plenty of opportunity to play with talented ensembles; you talked Her Grace into letting me go to Italy in very uncertain times; you suggested to Kirkland I'd make a decent substitute conductor. How didn't you help me?"

Until that moment, Val hadn't for himself admitted how much his father had supported him. He'd attributed those measures to his mother's influence, but even a duchess had limited reach when it came to matters financial and political.

"Money is not help," the duke said. "Of course you were going to have the best—you are my son. I would no more allow you to practice on an inferior instrument than I would have sent you to the hunt meet on a lame pony. What I mean is that *I could not help you*. St. Just and Dirt were off to the cavalry, and I certainly had useful advice for them both and enough influence that they didn't end up going directly to the worst of the fighting. Gayle is the family merchant, meaning no disrespect, and I've seen enough business transacted I can chime in knowledgeably from time to time if he asks for an opinion. Victor loved the social and political scene, and I've decades running tame through those halls. I had the perfect pocket borough picked out for him.

"But you… When you sat down on that piano bench, I felt as if you were alone in a little rowboat, no oars, no rudder, just waves and weather all around you, and I had no way to swim out and keep you safe. I know nothing about music—not one damned thing beyond 'God Save the King,' to which, mind you, I mostly just move my lips. I often wondered though, if you didn't choose music for that reason."

"What reason?"

"You did not want to be like me," His Grace said simply. "So you went where I could not follow. Not the least subtle, but appallingly effective. Fortunately, your mother could keep her eye on you, but it hasn't been easy, Valentine. But then, few efforts worth undertaking are, or so your mother has told me on many occasions, generally when the topic is her enduring devotion to me."

"Few efforts worth undertaking are easy," Val agreed, understanding perfectly where he'd gotten his determination and his willingness to maneuver boldly with little thought to the consequences.

"And hasn't this been the most interesting little chat?" The duke smiled at his son. "So how's the hand? And I will not peach on you to your mother."

"Better." Val held up his left hand and flexed it. "Much, much better. I just have to pace myself with it now."

"Why is that?"

"I'm working on a little project. Would you like to see it?"

"D'you think Worthington's staff is up to putting us together an actual meal?" His Grace tried to look indifferent, but his eyes gleamed like those of a man who'd waited nigh thirty years for his baby boy to invite Papa to see his toys.

"Beef roast is on for this evening. We can take trays in the music room, if you like."

"Well, why not? The rain might eventually let up, and I've always wondered whether Fairly has naked cupids plastered on every ceiling of his residence."

"Just in the bathing room," Val allowed, straight-faced.

"Don't suppose...?" His Grace let the thought trail off.

"Of course," Val replied, smiling openly now. "And then to the music room."

❦

Ellen was using the last of a pretty afternoon to separate a bed of irises along her springhouse—staying busy was supposed to help her forget a certain green-eyed, handsome man with talented hands, a beautiful voice, and a stubborn streak worthy of a duke. A man who

dwelled in her heart, just as she lived under the roof
he'd provided.

The extra iris roots were, of course, saleable, but
she'd had good markets over the entire summer and
had no real need of additional coin.

Val had seen to that.

"Lady Roxbury?"

The voice, so like Val's, caused her heart to skip a
beat, but as she raised her hand to shield her view from
the sun, her caller's face and form registered, as well.
For an instant—a joyful, unbelievable instant—she
thought it was Val, but then her senses took in the
different muscling, the lighter hair, the more austere
cast to the features.

"Lord Westhaven." It had to be he, for he'd sent
along a little warning note two days previous. Ellen
was faced with having to rise so she could curtsey.
Westhaven surprised her utterly by dropping to his
knees beside her.

He nodded at the flowerbed. "Irises, I'm guessing.
Can you spare a few? My wife and her grandmother
adore them, and our house is not yet landscaped. Anna
wants to do it herself, but there just hasn't been time
this summer."

"You have a new baby, don't you? They can be
very demanding, and of course I have more than
enough here to send some along to your countess."

He asked her to show him how to separate the
roots and soon had Ellen chatting about bulbs and
tubers and offering to send some of the daffodils she'd
separated, as well. She invited him in to tea, surprised
at how comfortably the time had passed.

He was a less vibrant version of Valentine but a man Ellen felt an inherent ability to trust. He had Val's instinctive sense of timing, too, as he steered her deftly but unerringly back to innocuous topics until the tea tray was delivered and the door to the parlor closed by the departing maid.

"How do you like your tea, my lord?"

"Later," Westhaven said quietly. "I like my tea later, though feel free to indulge if you're inclined. I think you'd rather hear what I came to say, though."

"I would," Ellen agreed, setting the pot down. "Or I hope I would."

"He loves you, you know." The earl frowned at her, an expression of considerable displeasure. "Valentine does. He hasn't said that to me, but I am to note your dress, your appearance, any evidence of ill health or poor spirits. I am to question the help while I'm here and wangle an invitation to spend the night—propriety and my countess's sensibilities be hanged—so I might reassure my brother the doors are conscientiously locked every night and the halls patrolled by a footman until dawn, and on and on."

He stopped, and Ellen realized her amiable companion from the iris patch had been just a well-crafted façade. This man was going to be a duke and was comfortable with both the authority and the power that entailed. He was a gentleman, but he was Val's brother and prepared to preserve his brother from heartache or folly at any cost.

Any cost.

Ellen added cream and sugar to the single cup of tea. "Then you must tell me, is he well? Is he sleeping?

Has his hand continued to heal, and please—if you tell me nothing else—is he happy?"

The teacup began to shake minutely in her hand, and she just managed to set it down before it would have shattered against the table when it slipped from her grip.

"He's miserable," Westhaven said slowly, his eyes narrowing on the teacup. "He's busy as hell, his hand is fine, but he's perishing miserable; so you, my lady, are going to accept my invitation."

Having spent weeks growing increasingly lonely and her nights increasingly convinced she'd made the worst mistake of her life, Ellen listened as carefully as she could to the earl's next words then nodded her assent. If it was what Valentine Windham asked of her, she would have accepted an invitation to garden in hell.

If she hadn't already.

※

"Mustn't gawk," the Earl of Westhaven whispered in Ellen's ear. "You look quite the thing, and you're in the ducal box. The entertainment is that way." He discreetly pointed to the stage and cordially seated her to his left.

"So is this Val's widow?" A jovial male voice sang out from the back of the box, and because she was watching her escort's every move, Ellen saw Gayle Windham *almost* roll his eyes.

"Percy!" a soft, female voice chided. "Really. Lady Roxbury is Valentine's friend and was his neighbor in Oxfordshire. My lady, Esther, the Duchess of

Moreland, pleased to make your acquaintance. I am Valentine's mother, and this scandalous old reprobate is His Grace, Percival, the Duke of Moreland."

Ellen would have fallen on her backside had Westhaven not had her hand tucked firmly on his arm. She curtsied, murmuring something polite, her mind whirling at the august personages before her and the casual manner in which they'd introduced themselves.

Maybe Val hadn't known his parents were using their box tonight, she reasoned. This whole trip to Town had been so odd, with Westhaven explaining only that Val wanted her to attend the opening night of the symphony's fall season. She'd been whisked to Town, spent the night in one of the most elegant townhouses she'd ever seen, presented with a peculiarly well-fitting bronze silk evening gown and all the trimmings, and now here she was.

"They're growin' 'em almost as pretty as my duchess out in Oxfordshire, I see," the duke said, beaming at Ellen.

Did dukes beam? Something in the mischief of his smile tickled her memory.

"You and Val have the same smile," she informed the duke. "And Your Grace"—she turned to the duchess, a stately, slender lady whose hair was antique gold—"Val has your eyes."

The duchess leaned close to whisper, "But I think Valentine has your heart, hmm?" She straightened and took her husband's arm. "Shall we be seated, Percy? One doesn't want to disappoint the crowds."

Westhaven stepped back, so it happened Ellen was seated between the duke and duchess, feeling nervous, excited, and thoroughly off balance. Where was Val? And why had he summoned her? Was this simply an outing for her? Was it a demonstration to Freddy that the Moreland consequence was being put in Ellen's corner?

The first half of the program started off in a blur as Ellen's mind continued to race and whirl from one thought to the next. She tried, in the dim lighting, to look around and see if Val might be watching her from a different box. Gradually, though, the music seeped into her fevered brain, and she began to calm. Maybe Val just wanted her to hear this music. The orchestra was in fine form, and Val's family was treating her with great cordiality.

Westhaven took her arm at the interval and informed her they would be strolling in the corridor. They barely escaped the confines of the ducal box when Ellen heard a familiar baritone rumbling behind her.

"If it isn't my favorite little gardener," Nick Haddonfield pronounced. "Give a lonely fellow a kiss, my lady, and I won't complain when you pinch me."

"Nick…" She smiled up at him, not realizing how much she'd missed him too, until that moment. When he wrapped his arms around her, there in the theatre corridor with half of polite society looking on, Ellen felt tears welling. "I've missed you."

"As well you should." Nick nodded approvingly. "Women of discernment always miss me, though I've missed you, as well, lovey. You did not answer my letters."

"A lady does not correspond with a gentleman,

your lordship," Ellen chided him, though her smile was still radiant.

Westhaven cast an assessing glance at Nick. "He's no gentleman. He writes a very charming letter, nonetheless. Next time, Bellefonte, you do as David and Letty do with Val. Val writes a two-sentence letter to David and then a four-page postscript to Letty."

"Strategy is always so tedious." Nick sighed. "Here comes one of my two favorite brothers-in-law." Ellen was hugged again as Darius Lindsey greeted her, looking strikingly handsome in his evening finery.

"I believe Her Grace will want to see you two," Westhaven decided. "Why don't you escort Lady Roxbury back to the box while I check on something backstage?"

A look passed between the gentlemen, something of male significance that had Ellen concluding Westhaven needed the retiring room. She let Nick and Darius each take an arm and was more than pleased when Her Grace invited them to stay for the second half. Westhaven slipped into the back of the box just as the ushers were dousing the candles.

"So this is the good part?" Nick asked from beside her.

"The party piece is always saved for the second half," Ellen explained, though it occurred to her belatedly, Nick had been to far more entertainments than she. "That way all the latecomers won't miss it."

"One wouldn't want to miss this," Nick murmured, only to be thumped on the arm by Darius.

She looked around one last time for Val, and then

she spied him, his progress being marked by the grow-ing hush of the audience as he strode across the stage.

Oh, he looked so handsome, so distinguished. He was too lean, maybe, though it was hard to tell when he was so far away, but how fortunate the lights caught his dark hair, his elegant, muscled form as he approached the conductor's podium.

What on earth?

He tapped a baton on the music stand and signaled to the oboist, who offered the pitch. When the squeaks, toots, and honks of tuning up were silenced, Val turned to face the audience.

"Ladies and gentlemen." His voice carried straight into the darkest corners of the hall and straight into Ellen's heart. "There is a slight misprint on tonight's program. We offer for our finale tonight my own debut effort, which is listed on the program as *Little Summer Symphony*. It should read, *Little Weldon Summer Symphony*, and the dedication was left out, as well, so I offer it to you now.

"Ellen, I know you are with me tonight, seated with my parents and our friends, though I cannot see you. I can feel you, though, here." He tapped the tip of the baton over his heart. "I can always feel you there, and hope I always will. Like its creator, this work is not perfect, but it is full of joy, gratitude, and love, because of you. Ladies and gentlemen, I dedicate this work to the woman who showed me what it means to be loved and love in return: Ellen, Baroness Roxbury, whom I hope soon to convince to be my lady wife. These modest tunes and all I have of value, Ellen, are dedicated to you."

He turned in the ensuing beats of silence, raised his baton, and let the music begin.

Ellen was in tears before the first movement concluded. The piece began modestly, like an old-fashioned *sonata di chiesa*, the long slow introduction standing alone as its own movement. Two flutes began it, playing about each other like two butterflies on a sunbeam, but then broadening, the melody shifting from sweet to tender to sorrowful. She heard in it grief and such unbearable, unresolved longing, she wanted to grab Val's arm to make the notes stop bombarding her aching heart.

But the second movement marched up right behind that opening, full of lovely, laughing melodies, like flowers bobbing in a summer breeze. This movement was full of song and sunshine; it got the toes tapping and left all manner of pretty themes humming around in the memory.

My gardens, Ellen thought. My beautiful sunny gardens, and Marmalade and birds singing and the Belmont brothers laughing and racing around.

The third movement was tranquil, like the sunshine on the still surface of the pond, like the peace after lovemaking. The third movement was napping entwined in the hammock, and strolling home hand in hand in the moonlight. She loved the third movement the best so far, until it romped into a little drinking song, that soon got away from itself and became a fourth movement full of the ebullient joy of creation at its most abundant and beautiful.

The joy of falling in love, Ellen thought, clutching her handkerchief hard. The joy of being in love and *being loved the way you need to be.*

Ah, it was too much, and it was just perfect as the music came to a stunning, joyous conclusion. There was a beat of profound silence and then a spontaneous roar of approval, a deafening wall of applause, cheers, foot-stomping, whistling, and calls for an encore. Val stood to the side, looking dazed and pleased, until the first violinist rose and gestured with his bow toward the podium. Even Ellen could hear the concertmaster happily yelling at Val to bow, for the love of God, and the applause did not diminish until Val turned, said something to his musicians, and held up his baton again.

The little drinking song served wonderfully as an encore, and the orchestra had to play through it yet again before the audience let the musicians and their conductor go.

In the ducal box, Ellen sat dazed and so pleased for Valentine she could not stop laughing and crying and being glad she had been there to see it. Her exile was now worthwhile. Through years and even decades of gardening in solitude, she would recall this night and those lovely sentiments tossed to her before all of London as if she were the prima donna on the stage.

And she would not—she would *not*—let herself worry that Freddy would get wind of this and pitch another tantrum.

"Come along." Nick took her arm when they left the box, and with his superior height, navigated her deftly through the crowds.

"Where are we going?" Ellen asked, for she did not recognize the path they were traveling.

"To meet your fate, my lady," Nick said, but his

eyes were sparkling, and Ellen didn't realize the significance of his comment until she was being tugged
backstage toward a growing buzz of voices. "The
green room is this way"—Nick steered her along—
"but for you, we will refer to it as the throne room.
Ladies and gentlemen…" Nick bellowed as he gently
pushed Ellen into a crowded, well-lit room. "Make
way for the artist's muse and for a large fellow bent on
reaching that punchbowl."

Applause burst forth, and the crowd parted, leaving Ellen staring across the room at Valentine where
he stood, a glass in his hand, still in his formal attire.
He'd never looked so handsome to her, or so tired and
happy and uncertain. He set the glass down and held
out his left hand to her.

"My Ellen," he said, as if introducing her. She tried
to make her steps dignified before all these strangers,
but then she was walking very quickly, then, hang it,
she pelted the rest of the distance right into his arms,
holding on to him with every ounce of her strength.
She did not leave his side when the duke and duchess were announced or when his various siblings and
friends came to congratulate him. She was still right by
his side when the duke approached.

"Well." Moreland smiled at his youngest son.
"Suppose I was mistaken, then."

"Your Grace?"

Ellen heard surprise in Val's voice, and pleasure.

"I kept trying to haze you off in a different direction, afraid the peasants wouldn't appreciate you for
the virtuoso you are." The duke sipped his drink, gaze
roving the crowd until it lit on his wife standing beside

Westhaven. "I was worrying for nothing all those years. Of course they're going to love you—you are my son, after all."

"I am that," Val said softly, catching his father's eye. "I always will be."

"I think you're going to be somebody's husband too, eh, lad?" The duke winked very boldly at Ellen then sauntered off, having delivered a parting shot worthy of the ducal reputation.

"My papa is hell-bent on grandchildren. I hope you are not offended?"

Ellen shook her head. "Of course not, but Valentine, we do need to talk."

"We do." He signaled to Nick, where that worthy fellow stood guarding the punchbowl. Nick nodded imperceptibly in response and called some inane insult over the crowd to Westhaven, who quipped something equally pithy right back to the amusement of all onlookers, while Val and Ellen slipped out the door.

By the light of a single tallow candle, he led Ellen to a deserted practice room. He set the candle on the floor before tugging her down beside him on the piano bench.

"I can't marry you," Ellen said, wanting to make sure the words were said before she lost her resolve.

"Hear me out," Val replied quietly. "I think you'll change your mind. I hope and pray you'll change your mind, or all my talent, all my music, all my art means nothing."

Sixteen

REMEMBER THIS, ELLEN ADMONISHED HERSELF. SHE ordered herself to recall the cedary scent of Val's shaving soap, the feel of his arm embracing her where they sat on the hard bench, the reassuring heat of his body still warm from the exertion of conducting a major work. To recall the beloved sight of his face, so grave and tired now that the excitement of the debut was ebbing.

Remember this, because it might have to sustain you for a long, long time.

"You need to know," Val began, "Freddy has left the country, and he is not expected back."

"Gone?" Ellen's jaw literally dropped. "Freddy detested travel by anything except curricle."

"He's better off on the Continent, believe me. Between Sir Dewey and Benjamin Hazlit, my private investigator, I have sworn statements sufficient to bring charges against Freddy on everything from conspiracy to commit arson, to attempted murder, to breaking and entering, and a host of lesser charges. I have a statement from the herbalist on the Roxbury estate. Freddy bribed her to teach him about poisons and further bribed her to sell him a supply of pennyroyal and to label it spearmint. She didn't untangle his purpose until your third miscarriage, and by then, it was too late. She suspects Freddy did kill the late baron, but we'll never know."

"I wish I could kill Freddy," Ellen said, staring at Val in shock.

"You won't have to," Val assured her. "He's in debt to so many people from whom one does not under any circumstances borrow, that they'll hunt him down and gladly make an example of him. Most damning of all, my father uncovered evidence Freddy has sold his vote in the Lords for coin, and that could cost him his title, should Prinny take him into dislike over it. Would you like that?"

"And the regent would benefit?"

"The regent would benefit handsomely."

Ellen shook her head. "It doesn't seem fair that one of the oldest titles in the land goes into escheat for the regent's convenience. Freddy has an heir, and he may be a decent enough fellow."

"He'll certainly be an improvement over Freddy, but the Roxbury estate is of no moment to me whatsoever. Tell me you'll marry me."

"You're sure he's gone?" Ellen asked, unable to keep her voice from breaking. "He'll stay gone? You're safe from him?"

"I am safe from him." Val held her gaze. "*You* are safe from him. I promise you this, Ellen, with my most solemn word. My family owns two shipping companies, and we'd spot him before he disembarked

at any domestic port. His ship was headed for Italy by
way of Portugal, because he already has enemies in
France. He can afford to run for a bit, since he took his
personal jewelry with him. Recall, though, that he's
alone, he doesn't speak the language, doesn't know
the customs, and I have friends who will keep an eye
on him in Rome. Will you marry me?"

"You're going to keep composing, aren't you?"
Ellen peered at him worriedly. "That music, Val. It
was...sublime. I could almost hear the frogs croaking
and feel the tears on my cheeks—well, I could feel the
real tears—and the flowers, I could smell them in the
sunshine during that second movement. I think the
Belmont boys were there too, and so was Marmalade.
You have to keep writing. You have to. Is your hand
all right?"

Val sat back and braced one of his hands on each
of her arms. "If I promise to keep composing, *will you
marry me?*"

"Yes." It was a simple word but the most *radiant*
in her vocabulary. Radiant like the notes of his symphony. "*Yes.* I will marry you, Valentine Windham,
and you will write music, and our lives will always
have something of the divine in them."

"Always," he agreed, hugging her to him.

And in his head, he heard a new tune: sweet, strong,
and clear, underpinned by sturdy, driving rhythms and
lush, generous harmonies. It was at once merry and
profound, and as he bent to kiss his prospective wife,
Val knew it might turn into something worthwhile,
when he had some time to work on it.

And as it turned out, Valentine Windham was

right. The working title of that piece, destined to be just as popular as his debut symphony, became, "Little Weldon Summer Christening."

Author's Note

Careful readers will note that St. Just explains to Valentine that St. Just's adopted daughter will hold the title on behalf of her legitimate heirs. This is in contravention of conventional wisdom telling us that adopted children would not have inherited titles. In the usual case, the conventional wisdom would prevail because an adopted child would not meet the criteria in the letters patent for most titles, which typically required the title to pass to "the oldest legitimate male natural issue surviving at the time of the titleholder's death."

Titled men could and did adopt children, but having letters patent reworded was a much trickier proposition. His Grace influenced the wording of St. Just's original letters patent, which put a very different face on the heritability of St. Just's earldom. Furthermore, in Bronwyn's case, I can assure my readers that both the Helmsley and Rosecroft earldoms included baronies among their predecessor titles, and among the old baronies, it was not at all unusual for female heirs to be able to hold titles in abeyance, sometimes for centuries. As for whether an illegitimate female might qualify, well, this is, as the scholars say, an area for further research—or a just a touch of literary license I hope the purists will find excusable.

Then, too, we know that Prinny's brothers and his sister, the Princess Sophia, had among them something like twenty illegitimate children, and I hope The First Gentleman might have found it in his heart to indulge a royal eccentricity on behalf of our dear Bronwyn's offspring. His Grace, when fixed on a goal, can be very determined and persuasive after all.

Acknowledgments

For a tadpole author to see her debut trilogy published in the space of a year is terrifically gratifying. This takes a lot of patience on the part of the publisher's staff, because the author is very much learning the process by the seat of her pants. My thanks go to Sourcebooks's publisher, Dominique Raccah, for many reasons; to my editor, Deb Werksman, for even more reasons; and to all the troops at Sourcebooks who've had a hand (yes, Valentine) in creating this lovely little book: Skye, Susie, Cat, Danielle, Madame Copy Editor, cover artist Anne Cain, and all the unsung heroes in marketing, art, bookmaking, and everywhere in between.

And there's one other person I need to thank: My first piano teacher. The late Kaye Rossi instilled in me a love of music that brings me joy to this day.

About the Author

New York Times and *USA Today* bestselling author Grace Burrowes's bestsellers include *The Heir*, *The Soldier*, *Lady Maggie's Secret Scandal*, *Lady Sophie's Christmas Wish*, and *Lady Eve's Indiscretion*. Her Regency romances and Scotland-set Victorian romances have received extensive praise, including starred reviews from *Publishers Weekly* and *Booklist*. *The Heir* was a *Publishers Weekly* Best Book of 2010 and *The Best Spring Romance of 2011*, *Lady Sophie's Christmas Wish* and *Once Upon a Tartan* have both won RT Reviewers' Choice Awards, *Lady Louisa's Christmas Knight* was a Library Journal Best Book of 2012, and *The Bridegroom Wore Plaid* was a *Publishers Weekly* Best Book of 2012. Two of her MacGregor heroes have won KISS awards.

Grace is a practicing family law attorney and lives in rural Maryland. She loves to hear from her readers and can be reached through her website at graceburrowes.com.

THE HEIR

An earl who can't be bribed. A lady
who can't be protected...

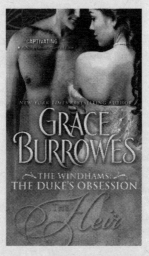

Gayle Windham, Earl of Westhaven, is the dutiful heir of the
Duke of Moreland. Tired of his father's unrelenting pressure to
marry, he escapes to his London townhouse for the summer,
where he finds himself intrigued by the secretive ways of his
beautiful housekeeper. Anna Seaton is a talented, educated
woman...so what is she doing here?

**"Luminous and graceful...a refreshing
and captivating love story."**

—*Publishers Weekly* Starred Review

For more info about Sourcebooks's
books and authors, visit:

sourcebooks.com

THE SOLDIER

New York Times bestseller

A weary soldier home from war. A beautiful
neighbor who could be his salvation...

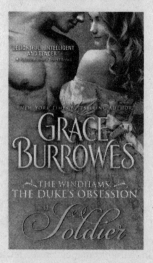

Even in the quiet countryside, Devlin St. Just, the oldest but illegitimate son of the Duke of Moreland, can find no peace. His idyllic estate is falling down from neglect, and nightmares of war give him no rest. Then Devlin meets his new neighbor...

**"A delicious, sensual historical romance
capturing the spirit of the time."**

—*Booklist*

For more info about Sourcebooks's
books and authors, visit:

sourcebooks.com

LADY SOPHIE'S CHRISTMAS WISH

Sophie's holiday is about to heat up...

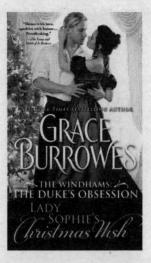

Lady Sophie Windham has maneuvered a few days to herself at the ducal mansion in London before she must join her family for Christmas in Kent. Suddenly trapped in Town by a snow-storm, she finds herself with an abandoned baby and only the assistance of a kind, handsome stranger standing between her and complete disaster.

NO EARLS ALLOWED

Award-winning author Shana Galen delivers
the Regency with wit, heat, and heart

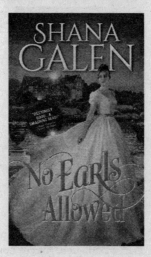

A veteran of the Napoleonic Wars, Major Neil Wraxall is as
honor-bound as ever. So when tasked with helping the head-
strong daughter of an eminent Earl, he can't say no...

Lady Juliana will do whatever it takes to restore a boys'
orphanage in her sister's memory. But the orphanage and its
charges need more help than she can give—she needs a hero.

"Bright, funny, poignant, and entertaining."

—*Kirkus Reviews*

For more info about Sourcebooks's
books and authors, visit:

sourcebooks.com

EARL INTERRUPTED

Acclaimed bestselling author Amanda Forester
delights with the story of a good earl gone bad.

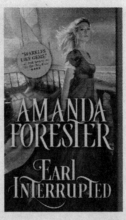

After restoring his fortune as a notorious privateer, Captain
Robert Ashton, Earl of Darington, goes to London in search of
a bride. Instead, he finds unknown assailants. He is shot and left
for dead. Life on the high seas was far calmer.

Enter demure Miss Emma St. James, who quickly proves
herself equal to any challenge, including saving Darington's
life. But she's betrothed to another. Now things REALLY get
complicated…

**"Forester's humor and memorable
characters sparkle like gems."**

—*RT Book Reviews*, 4 stars, *If the Earl Only Knew*

A LORD APART

Beloved author Jane Ashford takes you to a glittering Regency world you won't want to leave!

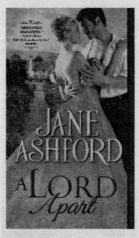

After his parents' sudden death, Daniel Frith, Viscount Whitfield, is struggling to unravel a web of chaotic family records. He is astonished to learn his father's will contains a mysterious legacy: a house left to a complete stranger. He knows nothing about the beautiful Penelope Pendleton, and he's not sure he wants to...until she uncovers an extraordinary secret hidden in the papers...

"A refreshingly different, sweetly romantic love story [readers] will long remember."

—*Booklist* for *Brave New Earl*

For more info about Sourcebooks's books and authors, visit:

sourcebooks.com

AN INCONVENIENT DUKE

When the duke starts searching for
answers...no one's secrets are safe

Marcus Braddock, former general and newly appointed Duke
of Hampton, is back from war. Now, not only is he surrounded
by the utterly unbearable **ton**, but he's mourning the death of
his beloved sister, Elise. Marcus believes his sister's death wasn't
an accident, and he's determined to learn the truth—starting
with Danielle, his sister's beautiful best friend. He never thought
Danielle might be keeping secrets of her own...

**"As steamy as it is sweet as it is luscious.
My favorite kind of historical!"**

—Grace Burrowes, *New York Times* bestselling author,
for *Dukes Are Forever*

Also by Grace Burrowes

The Duke's Disaster

The Windhams

The Heir
The Soldier
The Virtuoso
Lady Sophie's Christmas
Wish
Lady Maggie's Secret Scandal
Lady Louisa's Christmas Knight
Lady Eve's Indiscretion
Lady Jenny's Christmas Portrait
The Courtship (novella)
The Duke and His Duchess (novella)
Morgan and Archer (novella)
Jonathan and Amy (novella)

The MacGregors

The Bridegroom Wore Plaid
Once Upon a Tartan
The MacGregor's Lady
What a Lady Needs for Christmas
Mary Fran and Matthew (novella)

The Lonely Lords

Darius
Nicholas
Ethan
Beckman
Gabriel
Gareth
Andrew
Douglas
David

Captive Hearts

The Captive
The Traitor
The Laird

Sweetest Kisses

A Kiss for Luck (novella)
A Single Kiss
The First Kiss
Kiss Me Hello

True Gentlemen

Tremaine's True Love
Daniel's True Desire
Will's True Wish